Among my earliest memories was the cracked brown leather attaché case which my mother stored in the corner of the wardrobe. I had always thought she kept only chequebooks and bills in it. Now I got up and brought the case over to the bed and sat down again with it on my knee. I stroked the rusty catches with my thumbs.

'Don't open it now,' she said quickly.

I took my hands away from the catches.

'When you leave this room,' she said, 'when it's over and you leave this room, you are to take the case with you. Don't let your father see it. Do you understand? And when you're back home in London, then you can open it. Then you can decide what is to be done.'

Tom Macaulay has lived on four continents, working – among other things – as a journalist, a truck driver, an archaeologist and, for about seven sweaty hours, as a bush firefighter in New South Wales. Born in London, he settled for twenty years in Australia and holds dual Australian/British citizenship. Tom Macaulay is married, lives in Oxford and has a half share in a black Labrador called James.

The Warning Bell

Tom Macaulay

An Orion paperback

First published in Great Britain in 2009
by Orion
This paperback published in 2010
by Orion Books Ltd,
Orion House, 5 Upper Saint Martin's Lane
London WC2H 9EA

An Hachette UK company

1 3 5 7 9 10 8 6 4 2

A CIP catalogue record for this book is
available from the British Library.

ISBN 978-1-4091-0259-5

Typeset by Deltatype Ltd, Birkenhead, Merseyside

Printed and bound in Great Britain by Clays Ltd, St Ives plc

The Orion Publishing Group's policy is to use papers that
are natural, renewable and recyclable products and
made from wood grown in sustainable forests. The logging
and manufacturing processes are expected to conform to
the environmental regulations of the country of origin.

www.orionbooks.co.uk

Read it, my father, prune it of its faults,
And strengthen with thy praise what pleases thee.
And may God give thee in thy hands the green
Unwithering palm of everlasting life.

Walafrid Strabo

Acknowledgements

My father served from 1942 to 1945 on the original Air-Sea Rescue launch 2548. Called up at 35, he was a junior, though elderly, member of the crew. This book came forty years too late for me to ask him for guidance, but during my research it was my pleasure and privilege to make contact with two other wartime members of the crew, Bill Shepherdson and Laurie di Placito. Their help and encouragement were invaluable as were their remarkable memories of those years. Both knew, or knew of, my father. Which was a particular joy to me.

Posthumous thanks too to the late Dave Fellick, much loved Cox'n of 2548 during those years, and my gratitude to his son and daughter, Bryan and Elaine. They shared many of their father's stories with me, and showed me the exquisite model of 2548, which has found its place in the following tale.

Bryan and Elaine also alerted me to the survival of the real 2548, or what is left of her. She then lay derelict in a northern Spanish junkyard, far from her native element. Despite our father's stories about her, my brother Andy and I had never laid eyes on 2548, and in 2006 we were able to make a pilgrimage to see her for the first and last time. We both felt she had been waiting for us. Her fabric may be decaying now, but she has thrust herself – full ahead all three – into my novel. I hope that is some kind of a memorial to her.

Members of the RAF's Air-Sea Rescue and Marine Branch veterans' association, and other enthusiasts, were enormously helpful with photographs, anecdotes and research material. My thanks to all of them.

My indefatigable agent Mark Lucas and editor Peta Nightingale went far beyond the call of duty to keep this frail barque off the rocks (and me with it, occasionally). Nicki Kennedy and Sam Edenborough of ILA also laboured at the pumps to keep her afloat during both storms and doldrums. I can't thank any of them enough. Writing isn't the easiest row to hoe, but it must be one of the last professions where relationships don't stop at the commercial.

Thanks too to my publisher Bill Massey of Orion for his generous enthusiasm and many valuable comments, all of which have refined and improved the story.

The situation in Occupied France during the war years was a moral minefield of agonising complexity. Those times presented everyone with impossible choices, and. sometimes the most upright and courageous people faced the most impossible choices of all. I should like to thank all the fates that we in Britain never had to confront such challenges, and I hope I have treated the French circumstances with the reverence they deserve.

My lovely wife Jenny never faltered in her belief in this story, nor – incredibly – in me. How am I supposed to thank her for that? However, I shall try.

Long ago, and in another age, my father worked on the fishing boats out of Falmouth harbour.

I discovered later that he was thirteen when he first went to sea as a deckhand on his great uncle Jack's wooden trawler, a vessel which had been built so far back in the days of sail that it had to be adapted to take an engine. My father never talked to me about those times. He never really talked to me at all. But even now I imagine him at night on a pitching deck, a thin boy in oilskins too big for him, scrubbing fish blood off the planking, shovelling the quicksilver catch into the hold.

Fishermen of his generation knew the sea floor between St Anthony Head and the Breton coast better than they knew the road to Exeter. But after the Second World War, my father never went back to the great waters, as he called them. I should have realised that at some moment in the past he had broken faith with the sea, and that this haunted him. I should have realised that, down all the years that followed, he was trying to protect me in the only way he knew how. But as a child I was frightened when I heard him shouting at night, wild shouting and things knocked over – a lamp broken, a chair overturned – and under it all my mother's calm voice, soothing him until he was quiet again. To my shame, I felt only the injustice of his withdrawal, and never asked myself the reason for it.

When at last he did tell me about the night in 1944 which had thrown so deep a shadow over him, it was very nearly too late. Perhaps it actually was too late.

This is how it happened.

Prologue: 1944

A running sea muttered along the hull. The launch rolled a little. On the foredeck, Pilot Officer George Madoc braced his knee against the wheelhouse bulkhead and checked his watch. The luminous hands momentarily hurt his eyes with their brightness. It was 1.14 in the morning. That made it the 20th of March already. His twenty-second birthday.

He sensed the tide falling away beneath the boat, and could feel her tugging at her tether like a restive horse. Inshore, white water flickered as the St Cyriac Shoals rose above the surface. A tocsin bell tolled unseen in the darkness, as if from a drowned cathedral.

Great Uncle Jack would have called this a smugglers' night – the dark of the moon, ragged clouds drifting like gunsmoke, and the threat of dirty weather. George remembered a hundred nights like it on this very coast, the trawler thudding steadily homeward, fish flashing like ingots on the deck. A real smugglers' night. Uncle Jack would lean on the wheel and peer into the murk, chew on his pipe and spit over the side for luck.

George wondered what the old man would have made of High Speed Launch 2548, if he had been alive to see her – sixty-three feet of mahogany hull with a cutwater curved like a sabre and a top speed of forty knots. There were those who said the RAF should leave the sea to the Navy, but to George it was altogether fitting that the launch should be piloted by airmen: she was more of the air than of the sea, more gull than fish, with the thunder of her Napier Sealion aero engines and the jolt of grey seas spuming away behind her.

Beyond the Shoals he could just make out the dark mass of

the Breton coast. Once he saw a wandering pin-prick of light, a bicycle perhaps, with a poorly masked front lamp. He imagined a German soldier wobbling back to his billet, full of wine, dreaming of a blonde wife in Hamburg. But there would be other Germans on those cliffs tonight, men who were more alert, sentries leaning on the parapets of pillboxes, scanning the waters with their Zeiss binoculars. Everyone knew the invasion was coming soon, and the whole North Atlantic coast bristled with tension. George shrugged himself deeper into his duffel coat. It wasn't especially cold, but he could not seem to get warm.

'You wish to be flying back to England, Captain,' Lucien whispered, almost in his ear. 'Flying home over the waves in your fast boat.'

Lucien's eyes were startlingly white in the darkness, and were fixed on him like a cat's. The man's dark camouflage clothing and his blackened face and hands made the rest of him all but invisible.

'Your friends are late,' George said shortly. He didn't like to be surprised. He lifted his binoculars again to peer into the rising wind. 'I won't wait much longer.'

The seconds dragged by. George kept his binoculars to his eyes, rain speckling their lenses, hoping to shut out the other man, hoping he would take the hint and leave. But he did not leave. George could sense him hovering at his shoulder.

He didn't know why he felt the way he did tonight. He had reason enough to be on edge, with the launch wallowing off the St Cyriac Shoals and her huge engines cold and silent, but it was more than that. It was something to do with this quiet Frenchman with his classroom English and his face as black as a demon from the pit. Lucien wasn't the first agent George had ferried across – the fast wooden Air Sea Rescue launches were ideal for the task – but he was the first to unnerve him.

The cold wind slung a handful of rain over them both, and then curled back and slung another. Great blocks of water thudded into the sand ahead of them, and spray exploded over the Shoals. The launch swung and a cable groaned and the sea slapped against her stern. No matter what he had said, George knew he would wait a little longer yet. Someone was out there even now, a local fisherman perhaps, who could thread through the wire and the mines and the white shoalwater where no one else would venture; someone who knew the suck and rush of every channel and could find his way with no moon and all the shore lights blacked out.

'They've sent me to kill someone,' Lucien said, conversationally. 'I suppose you know that?'

'I just drive the boat. Thank God, that's all I do.'

'Ah, Captain, how you would like to stay pure.'

'I'm not a captain.'

'You don't like to risk your crew for an assassin. Your job is saving lives, not for ferrying killers. Am I right? But it is too late. We are all part of this madness.'

The Frenchman stood up, and for the first time George could see something of him in the light reflected from the water. He realised how young Lucien was, younger even than he was himself.

'He lives in St Malo, this man I must kill,' Lucien said. 'Runs a firm making precision instruments. He's a jolly type who likes a glass of wine with his friends and never hurt anyone in his life. An ordinary man, doing the best he can for his family and his people. There was a time when working with the Germans was the only option for men like him, but people think differently now.' Lucien paused. 'I'll use a knife, probably. That's what London will expect. It sends such an emphatic message.'

'You don't have to tell me this.'

'I've lost count of them, Captain, to tell you the truth. Though there is one I will never forget. A man in Nantes. I waited in the lobby of his apartment building for over two hours. It was very dark, and when he came up the stairs, it was all over in a moment. I wasn't to know his daughter had come down from Paris for the weekend. She was only eighteen or so, and looked remarkably like him. At least she did from behind, as she tried to find the lock. Looked quite different when she was dead, of course, but by then—'

'Shut up.'

'But no one could blame me for that. If they did, they'd have

4

to blame everyone else who played a part. The officer who gave the order, the people who trained me, the experts who forged my documents … Even the pilot of the plane who flew me across the Channel.'

George stared out to sea.

'How will we all be judged, Captain? I used to believe that Good would triumph, and that our blackened souls would be washed clean at the end, no matter what we had done, but now I'm no longer sure. Now I tell myself I am just the ferryman. That comforts me. Charon, that's who I am. I ferry the souls of the dead across the Styx.' He looked at George. 'Just as you ferry me.'

'No.'

'You cannot stand away from the shore forever, Captain. None of us can.'

George swung to face him, angry now. But as his eyes met Lucien's he saw such emptiness there, such despair, that he could give no voice to the sharp words that were on his lips. He turned away again.

'Perhaps it will be different this time,' Lucien said, his tone gentler now. 'Perhaps I will not do what they tell me to do. Perhaps this time there is a chance for me to find my way back. I shall take it if I can.'

The launch swooped into a trough and up again and both men gripped the cabin roof.

George ducked into the wheelhouse. MacDonald, the Australian Flight Sergeant and First Cox'n, was huddled against the bulkhead, his binoculars resting on the edge of the window and trained out into the night. Spray shone on his coat. George stepped past him and took the wheel, though this was properly MacDonald's role. Glancing towards the stern George could see Darby Allen crouched between his engines, his pale brow a question mark in the dark, waiting for the command. MacDonald moved his binoculars left to right, and then quickly back again.

'Red light, Skip,' he said. 'On the port quarter. Again.'

George felt the wheel twist in his hands as the sea nudged at the rudder; 2548 was restless, anxious to carry him away. She would respond at a touch. No one would blame him. The crew would thank him. *Full ahead all three.* The order that meant home, escape, freedom. Utter those words and they would be gone. They would be safe.

He left the wheel and climbed back out on deck.

In less than a minute the little boat nudged alongside, a cockleshell of a skiff with two figures in it. George caught a glimpse of a man reaching for the nets and behind him at the tiller a boy of perhaps thirteen who, astonishingly, smiled up at him with guileless pleasure. One of his crewmen took the thrown rope and made it fast, and there were hissed exchanges of French and English in the darkness. Lucien dropped a clinking bag over the side.

'It seems there is no escape for us, Captain,' he said.

Lucien swung himself over and found his footing on the nets. He gripped George's wrist, twisted his hand and pressed something hard and cold into his palm. A strange expression crossed his face, and then the boat fell away into the darkness.

I

Pablo handed his Mont Blanc pen to me across the leatherclad acreage of his desk. 'Two mill and change, you'll come out with. Plus the share option, and pension rights, healthcare and so on. It's not a fortune, but if you're careful, you won't have to work again. Which I suppose was the idea.'

'Isn't that everyone's idea?'

Pablo grunted in a noncommittal fashion, and peered at the label of the champagne bottle over the top of his half-moon glasses. I rolled the fat pen between my fingers.

'Well don't sit there staring at it!' Pablo bellowed. 'Sign the bloody thing!'

I scrawled my name and he snatched the document from me as if he feared I might have changed my mind at the last moment. He reached for his pen and tucked it away inside his immaculate jacket.

'Congratulations, Iain. You're a free man.' He leaned back in his oak captain's chair until it groaned. 'So it's to be bliss in Burgundy, is it? Passion in Provence?'

'Not sure where yet. Somewhere in France. A little place I can keep a pig.'

His chair came forward with a bump. 'A *pig*?'

'I always wanted a pig.'

He stared at me.

I grinned. 'Don't worry about us, Pablo.'

'I don't worry about *you*, you weird bastard. But you're even madder than I thought you were if you seriously imagine that the lovely Chantal is going to be happy digging in a dunghill and slaving over a hot Aga – even if she *is* French. That woman of yours is an adrenalin junkie.'

'I'm sure she'd be flattered, Pablo.'

'Where is she now, for example?'

'On her last assignment. Lebanon.'

'I rest my case.'

I smiled to myself. Pablo was secretly in love with Chantal, and sometimes not so secretly. I expect he fantasised about her in sweat-stained khaki, dodging bullets in some distant war zone with cameras strapped around her body. He wouldn't be the only man who did. It was different for me. I was married to her. I'd got past the fantasy stage some time ago and moved on to being worried sick every time she went off on assignment. Now, thank God, all that would change too.

I said, 'Chantal's spent enough time running around disaster areas with nothing more useful than a camera in her hand.' I raised my hand to silence him. 'Her words, not mine. She's already told the agency. After this trip, she's out.'

Pablo filled my glass, but the look of doubt never quite left his face.

I said, 'Don't you ever wish you could break the pattern, Pablo? Feel the sun on your back? Watch the sunset and not think about the office on Monday?'

'Is this a multiple choice question?'

'I want to build something new. That's all. Can you understand that?'

'So buy a Lego set.'

'We both want to build something new.'

'Get her one too.'

'You can say what you like.' I lifted my glass and gave him my biggest smile. 'Nobody's going to stop us now.'

I left his office an hour later and wandered through Covent Garden and down towards the river. I was euphoric from the champagne and from my newfound freedom. It was April, cold and bright, and the buses shone like big red toys. I sat on a bench by the Embankment and stared out over the flashing river. I was scared to death of boats, but whenever I needed space to think I loved to gaze at water. My office in Camden Lock – my former office – overlooked the piazza on the Grand Union Canal where young people in bright clothes crowded the Asian and Mexican food stalls in summer, and sipped latte on terraces beside the narrowboats. Through my windows the crystalline blocks of central London stood against the sky like Camelot in a Burne-Jones canvas, but it was the shining strip of the canal that my eyes always found.

I thought about the energy and optimism of that office, and the fun I'd had there. We designed on-line expert systems for the medical and legal professions, and our rooms hummed with hard drives and glowed with plasma screens and brainpower. The business had consumed me for nearly twenty years and the members of the team I had built up were the nearest I had to friends. For a moment, I couldn't imagine what life would be like without them.

But nobody would stop us now.

My mobile rang.

'Dad?' Kate's voice was urgent. 'It's Grandma.'

2

My parents' front room was as ugly today as I remembered it, with its heavy square furniture and dark curtains and the damp stain on the ceiling which had been there since I was a child. They had lived here more than half a century, but there were no ornaments, no paintings, no flowers, and no postcards on the mantelpiece, none of the busy clutter of a home.

A photograph hung above the mantel: my father, grim faced and awkward in his police uniform, on the day of his retirement. I knew even this was only on display because my mother had insisted. And the room was so very quiet. I remembered this Sabbath silence from thirty-five years ago, silence and dim afternoon light. Sunday mealtimes with glassy mashed potato, waterlogged carrots, a mat of beef, and the room heavy with the steam of overcooked food. Even now I felt a kind of panic, the fear that the gates might yet clang shut behind me and trap me here forever.

'Dad!' Kate said sharply. 'Stop pacing about. You're driving me mental.'

She sat on one of the hardback chairs at the dining table, still in the clothes she had been wearing when I picked her up from college in London: a turquoise top which showed some of her midriff, denim jacket and jeans. Her pale hair blazed in the half-light. She had never seen anyone dying. I wanted to re-assure her, but for the moment my own mind was too crowded. I just smiled at her, raised my hands contritely and forced myself to stand still beside the bookcase in the corner of the room.

The pair of photographs stood where they had always stood,

on the top shelf, in a jointed silver frame which was tarnished almost to black. There were three panels, but the middle one was empty. In the left panel, eight young men sat or sprawled on the deck of a launch at sea, crowding the narrow waist of the craft. Three of them sported jaunty RAF caps, a couple wore handsome white roll-neck sweaters, and one boasted a pair of old-fashioned sunglasses with round lenses. Another, older than the rest, was smoking a pipe. All eight of them were grinning. They were not merely cheerful, these men. They were unmistakably full of joy in that sunshine of sixty years ago.

Only two of these smiling lads wore their tunics. These two sat in the centre of the front row, turning their shoulders outwards so that the snapshot would capture their stripes of rank. One was a flight sergeant and the other a corporal, and both had raised their thumbs. All through my boyhood they had been my favourites, this pair of laughing young men. They looked indomitable. I would make up endless stories about them, naming them after my favourite movie characters or after personalities from my own secret world of adventure and escape. Usually I pretended I was the corporal. He was very young and remarkably handsome, fair haired and dashing. I liked his white knight good looks, but also his modest rank, which seemed to give so much scope for exceeding expectations, for surprising his superiors with his enterprise and bravery.

I had always longed to be able to do that myself. Perhaps that was why this picture had confused me from my earliest years. I couldn't understand how it was that these young men all looked so happy being my father's crew. It seemed to me that they could only be so pleased with themselves if he was pleased with them. Perhaps they were more competent than I was, good at important things I couldn't do well, and which I knew my father valued, like woodwork, or fixing engines, or looking into the skies and reading the weather.

'We should go in,' Kate said abruptly. 'I feel like I'm at the dentist's.'

'He's saying goodbye, sweetheart. Give him a minute.'

My daughter flicked back her hair in a characteristic gesture when she was stressed – half sullen, half defiant – and stared at the floor.

The other photo wasn't confusing at all. It showed a launch at speed in choppy seas, white spray pluming away behind her. Her bow had lifted out of the water and the RAF roundel and the tall numerals stood out: 2548. My father's boat. I picked up the picture from the shelf. It still affected me. Somewhere in space and time, as that speeding craft tore through the sea, these eight men would have been at action stations, drunk with exhilaration. And there, hidden behind the wheelhouse windows, my father would have stood, braced against the thumping of the launch through the Channel swells, his hands guiding the wheel with a horseman's touch. I was jealous of those young men. I always had been and even now, at close to fifty, I still was. Not since I was eight years old had I done anything with him that had made me drunk with exhilaration.

The door to my parents' bedroom opened. I put the photo down and turned to face my father. His face was wet with tears.

I said, 'Dad.'

I moved towards him and instinctively held my arms out to him. I had not done this for longer than I could remember, and for a moment I thought he would ignore me. He did not do that, but our embrace was brief and awkward, a clumsy collision like all the other clumsy collisions between the two of us. When it was over he stepped past me and walked away without a word.

I carried our bags in and dumped them on the single bed. Kate followed me, and sat down between the bags, making the bedsprings squeak.

She said, 'Did you speak to Mum?'

'Yes.'

'Is she coming back?'

'There's nothing she can do here, Kate. I told her we'd manage.'

She nodded, tight lipped, then lifted her head and gazed around her.

'This was your room,' she said.

'Yes.'

Whenever we came down to Plymouth I always insisted we stay in Betty Coleridge's bed-and-breakfast down the lane. I claimed the cottage was too small for us all, meaning that it was too small for me.

'It's a nice room.'

I hadn't expected her to say that. The room was a cramped box, but I had loved it once, the angles of the ceiling and the wallpaper with its pattern of grinning cartoon fish, peeling now at the corners. I remembered my father pasting that wallpaper up for me when I was about six years old. I had always thought of it that way, that my father had pasted the wallpaper up just for me. In those days this little chamber had been my secret cavern, where I kept my books and my treasures and watched these happy fish endlessly pursuing one another around the walls.

I sat beside my daughter on the bed. I put my arm around her and she rested the weight of her head against my cheek.

'You were his little boy once,' she said. 'And he was just your dad.'

I walked through the gloomy house into the dining room. The day was closing. I was his little boy once. I leaned on the table with both hands, and stared out over the twilit fields to the sea. Something caught my eye from across the room, the very smallest of movements, and I looked around and saw my father in his leather wing chair in the bay window. He was utterly still. I walked over and took the window seat opposite him.

I said, 'You didn't tell me she was so bad.'

'She wouldn't have me call sooner. She looked like she was coming good, then she took a fall in the night. The doctor wanted to take her in, but she wouldn't have it. Wanted to die here, she said.' His eyes were like stones. 'Only when she was settled would she let me call.'

I stared at the floor.

'She's leaving,' he said, his voice softening. 'That's all that matters now. She's leaving, and neither you nor I can call her back.'

Short as it was, this was the longest and most intimate conversation that he and I had shared for years. My throat tightened, and I knew this wasn't because of my mother, or not only because of her. He still had the power to do this to me, after all this time, even without meaning to.

'How did it get to be this way between us, Dad?'

I looked up and found his dark, unreadable gaze on me.

'I was cold with you, when you were growing. And since. I know it well enough. For what it's worth, it grieves me. More, maybe, than it grieves you.'

'Then why?'

He shook his head. 'It's too late. Your mother will be gone soon, and I shan't be far behind her. And then it won't signify no more.'

'It will always signify,' I said.

Beyond the clutter of lean-tos and beanpoles, green fields fell away to the estuary, shining like enamel in the last of the light. A catamaran was curving out of Plymouth on a creamy wake, passing to the east of the Plymouth Breakwater, the great man-made ridge of rock which broke the force of Atlantic storms and kept the anchorage safe. Off the Devon shore the lights of lobster boats and pleasure craft rode the darkening sea. But my father was seeing none of this. He was looking at something else altogether, and in my mind I was looking at it too: a pretty blue boat, upturned in a pewter sea, and not far away the tripod timbers of a channel marker standing out of the tide like a gibbet, hung with weed.

Yes, there had been a time when he was just my dad, and I was his little boy. There had been a time when he pasted up wallpaper with happy fish on it, just for me. But that had come to an end one day out there, among the flotsam on the grey water, when I was eight years old. He had thrown his arms around me in the cold sea that day, wrapped them around me and crushed me to him until it hurt. I had wanted him never to let me go. But he had. He had let me go.

When I looked up, his scuffed leather chair was empty. I had not even heard him leave.

3

I was to take the midnight watch. I pushed open the door of my parents' bedroom and noticed the smells again as soon as I closed it behind me – disinfectant and air freshener, and under it, something else, not quite disguised. Something sweet, fecal, troubling. The curtains were drawn and a lamp glowed yellow on the dressing table. I felt like a trespasser in here and I moved with reverence, not just because a woman was dying in the bed, but because this room had been forbidden territory all through my childhood, a place into which I never ventured.

My mother lay with her eyes closed and her grey hair spread in a fan on the pillow. She seemed impossibly small in the double bed. I could not remember seeing her hair undone like that, and it was as if she had momentarily regained some flowering of her youth. There was a drip stand next to her and a tube fed into a vein in her elbow through a plastic device bandaged to her arm. I sat in the armchair beside the bed and found her hand and took it between both of mine. It was weightless and cool, like a bird's wing, and I felt that if I held it up to the light I would have been able to see through it, as if she were already fading away.

After a while the silence made me uneasy and I got up and busied myself quietly around the room, tidying unnecessarily, adjusting the curtains, filling the carafe with fresh water. I put it down on the bedside table next to the single framed photograph she always kept there, and glanced at her face.

Her eyes sprang open. They were huge and flooded with a light I had not seen in them before. It made the hairs lift on the back of my neck. As if fearing I would start back she reached out and hooked her thin hand around my wrist and fiercely tugged me closer to her.

'He loves you, Iain.'

'Don't talk now.'

'He's always loved you. Don't you realise that?'

Moonlight lay across our joined knuckles.

At last she relaxed her grip and her clenched face softened. 'Iain, I know things haven't been easy.'

'They would have been harder, but for you.'

'Oh dear.' She gave me a small, tired smile. 'I can feel a speech coming on.'

'It was you who always stood up for me, Mum. It was you who'd come and find me when I had to go and hide.' I patted her hard fingers. 'It was always you.'

'I loved you both,' she said simply. 'I still do.' She drew a long breath. 'You have to put things right with him, Iain.'

I said nothing.

She gave a vexed sigh, as if my silence was no more than she had expected. 'Help me sit up.'

'You've got to rest.'

'I'll be dead in a few hours,' she said testily. 'I'll rest then. Now help me up.'

I lifted her, plumped the pillows behind her, settled her back against them. She asked for a drink. I tried to hold it for her, but her strength was returning and she waved me impatiently away and clasped the glass in both hands. When she had finished I took the glass and put it on the bedside table, and when I looked up again she was sitting with her hands crossed over the sheet, gazing steadily at me.

'Did you never ask yourself,' she said, 'what happened that made him so afraid?'

'Afraid?' I snorted. 'Dad was never afraid of anything in his life.'

'Oh, yes. He was very afraid of one thing.' And she looked steadily at me until I could hold her gaze no longer. 'You are a stupid, stubborn boy,' she said, softly.

I fussed with the corner of the sheet and waited for the

moment to pass. When I glanced at her again I saw with relief that her eyes were focused not on me, but on the photograph on her bedside table. It showed the simple stone which marked the grave of my older brother Callum, stillborn ten years before I had entered the world. She never spoke of Callum in front of me: neither of my parents ever had. The grave itself was barely two miles away in St Bede's churchyard, but so far as I knew neither of my parents ever visited it. Still, that sad and solitary photograph had stood beside my mother's bed for as long as I could remember.

I wondered what she was thinking now, as she gazed on it. Perhaps she was about to speak of that distant loss at last. I couldn't begrudge her that, but selfishly I hoped she wouldn't. I knew we had such a short time left together, and I didn't want this unknown dead boy in the way.

But when she spoke, it wasn't about Callum at all.

'Listen to me,' she said, speaking very clearly. 'Back in the War, in April of 1944, they sent your father across to the coast of Brittany.'

I looked at her blankly, wondering why she was telling me this. I already knew that, during the war, RAF Air Sea Rescue boats like my father's often hovered off the coast of France to pick up downed pilots.

Then she said: 'He didn't come back for two months.'

I blinked. 'For two *months*?'

'He went over to collect a man. A French agent. A … commando of some kind. And something awful happened.'

'What are you talking about?'

'Be quiet. Listen. Your father had taken this same man over there weeks before, in March, but something went wrong when he went to pick him up again and somehow your father was trapped there. Captured, I suppose.'

'Don't you know?'

But she ignored my question and stared into the darkness over my shoulder. Her eyes had a hollow look. 'When the boat didn't come home I thought George was dead. Nobody here seemed to know anything. It wasn't until October that a doctor called me from a military hospital, a place near Harrogate. George had been there for weeks.'

I couldn't make sense of this. 'And no one told you he was safe?'

'We weren't married then, or they would have contacted me. It's only that the doctor found my letters among your father's things and took pity on me. The thought of me not knowing.'

'But what had happened to him?'

'Your father had escaped somehow, and sailed back across the Channel in an open boat in June, just after the Normandy Landings. He'd even brought one of his crew back with him. He was a hero, apparently. But if that doctor hadn't called I would never have known any of that.'

'Mum, I don't understand. Why didn't he tell you himself?'

'He didn't tell me,' she said with great precision, 'because he never wanted to see me again.'

'What?'

'He wanted me to think he'd died that night in April '44. And part of him had.'

'That's rubbish. He adores you. He always has.'

She drew a deep breath. 'Iain, something followed him back from France. Something that never gave him peace. Oh, I found him again, helped him back on his feet. Then in 1948 we lost Callum and I thought that would finish him. But we picked ourselves up and kept going. And for years after the War it was better. You were born. It seemed a shadow had lifted, and life became ... good again. Not what it had promised to be, but good enough.' Her brow furrowed. 'And then he took you out on the water that day, when you were little. It started again from that moment. And after that it never left him alone.'

I sat back. 'You never told me any of this.'

'He made me promise. And I didn't know much myself. He didn't talk to anyone about what happened in France, not even to me. But it was something horrible. I know that. Something horrible.'

I took her hand again and sat silently holding it. Afraid? That was what she had said. And now I could hear it again, my father's harsh voice raised in the night while she soothed him, gentled him. That was fear? No one had ever told me that. But then I had never asked.

'I meant to tell you, Iain, so many times.' Her voice wavered a little. 'I kept some things – not much, but I always meant to show you.'

'What things?'

'Things he brought back from France with him. He told me I was to throw it all into the sea. He still doesn't know I kept anything from those days. But now someone's found the launch, and that can't be hidden.'

'His launch? After sixty years?'

'Just a few weeks ago. A man kept phoning about it, but your father would never speak to him. I tried to make myself call you, Iain.' Her breathing was growing ragged. 'But I'd promised him … and I thought … perhaps you'd come down to see us and I'd have the chance then … But you never did come …' She was silent for a few moments, then she said, 'Fetch my case.'

Among my earliest memories was the cracked brown leather attaché case which my mother stored in the corner of the wardrobe. I had always thought she kept only chequebooks and bills in it. Now I got up and brought the case over to the bed and sat down again with it on my knee. I stroked the rusty catches with my thumbs.

'Don't open it now,' she said quickly.

I took my hands away from the catches.

'When you leave this room,' she said, 'when it's over and you leave this room, you are to take the case with you. Don't let your father see it. Do you understand? And when you're back home in London, then you can open it. Then you can decide what is to be done.'

She touched my strong hand with her frail one as if she were the one offering me comfort. I could feel her slipping. I put the case on the floor and took her hand in both of mine and rubbed it and murmured to her.

She said, 'Your father was such a good man, Iain.'

I brushed a lock of grey hair from her forehead.

She smiled. 'Ah, you never knew him the way I knew him. Laughing. Always laughing. And with such courage. I can still see him, standing there on the cobbles outside Constable's Gate at Dover Castle, waiting for me to come off duty. He'd bring his motorbike up from the town. I used to linger in the shadows inside the gateway, behind the guard hut, just so that I could watch him standing there, leaning on that old motorbike, waiting for me.' Her smile drained away. 'I don't like to think what must have happened over there to change him so.'

I ran the backs of my fingers down her cheek. Her skin was cool and damp. Her eyes sought for mine in the darkness, and it was as if she had come floating up from the depths of a pool. She lifted herself towards me and I slipped my arm under her thin back to hold her. I could feel her breath against my cheek.

'They were like wolves,' she whispered. 'The memories. Slinking after us down the years, like wolves in the dark forest, waiting for their chance to pull him down. You mustn't let them pull him down, Iain. Even now. Promise me that.'

I promised, not knowing what I was promising, nor how I could refuse, and at that moment not caring.

She grew still and heavy against my arm. I settled her back on the pillow and talked softly to her until her breathing steadied. Her eyes were still open but I could no longer tell whether they were focused on me. I sat with her for a full hour after that, stroking her hand in the night. Even though I watched for it – and I watched like a lynx – I was unable to identify the precise moment when she died.

At a little after four in the morning I closed her eyes. I settled the blankets around her and kissed her forehead for the last time. After that I sat for a while longer in the dark room, and then I took the old brown attaché case out to the car and locked it in the luggage compartment and came back in to wake my father.

4

Only a handful of mourners came back to the cottage, to stand around in a morose little group for an hour or two, nibbling food they didn't want. Now the last of them had gone, the last taxi winding away down the lane. I slipped out into the grey afternoon. The winter greens in the vegetable garden lay drab in the wan light. Below, the Channel shone like steel. I saw my father at once, standing at his favourite vantage point on the cliff path, high above the cottage. He was gazing seaward, his brown coat flapping. I pulled my jacket around me and set off up the slope. He stood with his back to me, leaning into the wind like an old tree. A few spots of rain were driving in now, but he didn't seem to notice.

I walked up and stopped beside him, willing him to face me. He did not. I said, 'You know we'll have to leave soon.'

'Go back to your life in the city, Iain,' he said to the sea. 'You're best away from here. You were always best away from me.'

'It doesn't have to be like this any more, Dad.'

'It's not the time to speak of new beginnings.'

'Maybe it's just the right time.'

Finally he looked at me. 'You go on your way now, Iain. It's better you do.'

If he had just opened the door to me then, even the merest crack ... But then again, perhaps nothing we did or said could have changed things. At that moment, at least, it felt that way. I hesitated, on the point of retreating, but below me I glimpsed Kate standing outside the back door of the cottage, her face tilted anxiously towards us and her fair hair streaming in the wind. I swung back towards my father and stepped in front of him, onto the very edge of the cliff.

'What happened in France all those years ago, Dad?'

He did not move, but I saw the pupils of his eyes shrink to black dots.

'Don't think badly of her,' I said. 'She told me about Brittany.'

'What about it?'

'Not much. How you went missing. She thought it might help us if I knew. What happened to you there, Dad?'

'The world's past caring about all that.'

'I care about it. You suffered and so we all suffered. Everyone around you suffered. And you couldn't even *tell* us?'

'It couldn't have profited you. It cannot profit you now. It would have been better if your mother had kept her peace, God bless her.'

'She did for as long as she could, Dad. But now I can't unknow this thing. I can't just pretend she didn't speak.'

His shoulders rose and fell. 'What do you want?'

'What do you think I want? I want us to salvage what we can before it's too late.'

He turned his head, shifting the focus of his gaze far out towards the horizon once more. I realised that he wasn't going to answer me. I had thought he might be angry, or stricken, or remorseful. But it hadn't occurred to me that he would simply stay silent. It filled me with a kind of panic, as if – having finally glimpsed him – I could see him slipping away from me again and was unable to stop him.

He made to move away but I took his arm and held him.

'Dad, help me understand. Why has it been the way it has between the two of us?'

He met my eyes at last, and I saw that his own were full of pain. Gently he freed his arm from my grip. 'Let it be, Iain.'

He stumped away up the flank of the hill, and I stood there like a fool in the rain, watching him as he kept plodding up and up, towards the cliff top and the pewter sky. The wind began to strengthen, blowing in from the Channel. I could hear it sweeping through the grass and I felt the rain running down my hot face.

I drove home down the A303 across Salisbury Plain, the tyres sibilant on the wet road and Kate curled asleep in the seat beside me. Stonehenge stood like a ring of grim sentinels against a rinsed sky. This was the route I had followed when I had left home as a teenager. No, I hadn't left: I'd fled. I hadn't known where I was going to stay when I got to London. I hadn't known anything much at all except the need to escape, and the need to make him sorry by my escaping.

I had hitch-hiked from the West Country over two January days, with twenty-three pounds in my pocket and nothing in my backpack but one change of clothes and a burden of rejection I could no longer shoulder. I had stuck my thumb out at every passing car along this route, and even now every lay-by and landmark held a memory for me. In that bus shelter outside Honiton I had tried to sleep through the first iron-hard night. On that drystone wall on the Salisbury road I had waited for three hours in driving sleet, until, out of pity, a local farmer had picked me up on his tractor and taken me a couple of miles. I had tried to look tough and capable as I clung behind his shuddering cab. But I was neither. I was merely young and scared.

Most vividly of all, I remembered endlessly scanning the grey country roads, looking for the police my father would surely have alerted. I had watched for the white patrol cars through the bitter day as I moved further and further northeast, through Devon and Somerset and Wiltshire and nearer to my goal. I wasn't sure now what I would actually have done if, as winter darkness fell for the second time, a police car had cruised past with a couple of warm beefy constables inside.

It didn't matter. There had been no police. My father, who was a veteran sergeant in the Devon and Cornwall force by then, and could have called in all kinds of favours, had never even reported me missing. I had always assumed that this was my punishment.

But now as I drove I kept hearing my mother's voice whispering to me in the night. Afraid. She had said he was afraid. And I realised that what my father had told me just yesterday was literally true, and had long been true: he believed I was better away from him. He had wanted me gone from that place and from him, for my own good. I glanced down at my sleeping daughter. I wondered what could drive a father to wish for such a thing. And I thought of the old leather briefcase lying still unopened in the boot.

5

I awoke at five to the sound of the wind buffeting the picture windows. Chantal breathed softly beside me and I was comforted by her presence. I had been dreaming, and a confused patchwork of images still crowded my mind – a launch pitching on a black sea, men hunched in duffel coats, luminous surf breaking over a sandbank. I could taste tension, and knew I wouldn't sleep any more. The curve of Chantal's warm back tempted me for a moment, but she had arrived home very late the previous evening. She was exhausted, and needed all the rest she could get. I got up and dressed quietly.

I settled myself at my desk. London was a mass of lights. The sky over Docklands was still dark, the river a mercury serpent slithering eastward. A loose hoarding banged like a cannon in the rising wind and made me think again of a storm at sea, way out there to the east, beyond what I knew and understood. I lifted the brown attaché case onto the desk and clicked open the catches.

Gas bills, bank statements, chequebook. I took the papers out, flicked through them quickly and stacked them on the desk to my left. At the bottom of the case was a fat buff envelope, and under it a folder of faded green cardboard, its corners pulpy. I had never seen either before. I took out the envelope and opened it.

She had kept my old school reports right back to primary, and childhood drawings of stick people with straw hair, and a letter I had written to her while on a French exchange trip, scribbled on the back of a menu. There was a photograph of me setting off for my first day at St Edmund's Grammar, my satchel over my shoulder, and a colour picture of my wedding day eighteen years ago. I could fix the very moment that photo had been taken: I couldn't stop smiling, I remembered, with Chantal dazzling at my side.

At first my father had refused to come to the wedding. I was hurt and angry, but Chantal would not hear of him staying away, and she and my mother had managed it somehow. He had been gruff and silent as ever, but he had at least been there. We owed such rapprochement as we had been able to achieve to that day, and I had started going down to see them again after that, a hurried visit every few months, but a visit nonetheless.

I had no idea my mother had kept any of this. She never spoke of such things. But the pictures and the papers were well handled, and it was evident that she had often taken them out and looked through them. I sifted through the little pile of memories under the desklamp. All that remained of a life of over eighty years, and it would fit in a shoebox. It was a little while before I could bring myself to put it all back into its envelope and set it aside, next to the bills and the bank statements.

I opened the green folder and the contents slipped out onto the desk. I found myself staring at an odd little collection of relics: a flattened Senior Service cigarette packet with its logo of a clipper ship in full sail; an antique coin; a small square snapshot, now fading to sepia; a yellowed article from an old newspaper and a much more recent one clipped from a colour magazine.

The newer of the two articles was stapled to a compliment slip and had been cut from a recent issue of a French tourist magazine. It was crumpled and stained with grease and what might have been tea. I translated the title to myself as: 'FAST LADY COMES TO SAD END'. There were a few lines of racy copy, and though I merely glanced at them I caught the name of a village – St Cyriac-sur-Mer, Brittany. The picture itself hardly looked as dramatic as the caption promised. A group of elderly men in wet-weather gear stood on the muddy bed of a tidal river at low water, grinning bravely in the rain. The riverbank was overhung with willows and fringed with reeds. One of the men carried a miniature French flag, and one of them a British.

Behind them loomed a dark shape, like the carcass of a whale, overshadowing its hunters and partly screened by the willows on the bank. The pale disc of an RAF roundel was visible on the hull. The tall numerals were faded and half hidden by dirt: 2548.

The second cutting was so faded and brittle that I had to move it directly under the light to read it. It was from an issue of the *Kent Courier* dated 22nd March, 1944, and it read:

YOUNG WOMAN'S DEATH 'SUSPICIOUS'

Dover police have not yet released the identity of a young woman found dead in a flat in the Buckland area of the city on Friday last. Detective Sgt Adrian Proctor confirmed that police are treating the death as suspicious. The woman is believed to have been a member of the Women's Royal Naval Service.

Printed across the top of the cutting, in my mother's neat handwriting, was the name 'Sally'. Was that the name of the dead girl in the article? It looked like it. But I couldn't remember my mother ever mentioning anyone called Sally, nor what was presumably a murder in Dover.

The coin was a sovereign with George VI's head on it, and dated 1944. I turned it in my fingers, rubbing the gold with the ball of my thumb until it shone.

The sepia snapshot would fill the third panel of the triptych on the bookcase in my parents' cottage. My father, in his early twenties, stood black-bearded in a white Air Sea Rescue sweater, an RAF cap set at an angle on his head. He was smiling, his eyes closed to merry slits, like some devil-may-care pirate. Beside him, her arm around his waist, my mother stood in her Wrens uniform, the pride of possession in every angle of her body. Her cap was in her free hand and long-ago sunshine glinted on her blonde hair. She was almost as tall as he was, but looked half his size, and she was quite lovely.

Behind the two of them was a grey blur of beach, a groyne, ridged water. I stared at the photo, held it to the light. I had never seen him laughing in a photograph before. For years I had not seen him laugh at all. I had to search my memory before I could find an image of him which came close to matching this young buccaneer, and when I did it was a long, long way back.

I went through them all again without learning much more, except that on the back of the cigarette packet was a map of some kind, cross-hatched squares of buildings, stylised waves, jotted numbers. It was clearly the plan of a complex of buildings, four of them set back from a beach. A pier or landing stage jutted out into the waves, and close to it were scrawled the letters *LW*. Just behind the shoreline a fifth building was drawn in more detail than the rest, with individual rooms. An odd design – a box with three lines across it – was marked in the centre of the main room, and beside it measurements in feet and inches. The card was waterstained and the lines uncertain, but I was certain that the map had been drawn by my father.

None of it meant anything to me.

I fired up the computer and began to run searches. I went onto a Brittany tourist website and found St Cyriac quickly enough. The map showed a small village tucked into a fold of the rugged north Breton coast perhaps one hundred kilometres west of St Malo. The place lay on the western bank of a modest river which emptied into the broad central reach of the English Channel.

I magnified the stylised map until I could read the name of the river. The Vasse. I ran Google Earth, keyed in St Cyriac, and after a couple of tries a jumble of fuzzy pastel cubes filled the screen, irregular blocks of houses beside a gunmetal sea with dull green hills behind. I could make out the foreshortened tower of a church, trees in the churchyard and in the centre of the village an open square with toy cars parked around it.

There was a quay and against it a miniature harbour. The Vasse, darkened by overhanging trees, opened into a small estuary just to the east of the village centre, and its outflowing water spread a rusty stain on the sea.

I went back to the Brittany website. The breathless text told me that the village itself was less renowned than the St Cyriac Shoals two kilometres offshore, for centuries a deathtrap to shipping seeking to shelter from the Biscay storms. As a result, the tiny harbour at St Cyriac had never grown beyond a fishing port. I hit the print-out button and sat thinking while the printer whirred.

The homepage of the RAF Air Sea Rescue and Marine Craft Section veteran's association led me to an archive of photographs of launches, pinnaces and tenders. Most of the craft shown had been lovingly restored, and were pictured at sea with smiling enthusiasts aboard.

I spent some time searching this gallery, until I found the image I wanted. It was in brilliant colour, and showed a boat which looked to me almost identical to 2548. She was on sea trials after restoration, a Type 2 High Speed Launch, 63 feet long, originally built in 1939 at the British Powerboat Company's yard in Hythe, near Southampton. In those days she had been powered by three V12 Napier Sealion aero-engines, the accompanying text told me, generating 500 horsepower apiece, but these monsters had been replaced long ago by solid General Motors diesels. In the picture, the vessel was moving at speed through a choppy sea, her cutwater slicing the water in a plume of spray, under much the same conditions as 2548 in the old black-and-white shot on my parents' bookcase.

I took the French magazine article with its picture of 2548 beached at St Cyriac and stuck it on the wall beside my desk. Then I printed out the new photo and stuck that directly below it. The boats made a poignant contrast, the one vivid and glamorous, the other derelict and all but forgotten. I turned back to the computer and searched the site again. There was a good deal more information about Type 2 launches, but I could find no reference to 2548 or to my father.

I became aware that the shower was booming in the bathroom down the hall, a comfortable, domestic sound. Almost as soon as I registered it, the sound died away and I heard Chantal in the kitchen. In a moment she came into the study wrapped in a towel and carrying two mugs of coffee. She didn't speak. She put the mugs down on the desk and stepped behind my chair and put her arms around me. I could feel the weight of her breasts on my back and could smell the steamy warmth of her body.

I said, 'Has the Foreign Legion come to rescue me?'

'The camel's in the car park.' Her glance fell on the pile of school reports and souvenirs I had put to one side. She hugged me back against her. 'I'm sorry, *chéri*. I liked your mother. You know I'd have come back if you'd asked.'

'There was nothing you could have done.'

'And Katrine?'

'She's dealing with it. She was great.' I reached up to stroke Chantal's bare arm where it lay across my chest. 'How was Lebanon?'

'OK.' She sighed. 'Doesn't matter now, does it? That's all history.' She tapped me in a matronly fashion on the top of the head. 'You should get some sleep.'

But she didn't expect a reply to that, and very soon sat down beside me at the desk, leaving one arm resting across my shoulder. Then she noticed the little collection spread out on the desk before me. I could feel her surprise.

'What's all this?'

'It was in the briefcase. I started to tell you last night, but I think you went to sleep halfway through.'

'I wasn't asleep.' She prodded the items on the desk. 'Only I thought maybe there'd be old love letters in it. You know, brittle envelopes, faintly perfumed. Call me romantic.' She wrinkled her brow. 'But newspaper cuttings? Pieces of eight?'

'It's a sovereign. There's a map, too. But maybe this is more what you had in mind.'

I picked up the picture of my parents and handed it to her. She looked closely at it, turning it first one way and then the other.

She said, 'He was handsome. They both were.'

'I suppose so.'

She put down the photo and touched the other things in turn. She let her finger rest on the magazine cutting with its picture of the beached hull.

'Some RAF museum sent him that,' I said. 'It looks as if Mum rescued it from the garbage. It's dated a couple of months ago.'

I showed her the compliment slip attached to the cutting. It had a blue letterhead which read 'Tangmere Military Aviation Museum' and gave an address near Chichester. There was no message, but someone had scrawled an illegible signature on it in ballpoint. Bickerton, I thought. Or maybe Biddington.

I said, 'He disappears for two whole months in Occupied France but he never tells anyone about it. How crazy is that?'

'Pretty crazy.'

'I never knew anything had happened to him in the War. Not anything bad.'

'War's always bad.'

'But how could I not have known about this?'

She squeezed my shoulder. 'You can only know what people tell you, *chéri*. If he didn't tell you the truth, you can't be blamed for making up your own version. Trust me. I'm a journalist. I do it all the time.'

'His boat turns up after sixty years, and he doesn't want to know?'

'Not everyone wants to remember. Some people try very hard not to.' She turned the cutting with one fingertip and looked at it. 'Did she say anything more, your Mum?'

'That my father loved me. That he'd always loved me.' I kept my eyes on the cutting. 'That's what she said.'

'Well, then.' She stroked the back of my head. 'Well, then.'

The wind threw rain like buckshot against the window. We sat close together. I pulled the snapshot towards me and stared down at this jaunty pirate, this man I had lost sight of so long ago, and she followed my gaze.

'Chantal, what happened in Brittany in 1944?'

'Iain, *chéri*, I can't make sense of shiny modern wars, let alone ones that ended six decades ago. But I expect the same madness happened in Brittany as happens everywhere else, in every other crazy fucking war.' She looked again at the snapshot. 'When are you going to speak to your father about this?'

'I don't think I know how.'

'Your mother didn't give you all this so you could forget about it.'

'No.' I gathered the items into the folder and closed it. 'I don't know how to do that either.'

I could hear the mournful sounds of Kate's viola as she began her practice, and I realised it must be gone seven. Chantal perched on the edge of the desk and sipped her coffee, regarding me gravely. I thought she was more lovely than any woman had a right to be at this time in the morning.

'I've got to go to this St Cyriac place,' I said.

'Yes, I can see that.'

'And I want to talk to the people at this museum, too. Maybe they can tell me something.'

'You do what you need to do, *chéri*. We can put off starting the rest of our lives for a few days.' She leaned forward suddenly and kissed me hard. 'I'm on your side, Iain. I always have been and I always will be.' She slid off the desk and left the room without another word, and very soon I heard her in the bedroom, singing to herself as she dressed.

When Chantal had left for the office I walked out of the study and down the hallway and stood outside Kate's door, letting her music flow through me. I tapped softly and she called 'OK!' without pausing in her playing. Kate sat with her back to me. She had switched on just one lamp, in the corner of the room, and the light of it shone on her pale hair and on the glossy curve of the viola's shoulder. I saw her face reflected in the blue window and realised that she was playing from memory, her eyes closed. The music was something deep and sonorous. I didn't recognise it, but then I never did.

She stopped playing, leaving a long bass note vibrating in the air. When I looked again at the reflection I saw her eyes were open and she was calmly regarding me in the glass.

'That was beautiful,' I said.

'Dad, you're tone deaf.' She put the instrument on its stand and turned her stool to face me. 'You wouldn't know Brahms from Black Sabbath.'

'Well, it looked beautiful. It felt beautiful.'

I sat down by the desk, under the lamp, and gave her my most self-deprecating smile. Kate put her bow down on the floor and crossed her arms over her chest.

'You look exactly like a hyena.'

I didn't seem to be doing too well. I rearranged my face. I said, 'I'm out for the day, Kate. I'll be back this evening.'

She nodded. 'So what was in the case?' she said.

'Some things I need to check up on. It might delay us a day or two. Getting away. I'm sorry.'

'That's cool. I'll live.'

I leaned over and kissed her. 'Maybe we should all go out for a meal tonight, when I get back?'

She made apologetic eyes. 'Sorry, Dad. Some of the guys are coming round from college. Kind of a goodbye party for me.'

'They're coming here?'

She raised her eyebrows. I had never objected before. 'That's OK, isn't it? I cleared it with Mum.'

'Yes. Yes, of course it is.'

I was obscurely disappointed all the same, and I suppose it showed in my face, for Kate said suddenly, 'Dad, are you all right?'

'I'm fine. Why?'

'Only it must be the pits, losing your Mum.'

'I'm all right, sweetheart.'

She gave me a long and unconvinced look. 'But then maybe your Mum isn't the problem,' she said.

6

I parked the Discovery on the gravel outside Tangmere Military Aviation Museum at a little after eleven. There were no other vehicles in the car park.

The reception area occupied the low wooden buildings of the old squadron offices and behind them the original airfield stretched away flat and empty, a sea of long grass rippling in the wind. To one side of the entrance stood a green-painted scout car with a mannequin at the wheel sporting a handlebar moustache and dressed in a too-large RAF uniform. On a patch of grass nearby men in overalls were working on a bright red jet aircraft which stood on flat tyres. The engine cowlings were open and someone was saying, 'Hit the fucking thing, Jock.'

The severe elderly woman behind the reception desk poked the compliment slip with her fingertip. 'That's Billy Billington's signature, if that's what you're asking. Flight Lt Rodney Billington, OBE. But everyone calls him Billy. He handles our correspondence.' She said this as if I should have known, and added with satisfaction, 'He doesn't come in on Mondays.'

'Maybe I could contact him at home?'

She gave me a steely look. 'If it's so important, I suppose I *could* telephone him.' She used the phone at the desk, an ancient instrument in black Bakelite with a twisted brown cord, which I had assumed was an exhibit. 'Billy, my dear? There's a chap here most insistent to see you. Yes, I've told him that, but ...'

I could hear the distant voice down the line, feisty, indignant.

'Yes,' the woman went on, 'I told him that too. His name's Maddocks.'

'Madoc,' I corrected automatically. 'Iain Madoc.'

The squawking voice on the line stopped for long enough for the woman to frown in puzzlement, then it started again, sounding even more animated.

'Oh,' she said in surprise. 'Well, only if you feel up to it, Billy. But—'

I heard the click of the distant receiver as it was replaced.

She raised her eyebrows and hung up. 'Apparently he's coming in after all. You might have quite a wait. He's very elderly.'

'I'll have a look around, then, if I may.'

I turned away and she barked, 'We do charge for tickets, thank you *very* much,' and moved her shoulders, pleased to have re-established her authority.

I spent the next half-hour mooching around the museum. It depressed me a little, the chain of dark rooms cluttered with bits of aviation history: a polished wooden propeller, a torn fragment of aluminium with a swastika painted on it, more mannequins in ill-fitting uniforms, German, British, Canadian, Polish. Glass cases crammed with medals and faded ribbons, photographs of carefree young men, long dead. And their pathetic possessions: a pocket compass, a Parker fountain pen, a letter from mother with cursive handwriting on very small sheets of lavender paper. I imagined a vicarage in Norfolk and a woman writing at a garden table in the warm summer of 1940, while the birds sang and a lawnmower churned and the world fell apart.

'The living dead,' the voice boomed from behind me, making me spin round.

A bulky old man sat in a wheelchair, looking up keenly at me. His face was dramatically disfigured, like a wax mask half-melted. His eyes were extremely bright, and I realised after a second that this was because he had no eyelids.

'Not bad,' the old man said. 'Most people jump a foot in the air. It's one of the few amusements I have left.'

'Mr Billington?'

His hand felt odd in mine and it took me a moment to realise that he had fewer than the normal number of fingers.

'You must be George's boy,' he told me. 'I hoped it might be old Georgie himself. Didn't expect it, but hoped. So what's he gone and done? Died at last, I suppose. Took him long enough.'

'No. He's well. Comparatively.'

'Being well is always comparative at our age.'

'What did you mean about the living dead?'

The old man pinwheeled his chair and propelled it between the cabinets so that I had to step smartly to follow. 'It's an African thing,' he called over his shoulder. 'The dead stay with us, to help or hinder us, until the last person who remembers anything about them has gone to follow them. Mumbo jumbo, probably, but that's what you get for reading *National Geographic*.' Billington sped down the corridor until he rolled between the tables of the mocked-up NAAFI canteen and out through French doors into the open air. He pivoted to face me. 'And that's what we try to do here. Keep the memory alive. Forlorn hope, but some of us old fools feel we owe it to them. This whole place is nothing more than a shrine to ancestor worship when you get right down to it.'

He propelled the wheelchair away again before I could speak, down a flagged passageway, through a rustic arch and onto a patch of lawn beyond. I followed him into a pleasant garden of rose trellises and young trees. It was cool, but a thin sun had broken through, and I was glad to be under the wide spring sky and to feel the pressure of the open air on my face. Billington wheeled himself over to a bench and parked his chair near it.

'Take a seat, young Mr Madoc.'

I did. There was a plaque on the back of the bench which read: *In memory of members of the Air Sea Rescue and Marine Craft Section of the RAF who died in the Second World War: 'They gave their lives to save others'*

Billington squinted at me with his glittering hoodless eyes. 'I must say, you're not a bit like George. More like your mother. Tall and fair and slender, she was, I remember. I can still see the way she walked, the way she held herself. We were all green with envy.'

It was strange to hear my mother described in this way. I had seen a certain quiet grace in her – I recognised this even as a child – but I had never thought of her as beautiful. Perhaps if I had not so recently seen that old Box Brownie photograph I would have thought Billington was merely romancing the past, but now I could not forget the way she stood so proudly in her Wrens uniform, her fair hair shining in the sun. And my father beside her in his regulation white sweater, raffish and powerful.

'How is your mother?' Billington demanded.

'She's dead,' I said.

His question had come too suddenly for me to compose a gentler answer. It was difficult to detect any change of expression in the ravaged face, but when he spoke his voice was momentarily stricken.

'When was this?'

'Last week.'

'What could be so urgent it brings you here at such a grim time?'

I took the cutting out of my wallet. 'You sent this to my father.'

The old man took the paper, handling it with surprising dexterity between his stunted fingers. 'Certainly I did, and I see he treated it the way I thought he would.'

'But you sent it anyway.'

'I could hardly keep a thing like that from him. Old 2548 turning up the way she did, right there in St Cyriac? I tried phoning him about it, but he wouldn't take my calls.' He handed the cutting back. 'Some anorak spotted her in the river Vasse last year. Some of our chaps went to have a look at her, and the local tourist paper printed the story. I had to send it to George, even though I knew he'd take no notice.'

I smoothed the article on my knee and stared at it for a while, at the dark curve of the hull rising from the mud, the grinning elderly men in waterproofs waving their little flags in the drizzle. I folded the paper and tucked it into my pocket.

'Did you know him well, Mr Billington?'

'George? Of course. I was adjutant of ASRU 27 at Dover. Air Sea Rescue Unit. Shore duties.' He jabbed one webbed hand at his face. 'You probably think I got this battling through burning oil to rescue some poor devil of a pilot. Not a bit of it. Car

37

accident in my brother-in-law's Hillman. Weston-Super-Mare, on the way back from the pub. I never even got to sea. But I knew George all right.'

'It's just that I've never met anyone who knew him in those days,' I said.

'Well, there you are. Finally I'm first at something.' He paused. 'I was sorry he wouldn't let me speak to him on the phone. I only wanted to thank him, you see. It's all I did want, really, to thank him before they ring down the curtain on the pair of us. He was kind to me, your father. He was a good man. A gentle man. Rare gift, you know, not just having courage, but to be able to share it. Rare in any man, especially a young one.'

'I'll thank him for you.'

Billington looked up at the pale sky, and back down again. 'I'd be much obliged to you if you would.' He made a sound somewhere deep in his throat. 'Very much obliged.'

I let a moment pass. 'Mr Billington, what happened to him at St Cyriac?'

He peered sharply at me. 'Why ask me?'

'I thought you'd know something about it. As adjutant.'

'Mr Madoc, the last time I saw your father he was at the wheel of 2548, slipping away from Dover ferry dock that April afternoon. He never came back to Dover so far as I know. I was posted overseas myself in May, and nothing had been heard of him or the boat by then. I only heard years later that he'd managed to get out.'

'And the rest of the crew?'

'I gather he brought one out with him. Don't know who. The others were POWs for the duration, I expect.'

'So the boat was captured?'

'Logical assumption, since it's still in one piece over there.'

'You didn't try to make contact with any of these men after the War?'

'I was overseas for nearly ten years after '44. Malaya, Hong Kong. Never kept up with the Section.' He made an impatient gesture. 'If you want to know this sort of thing, you really must ask your father.'

'He won't talk about it.'

'Well, then,' he said, as if that explained everything. 'St Cyriac was a balls-up, young Mr Madoc. Just like every other balls-up in wartime. Not even an important balls-up in the grand scheme of things. There's no more to be said about it.'

'I'm sorry. I can't leave it like that.'

'Can't you indeed?' he flared. 'And why is it suddenly so important that you know? This isn't even your story. You weren't even born! Why does it matter what we old fools choose to remember and choose to forget?'

'Do you have a son, Mr Billington?'

He hesitated, caught off guard by my question. 'Three of them. What of it?'

'Do you ever talk to them about those days? About the War? About your friends back then, and the funny or sad or stupid things you did together?'

He stared at me for a few moments. 'I bore them rigid, if you must know,' he said at last. 'Endlessly. And the grandchildren. They humour me, but they think I'm talking about the Land that Time Forgot.'

'I'd have liked my father to bore me every now and then, Mr Billington. I'd have liked him to feel that he could bore me whenever he wanted. But he never did. He never talked to me about those days. I'm coming to think that's why he never really talked to me at all.'

For some seconds he sat softly thumping the arm of his wheelchair. I don't know what it was about him – his age, I suppose, or the vulnerability suggested by his disfigurement and disability. Whatever it was, I found I couldn't hold back now.

'I worshipped him, Mr Billington. And for a while he was what every kid wants from his father. But then when I was eight years old something happened. A boating accident. It wasn't very serious. Nobody died. Nobody was even hurt. But he was never the same after that. A few days ago, when she was dying, my mother said that accident had brought back something which happened to him in the War. Something horrible, she said. That was the word she used. Horrible. I need to know what it was.'

Billington kept his lidless jackdaw eyes fixed on me for a long time. Over the fence I could hear the wind hissing in the long grass of the abandoned airfield.

Finally, he said, 'Your father was sent over to St Cyriac in March of '44 to drop off this mad Free French Johnny. Codename of Lucien.'

'Lucien?'

'Correct. Some sort of a resistance organiser fellow. Trained assassin, more like. The drop-off went all right, but in April George was sent back to pick this chap up again. And that's when everything went belly-up. I don't know what went wrong over there. But that was the sequence of events.'

I took out my wallet and held the flattened Senior Service packet up for him to see, with its sketch map scribbled on the back.

He frowned. 'What's this?'

'I found it among my mother's things. I wondered if it meant anything to you.'

He peered at it for a moment then shook his head. 'Should it?'

'Or this, maybe?'

I tipped the gold sovereign into his palm. He rolled it between the stumps of his fingers, examining both sides.

'Cloak-and-dagger types were given gold sovereigns as emergency funds,' he said, handing the coin back. 'They still are, I believe. I expect that's what this was.'

'You mean this man Lucien gave it to my father?'

'That's possible.'

'For good luck?'

'Who knows? Though if you ask me Lucien wasn't the sort of cove who'd bring good luck to anyone.'

'Why do you say that?'

'There was something about him. I remember the first time I saw him. He was just sitting there in the CO's office in that black get-up, smoking these foul cigarettes. He was supposed to wait for the CO to invite him to smoke, but Lucien didn't bother about that, and nobody quite had the nerve to tick him off. I shouldn't think he was more than nineteen or twenty, but he looked like Old Nick in all that commando gear, with his face blacked up. Slightly unhinged, in my view. Very polite and correct, spoke good English. But he gave you the feeling he'd stick a knife into you as soon as look at you. Which was his job, in point of fact, sticking knives into people.'

'Did my father feel that way about him too?'

'More so, I'd say. When he was due to go over and pick him up again, George didn't want the job. I'd never seen him windy. I'd never heard him sound worried about anything. Of course, we had to send him anyway. No one knew that coast like George did. But if he had some sort of premonition, it seems it was correct.' Billington huffed a bit and rocked around in his chair. 'Look, I think I've said quite enough, don't you? It hardly seems up to me to talk to you about matters your father quite clearly would rather forget.'

'I expect you're right.' I got to my feet. 'Just one last thing, Mr Billington.' I took the faded *Kent Courier* cutting from my wallet and showed it to him. 'Does this ring any bells?'

He stiffened, and I watched the wary light hardening in his eyes as he read it.

'No,' he said. 'It does not.'

'You can't think of any reason why my mother would keep an article about a girl found dead in Dover back in 1944? A Wren called Sally?'

'You're assuming that was her name.'

'Wouldn't you? It's written on the cutting.'

He grunted, but didn't deny it. 'Your mother was a Wren. Perhaps they knew one another. How would I know?'

I rested my hand on the back of the bench and drummed my fingers on the warm wood. I waited for him to say more, but by degrees his glittering eyes were focusing somewhere in the past and I knew I'd get nothing more out of him. I leaned forward and placed my hand over his on the arm of the wheelchair. The old man stared down at my hand covering his own mutilated one. I thought he might pull away, but he did not. Instead he took a couple of deep breaths, gradually recovering his composure.

'I'll tell you something about your father, Mr Madoc,' he said eventually. 'Might help, might not. George could have had what they used to foolishly call a "good war". Could have gone into the Navy. The Senior Service.' He curled his lip a little to show what he thought of such nonsense. 'Instead, he ended up with the lowest commissioned rank it's possible to get, in command of just about the smallest vessel afloat. And do you know why? Because he wouldn't kill. He abhorred the very idea. He came close to being interned as a conscientious objector. And let me tell you, in the Second World War they didn't think there was anything very noble about that. Then somebody suggested the Air Sea Rescue to him. Not glamorous. Not safe. Not an easy option. But *saving* life, not taking it. And that's the path he followed, to the great privilege of all of us who knew him. To the lasting gratitude of all the men he pulled from the water, and their families, their children and grandchildren. All the men – British, French, German, American, whatever – whom he never abandoned, when everyone else had given up hope. And he never abandoned anyone. I want you to remember that, Mr Madoc. He never abandoned anyone.'

I sat in my car outside the museum for some time after I had left Billy Billington, staring out over the airfield. The early spring sun washed primrose yellow over the meadowland, and then shrunk away, leaving the fields dull and wintry again. A coach pulled up on the gravel and discharged twenty or thirty elderly men and women in overcoats, some with sticks, some wearing veterans' berets with badges on them. Across the carpark one of the men working on the scarlet jet aircraft was belting something in the cockpit with a big spanner.

I looked across at the glass doors of the museum. A shrine to the living dead, Billington had called the place, to the shades that still flickered with life so long as someone remained to conjure them from the past and give them honour – not even honour, but the simple respect of memory. He had been speaking from the heart about that, but not everything he had said had been so frank. I knew I had not imagined that.

I saw again the slight retraction of his head, tortoise-like, when I had shown him that faded cutting, the hunted light in his eyes. For a second I considered going back in and asking him outright why he hadn't been honest with me, but I pictured his outrage and his dismay and I didn't have the heart for it.

But I didn't have to go straight back to London either.

7

Three hours later I parked in a multi-storey close to the centre of Dover.

The Library and Discovery Centre occupied a futuristic block in the Market Square, all cantilevers and glass walls. A middle aged woman with tawny hair sat behind a reception desk in the foyer. She looked bored, but her interest sparked up at once when I showed her the cutting.

'A murder?' She scanned the article and opened her eyes very wide. 'How exciting!'

'I'm wondering if you can help. There's something I want to know about this.'

'Try me.'

'I want to find out who the dead girl was. This Wren, presumably Sally something-or-other. How would I go about that?'

She frowned in concentration. 'Well, when this was written the police obviously hadn't identified her. But as soon as her full name was released they would have reported it.'

'That's what I thought.'

'So you'd have to find some later issues of the *Courier* and look through them.' She put on reading glasses and looked at the article more closely. 'We don't keep anything this old, I'm afraid. Your best bet would be Kent County Archives. They have all the local papers on microfiche, going back to year dot. That's up at Maidstone.' She glanced at her watch. 'But you wouldn't make it before they closed today. Still, I imagine it isn't all that urgent after sixty-odd years.' She caught my expression. 'Or is it?'

'I suppose not. But it feels that way.'

'I see.' She nodded and thought for a moment. 'In that case, you could always go direct to the *Courier*.'

'The newspaper? It's still in business?'

'Oh, yes. Take more than a little war to finish them off. I think they still keep the originals at their office.'

'Would they let me see them?'

'They would if I asked.' She winked. 'The archivist's a friend of mine. You want me to give her a ring?'

The *Kent Courier's* offices were a couple of miles down the Canterbury road. I had been expecting something modest and old fashioned to fit my view of regional papers, but this was a modern block with a lot of glass and steel and a gatehouse at the entrance. A security man buzzed me through. By the time I got into the marble foyer a round woman, swaddled in bright woollen clothing, was already waiting for me, drumming her fingers on the reception desk.

'Mr Madoc? I'm Melanie Townsend. Jane Hatton at the Museum called me about you.' She took my hand. 'You're doing some research into wartime crimes, I gather? Down from London, did she say?'

'Well, yes. That is—'

'My daughter's at London. University College.' She was already leading me towards the lifts, her heels clicking on the parquet. 'One of her courses is criminology. That's your line, I suppose. Or history, is it?'

'Not exactly, but there's a particular murder—'

She glanced at her watch and ushered me into the lift. 'Yes, I'm sorry to hurry you, but I'll have to leave in about half an hour. So we'll go straight to it, if we may.'

I kept quiet after that. On the second floor I followed her down a long corridor and into an open plan room furnished with maplewood tables and computer terminals. The walls were ranked with broadsheet-sized bound volumes with cracked leather spines. I handed her the cutting. She took it and put on her glasses.

'So,' she said, 'the 20th of March, 1944.'

She was reaching for one of the oversized volumes. I helped

her heave it down from the shelf. It was extraordinarily heavy and came to rest on the desk below with a thud. It contained bound copies of ancient newspapers, yellowed and spotted, and it gave off a smell of dust and age. She turned up the original story within a few moments.

'Here we are. But there'd be a follow-up for sure, when they identified her.' She lifted over the soft pages. 'It's just a question of finding it.'

Murky photographs, columns crowded with newsprint, advertisements for Bird's Custard, Ovaltine, Tetley's Tea, War Bonds. I saw it even before she did, the cheeky schoolgirl face on the front page of the 28th March issue, a plump face with dimples, grinning from under a uniform cap. The caption was in blockish type: 'Savage killer sought for Wren's death'. I put my hand on the page to stop her turning over.

Police have appealed to the public for help in tracking down the killer of 19-year-old Wren Sally May Chessall, whose body was found last Friday in a flat in Buckland, Dover. Detective Inspector Charles Hopkiss of Kent Police, leading the investigation, described the murder as 'particularly brutal'. He said that he would like to hear from anyone who was in Brent Street, Buckland, on the night of Wednesday 15th March or early in the morning of Thursday 16th March. Inspector Hopkiss confirmed that the murder weapon, believed to be a commando dagger or similar knife, has yet to be found.

I looked at the saucy 1940s face in the picture, smiling, cap at an angle. Sally May Chessall. I still didn't recognise the name. I didn't recognise anything about the story. I read on, not knowing what I was looking for until I reached the last paragraph. Then I stopped and re-read it.

Miss Chessall was stationed at RN Dover Command, Dover Castle, where friends described her as 'popular' and 'outgoing'. Her unit was reported to be 'deeply shocked' at the tragedy. Miss Chessall failed to report for duty on Thursday morning. On Friday evening, her colleague Leading Wren Joan Fordyce became concerned and called at Miss Chessall's lodgings, where she made the grim discovery.

Melanie Townsend glanced at me. 'Well, that's got your attention. Answer a question, does it?'

'Joan Fordyce was my mother.'

'Was she now?' She looked at me in owlish surprise. 'Well, there may be more about this, you know, especially if they caught the chap, and there was a trial or whatever. But you'd have to come back tomorrow and look through all the files. We don't have it on disc, I'm afraid.'

'Thanks.'

'Glad to be of help.' She bustled a bit, anxious to get rid of me. 'Look, I'm so sorry, but I really must close up now.'

I left the building and walked back to the car. It was dark now and the evening rush hour was under way beneath a steady drizzle. I drove back into town and found a café and sat there with a mug of tea and a bacon sandwich. The original cutting lay on the table in front of me in a plastic sleeve. The story had led me down a blind alley and I felt slightly foolish. The cutting had nothing to do with my father. Instead it was merely a memento my mother had kept of a long ago drama, and of the cameo role she had played in it. It was part of her history, not his, and all my father's mysteries remained as dark as ever. For some reason, this fired my determination more than success would have done.

I finished my sandwich and walked through the city centre and up the narrow shining streets. I had just wanted to get some air while I pondered my next move, but I found myself following the signs to the castle. The road climbed out of the bustling centre, past wealthy residential houses, and looped steeply up through wet green banks.

I was out of breath by the time I saw the castle walls floodlit against the evening sky above me. I stopped. Rain swarmed in the yellow light. It hadn't been like that in those days. Back then it would have been pitch dark, all lights shrouded in the blackout. I walked on along the perimeter road which followed the curtain wall. Constable's Gate, she had said. I set off again, following the road around for some distance, ducking under a barrier beside an empty kiosk. And quite suddenly I saw it on the far side of the moat, an ancient stone barbican, its huge studded gates hinged back against the wall and the lights of the castle shining on the wet flagstones within.

He used to ride his old motorbike up here and wait outside, my mother had said, standing in that way of his, with his legs planted apart on the cobbles. She had hidden in those shadows within the vaulted entry of the gate for a minute or two each night as she had come off duty, just so that she could feed on the sight of him standing here, waiting for her.

Down in the port a siren sounded. I turned my head. From where I stood, high above the town, I could see a ferry, twinkling with lights, nosing out of the harbour mouth to the open sea. I took out my phone and called the flat. Kate answered at once.

'Oh, hi Dad.' I could hear music in the background and the clink of glasses. She said, 'Where are you?'

'I'm in Dover.'

'Oh, yes?'

There was a giggle from behind her and a girl's voice said, 'Brett, not in the *sink*!'

I said, 'Is Mum back yet?'

'No. She's got more sense than that.'

'I'm thinking of staying overnight. Will you let her know?'

'Sure. Of course.'

I paused. 'Do you need me for anything?'

'Need you?' She laughed fondly. 'You're a liability.'

I watched the dwindling ferry, its wake churning white. 'I might stay away for a day or two. I'm thinking of going over to France.'

'Right,' she said, with more attention now.

'I'll give you a call tomorrow and tell you what's going on. OK?'

She was silent for a couple of beats, long enough for me to wonder if we'd lost the connection.

'Kate?'

48

'I knew it,' she said.

'Knew what?'

'That he was just your dad. And you were just his little boy.'

8

The fields on either side were heavy with rain. I had been driving for an hour or more down winding coastal lanes and no longer knew exactly where I was, but I assumed I must be somewhere near St Cyriac by now. I came over a small humpbacked bridge across a river, and slowed to get my bearings. On my left, set back from the road, stood a fine old house with tall windows and ornamental turrets. I glanced at it and overshot the turning to the village, so that I had to stop and back up.

I drove down a narrow lane between stone walls, catching a glimpse of houses and slate roofs and a quadrant of iron-dark sea. The lane opened into a village street – boulangerie, Citroën garage, minimarket – and abruptly I was in St Cyriac. Most of the shops were shuttered against the gloomy afternoon. Another hundred metres and I emerged into an unexpectedly handsome square surrounded by buildings of honey coloured local stone.

The Hotel de Ville looked out over a small park set with plane trees and benches. A large grey church stared across the open space from rising ground on the other side. There were puddles of rainwater on the gravel and the benches were deserted. Between the buildings I saw a harbour wall and boats.

I parked and got out. Three middle-aged men in anoraks and woollen hats, all with binoculars slung over their shoulders, were unloading backpacks from the boot of a car, but otherwise the square was empty. It was peaceful in the soft afternoon light. Drops fell from the leafless branches above me, thunking onto the Discovery's bodywork.

I looked around the square, wondering where to start. A school behind black railings, a pharmacy, gloomy Bar des Sports, estate agents, solicitor's office, Credit Agricole bank, photo shop. The buildings along the seaward side were mostly residential, two-storey houses and guesthouses with mansard flats which, on the far side, must look directly out over the Channel.

A rose arbour stood in the square immediately opposite the church. I walked over to it and glanced inside. At the far end was a bas relief carved in grey and pink granite. The stone wings of the monument curved towards me on either side to form benches, and into the backs of the benches were cut the names of the dead from both world wars, and from Algeria and Indo-China.

I walked up to the bas relief under the arch of roses. I had expected a soldier in heroic or tragic pose, but this was a family group – a smiling dapper man, an elegant woman, and a girl with large sad eyes. The inscription underneath read simply: *Famille Rosen* – 1942.

I left the monument and turned down an alleyway between two fine old houses. Stepping out onto the seafront was like emerging from a quiet wood directly onto a windswept plain. The sea stretched away grey and broken under a bruised sky. A formation of high-flying geese cruised seaward, honking faintly as they went, and out on the harbour wall a knot of watchers in rain gear followed them excitedly through binoculars. They were the only people in sight.

I strolled left, towards the harbour. A score of boats rocked here, six or seven fat little fishing craft and oyster boats, a ferry kitted out for day trips but still sheeted down under tarpaulins awaiting the start of the season, a couple of rental yachts and a port authority barge. But almost at my feet lay easily the most handsome vessel in the basin, an exquisite cabin cruiser about eight metres long, with brass fittings, a spoked wheel and polished decks which might have been teak. Even I could see it was an antique, perhaps as old as the craft my father had skippered, though this vessel had clearly been built for pleasure and style. A tarpaulin was stretched over the bow and through the cabin window I could see tools laid out and lengths of timber. Someone was evidently in the process of restoring the vessel, and lovingly. Its name, *The Gay Dog*, was lettered in a burgundy scroll on the transom.

A bell jangled as a door opened behind me, and I turned and saw a steamy restaurant window with lights glowing behind dribbling glass. I crossed the road and went in. It looked as if most of the population of the village had taken refuge inside. The tables were crowded and the bar, with its rows of china beer pumps and old-fashioned mirrors, was two deep with people, shoulder-to-shoulder.

I leaned in a corner, hoping a seat would materialise somewhere. I liked the feel of the place, and didn't mind waiting. There were opera posters on the walls and, close to where I stood, framed black-and-white and sepia photographs of old ships and buildings. The proprietor appeared magically at my elbow, a handsome fleshy man of about forty with a fine moustache and a gold ear-ring.

'A table, M'sieur?' Before I could answer he gestured at two youths hunched over a window table and roared, 'Move your backsides, you idle layabouts! Make room for some quality custom there!'

The youngsters – working lads in sweaters and parkas – grumbled while the owner stood in magnificent disdain, one hand on his hip and his head thrown back, but they rose and drifted off to the bar. My host led me through the crowd, seated me with extravagant courtesy, and began to polish the tabletop. He cracked the napkin like a whip and tucked it into his apron.

'Staying for a while, M'sieur?'

'A few days.'

'Congratulations. You're the first this year. You've extended our holiday season all by yourself. In fact you may *be* our holiday season.' He drew himself up and offered me his hand. 'I am Henri. And you are welcome. But if you're planning to stay in the village I hope you've booked.'

'At this time of year?'

'It's the migratory geese, M'sieur. They gather out on the Shoals. Please understand I've nothing against geese. Very good roasted with apricots. But the people who observe them are rather odd, and these odd people have taken over most of the rooms in town.' He produced his order pad with a flourish.

'But you could always try Evangeline Didier's. She's so strange that even goosewatchers steer clear of her. I can't say I'd exactly recommend her place, but at least no one else is likely to be there.'

'It sounds perfect. Where can I find it?'

'You can't miss Evangeline's. It's a ghastly three-storey monstrosity just behind the library, painted the colour of mould.'

'Thanks.'

'Though perhaps you too are interested in migratory geese, M'sieur?' he went on, apparently in no hurry to take my order. 'I must say, you don't look quite peculiar enough.'

'I'm on a different mission. I'm looking for an old boat.'

'We have plenty of them around here. Almost as many as geese.'

'One old boat in particular.' I took the magazine article out of my wallet and spread it on the table for him to see.

Henri looked down at the picture and pulled down the corners of his mouth. 'You'd do better with a new one, M'sieur.'

'You don't recognise it?'

He shook his head. 'They all look the same to me.'

In a village this size I had assumed everyone must know about the old launch, but if Henri did, he seemed determined not to admit it.

I said, 'It's supposed to have been here since the War.'

'The war, eh? Which war would that be, now?' He swung back towards the bar, where a tall and beautiful blond man was pulling glasses of Kronenbourg lager. 'Gunther? Did you ever hear of a war around here?'

The tall man sliced foam off a glass with a spatula and flicked it into the sink. 'Nah,' he said, without looking up. 'I would have noticed that.'

'I'll have a *grand crème*,' I said, weakly.

9

By the time I left the café the rain had started to fall again.

I stood for a while on the quay, between the iron bollards and the piled lobster pots. The small adventure of getting here was over, and I felt tired and deflated. But I thought that I should be making some effort, so I trudged along the front for a few hundred metres, following the promenade. Behind the cottages lay a patch of open ground, a child's playground, deserted in the rain, and beyond that a flash of what must be the River Vasse. I crossed the playground to the water's edge. It wasn't broad – I could have thrown a stone halfway across – but the steepness of the little valley in which the river flowed suggested it might be deep. The water was overhung with trees, the sliding surface black in the failing light and stippled with rain. On the point opposite me, half swallowed in the undergrowth, I glimpsed a jumble of broken concrete, an old blockhouse, perhaps. There were no other buildings on the river bank.

In the estuary of the Vasse. That was where the boat had been found. Did that mean here? There was no sign of any boat or of anything else unusual, just this deep, swift little river winding down through the woods from my right. If the boat was somewhere along these wooded banks, it could be anywhere. Perhaps it was no longer here at all. The rain strengthened, drops slapping through the leaves above me. Had there even been a war? Oh, no. Henri and his friend Gunther would have noticed that.

I plodded back into the square, got my bag from the Discovery and made my way to the guesthouse.

Madame Didier's false lashes sat on her eyelids like large spiders.

She reclined against the doorframe, and looked me sourly up and down, moving only her eyes. They were large blue eyes, like a child's marbles, and fitted only approximately into their sockets.

'You wish to take a room, Monsieur?'

'Henri at the café recommended you, Madame.'

'Ha!' Her bark of laughter startled me.

I began to lose confidence, standing in the street with the rain falling on me and this dour old woman observing me like a specimen.

Finally she said, 'This establishment has not been open for business for three years, Monsieur. Not since Jean-Luc was carried off. My husband, that is. That was.'

'I'm sorry to hear that.'

'Don't be. He was carried off by the wife of the man who empties the *fosse septique*. They deserved one another.'

'I'm sorry to have troubled you, Madame.' I turned to go, mentally cursing Henri for having sent me.

'Don't run away,' she commanded suddenly. 'Perhaps something may be arranged. Come.'

I didn't have the courage to refuse her summons and I followed her through the door, closing it behind me. The house was dim and congested. Glass-fronted cases crammed with cheap porcelain figurines flanked the corridor, and above them the wall was crowded with framed black-and-white photographs of a much younger Madame Didier in sequined gowns posing with men in dinner jackets.

I followed her into a large room so cluttered with overstuffed furniture that it seemed small. A bald man in shorts sat in an armchair eating peanuts and drinking Stella lager from a bottle. He leapt to his feet so quickly that he had to catch the glass dish of peanuts before it fell. He stood blinking from me to Madame Didier and back again.

'Gaston, prepare the Camellia Suite,' she ordered, 'and take the gentleman's bag.'

He grabbed my bag and fled with it.

'Gaston is an uncultured yokel.' Madame Didier settled into a brocade armchair and waved me to the one opposite. 'But he has his uses. He empties the septic tank. A most necessary function.' She lit a long white cigarette and grew languid. 'I will tell you the truth, M'sieur. There were times when I considered pushing Gaston's little slut of a wife into that same *fosse septique*, but my husband was so besotted that he would only have jumped in to rescue her. Not that he would have been able to distinguish her from all the other shit.'

She tapped the ash from her cigarette into a brass Moorish pot. I heard a wet snuffling beside my chair and an elderly boxer dog shambled into view, stretched, and without further preliminaries attempted to mount my left leg. I prised the dog off, but instantly he grappled my shin again. I dislodged him with a struggle, and he lay down on the rug and gazed at me, grunting with lust.

Madame Didier blew out a long stream of smoke but said nothing.

Desperate to make some normal conversation, I said, 'You've lived in St Cyriac for some time, Madame?'

'All my life, M'sieur. My aunt and uncle owned the house before me.'

'Well, in that case, Madame, I wonder if you'd be able to help me with a little research I'm undertaking?'

'Research?'

'I realise this was long before your time, Madame, but I'm investigating events that took place here during the War.'

She stared at me coldly, disdaining my flattery.

I pulled the magazine cutting out of my pocket and held it out to her. 'Perhaps you recognise this vessel?'

Her face clenched, and I knew at once that I had overstepped some mark.

She said, 'I was much too young to understand what was happening during the War, M'sieur.' She made no attempt to look at the cutting but sat gazing at me through her cigarette smoke for so long that I began to find it unsettling. 'There are a lot of stories from those days. Or perhaps only one, told by many different tellers.'

I waited but she didn't elaborate and a moment later Gaston reappeared and led me up to the room.

The Camellia Suite was at the very top of the house, wedged under the angle of the roof, and it was as tasteless as any room I had ever stayed in. A glass cabinet of crystal animals stood beside the door and a huge print of Landseer's *The Stag at Bay* hung on the wall beside the bed. A child's chest of drawers, thick with blue paint and with two of its knobs missing, sat under the mansard window. On it was a burn-scarred Cinzano ashtray and a Lladro ballerina.

I shut the ballerina and the ashtray in the top drawer and pushed open the window. The view gave out over angled slate roofs, dark with the rain, and the backs of the houses along the seaward side of the square. Beyond that lay the wide black expanse of the sea. The air was cool and rainwater clucked miserably in the gutters.

I sat on the end of the bed, and asked myself what in God's name I thought I was doing here.

10

The weather was still dull the following morning. I ate croissants and drank coffee in solitary state at a card table set up in the sitting room, served by a terrified Gaston. Of Madame Didier there was no sign. It was utterly quiet, and the ringing of my cutlery sounded like a fire alarm.

I escaped as soon as I could and spent an hour wandering round the wet streets. I fooled myself that I was exploring the little town, but the reality was that I had no idea what to do next. Someone, presumably, must at least know about the boat: I asked in the pharmacy and the minimarket. The pharmacist was Vietnamese and the manageress of the minimarket came from Lannion. Neither of them knew what I was talking about.

In a moment of inspiration I thought of the local library. I found it, housed in a modern annexe beside the Hotel de Ville, but the sign on the door told me it was only open three days a week, and today was not one of them.

I wandered back across the square. I felt very much a stranger here. I thought of Chantal and Kate, already packing, I guessed, for our new life. I was holding that up with this ridiculous quest. The sight of the Discovery parked under the trees was almost enough at that moment to tempt me to give up the whole thing.

Still debating that with myself, I walked over to the war memorial under its rose arbour, and ducked in under the dripping branches. I moved close to the monument itself, that sad little family group – portly father, handsome mother, the girl with huge eyes.

'The Rosen family,' a man's voice said from behind me.

He was sitting at the end of the bench quite close to where

I stood, but so lost in the gloom of the arbour that I had not noticed him. He was an old man with a white moustache and white hair tucked under a beret. A very old man, I saw now. He was slightly built and wore a fawn gabardine coat, dark with moisture on the shoulders, over a maroon cravat and a tweed jacket. His brogues shone like conkers, even in the dim light. He had kindly blue eyes and the dignity of a patrician.

I said, 'Who were they? The Rosens?'

'Gustave was our mayor at the start of the Second World War. That's him, his wife Rachel and daughter Madeleine – Lena, as everyone called her. Jewish, of course.'

'Ah.' I looked again at the monument.

'They were taken in 1942.'

'They must have been terrible times,' I said.

'Terrible, yes, and in many different ways. It is a curiously corrosive experience to see foreign soldiers marching through the streets of one's village, and the swastika flying from one's Town Hall.'

'I can imagine.'

He smiled. 'Forgive me, but I'm sure you cannot.'

There didn't seem to be anything I could say to that.

'Are you English, M'sieur?' he asked after a moment. 'I thought I detected the slightest of accents.'

I told him he was right.

'And yet your French is excellent.'

'My wife's French. She's a fearsome teacher.'

'Now I understand.' He rose to his feet and peeled off his glove and extended his hand. 'Pasqual. Dr Yves Pasqual. Welcome to St Cyriac.'

I fumbled to take his hand, which was thin and delicate. His old world courtesy took me by surprise, and in my confusion I failed to introduce myself in return. I was about to put this right, but by then he was already speaking again.

'Tell me, M'sieur, do you English also erect monuments to the least glorious moments in your history?'

'It's a national pastime.'

He moved past me, closer to the sculpture. Leaning on his

stick he stretched out his hand and with great tenderness he touched the raised stone figures.

'An old man's sentiment. I knew the Rosens rather well. They were a fine family.'

I stepped back to allow him his moment of contemplation, and, as I moved, the bulk of my wallet and the relics it contained shifted in my pocket. It struck me suddenly that meeting this old man might be an extravagant piece of good fortune.

I said, 'I expect you know everything there is to know, M'sieur, about St Cyriac during the War years.'

He glanced at me shrewdly. 'Less than you might think. I was away for much of the War. In the Army, you know.'

'It's just that—'

But before I could continue he straightened, drew on his gloves, and lifted the peak of his cap to me. 'Please enjoy your stay in our village, M'sieur.'

He walked out into the wet grey afternoon and made his way, frail but erect, up the hill and past the church. There were a few people on the streets now – a taxi-driver parked by the kerb, a woman with a baby in a pushchair, a man carrying shopping bags. I noticed that all three of them greeted the old man respectfully as he passed, and he exchanged a friendly word with each of them. I watched his thin back until he was out of sight, and then I sat for some time in the cool gloom, obscurely ashamed of my clumsy approach to him.

After a while I got up and walked down to the little harbour. Just as it had been yesterday, Henri's café appeared to be the centre of things in St Cyriac. It was lunchtime, and the long bar was packed with men drinking coffee or beer. I made my way to the same table I had taken yesterday. Henri appeared almost at once, cracking his napkin.

'*Grand crème* again, M'sieur? Or something more stimulating? You look as if you could use some stimulation.'

'You're right,' I said. 'I'll have a rosé.'

'Excellent choice! Coming right up! And you'll be eating?'

'Maybe. Why not.'

He beamed and vanished between the tables. Some instinct

prompted me and I took the magazine article out of my wallet and spread it out in front of me. Henri was back almost at once with my drink and a menu. Before setting them down he bent to polish the table once more, unnecessarily, then stopped, arrested by the sight of the article with its photo.

'That again,' he said.

'My father commanded it,' I said, watching his face. 'This boat. During the War. That's why I want to find it.'

Henri stood back with his hands on his hips, eyes wide. 'Your father?'

'That's right.'

'This isn't a joke?'

'No. I don't think it was a joke back then, either.'

He held my gaze for a long moment.

I sipped my wine, put the glass down. I said, 'What?'

He shook his head in wonder. 'Well, now, M'sieur, personally I don't care much for all that wartime nonsense, you understand. But you really mean to say the commander of that boat was your father?'

'You know about this story, then?'

'I know that if your dad was the skipper of that old tub he was about the most exciting thing that ever happened in St Cyriac.'

'So you *do* recognise the boat?'

Henri ignored that. 'He's not still alive, is he?' he said. 'Your father?'

'As a matter of fact he is.'

'And has he come with you? Is he here?'

'No, but—'

'Pity, pity. Still, you're here.' He stood staring at me, still shaking his head. 'Your father! Imagine that.'

I let him go through these theatricals for a while, then I said, 'Henri, can you handle a stupid question?'

'Try me, M'sieur. I've had quite a lot of practice.'

'What did my father do here?'

He frowned. 'You don't know?'

But at that moment someone called for him from across the café.

61

'All right!' he bawled over his shoulder. And then, swinging back to me, 'Impatient rabble. No, look, M'sieur, I didn't grow up here. There are half a hundred people in St Cyriac who know more about this than I do. I'll put out the word that you're in town, if you like. Meanwhile at least I can tell you where the boat is.'

'I thought you'd never seen it before.'

'That's before I realised you were the son of our local hero. The boat's near Daniel Bourgogne's yard.'

'Where's that?'

'A few hundred metres upriver. Though if you'll take my advice, you'll forget this old wreck and get Daniel to make you something with a bit of style. He's just rebuilt *The Gay Dog* for us. Gunther's putting the finishing touches to her himself. Did you happen to notice her?'

'I believe I did. She's beautiful. But—'

'But of course, it's this old tub or nothing for you, M'sieur, I understand.' He sighed. 'Take the path the far side of the square. Just walk down the alleyway past the photo shop, you'll see it. Follow the track up the river. The old boat's up against the opposite bank. You can get across at the boatyard.'

Someone shouted for him again.

'Coming!' Henri roared. 'Good God, can't you ignorant bastards do anything for yourselves?'

And he was gone, cruising off between the tables, slapping his napkin left and right.

'Thanks,' I said to his retreating back, but I don't think he heard me.

II

This was progress at last, and my spirits lifted. I contained my impatience and treated myself to lunch and a second glass of rosé. It was after two before I left the café.

The sky began to clear before I had even crossed the square.

I followed Henri's instructions, emerging on the riverbank a little above the spot where I had stood yesterday, and this time quickly saw the path. The Vasse flowed dark and smooth in its steep little valley under the trees. I could see that the current ran fast here as it swept out into the sea.

I turned right, upstream, and within a few metres the path became a muddy track, perhaps originally a towpath. The houses of the village were lost to view behind banks of wet hawthorn and alder. I walked on for a few minutes, picking my way between the puddles. It was very quiet, and I was startled when a family of coots burst out of the reeds almost at my feet, ploughing the water into furrows. The birds sat in midstream, riding the current, watching me, two adults and three sooty chicks. Their sharp indignant cries echoed under the dripping trees.

I saw the launch before I realised that I was even looking at her. She lay tilted to one side against the far bank of the river, drowned in the shadows, the fronds of waterside willows screening her. On the bow the phantom numerals 2548 still showed, and beside them the RAF roundel.

I stood there for some time, looking at her. When I was ready I followed the path a little further, looking for a way across the water. After a few metres I could see round the bend of the river. Bourgogne's boatyard lay just ahead, a cluster of modern buildings, a boatshed built out over a concrete dock, a parked Nissan four-wheel drive with a boat trailer. Beside the boatshed stood a rack of plastic kayaks in red and yellow and some sailing catamarans. A sign advertised them for hire. The yard was deserted. Half hidden among the trees on the opposite side stood a small cottage built of the local stone, with a fenced garden and lights on in the front windows.

At the boatyard itself pontoons connected by gangplanks spanned the Vasse. I crossed the concrete dock and stepped gingerly down, feeling the timber sag in the dark water under my weight. Upstream I saw a patchwork of cress beds with low concrete walls and I heard the rushing of the stream through iron sluices.

I quickly climbed the muddy steps onto the far bank and walked down the path. For a moment I could see nothing through the screen of reeds and willows except the flicker of light on the river. I stopped. I swept aside the trailing branches and the launch was suddenly there, just an arm's length away, leaning slightly towards me.

There seemed to be no metalwork left on the hull, no railings or fittings. The wheelhouse and all the upper works had vanished, but someone had built a makeshift sliding roof of marine ply over the main cockpit and had stretched a green tarpaulin over the forward hatch. Where the original decking was visible beneath the patches it was sun-bleached to silver. The varnish had peeled from the hull and I could see the diagonal lines of the strakes.

I took a couple of steps forward to the edge of the bank, letting the wet willow trail across my shoulders, soaking my jacket. The launch was no longer a blur of speed and drama from long ago, captured on a murky photograph. She was a presence, and a far more emphatic presence than I had imagined, heavy and solid and much bigger than I could have guessed, a real thing that I could touch, if only I stretched out my hand. I stretched out my hand.

The hatch slid back with a bang and a man's head loomed from the dark of the hull. I leaped back, slipped on the mud and had to clutch a branch to stay on my feet.

'Hello,' the man said, blinking guilelessly at me.

He was elderly, certainly over seventy, but somehow he didn't look it. His sunbrowned face was unlined and framed in a halo of soft white hair, and there was a curiously childlike quality about his blue eyes. He was wearing old-fashioned working dungarees, the sort the French used to call *bleus*, and I saw now that he was standing on a short ladder leading up from the waist of the vessel. He came up a couple more steps, pushed the hatch cover fully open and stepped out onto the deck.

'I heard someone,' he said. 'I thought it was Daniel. He's my friend. But you're not Daniel.'

'No, I'm sorry but I'm not Daniel.' I let go of the tree and dusted lichen from my hands, trying to regain some aplomb.

'And then I thought maybe it was M'sieur Heron. He's my friend, too.'

I looked at him.

'He comes quite often,' he went on. 'We go fishing together. He's very clever. He catches fish in his beak.'

'I'm afraid I'm not M'sieur Heron either,' I said, carefully. 'I'm Iain.'

'That's a funny name.'

'Yes, it is. It's English. Sort of.'

'I'm Dominic.'

'Well, I'm pleased to meet you, Dominic.'

I slithered down to the edge of the bank and held out my hand. He looked at it with something like awe. I got the impression people didn't often shake hands with Dominic, and with my paw stuck out in front of me I began to feel stupid. Despite his years he seemed not quite old enough for such formality. All at once he seized my hand and pumped it and beamed at me, and his eyes filled with the sunniest pleasure.

'Iain, would you like a sausage?'

I retrieved my hand. 'A sausage?'

'I cook them on my little stove down below. Daniel says I shouldn't but I'm very careful.' He said this again, making his face solemn. 'I'm always very careful.'

I glanced past Dominic through the hatchway and down into

65

the hull of the launch. I caught a glimpse of gloomy space, of curved frames and planking.

'Actually, I've already eaten,' I said.

'Not my sausages, you haven't. Come along!'

He scampered down his ladder so that I momentarily lost sight of him. It evidently didn't occur to him that I might not follow.

I put one foot on the top strake and checked that the hull was thoroughly grounded. It was low tide. The mud around the old launch was printed with bird tracks, and a dirty white mooring buoy and a couple of barnacled tractor tyres lay stranded on it. The flowing water was several reassuring metres away.

I swallowed hard, and stepped onto the deck. My footfalls echoed through the hollow hull as if through the soundbox of some huge musical instrument. I got onto the ladder and perched uneasily there, my hands clamped on the edge of the hatch. I could see Dominic working busily below me, lighting his stove, turning sausages in a pan, still talking about his friends in the village, about the visitors who came to see him. He didn't seem to need me to answer immediately, so I let him rattle on while I stood on the ladder and let my courage build up again.

The deck curved away from me at chest height, the river shining like enamel beyond the tapering bow. Further downstream, through the leaning trees, I could see the houses of the village clustered on the left bank of the river, and the wide steel sea beyond. For a second the trembling light on the water gave me the illusion of movement, and I had to close my eyes and hope the feeling would pass. It did pass, more or less, but not before I found myself wondering how often my father had stood on this very spot, scanning the grey seas and the grey skies. I wondered what that must have felt like for him, with his hands on the quivering wheel and the engines thundering through the soles of his seaboots, and the lads of his crew squinting into the murk, gripping the hatch edges as the launch heeled, baring their teeth at the rush of it.

Dominic popped his head up beside me and looked directly into my face, smiling his innocent smile. 'You're frightened,' he said.

'It's boats.'

'It's not boats,' he replied easily. 'It's the sea. It's the deep, dark sea.'

I opened my mouth and closed it again.

'Don't be frightened, Iain.' With great gentleness he touched the back of my hand where it gripped the side of the ladder. And he added, as if this were somehow relevant, 'Your sausage is ready.'

He moved away and I took the last couple of steps down. It was a low shadowy space but surprisingly roomy. There were some plywood partitions up forward, where light washed down from the circular forepeak hatch, and some rudimentary benches which might originally have been the bases for bunks. I could feel the damp in the air and, beneath the savour of Dominic's sausages, the place smelled dankly of mud.

I saw that he had arranged the central area into a den. There was an old wicker chair, a makeshift table, and a lopsided book-case with a stack of Tintin comics on it and half-a-dozen packets of biscuits. His small camping Gaz stove was set up inside a tin box directly under the hatch so that the fumes and smoke rose into the open air. I had the impression of a child's camp or tree house, a place of private refuge, filled with bric-a-brac discarded by the grown-ups. On the table I noticed a large sky-blue china elephant and a tube of glue.

'They'd broken jumbo's trunk off,' Dominic said, and pulled a sad face. 'I had to make him better.'

I looked closely at the china elephant. It had evidently been in a hundred pieces, and must have taken enormous patience to repair.

'You've certainly fixed him up, Dominic.'

'Yes, I make models too, you know.' He smiled broadly. 'You can have the chair.'

It seemed that this might be my reward for saying the right thing. I sat down. Dominic crouched over his cooker, humming to himself while the fat sizzled and the scent of herbs and garlic rose around me and filled the belly of the launch.

I said, 'Do you live here, Dominic? On the boat?'

'Oh, no! Daniel would never allow that.' He turned off the gas and took the pan away from the heat, and in the sudden quiet I could hear the silky run of the river. 'I have a little flat in the Old Mill. It's nice there. There's a television and everything and Madame Duquesne keeps an eye on me. That's because I'm not quite right in the head.'

'Oh,' I said, startled. 'I see.'

'But I come here most days because I like the river and the fish and the birds.'

He forked a fat sausage onto a tin plate and passed it to me, and stood crouched under the low deck, pleased with himself, waiting for me to eat. I speared the sausage with the fork and nibbled a piece off one end. It was very hot and very good and I told him so. Pleased, he served his own sausage and settled down on the floor to eat.

'I like the boat, too,' he said. 'I look after her.'

'I can see you do. My father would be happy about that.'

He stopped chewing as this registered with him.

'Long ago,' I said, 'this used to be my father's boat. Back in the War.'

Dominic's mouth fell open and he gazed at me with his wide blue eyes.

I said, 'That's why I've come to see her.'

He swallowed hastily. 'Your father was a great patriot, then. A *very* great patriot.'

I meant to say something funny, the way I might have answered a child, but I found that I could not. A great patriot. I had never thought of my father that way. I did a rapid mental calculation of Dominic's age: I guessed he would have been twelve or fourteen at the end of the War. I put my plate down on the deck.

'You were here in those days, Dominic? In St Cyriac?'

'Me? I've always been here.'

'Maybe you know what happened to my father when he was here. Maybe you even saw him?'

'Oh, I couldn't say,' he answered brightly.

I suppose he could have meant merely that he was unable to recall but, oddly, I didn't think so.

'Well, what about this boat?' I said, changing tack. 'Did you see her back then?'

He thought about this question for a minute. 'I saw her the day the Germans pulled her off the Shoals,' he said. 'The day after all the shooting.'

'There was shooting?'

'Lots! I heard it. The Germans had a big gun up on the cliff top. They were very good shots.'

For some reason I had not imagined real gunfire, with real danger. I had assumed the launch must have been captured at sea. I had pictured a dignified surrender to some serious warship out in the Channel. Some courtly nonsense out of Ealing Studios: *For you, chentlemen, ze war is over.* Now in my mind I saw tracer fire crawling out from a dark shore and I tasted the fear of the men as they watched it probe towards them.

'There was lots and lots of shooting,' Dominic went on happily. 'Bang-bang-*bang*! Then the next day they towed her in here.'

'What happened to the crew, Dominic?'

'Oh,' he said almost negligently, 'they died.'

'Died? What – all of them?'

He screwed up his face and counted on his fingers. 'Six, no ...' He held up seven fingers. 'That many. They're asleep now, in the churchyard in the village.'

'Seven of them? Seven of them were killed in the shooting?'

'Not exactly,' he frowned, anxious to get this right, not to mislead me. 'Some of them drowned. They were washed up later, and the crabs had tried to eat them.' He made a face. 'Can't blame the crabs. They were only having lunch. Afterwards the people in the village put the dead men in holes in the ground. Very deep, they were, the holes. They put them into boxes, and then into the holes, and filled the holes in. Very sad. Even the German soldiers were sad.'

I knew Dominic had sensed my shock but I couldn't hide it. Seven men. Seven young men. The very same lads I had stared at with such envy all through my childhood in the photograph on the bookcase, raffish and cocky, clowning for the camera in their roll-neck sweaters and caps, the two in the front showing their stripes. I knew each of those faces so well that I felt a little as if I had lost relatives.

I said, 'Dominic, would you tell me about those times?'

'Tell you what about them?'

'What happened to this boat, for example. What happened after she was towed in? What happened to the people on board who didn't die?'

He sat gazing placidly at me. I wondered if somehow he hadn't heard me, so I tried again.

'I'd really like to know. Can we have a talk about it all?'

He gave me his sunniest smile. 'No.'

'We can't?' I stared at him. 'Why not?'

'Father Thomas told me never to talk about all that.'

'Father Thomas?'

'He's at the church. Haven't you heard about Father Thomas? He knows everything. And he says I can keep secrets better than anyone.'

'What kind of secrets?'

'If I told you, they wouldn't be secrets, would they? Even I know that!' He laughed. 'Of course, if Father Thomas says it's all right, then I could talk to you. Only he always says no.'

I considered all this for a moment. 'I'll tell you what, Dominic. If I go along to the church, maybe I can ask Father Thomas myself. Would that do?'

'Oh, yes! Anyone can talk to Father Thomas.' He smiled, delighted that between us we had found a way through this moral maze. He opened his eyes very wide. 'Shall we have another sausage?'

I walked back along the towpath, turning the scene over and over in my mind. I was so absorbed that only when I reached the boatyard did I notice that the lights were still on in the house among the trees. Standing in the front window was a tall woman with short, no-nonsense hair. Her arms were crossed over her breast and she was quite obviously watching me.

I raised a hand to her, but she neither responded nor made

any attempt to take her eyes off me. When I had crossed the Vasse and started back down the other side I looked back and could still see her dark silhouette in the yellow rectangle of the window.

12

It was early evening by the time I got back to the square, and the rain had started to fall again. I stopped at the iron gate of the churchyard and looked up through the dripping trees at the headstones and mounds, half-hidden in the grass.

I had intended to go in immediately and find the graves of my father's crew, and then to seek out this Father Thomas. But the graveyard was gloomy and the church looked cold and empty. Standing there in the wet evening, tired and a little overloaded, I lacked the spirit to tackle all this right now. Tomorrow would do fine.

I went back to the guesthouse and crept back up to the Camellia Suite, hoping to escape detection by Gaston, Madame Didier or her amorous dog. I made it. I locked the door behind me.

It was still early, not six o'clock. I was pleased with my day's work, especially after such an unpromising start. I supposed at some stage I would have to go and find something to eat, but I wasn't hungry yet. I kicked off my shoes and stretched out on the bed. It was surprisingly soft.

I wasn't sure what had awakened me; perhaps the unfamiliar shadows of the angled ceiling, or the small knocking of the open window against its fastening. The wind had risen and the net curtain billowed into the room, filling like a parachute.

I rolled over to sit on the edge of the bed and checked my watch. It was three in the morning. I got up to tie back the curtain and close the window, but stopped there, looking out at the night sea. Way, way out, I could see a long flicker of white which shivered, faded, and then grew luminous again. The Shoals, exposed now as the tide dropped. I stared out, fascinated, imagining acre upon acre of white water and bursting surf, mill race currents roaring through hidden channels as the tide drained. If I listened hard I could hear the dull booming of the sea breaking on those dark sands in the night.

And then something else. Carried on the wind, from a great distance, I could just hear the peal of a bell. A warning bell.

The tiny sound seemed both awful and thrilling – I thought of a great bell-buoy, lurching on black water, groaning against its chains. I wondered if there had been a bell-buoy like this one out on the Shoals sixty and more years before, and if my father had heard it back then, riding the black waters in his sharp-prowed launch, butting the suck and rush of the tide, struggling to reach a man called Lucien while the guns fired from the cliffs and the tracer fire came in search of him.

All for nothing.

The guns found their range, seven young men died, and my father's life was dislocated forever.

I stood there listening for a very long time before I closed the window and shut out the night. But I could not shut out the wild sensation that this bell tolling in the night was a signal just for me.

13

At eight-thirty the next morning I opened the iron gate into the churchyard. The air was damp and herbal and gulls chimed in a white sky as I climbed the path between yew and beech trees.

I saw the graves almost at once, seven Commonwealth War Graves Commission limestone headstones under the yew tree by the wall, the neatly clipped grass over the mounds speckled with buttercups and daisies. They lay in two rows. Each headstone was sculpted with the RAF crown and eagle, and under it a name. Aircraftman 1st Class S. D. Allen, 38; Aircraftman H. Underwood, 26; Flight Sergeant P. E. MacDonald (First Cox'n), RAAF, 22; Aircraftman D.R. Evans, 17. I recited each one to myself in a whisper. K. T. Tucker, F. O. Pisani, L. T. Sheldrake. And under each one: *Died 20 April 1944*. I had never known their names before, and it saddened me to read them now, and to see their youth set out so starkly before me.

I could match some of them readily enough with faces in the photograph on my parents' bookcase. The pipesmoker in the picture would be Allen, at thirty-eight the old man of the crew. What had his role been? Father confessor, counsellor, the voice of wisdom? Beside him lay seventeen-year-old Aircraftman Evans – he must be the slight, dark haired boy in the second row of the photo, his arm hooked defensively around the radio mast, as though afraid he might fall overboard. And the sergeant in the front row, that would be MacDonald – an Australian, I saw from the headstone; I wondered what cascade of petty circumstances had drawn him from the warm south to die on the windy coast of France.

Seven graves. There had been eight men in that photograph

and my father would have been behind the camera. Just one other man had cheated death that night, the crewman my father had brought back with him to England. Ironically, the only member of the crew to survive was now the only one whose name I didn't know.

I stood up slowly, then walked around to the west porch of the church and pushed on the double doors. They swung open at my touch. The space inside was cavernous, lit by the morning sun streaming through stained glass.

I could see nothing at first against the glare, but as my eyes adjusted I made out a figure near the altar, setting out hymn books on the front row of pews. He looked up as I approached, and stood waiting for me, a small and energetic man of about my own age, with a polished pate, brown from the sun, and dark, merry eyes. He wore a blue denim shirt, jeans and white trainers with reflective patches which blazed in the light. A pair of fashionable sunglasses hung on a cord around his neck.

'Father Thomas?' I asked, tentatively. He didn't look like any priest I'd ever seen.

'I'm afraid not. But I can take you to Father Thomas if you want.'

Before I could reply he set down his hymn books and led me around the back of the altar. There was a small chapel to the Virgin off to the right – three ranks of pews, twinkling candles, a vase of lilies – and beyond that a heavy door set into the wall. He reached up for a large iron key, inserted it in the lock, pushed the door wide and stepped inside.

It was a plain stone cell with eight hardback wooden chairs in it, and it smelled of stale air. The light was dim, filtering in through a diamond-paned casement deeply overshadowed by the trees outside. The little man walked in and lit a candle, one of a line of votive stubs set in a sand tray. By the flare of it I saw, set into a niche in the wall, the bronze bust of a man; a hard face with a hawk-like nose. Under the bust was a brass plaque, and on it the words: '*Fr Thomas Montignac, né* 12 *Decembre* 1900, *fusillé par les Allemands* 14 *Juin* 1944.'

The candlelight flickered over the crags of dark metal, so that the face seemed to frown and sneer in quick succession. I looked sharply around at the little man.

'Meet Father Thomas,' he said, and gave me a wry smile. 'I'm afraid I have the advantage of you. Your name is Madoc, right? Your father was the captain of that wreck in the river, and you've been down there talking to old Dominic.'

'You're very well informed.'

'This is St Cyriac, M'sieur Madoc. By now everyone in the village knows your blood group, your passport number, and the e-mail address of your uncle's mistress. What I don't know is your first name.'

'It's Iain.'

'And I'm Felix. OK? Like the cat. I'm the priest here these days.'

'So this was Dominic's idea of a joke, was it, sending me up here to talk to a man who's been dead for sixty years?' I felt foolish and I couldn't keep the resentment out of my voice.

'No, no,' he said gently. 'Dominic was just sending you to speak with the cleverest person he knows. See it as a compliment.'

'I'm not with you.'

'Dominic's family abandoned him when he was a kid. Dumped the boy in the church porch and vanished. In those days people weren't as enlightened about simple souls like him. Father Thomas fed him, found him jobs to do, protected him. And as far as Dominic's concerned Father Thomas never went away.' Felix saw that his explanation had silenced me. He touched my arm lightly and steered me out of the chamber, and then bustled back to lock the door behind us, so that iron clashed in the stillness. I walked ahead for a few steps and stopped, waiting for him. The church lay silent and still around me. The soles of the little priest's trainers hissed on the stone as he came up to me.

'Henri says you don't know what happened to your father here in St Cyriac. Can that be true?'

'It's true.'

He shook his head then led me to the west door and out into

76

the bright day. I began to feel as if I'd wandered into someone else's play and didn't know the script.

'Thomas was shot by the Germans in front of the altar,' he said, as we walked between the yew trees, 'so he's something of a saint around here. St Cyriac library treats his diaries like fragments of the True Cross. We used to keep the old boy's statue in the gardens, but the inscription upset some of our European partners, so we moved him inside.'

We rounded the corner of the church and Felix stepped off the path and pushed through a screen of laurel bushes whose dry leaves crackled underfoot. Concealed behind the foliage a flight of stone steps led down to an arched wooden door. He shoved it open and ducked inside.

'Come on in,' he called from the darkness.

I followed him, sensing cold air against my face and the taint of decay. Half-a-dozen ancient striplights flickered into life in the vaulting. I saw a forest of squat stone columns with square plinths and sarcophagi along the walls. A cushion of white fungus bulged from the foot of the pillar beside me. On the ground next to my foot lay a mummified toad. Felix walked briskly down the length of the crypt's central aisle. Halfway along he stopped and faced me.

'Father Thomas used to hide people down here, Iain. Men dodging the work battalions, escaped POWs, deserters. But finally in June '44 his luck ran out, and the Germans caught up with him. There were two men in hiding here when the soldiers came. Father Thomas refused to give them away.' He paused. 'One of those two men was your father.'

I realised I had been holding my breath and forced myself to release it. I put out my hand and rested it on a pillar, grateful for the cold kiss of stone.

'Thomas Montignac had been hiding your father and his friend here for nearly eight weeks,' Felix went on, keeping his eyes on mine. 'There was no light. Very little air. The tombs were still in use, and it could be pretty gruesome. That entrance was kept locked in those days, so when they replaced the flagstones in the chapel, whoever was down here was sealed in. There was no question of getting out, not even at night, not even for an hour or two.'

'So how did they escape?'

'While the Germans were interrogating Father Thomas, a bunch of local lads broke that door open and got them out. Bundled them down to the boatyard and into a dinghy. That's how I heard it.'

I looked around me. Eight weeks. The chill, the darkness, the scrape of every shoe on the flagstones above. The dread every time the trap was heaved open and light spiked into the gloom. Felix came back up the aisle to me.

'Iain, let me take a priestly guess. You're confused that your father didn't confide in you about all this, right? Confused and maybe resentful.'

'I suppose I am.'

'But think about it. Locked up in here for two months, in constant fear? I don't think that's something a man would want to share with his innocent young son. I think a man might prefer to leave his child untainted by an experience like that.'

I said nothing.

Felix took my arm. 'Let's go out in the sunshine.'

He locked the crypt door behind us and we walked back up to the bench overlooking the graves. It was a brilliant cool morning, and I was glad of the space and the free air.

I said, 'You're saying this priest died for them?'

'Thomas died for his beliefs, not just for your father and his pal. Thomas would have seen it as his duty, a chance to balance the books a bit.'

'His duty?'

Felix tore off a grass stem and chewed it. 'Your dad and his crew had risked their lives to bring over a Free French agent. A few weeks later they risked their lives all over again to come back and fetch him. Only this time they didn't get away with it, and seven of them lost their lives in the attempt. Thomas's sacrifice was payback time. That's my guess.'

I grappled with the idea of a man who would give his own

78

life to settle such a debt. That train of thought triggered a new question in my mind.

'What happened to the agent? This Lucien?'

'He died with the rest of your father's crew when the launch was hit.'

'He's buried here?'

Felix shook his head. 'His body was never found. That's not unusual on this coast. It's a bit unusual they found all the rest of them. Awful waste, huh? Your dad brings him over, and he spends a month here dodging the Germans and organising the resistance. But in the end there isn't any resistance because the Landings happen in Normandy instead of here. And on top of that he gets himself killed – and seven young men who try to get him out. There's not many positives in that.'

I sat gazing out over the neat rows of graves. I thought about Lucien and his meaningless mission, and of the men who had died trying to save him. I thought again of Father Thomas and of his own sacrifice. Perhaps I could understand after all something of why he had done it – to try to make sense of the loss of all these young lives.

Over the years Chantal had brought back similar stories from her war zones, stories of ordinary people and their capacity for heroism and sacrifice. These tales used to move her in the telling, often to tears, but lately I'd noticed a weariness in her. It was testosterone and lack of imagination that drove men to heroism, she'd said bitterly after a recent assignment to Iraq. Nothing more. She was tired and depressed after that trip, so I didn't argue. I wanted her to resign and was glad she was growing tired of it all. But just the same I thought she was wrong about this, and sitting here in the quiet churchyard, I was sure of it. For there was no escaping the truth. This wasn't done in hot blood: the priest had a choice, but he had still given his life for my father and his companion.

Felix took the grass stem out of his mouth and slung it away.

'Talking of fathers,' he said, 'I gather you met mine yesterday.'

'I'm sorry?'

'Down at the Rosens' memorial. Nice old boy in a beret?

White moustache? He told me he'd met a wandering Englishman asking about the past. I put two and two together.'

'That was your father?'

'He's the guy you need to talk to if you really want to know how things were back then. He's been here since the Flood. Trained as a doctor after the War and delivered half the population of St Cyriac.'

'He gave me the impression he didn't want to talk about the old days.'

'Ah, but then he didn't realise who you were. He knows all there is to know. He was the mayor until the end of the War. Took over from Gustave Rosen.'

'Really? He told me he was away in the Army.'

'That's just him giving you the brush-off. He was at the cavalry school at Saumur, but then he was wounded in the battle for the Loire bridges in June 1940, and that was the end of his war. After that he was a prisoner for a while, then he came back here in early '42.'

'And became mayor?'

'He didn't want the job. He'd been friends with Gustave Rosen, and he hated treating with the Germans. Still, he got his own back by helping the Resistance whenever he got the chance. He got the Croix de Guerre at the end. De Gaulle wanted to award it personally after the Liberation, but of course Papa wouldn't have that.'

'Why of course?'

'We're old Breton nobility, the Pasquals.' Felix rocked his head mockingly. 'Very grand. Very ... well connected. Not great de Gaulle fans, us *aristos*.'

'And he was in the Resistance too? He must be quite a character.'

'He didn't run round with a Sten gun and a beret. But he helped out where he could.' Felix gave me a sideways look. 'Like the night your father escaped. Papa was one of that group. He didn't lead it, but he was one of them. So you see, if it hadn't been for my dad, yours might have died in St Cyriac, and you'd never have been born. Makes us brothers in a way, wouldn't you say?'

I put my head back and looked up at the shifting trees. 'Would your father talk to me about all this, Felix?'

'I don't think I could stop him, once he finds out who you are. We'll go over to my place right now, have a drink, fix a time.' He got to his feet.

We went through a gap in the wall and across a gravel driveway to the rectory. Rosemary grew in terracotta pots beside the steps to his front door and made the morning aromatic. Felix unlocked the house, and I followed him along a low corridor. He went into a small bright kitchen, opened the fridge and took out an unlabelled bottle of white wine.

'Go on through,' he said over his shoulder. 'Make yourself at home.'

I did as I was told, and walked into the main room. I felt a little dazed, and was glad to have a moment to myself. The room was cool and light, with a slate floor and two shallow steps down into a conservatory which looked onto a walled garden, vivid with spring flowers. Over the far wall was a view out to the port and, between the masts of the yachts, to the wide sea beyond. The room was calm and well ordered, with a wall of books, a chair set under the window with a reading lamp on a sidetable, a modest desk with a computer and a block of white paper squared beside it. A framed photograph on the wall showed a much younger but already bald Felix in a striped rugby jersey, standing in a team line-up.

He appeared with a jingling tray and saw me examining the photo.

'When I was young and reckless, I played for Rouen. Well, Rouen Reserves. I played fly-half, which means you get trampled by fourteen troglodytes from one team and fifteen from the other. At that stage in my life I was a good deal more concerned with the present than with the future, let alone the past.' He carried the tray down the stairs into the conservatory and set it on the table, waved me to one of the white wicker chairs and took a seat himself. He poured the wine. 'To bygone tragedies. And to what they can teach us.'

I touched my glass to his. I looked out at the boats, but I kept thinking of the chill darkness in the crypt – that utter darkness – day after day, week after week. And the terror. I couldn't get it out of my mind. I saw that my glass was empty, without knowing quite how it had got that way. Felix filled it again. I shook myself, took the plastic sleeve out of my jacket pocket and showed him the sketch my father had drawn on the back of the Senior Service cigarette packet.

'What's this?'

'My father brought this back from St Cyriac in 1944. I think he drew it. I was hoping you might know where it is.'

He took the card from me and produced a pair of reading glasses.

'Buildings by a beach, right? And this is a pier, is it, or a dock of some sort?'

'That's how I read it.'

'And a house here? And a little square inside it ... And these numbers?'

'Measurements, maybe. They're in feet and inches. Do you know the place?'

'Hardly.' He folded his glasses away. 'There are half a hundred properties up this stretch of coast with landing stages or piers of one sort or another. In the old days every farm had one – it was easier to get around by sea than by road. You'd have to go and look at them all to get any real idea.'

'So maybe I'll go and look at them all.'

He glanced doubtfully at me. 'That's a tall order, Iain. You don't know for sure if it's anywhere near here. Besides, if the map was drawn during the War, this place could have changed out of all recognition. It may not even exist any more.'

'Still, I have to try.'

'You *have* to?'

My own earnest tone embarrassed me. 'It feels like I have to.'

I took the map back from him and examined it again, the ink mottled by rain or seawater and that odd design in the centre, like a barred window. When I looked up I caught him watching me.

'This is your very own Grail Quest, isn't it?' he said. 'Well, far be it from me to interfere with a man's search for grace.' He got to his feet and crossed to the computer desk. He opened a drawer, took out a palm-top and touched the stylus to the screen. 'There'll be others who want to meet you, apart from Papa. Between them, all those old timers should be able to answer your questions. How about Henri's? About eight o'clock?'

'You mean tonight?'

'If we gave them any longer the Commune would organise a civic reception. Bring your mysterious map and we'll ask Papa about it. He's got a memory like an elephant.'

The room was suddenly filled with the swelling sounds of the Hallelujah Chorus.

Felix said, 'I'd better get that. One of these days it'll be God.' He pulled a slim mobile out of the top pocket of his shirt and snapped it open, listened for a moment and spoke briefly into it. He closed the phone. 'Duty calls, unfortunately.'

He began to gather up bottle and glasses, refusing to let me help. But he didn't move away at once, and when he had finished clearing the table he stood there for a few moments with the tray in his hands.

'Iain, you haven't come here to St Cyriac looking for some old boat and a story of derring-do. You've come looking for your father.'

'Yes,' I said. 'I have.'

'Let me put my priest's hat on for a moment and give you a word of advice. If you truly want to find him, you won't do it by standing at the top of the cellar steps and shouting into the shadows. You'll have to go a little way into his world to look for him. Sometimes that requires a leap of faith.'

I laughed uneasily. 'Sounds like a leap in the dark.'

'I hope not. The dark's not always an agreeable place to be.' He marched away through the house, replaced glasses and bottle in the kitchen, showed me out and trotted up the steps past me. The sun had vanished behind clouds again. He said, 'Do you think I'll beat the rain?'

'No.'

'There, you see? That's why you need faith.'

He walked the few steps to his car – a canary yellow 2CV with a striped awning, folded back – and swung himself into the driver's seat. The little engine popped like a lawnmower. He shouted a farewell, rammed the car into gear and roared away, scattering gravel, one hand waving over his shoulder. The rain began to fall, fat drops slapping through the leaves of the garden trees.

14

At about six I showered and changed, left my mobile on charge, and went downstairs.

'You will take sherry, M'sieur?' Madame Didier intoned as I passed the living room door.

Surprised at this invitation, I stepped into the room. She was lounging with her back to me in her brocade armchair, wreathed in cigarette smoke, her hair wound up in a pale-blue turban. There was a large gilt-framed mirror on the wall above the fireplace, in which I realised she followed every movement along the hall and up and down the stairs. She rose and crossed to a fabulously ornate glass and chrome drinks cabinet.

'It is unthinkable for an Englishman of quality not to take a little dry Amontillado as an aperitif before dinner. That rogue Henri may be charming, despite his ambivalence in matters of romance, but you may be sure that he will have nothing like this on his wine list.' She handed me a cut glass goblet, only slightly cracked, with an inch of straw coloured liquid in it. 'Given to me personally by Albert Camus, with whom I was – how shall I put it? – on excellent terms.'

I couldn't see any way of escaping, so I thanked her and took the glass. Jasper, the Boxer dog, shambled in, saw me and shook his chops lasciviously so that a dumbbell of drool flew up and hung from the moulding of the mirror.

'Father Felix tells me there is a gathering in your honour tonight,' Madame Didier said, as if nonchalantly.

'And will you be joining us, Madame?'

'I regret I shall not.'

'It was rather short notice.'

She eyed me through the smoke. 'It is not a matter of notice, M'sieur.'

I sat sipping my awful sherry, perched like a schoolboy on the edge of my chair, waiting for the explanation I knew would come.

'This gathering concerns the War, I imagine?' she asked.

'Yes. Or rather, my father's time here during the War.'

'People will tell their stories of those years,' she said. 'What kind of a place St Cyriac was when your father was here. How he was hidden. How he and his companion escaped. Who was courageous enough to help them. These are the stories you would like to hear, I think?'

I put my glass down. 'Yes. I would like to hear about those days.'

She ground out her cigarette and lit another with a gold lighter, blew a plume of smoke at the ceiling. 'My uncle owned this house during the War. He was a member of the Lu Brezon. Have you ever heard of the Lu Brezon, M'sieur?'

'I'm afraid not.'

'It was a movement dedicated to Breton independence. Independence from France, that is. Brittany was only incorporated into France in the sixteenth century, and that was too soon for most Bretons. The Lu Brezon was all about Breton dress and Breton bagpipes, Breton poetry, the Breton language. All slightly ridiculous, but not so different from your Irish Republican movement, perhaps. Then in 1939 France was at war and suddenly the Lu Brezon, like your IRA, was not so ridiculous any more. Some in the organisation collaborated with the Germans during the Occupation, just as some Irish fought for Hitler. They assumed a German victory, like everyone else, and thought collaboration would help their cause when the War ended. The Lu Brezon refused to recognise the new French Government at Vichy. An extremist Lu Brezon militia was even formed to help fight the Resistance.' She looked at me. 'Members of that militia wore Waffen SS uniforms.'

I couldn't hide my surprise.

'My enemy's enemy is my friend,' she said. 'Do you see? For

Bretons to wear French uniforms would have been to identify with the traditional oppressor, which was France, not Germany. That's how the Lu Brezon saw things.'

'I didn't realise, Madame.'

'Only a small number of passionate and misguided people went as far as that.' She leaned across and poured me more sherry. 'My uncle was not one of them. He was a foolish old dreamer who played Breton songs on an accordion in the café. Everyone here knew he was harmless. Most of them had grown up on his songs and stories of old Brittany. The lost city of Ys, King Gradlon, Merlin and Morgane la Fée and the Forest of Broceliande. Fairy tales. But he had been a member of Lu Brezon, and at the end of the War, he found he had been mixing with the wrong friends …

'I stood at that window and I watched while people waving the *tricolour* burned his books and smashed his instruments, and made him parade around the square in a German helmet. I watched while village women who had fawned over German officers cut off my aunt's hair with garden shears. They had to leave St Cyriac, of course, my aunt and uncle. Neither of them lived very long after that.

'I don't blame the local people, M'sieur. They were merely frail and frightened creatures. No one knew the war was going to end in 1945, nor that the Allies would win it. Collaboration was not then a dirty word. Indeed, the government ordered it. Everyone compromised in one way or another. Afterwards, some wished to pretend they had been true *resistants* all along, as much for their own self respect as anything else, so they turned on anyone who had collaborated more openly than themselves. I understand these things. But still, it was hard for a child to watch.'

'Didn't anyone speak up for your aunt and uncle?'

'Dr Pasqual did. He strode into the crowd and put a stop to it. I can still see him, just a young man he was then, even though he was mayor, but he carried such authority about him. He was quite alone, but no one dared face him down. He was outraged. I remember him shouting, "Is this the St Cyriac we suffered for?"

For that I thank him, and will always thank him.' She stubbed out her cigarette in the brass dish. 'But perhaps you can understand why I do not wish to attend his dinner and talk about the War and our people's heroism in adversity.'

15

I took my time walking through the quiet streets. Madame Didier's ugly little story darkened my mood. The Occupation was no longer some distant drama, but very real, very close to me, and much more than just a component of my father's tragedy. I knew I should have seen this before. I knew that if I had been French I would have understood it instinctively, and for a moment I was uncomfortable with myself.

But quite soon I could hear the party in full swing – laughter, voices raised, the chime of glasses. The evening was fresh but three terrace tables had been nudged together and as I walked along the quayside I saw Gunther, Henri's blond partner, setting up a space heater under the awning. Felix was in white jeans and a sailing jersey, with redundant sunglasses pushed up onto his brown scalp, looking even less like a priest than when I had first seen him.

'Iain! Iain Madoc!'

He pushed back his chair and came bounding to meet me amidst a little storm of greetings and good humoured applause. Chairs were scraped back and Henri was summoned and another table dragged up; in the reorganisation somebody knocked over a wine glass to catcalls and jeers, and several more bottles of wine were ordered to compensate, and people shuffled up to make room for me.

Felix's father was sitting not quite opposite me and a little to my left, sporting a linen jacket and yellow bow tie. I could picture him with a straw hat and an easel, Monet-style, trying to capture on canvas the changing light of a summer afternoon. His face lifted as he saw me, and he smiled as his eyes met mine, but before we could speak Felix was in action again, sweeping his arm around the table and delivering quickfire introductions which lost me almost at once. I caught the first few names: Daniel and Marie-Louise Bourgogne, who owned the boatyard; Sylvie Bertrand, music teacher at the local school; Sergeant Freycinet, St Cyriac's elderly *gendarme*. I was still trying to memorise these when he started again: Jean Bonnard, the local builder, and his wife Lucille; Jean-Pierre Le Toque, whom Felix described as the only eco-friendly fisherman in Brittany because he hadn't caught a damned thing for a month; Marc Garnier, owner of St Cyriac's recycling business – 'that's what we used to call the junkyard.'

The victims of Felix's jokes heckled him in reply or raised ironic glasses to me. I tried to fix one or two of their faces in my mind, but in those first few moments it was only Marc Garnier who caught my eye. He was a thin old man with sparse hair, and he gave me the instant impression that he didn't much want to be here. I noticed that he wore a hearing aid and I wondered if noisy gatherings were difficult for him.

Daniel Bourgogne leaned over to me. He was about my own age, with a tanned outdoor face and short grey hair. 'I saw you down at the boatyard yesterday,' he said, 'looking at your father's launch. I would have come out, but I thought maybe you wanted some time to yourself – not that Dominic would have left you much of that, the old rascal.'

'He's not here tonight?'

'Dominic and alcohol don't mix.' Bourgogne tapped his temple in a knowing fashion. 'But everyone loves him. Especially my Marie-Louise.'

She was about forty, heavily built, with big shoulders and short dark hair. She held out her hand and as she did so I realised that she was the woman I had seen the day before, standing in the window of the cottage by the river, watching me.

'We've met,' I said, taking her hand. 'Or at least we've seen one another.'

'Oh, that was you?' She grew flustered. 'I'm so sorry. It's just that I like to keep an eye on Dominic, you see. I didn't mean—'

'Old Dominic is family to us, you understand,' Bourgogne

said, by way of explanation. 'We get a bit over-protective.' He smiled and squeezed his wife's waist and a blush bloomed up her neck and over her broad face and made her look girlish, which sat oddly with her solid build.

Felix's father rose to his feet, and the conversation died away.

'You'll forgive me, my friends,' he began, 'but I shan't stay long tonight. I don't often accept Henri's generous hospitality these days, but when Felix told me who it was I had met in the square yesterday, I could hardly stay away. Indeed I feel that somehow I should have recognised our visitor at once, given how closely our histories are intertwined. So let me say a few words about that history. And then, perhaps, we can let it rest in peace and enjoy our dinner.'

The café was quite silent now. I realised that Dr Pasqual was about to make a speech, a few words he had prepared and rehearsed. The formality of it touched me, and the fact that the entire party was prepared to sit like schoolchildren and listen to this frail old gentleman. It was the first intimation I had of the respect and the affection he commanded. Not quite the first: I remembered him walking away up the street the day before, dispensing a greeting here, a compliment there, like some seigneur of earlier days. Old Breton nobility, Felix had said, with a mocking roll of his eyes. I found it endearing.

'Iain, you've been told,' Dr Pasqual said, turning to me, 'that I was instrumental in helping your father to escape on that dreadful night when Thomas Montignac was killed. But you must know I was a very small player in that drama. There were three others, and they deserve to be named here tonight. Our leader was Mathieu Garnier; then there was Guillaume Le Toque and Paul-Louis Bonnard. Such were the names of those brave men.

'All three are long dead, but their relatives are around this table – Mathieu's brother, Guillaume's nephew, Paul-Louis' grandson. And of course others in the village helped, and put themselves in danger to do so. Some provided food for the fugitives, or carried messages, or kept watch. Many of *their* relatives are here also. Indeed a lot of people risked a great deal that night. Thomas Montignac risked everything and lost.

'But in the end, it was your father who made it all worthwhile. Why do I say this? Because he brought us hope, and tried valiantly to help one of our own. And then, when things went so horribly wrong, he endured untold hardship to save his companion and himself, and escaped to his homeland, and to life.' He lifted his glass and his voice grew passionate. 'My friends, I give you the toast. To *life*.'

There was a commotion of raised glasses and raised voices, and for a moment a little knot of people hemmed me in. When they stepped back and I looked across the table the old man was gone. I could hardly believe that he had left already. I had needed more than a decorous speech from him. I might even have left the table and gone after him, but food arrived at that moment – seafood, cheese, crêpes, *frites* – and more wine. Much more wine.

Suddenly, with the formality over, everyone wanted to talk. The music teacher Sylvie Bertrand, an elegant woman in her thirties, laid a hand on my arm and asked me something about my family. Before I had finished my answer Le Toque, the beaming red gnome of a fisherman, was demanding my opinion of EU halibut quotas. I kept looking over their shoulders into the café, but I could see no sign of Dr Pasqual. Henri drifted between the tables, collecting plates, dispensing wine. Music started to play. My glass was empty yet again and someone filled it. The sky had grown luminous and beautiful over the sea, and my disappointment faded as the party grew noisy and boisterous around me.

I was caught by surprise when Felix moved up behind my chair and spoke softly into my ear. 'Iain? A moment?'

I followed him into the dark interior of the café. One of the booths at the back was softly lit, and Dr Pasqual was sitting there with a milky glass of Pernod in front of him. He rose a little stiffly and offered me his thin hand.

'Iain, you must forgive me for hiding in here. Please sit down.'

I did so. A burst of laughter and a tinkle of glasses drifted in from outside.

Felix said, 'The natives are getting restless.' He gave me a wink and walked out towards the party.

'Felix is a very good son to me,' Dr Pasqual said, watching him go. 'When he was ordained he could have had a ministry almost anywhere. Paris. Overseas. There was talk of a post at the Vatican. But he chose to come back to St Cyriac. He denies it, but my dear wife was gone by then, and I'm sure he came back because of me.' He smiled and folded his hands across one another. 'But this isn't what you want to hear, I know.'

'Dr Pasqual—'

But he raised his hand and silenced me. 'Forgive me. But let me guess what's going through your mind. I don't think you are satisfied with this – how shall I put it? – this comic book adventure story. I think you are troubled by your father's reaction to what happened here. I think you suspect it was not glamorous in the least. And you are right.'

I did not speak.

'Iain, your father and his companion were in that crypt for two months. The few people in the village who even knew they were there did their best for them, with food and medical help and so on. Sylvie Bertrand's grandmother was a nurse. Marie-Louise's two uncles owned the boatyard and supplied the dinghy in which they eventually escaped. But I'm afraid there were others who regarded Father Thomas as a dangerous zealot for hiding refugees, and in the end somebody betrayed him.'

'Do you know who?'

'No,' he said. 'And I wouldn't trouble to find out. No doubt they are long dead by now, and besides, I wouldn't even blame them very much.'

He must have seen my surprise.

'Things were not simple back then, Iain. Ordinary people had families to protect. If St Cyriac's priest had been found sheltering refugees it would have posed the most appalling risk to the whole community. There were German troops everywhere. They expected the invasion at any moment, and they were afraid. And it is when they are afraid that human beings are at their most brutal.'

I could think of nothing to say. Once again I had the uneasy feeling that in trying to resolve the questions which confused me I had somehow glossed over human confusion of colossal scale.

Dr Pasqual braced his shoulders.

'Two months down in that damned crypt. It's hard to imagine, isn't it? Your father and his comrade were in a bad way when we came for them that night. Your father had a leg injury which had never properly healed. The other man was so deeply shocked that I never heard him speak a word.'

'But you got them away.'

'Barely. The Germans were beating on the church door above as we took the two of them out of the crypt. Thomas went back to face the soldiers, to stall them. He must have known what would happen to him. And in a little while, we heard the shots. It was Mathieu Garnier who kept us together, or I think we might have panicked then. He was a born leader of men.'

Dr Pasqual took a sip of his drink.

'God knows how we got away with it. We had to walk them right through the village, expecting to blunder into the Germans at any time, but the patrols must have been drawn to the church by the shooting. All I can really remember is the church clock striking midnight as we led your father and his friend through the streets. Those midnight chimes will always stay with me.' He collected himself. 'Mathieu Garnier took the two Englishmen down to the boatyard. I went back to the bridge over the Vasse with Guillaume and Paul-Louis in case the Germans returned. Fortunately, they did not. We had, I think, one ancient rifle between us.'

'And my father sailed away from the boatyard?'

'I watched from the bridge as the tide carried them out, the two of them crammed into that little boat, and I thought they must be spotted at any moment. There was a German blockhouse right on the point, but the tide runs so rapidly on the ebb that it only took a couple of minutes for them to get clear. Less than that, perhaps. Even so, they were very lucky. We were all very lucky. It makes me tremble to think of it, even now. Mathieu told me later how when they got to the boatyard your father took one look at that dinghy, and said, "I'll take my chance with the sea." Mathieu didn't speak much English but he remembered that well enough.'

Yes, I could imagine my father not waiting for anyone's permission, but bundling his wounded comrade into the boat and unmooring with quick fingers. So long confined, and to feel the little dinghy rocking under his hands, straining to get away. Taking his chance with the great waters. I pictured a tiny cockle-shell of a craft, a blur on black water beneath overhanging trees, whirled on that sliding tide under the gunslits of the blockhouse towards the open sea and the siren call of freedom.

Dr Pasqual spread his hands. '*Voila*. There you have it. I make it sound very noble, don't I? But I'm afraid none of us thought they would get further than the Shoals. In our hearts we were only glad that the two of them had gone, and taken the burden of danger with them. Not quite so heroic put that way, is it?' He smiled sadly at me.

I said, 'You knew he'd made it home?'

'I had that satisfaction. I made some inquiries after the War.'

'But you never contacted him?'

'I felt the prerogative was his. And I understand why he chose silence.'

I sat quietly after he had finished. I liked this white-haired old man. I liked to hear him talking about the past. It was what old men were supposed to do, to pass down such stories. It was what fathers were supposed to do.

Dr Pasqual reached for his stick and drew it towards him. 'There was a time when I could ride all day and dance all night,' he said. 'No longer, I'm afraid. But I should very much like it if you would come up to the house one day so that we can talk further. I shall be away for two days at a rather tedious reunion. But Tuesday afternoon, perhaps? At around four? If you can bear to listen to an old man's ramblings for an hour or so I could at least lighten the burden with some excellent armagnac.'

'I'd like that.'

'If you'd excuse me now, I am rather tired.'

'Dr Pasqual, can I ask you just one more thing before you leave?'

'Of course.'

I took the sketch map out of my pocket and slid it across to him. 'My father brought this back with him. I wondered if you might recognise it.'

He took his hand from his stick and sank back into his chair. 'Iain, could I impose upon you to pour me a glass of water?'

I noticed his pallor for the first time. He had wanted to get away without betraying his frailty, and I felt bad that I had not allowed him to go. I poured him a glass from the carafe and moved it across the table. He did not take it at once. His hands were busy with the map, turning it into the light, lifting it close to his face. I saw the muscles clench around his eyes and mouth.

'Dr Pasqual? Are you all right?'

He looked up distractedly. 'A touch of angina. It afflicts me from time to time.' He put the drawing down between us, reached in his jacket pocket and took out a small silver box, shook out a couple of pills and swallowed them with a sip of water. He lifted the map again. 'Your father drew this?'

'I'm pretty sure he did.'

'And you believe this location is somewhere near here?'

'I assume so.'

'And yet it's hard to see how he could have drawn a map of anywhere local during his time in St Cyriac. Or why. He couldn't have left the crypt.'

'I can't explain that.'

'Strange.' He frowned. 'I'm afraid this doesn't look familiar to me. I'm sure I should recognise the place if it was nearby. What is this, a breakwater of some sort? It appears to be quite distinctive. But I can't call to mind anywhere like this.'

'It was just a thought.' I took the map and folded it back into my wallet.

Dr Pasqual rose, and I made to stand too, but he waved me down. 'No, stay, please.' He stepped out from behind the table and carefully smoothed his jacket and adjusted his tie, an old man who would not give up his dignity, even though the burden of memory and of the years was wearing him down.

'You have a good life, don't you, Iain?' he asked unexpectedly. 'You have a family. And you have done well in the world. Isn't that so?'

It was very quiet in the room. The sound of jollity from outside seemed to float in from another dimension. 'Yes,' I said. 'We have a good life.'

He smiled that smile again and with it his strength seemed to return.

'You've no idea what a comfort it is to me to know that in some small way I helped achieve such a thing,' he said. 'But you must not forget that, without your father's steadfast courage, it would never have happened.' He shook my hand and gave a small courtly bow. 'Until Tuesday.'

Then he was gone, his stick tapping on the floor of the café. I waited for a while, looking at the half-finished glass of Pernod on the table. I could understand why Felix so loved the old man, and I felt a quick stab of jealousy, and was ashamed.

I let myself out of the side door and, skirting the light and noise of the party, I walked across the promenade to the edge of the quay. The spring air was cool on my face. *The Gay Dog*, her decks polished and gleaming, bobbed at my feet. Black water slopped between the hulls of the boats, and truck-tyre fenders creaked in the dark. Felix stepped up beside me and put his arm around my shoulders.

'I couldn't help overhearing. An invitation to the family seat, no less! It's that mouldering great pile the other side of the coast road, by the way.'

'With the turrets?'

'Castle Dracula,' he sniffed. 'All ferroconcrete nymphs spewing into fountains. It's not actually that huge when you get up close to it.'

'I'm honoured.'

He glanced at me. 'The old boy likes you, Iain. He doesn't take to everyone.'

'I like him too.'

'Good. You can share him, if you like.'

'I'm sorry?'

'My old papa. Consider him half yours.'

I held his gaze. 'I have tried,' I said, 'with my father. He just ...'

'I don't imagine it's easy.'

'Can I tell you something, Felix?'

He looked at me curiously. 'Go ahead.'

'I woke up late last night. Couldn't sleep. I stood at the window for a while, listening to the warning bell out on the Shoals. And I began to wonder if my father had heard something like that, all those years ago. Just that sound in the night, it made me ask myself what it must have been like for him. Waiting there in the darkness. Fearing the worst every minute, and then the worst happening. And what that might have done to him. That, and everything that followed.'

'I see.' Felix paused. 'You know what, Iain? When it comes to entering his world, you might be making more progress than I gave you credit for.'

'What do you mean?'

'There hasn't been a warning bell on the Shoals for fifty years.' He grinned at my expression. 'Don't let it get to you. The sea plays all kinds of tricks at night.' He chuckled, clapped me gently on the shoulder, and sauntered back to the party.

16

I awoke the next morning with a hangover and an unquiet mind.

I threw the bedclothes off to let the cool air from the open window wash over me. Last night, when I got back from the party, I had stood at that window for half an hour or more, drinking in the clean night air, listening to the sea and the steady hiss of the wind across the rooftops. Once I heard a distant ship's siren. But I could not recapture the sound of that bell, nor anything I might have mistaken for it.

I showered and dressed, and went downstairs. The sitting room reeked of cigarette smoke and dried flowers. Little Gaston was dusting the china ornaments on the windowsill. I slipped out through the front door before he could see me.

It was fresh outside, with a pale sun breaking through and a breeze flapping the shop awnings. The church clock struck eight as I walked into the square. St Cyriac was coming to life around me. A yellow mail van came popping down the street, shutters clattered, and people queued for bread at the boulangerie on the corner. Cars pulled up outside the gates of the school and kids kissed their parents and ran inside, shouting to one another, bags and scarves flying. I glimpsed Sylvie Bertrand standing with a knot of other teachers on the school steps. The scene was lively, colourful and reassuringly normal. It should have made me feel better.

On the riverside path the willows were noisy with birds. I crossed the Vasse on the wallowing pontoons at Daniel Bourgogne's yard. A few of his men were already at work and in the main boatshed a circular saw was whining, but nobody paid any attention to me. This time there was no light in the windows of the house among the trees. I walked on down the track until I could see the stern of the launch through the curtain of branches, and then the whole length of the hull.

Dominic was sitting right up at the bow. I could see his blue-clad back and the sparkle of early sun on his hair. The sight of him gave me a comforting sense that at least one part of the world was as it should be. He turned as I approached.

'Hello, Iain! Have you come visiting?'

'If that's all right.'

'Oh, yes!' he said. 'I like visitors very much. I bet you want a sausage?'

I swallowed hard. 'Maybe a little later, Dominic.'

'Come aboard, anyway,' he said, and added, 'Don't be frightened. We can't float away when the tide's out.'

I steeled myself and stepped onto the deck and sat down quickly a couple of metres away from him, my back against the raised edge of the hatch.

'You can come up here, if you want.' He patted the deck beside him. He was sitting on the very peak of the bow, his legs hanging down over each side.

'I'm fine here, thanks.'

I glanced over the gunwale. The river cut in close to the bow of the launch but there was still a reassuring stretch of mud between the hull and the water, and I began to relax. It was pleasant here in the sun, with the deck warm beneath me.

'You're my second visitor today,' Dominic said.

He pointed ahead and I saw a heron among the reeds not five metres away, standing like a blade of slate in the shallow water. Dominic grinned back at me, his face framed by the leafy branches, like some woodland spirit. I felt a great peace in the air near him and I rested my head back against the hatch cover and half-closed my eyes so that the light glowed red. When I opened my eyes again Dominic was winding in his line so rapidly that his hands blurred. A silver bass came dancing up. He caught the fish in his free hand and murmured to it as he unhooked it.

'Dominic?'

He was still busy with his fish but he glanced over his shoulder to show that I had his attention.

'I heard a bell the other night, Dominic. Out on the Shoals.'

'Did you?' His voice was light. 'You heard the warning bell, then.'

'Only they tell me the warning bell was taken away years ago.'

'That's right, it was.' He seemed to see no contradiction in this. 'I was in the boat that went out to cut it free and tow it away. It was *huge*. Like an iron house! All rusty, with weed under it. And it made this horrible ringing! *Dong! Dong!*' He made big eyes at me and rocked his head. 'We couldn't stop it ringing when we towed it out and sank it in the deep water. I think it didn't want to go. We could even hear it under the sea for a while as it sank. *Dong! Dong!*' He repeated this, making the sound fainter with each repetition. '*Dong! Dong!*'

'Do you remember when that was?'

'Oh! Ages and ages ago. They put in one of those new sirens instead.'

'So I must have heard something else, mustn't I? An anchor chain, maybe, or some sort of an echo.'

'You know, Iain, it's a funny thing, but that's what everyone tells me when I hear it.' He freed the bass at last and tossed it back into the river, and we both watched while it darted away into the depths.

I said, 'Do you hear it often? The warning bell?'

'Of course I do. Whenever something's wrong in the village.' He beamed at me. 'But then, I'm not right in the head, am I?'

I didn't ask him any more questions. I realised that Dominic didn't work to the same logic as other people. Also, and for some reason I couldn't explain, rational answers didn't matter quite so much to me when I was around him. The world he occupied did not operate to the usual rules, and when I was in it, neither did I.

I leaned back against the hatch cover as Dominic, humming to himself, threaded more bait onto the line and cast expertly out into the silky water. It had strengthened into a brilliant spring morning, and the sky above the overarching trees was cornflower blue.

'Iain?'

'Yes?'

'Did you talk to Father Thomas?'

'Father Thomas wasn't in a very talkative mood. I spoke to Father Felix.'

'Oh, he's a great friend of mine, Father Felix! But he wasn't here in the old days. He didn't know your papa.' Dominic started humming softly again, hunched over his hook and line. And then he said, without looking up, 'They weren't his fault, you know. The bad things. I know your papa thought they were his fault, but they weren't. Not really.'

I rolled my head to look at him. 'You mean the bad things that happened to his crew? And to Father Thomas?'

He lifted his face to me and smiled. 'No,' he said. 'I don't mean that.'

I waited, but he didn't say any more and in a second turned his attention back to his fishing gear and began to hum his tune again.

'I can't read,' he said, after a while. 'But you can, can't you? If you read Father Thomas's diaries it would be like talking to Father Thomas himself. And Father Thomas *was* here in those days, and he *did* know your papa. And he put everything in his journal. I used to sit and watch him writing it every night, up at the rectory. Lots of diary books, he had.'

'Father Felix says the diaries are in the library, Dominic. Is that right?'

He smiled at me. 'There are some diaries there, yes.'

Over his shoulder I caught a flash of movement and I saw that the heron had taken a small fish which thrashed in its beak. The bird tossed back its narrow head and gulped down the glittering prize, its white ringed eye glaring straight at me, greedy and triumphant.

17

Later, I walked back to St Cyriac's tiny local library in its glazed annexe next to the Hotel de Ville. The librarian at the front desk was an unreasonably pretty woman in her late thirties. She wore jeans, a tight blue tee-shirt and enormous glasses, and introduced herself as Christine Tremblay.

She listened politely to my story, but I sensed that the St Cyriac bush telegraph had already told her all about me. She seemed genuinely pleased with my visit, although probably in the sunny tedium of St Cyriac's library she would have been pleased to see anyone.

She sat me at one of the blond wood tables and in a few moments came out of the archive room with three small journals bound in black leather. They were well handled, and the leather was scuffed and pliant. The books formed a set, and in each case the year was embossed on the spine in gold: 1939, 1940, and 1941. Mademoiselle Tremblay was wearing a pair of white cotton gloves and she brought another pair for me, which she set down on the table beside the journals.

'I suppose we should observe the proprieties.' She gave me a look from behind her glasses to show she thought this rather a bore. 'Though it's hardly a first edition of Racine.'

I pulled on the gloves, took the first volume and flicked tentatively through a few pages. The book was about half the size of a regular paperback novel. The pages were lined, and densely covered with fierce angular handwriting in blue ink. I scanned a paragraph at random. It listed attendance at Vespers one evening in December, and went on to wax indignant about the price of fish in Lannion market. I riffled through the pages, releasing a faint and musty odour. I put the book down and took up the second volume, the journal for 1940.

Sunday, 14 September
Two Wehrmacht officers came to church this morning. They introduced themselves as Major Leunig and Leutnant Reimann of the Todt Organisation, and asked my permission to bring some of their labourers to mass. I could see these unfortunates gathered near the west door. Most were Polish Catholics, the major told me, and he added (knowing that this would win me over) that these men had not been able to take communion or make confession for over a year, and they earnestly longed to do so. However they could not be allowed to attend without their German escort, so would I permit both soldiers and prisoners to take part in the service? Of course I agreed.

They were a sorry crew, these forced labourers, twenty or so dissidents and activists one assumes, and other transgressors against the Reich. A few may have been gipsies. One or two looked half-witted. All were gaunt with hunger. But while I could not withhold my pity for the hardships they must endure, I could not help comparing their cowed demeanour with the evident self-respect of the two German officers. These young men were correct in every detail: courteous, dignified, quietly spoken. I could not fault them. Both, they told me, were Bavarian Catholics, and were themselves glad of the opportunity to practise their faith.

While my pride rankled at seeing the invader in my church, part of me felt that any nation that could call upon such young men to command its armies must at the very least have respect for order and discipline and the rule of law – respect in which our own poor country has been sadly lacking in recent years. One is grateful for solid French families like the Pasquals, who remember the old ways, but there are few enough of them. I found the encounter with these German officers confusing, and I have prayed since for guidance, but as yet without regaining complete spiritual calm as regards this matter.

I closed the book softly. It was strange to read the words of the little town's dead martyr, written in his own hand: stranger still to find those words so banal. In my mind's eye I saw an irascible and pedantic man, a man committed to structure and form. It was pretty clear that Father Thomas admired the immaculate German officers, and that his pity for the slave labourers was tainted with contempt. I wondered how such attitudes had gone on to evolve in the heart of this man, who four years later was to die at the hands of just such soldiers of the Reich, in defence of people who by then were not so very different from the wretched labourers he had so grudgingly allowed into his church that Sunday in 1940.

'It's not all like that,' Mlle Tremblay said.

I wasn't sure whether she had been there at my shoulder all the time.

'Most of it's rather boring,' she said. 'Mildly scandalous social observation. Who was sleeping with whom. Who came to Church and who didn't.'

'You've read it all?'

'Reverently, if without much joy. Father Thomas was a hero, after all.' She wrinkled her perfect nose. 'Personally I'm rather distrustful of heroes in history, aren't you? They're never quite what they seem, when you look closely.'

'Does that include Father Thomas?'

'I'm sure he did everything they say he did. He certainly died heroically enough. Still, for me it's not the heroes who make history interesting.'

'No? What do you think makes it interesting?'

'The way great events affect little communities. What the ordinary people felt at the time, not the way they think they ought to have felt, when they talk about it afterwards. But that's not how people want to see the past. Not in France. Perhaps not anywhere.' She picked up one of the journals and flicked carelessly though the pages. 'You'll have noticed that they only go up to 1941, years before your father came here. If you were hoping for some insights into his experiences I'm afraid the journals won't be much use to you.'

'I was thinking the same thing, but Dominic was very keen I should read them.'

'Dear old Dominic! You know he can't read or write himself? He probably hasn't a clue what's in the diaries and what isn't.'

'I gather Father Thomas was like an earthly father to him?'

'That's the story I heard, too. Dominic was devoted to him, apparently.'

'So there's no telling what he might have known about the priest and his diaries.'

Mme Tremblay pursed her lips, unconvinced. 'Well, perhaps he knows something the rest of us don't. It just doesn't seem too likely.'

I turned back to the books on the desk in front of me. 'Why do they only go up to 1941?'

'Father Thomas got involved in the Resistance during 1942, and I suppose you don't put that kind of thing on paper.' She lifted one eyebrow. 'Though there's an alternative version, if you choose to believe it.'

I opened my hands, inviting her to go on.

She said, 'There's a local folk tale that Father Thomas went on keeping his journals *after* he joined the Resistance – dishing the dirt on all sorts of people. Who was collaborating, who was profiteering, who joined the Resistance five minutes before Liberation. All that, and maybe some more important things, too.'

'And do you think that story's true?'

'Well, if any more of Father Thomas's diaries ever existed, they've conveniently disappeared since.' She shrugged. 'But I suppose it's not out of the question, and it is the kind of thing people like to believe. I'd quite like to believe it myself.'

I opened the journal for 1941 and flicked to the back. The last entry was for the 30th of December of that year. The St Cyriac farmers were a bunch of scoundrels, Father Thomas fumed in his cramped, repressed handwriting. The price of cabbages was simply extortionate. How was a poor priest to live?

Mlle Tremblay said, 'Last year I put together a local history project. "St Cyriac at War", it was called. Would you like to see it?'

'Very much.'

Pleased by my interest, she went back to the archive room, returning in a couple of minutes with folders cradled in her arms. She dumped two box files and a sheaf of photographs on the desk. The files were new, of marbled cardboard, with neat labels. The handwriting on the labels was small and precise.

'I hoped maybe the local schools might use it,' she said wistfully, 'but nobody's really interested in this stuff any more.'

I opened the first box file and was surprised to find a large colour print of my father's launch on top of it, the same picture which had appeared in the magazine cutting my mother had left me. The curved hull of 2548 swelled out of the muddy riverbed, while the elderly enthusiasts waved their toy flags in the drizzle.

'Funny old men,' she smiled fondly. 'They spoke such awful French! I adored them all.'

I caught a whiff of her perfume as she bent forward and I allowed myself a moment to imagine what the worthy volunteers from Tangmere Military Aviation Museum must have thought about Christine Tremblay.

'Dominic's not in the photo,' I said.

'Dominic doesn't like cameras. I sometimes wonder if it's even possible to photograph him. I always have the feeling that he just wouldn't appear on the print, like Pan or something.'

She took the second of the box files and helpfully unpacked it on the desk beside me: plastic sleeves holding documents and cuttings, maps, copies of wartime regulations, lists of curfew times, blackout instructions, ration cards.

'St Cyriac had it easier than a lot of villages,' she said. 'It wasn't bombed and it wasn't directly involved in the fighting. Also its two wartime mayors, first Gustave Rosen and then Dr Pasqual, both did their best for the local people. But there were the usual hardships. Under the *Relève* scheme a lot of the young men were sent to Germany to work in exchange for French POWs. Others were just called up for forced labour.

'Then there were the *Ravitaillement* regulations, where French authorities requisitioned food on behalf of the Germans. They seized all the local horses for the Wehrmacht, too, and cars and trucks, not that there was much fuel for them in any case. Where people managed to hold onto their vehicles they ran them on gas or charcoal. Mostly they got around on bikes with these funny little twenty-five kilo trailers on the back. By the end of it the Germans were even requisitioning the bikes.'

She set out some black and white photos on the desktop: a bicycle with a home-made trailer just as she had described, a taxi with a bulging gas bag on the roof, a row of skinny horses lined up beside the road with a German corporal and a French *gendarme* standing guard. Several of the pictures showed German soldiers in the streets of St Cyriac, on parade in the square, relaxing at pavement cafés, lounging beside a parked armoured car. In one shot three workmen were using crowbars to lever up the plinth of a statue.

'That caused a bit of a fuss,' she said. 'Joan of Arc used to stand in the main square – just outside there, where the war memorial is now. They melted her down for the bronze, along with all the railings in the village and a couple of Crimean War cannon and pretty well everything metal they could shift. There was a lot of resentment about all that.'

I looked at the photo. I could see now that it had indeed been taken in the village square. I could make out the Hotel de Ville in the background with the swastika draped from the upper balcony.

'Ah. Now take a look at this.' She lifted out a slim cardboard folder and set it down on the table in front of me. Inside were photocopies of forms with the RAF crest on the letterhead. There were seven of them, listing ranks, military numbers, places and dates of birth.

'Your father's crew,' she said. 'The ones who didn't get home.'

I sat up straight. 'Where did you get this?'

She smiled at my surprise. 'From your Royal Air Force archives. I gave them the names and ranks on the gravestones and they sent me these copies.'

I leafed through the papers, wondering how many people remembered any of these men now. Maybe an ancient lover could summon up from the past the clump of military boots on a stair, the taste of untipped Capstan on a man's lips, a night of passion between coarse boarding house sheets. An elderly lady somewhere might recall that last family Christmas, her big brother wearing a paper hat, drinking pale ale from a dark bottle. Today, these lads survived only in the fading memories of others. Not for much longer. Soon they would be eternally in the shadows, along with everyone who had ever known them.

A thought struck me. 'Just seven? There were nine in the crew.'

'I only asked for information on the men buried in the churchyard. They were the only names I had.'

I spread the photocopies on the desk in front of me and looked through them once again. I re-read the details for MacDonald, the Australian Flight Sergeant. I noticed he was the only NCO listed. I remembered he was the only NCO in the churchyard too, according to the headstones. And yet there had been a corporal in the crew: he was shown in the photograph on my parents' bookcase. I could picture him clearly – my friend in the front row of that old picture, sitting next to MacDonald, the two of them making a game of showing off their stripes.

The missing man was very young, I remembered, and strikingly handsome, with a mop of fair hair. He was the one I used to cast in my imagination in the most dashing roles – the squire to the Flight Sergeant's knight, or the kid deputy who saves the Sheriff's life. I used to identify with him. So this must be the man my father had brought back across the Channel. I wondered if he was still alive, and whether I might still be able to trace him.

Before I could get this idea to settle, Christine Tremblay had pulled a thick plastic ring binder towards me. 'And here's something else.'

In a translucent sleeve, right at the front, was a good quality black-and-white picture of a mother and father and a girl of perhaps twelve, all of them soberly dressed in 1930s style, the parents smiling in the sunshine as they posed at the door of a high street office. Behind them on the wall was a brass plaque which read: *Gustave Rosen, Notaire*. Standing next to the girl was a dark good-looking boy of fourteen or so with his chin self-consciously lifted. The girl's left hand lay in his right and his attitude seemed to defy the viewer to mock this open intimacy.

I said, 'These are the people on the war memorial.'

'The Rosens, yes. But look at the boy.'

I peered at the dark and handsome face. 'Who is it?'

'That's Robert Hamelin.'

'Who?'

She was puzzled by my ignorance. 'Robert Hamelin, the agent your father brought across the Channel in 1944. The man he was trying to pick him up the night of the wreck. You didn't know?'

'I only knew him as Lucien. His codename.'

'Well, that's him. Lieutenant Robert Hamelin of the Free French, as he was to become. There's a memorial to him in the churchyard, an obelisk near the airmen's graves.'

'Really? Felix didn't mention that.'

'Well, perhaps it's gone now. It was in pretty bad condition when I last saw it, and that was years ago. But there used to be one there.'

I frowned. 'I don't understand. This Lucien – this Robert Hamelin – why's he in the picture with the Rosens?'

'He was virtually part of the family. The Rosens were wealthy – they had a big place called La Division, an old farmhouse just up the coast. Robert was an orphan and they adopted him. I'm not sure if that was official, or if they just took him in and gave him shelter. Anyway, that was before the War.'

'I had no idea there was a connection between him and the Rosens.'

'Oh, yes. It was the fact that he was so close to the family that drove Robert to join the Free French when the Rosens were arrested in 1942. At least, that's my reading of it. Robert was seventeen or so by that time, but he'd have been a couple of years younger in this photo. Just a child, really.'

I looked hard at the picture. I could tell that the sculptor of the Rosens' memorial had used this very print as his model, omitting the boy. Gustave Rosen was plump and pleased with life in his important suit. His wife stood at his side, a slender woman with a dashing black hat, worn at an angle which made her look devil-may-care and feisty. The girl was dark and very pretty and had large lustrous eyes. Christine Tremblay saw the hold the picture had on me and took the print out of its sleeve and slid it over to me.

She said, 'I'll find you a copy before you go, if you'd like one.'

'Thanks,' I said. The photo was creased and fading slightly to sepia. 'This is the original?'

'They say it was found at La Division, after the Rosens were taken away.'

I had a vivid image of the photo, propped on a table in the kitchen, perhaps. I couldn't take my eyes from those two young faces. A dark boy with his sweetheart's hand in his. Children, both of them. I remembered how Billy Billington had described the Lucien of just a few years later: dangerous, unstable, the Prince of Darkness. How had this boy become that man?

'Turn it over,' Christine Tremblay said.

I did as she told me. On the back of the photograph, written in soft pencil, were the words: *Robert, je t'attendrai jusqu'a la fin du temps – Lena.*

The handwriting was firm. I stared at it, perhaps the last surviving fragment of anything written by this long vanished Jewish girl. *I will wait for you until the end of time.* I felt an obscure sense of shame even to be reading of such desolate longing, knowing it to have been unrequited, as if it were an intimacy I should not have been allowed to see. When had she written it? As a car full of armed men pulled up outside and she knew the moment had come at last? Where was Robert at that moment? Presumably, and mercifully, he had been away from the house. She had scribbled this message and left it for him to find when he returned. Perhaps he had indeed found it, and – in anguish and desperation – had started his own journey at once, leaving everything behind in that desecrated farmhouse: memories, hope, and even some part of his own humanity.

'Robert Hamelin and Lena Rosen,' Christine Tremblay said, and I saw that her eyes were full of tears. 'St Cyriac's own little Romeo and Juliet tragedy.'

I took a last look at the photograph, and wordlessly slid it back to her.

A few moments later I left the library and walked across to the churchyard gate. I climbed the path to the RAF graves. I meant to look for Hamelin's memorial, but it was already past two o'clock and I was tired and I hadn't eaten. I gave myself a break, and sat on the bench by the graves and watched the sparrows taking dust baths beside the track.

I could not quite get things ordered in my mind. Why, for instance, had Dominic insisted I read the old priest's diaries? He had hinted I would learn more about my father's time here. But how could the diaries help me? They did not extend beyond 1941, more than two years before my father had come to St Cyriac. Perhaps Dominic was, after all, just a crazy old man who made up stories.

I gazed up through the branches of the beech tree, hazy with new buds, at the bright sky beyond. The air was rinsed and clean, the village itself washed in pure light, as if nothing dark could ever have touched it.

It was when I lowered my eyes that, without even looking for it, I saw the obelisk. It was grey granite, about a metre high, tilted into the deep grass near the churchyard wall just beyond the RAF graves. I walked over to it between the mounds. The stone was cracked and weathered, and mallow and dock grew thickly around it. I knelt and brushed at the moss on the plinth, as soft as an animal's pelt, and scraped it back from the stone.

LT ROBERT HAMELIN
Thy way is in the sea, and thy path in the great waters:
and thy footsteps are not known

I took a moment to recognise it. Psalm 77. My father's favourite verse.

18

The next morning was Tuesday. I was to meet Dr Pasqual in the afternoon, but that gave me six or seven clear hours. Even so, for a few moments over breakfast in Henri's, I dithered. My search for a place with a jetty – a house which probably didn't exist any more – was beginning to feel pretty foolish. I didn't even know for certain that my father had drawn the map: it could be a total blind alley, like the business of Sally Chessall.

And yet I had come this far. My personal Grail Quest, Felix had said, not altogether cynically.

I went to my Discovery, drove out of the village and headed south.

I stopped at St Brieuc and found a bookshop bigger than anything St Cyriac could offer, where I bought a sheaf of local maps covering the coast. A couple of kilometres out of town I parked at a seaside hotel and drank coffee in a dining room overlooking the grey Channel.

I spread the maps out on the table beside me. I have always loved maps, with their promise of discovery, their thick paper and delicate printing. These were of the largest scale I could find, designed for walkers, and they marked every farm track and stand of timber and house within ten kilometres of St Cyriac. I could see every detail of the village: the bridge upstream from the boatyard, the patchwork of cress beds, and the boat ramp and clustered buildings of the yard itself. I could see the blocks of the houses around the little harbour, the village square and the church on its mound of rising ground.

I propped my father's sketch up against the water carafe, folded my new map to a workable size, and studied the rugged shoreline ten kilometres southwest from the Vasse, tracing its folds and turns with a fingertip. I marked every hamlet or coastal farm which boasted what could pass for a pier or a jetty, and I repeated the exercise along the shoreline to the northeast. I settled on ten candidate locations, three to the east direction and seven to the west. When I had made my choices I took my bundle of charts out to the car.

It was not yet eleven. By a little after midday I was within the search area I had marked on the map. I pulled into a lay-by and checked my position, then turned left onto a narrow side road which wound through steep lanes towards the sea.

The first place proved to be a brand-new holiday marina, still under construction. I drove down a churned track with the leaves of the hedgerows on either side white with dried mud, and pulled up by a site office. Men in hardhats were using yellow earth-moving equipment to clear scrub from beachfront lots. Beyond half-built chalets I could see a landing stage of steel and timber. It had been there longer than the new development but even so it couldn't have been more than a few years old. I turned the car around and followed a lurching truck back to the road.

The second choice looked more promising. I couldn't get all the way to it by car and had to park, then hike over a low promontory to see it. Below me and a couple of hundred metres away, a derelict wooden pier, half-collapsed, poked out into the surf. It at least looked old.

I started down the slope, and stopped on the windy hillside to get a better look. Two big tin-roofed sheds stood on open ground nearby, an old rusting crane in front of one of them. My father's drawing did show buildings of some kind standing back from the shore, but on his sketch there were four of them. The two sheds below me were in the wrong position, and there was no sign of any house near the beach. I trudged back up the hill.

I got as close as I could to the third candidate along a corrugated track through a coastal reserve choked with wind blown gorse. I left the car and walked for nearly a mile along a deserted beach to get to the jetty shown on my map, but when I got there it turned out to be a storm water outfall of some kind, a rusty pipe carried on trestles out into the sea, where its effluent stained the water brown. Cormorants perched on the pipe, drying black wings in the sea wind. There were no buildings of any kind.

I plodded back to the car and sat there while the wind threw sand against the bodywork.

19

I drove back to St Cyriac, and went straight to Madame Didier's to change. I had a late lunch at Henri's and then walked through the village and across the coast road to the Pasqual house.

It was a cool, damp afternoon, the hedgerows and the fruit trees in the gardens alive with birds and bursting with buds. I walked in between shabby grey gateposts with stone gryphons on them and then followed a driveway for a couple of hundred metres to the front of the house. There were weeds pushing through the cracked tarmac and the lawns to both sides had reverted to meadowland dotted with wildflowers.

As Felix had suggested, the house was smaller than it appeared from the road, but it was still impressive enough, with wide square downstairs windows and turrets on the corner rooms upstairs, their conical roofs clad in grey slate. A stone fountain formed the centrepiece of the carriage turn. Some particularly ugly concrete cherubs clamoured around a naked woman who might have been Venus. The fountain was not working and the statuary was mossy and neglected, but the basin below was luxuriant with lilies, which made it beautiful. I saw a golden carp shimmer beneath the pads.

'M'sieur Madoc?'

I looked up from the water. The big main door had swung open and a plump and cheerful woman in a grey woollen dress stood in the doorway.

'Come in! Come in! Dr Pasqual's only just got back, but he's been looking forward ever so much to your visit.'

She hurried down the steps and ushered me into the dark hallway, took my jacket and hung it on an old-fashioned coat rack. Around me I glimpsed heavy panelling and a long wooden staircase and subfusc paintings. Far above an art nouveau skylight glowed in coloured glass.

'I'm Jeanne, M'sieur,' the woman chattered on, fussing so busily around me that she was out of breath. I guessed she was in her sixties, but that didn't seem to slow her down. 'I look after Dr Pasqual. Have done for years. You just go on into the study. The doctor's in there already.'

The study was pleasantly dim, and smelled of beeswax and old books. The walls were crowded with trophies of a long life. Some of these seemed so archaic that they were nearly comical: cavalry sabres crossed over the fireplace, a marlin mounted in a mahogany case, stuffed birds of prey perched in aggressive poses on top of the bookcase.

I liked the room at once for its genteel shabbiness and its unashamed masculinity. I liked the cracked leather armchairs by the hearth, and the photographs in their tarnished silver frames, and the faded Turkish carpets on the floor. It reminded me of a gentlemen's club which had seen better days. A fire had been laid in the hearth but had evidently remained unlit during Dr Pasqual's absence, for the room was a degree or two too cold for comfort.

He was standing by a little rosewood desk on the far side of the hearth. I couldn't see him clearly in the half-light, but he lifted his head and smiled at me, and first his white hair and then the rest of him materialised like some benign and courtly ghost.

'Iain! I'm so glad you could come.' He took a step forward to shake my hand. 'I've found at least something that might interest you.' He turned back to the desk and opened a brown paper envelope which lay there, clicking on the desklamp as he did so. He shuffled through a sheaf of photographs before handing one to me. 'Here we are. The Four Musketeers who helped your father and his comrade to escape.' He snorted. 'We don't look so very intrepid, do we?'

In the snapshot the four men looked as if they had been unwillingly shoved forward from the crowd of revellers. I could see men, women and children behind them, smiling, raising glasses, waving flags, sporting rosettes. Two soldiers in American uniform were flanked by laughing girls with flowers in their hair and their right knees raised in a dance routine.

'That's Bonnard on the left,' he said. 'I'm next to him. The tall willowy one is Le Toque. And here's Mathieu Garnier. I believe that's the only photograph that catches us all together. It was taken just after the Liberation.'

Dr Pasqual was right. He and his little group did not look intrepid in the least. They looked awkward, embarrassed. I studied them in turn under the lamp. Paul-Louis Bonnard had low brows, a broken nose and the powerful physique he had passed on to his grandson, the builder. The young Yves Pasqual, terrier-small beside him, stood to attention as if enduring some ceremony he hoped would soon end. Le Toque was excessively tall, etiolated, his eyes fixed on some distant horizon far above the photographer's head. Mathieu Garnier was thin-faced, not physically impressive, and no taller than Pasqual. But he had a certain tough presence, and I noticed in particular his very light eyes which glared defiantly, straight into the lens.

Jeanne came puffing into the room, scolding the old man for standing about in here without lighting the fire. She stooped and lit it herself and bustled around the room snapping on lights, so that in a second the afternoon outside was thrown into evening and flags of yellow light were reflected in blue windows.

I handed the photograph back to Dr Pasqual. He slipped it into the envelope and then into a drawer. He waved me towards one of the cracked leather armchairs. The last of the kindling spat and popped and the fire began to draw. Dr Pasqual arranged a screen across the hearth and flame sparkled on brass.

'What were they like, those lads?' I asked.

He pursed his lips, looking into the fire. 'A cross-section of young chaps, might have been from any French village. Bonnard was a born troublemaker, a brawler long before the Germans got here. He was the same with any kind of authority. Poor Le Toque was a teacher, a hopeless romantic.' He glanced at me. 'And Mathieu Garnier was a communist.'

'Which you were not.'

'Good heavens, no!' He laughed. 'My family were the very worst sort of *petite noblesse* – not really rich, but dreadfully proud of their aristocratic connections. Such awful snobs! It makes me wince to think of it now.' He laughed again, shaking his head, but then his voice grew serious. 'Arrogant elitists, anti-Republicans, traditional conservatives. Even anti-Semites, some of them. It's no wonder Petain appealed to them so strongly. I fell out of love with all that quite early on, Iain, but I won't attempt to exonerate myself entirely. We all thought Petain was our best hope immediately after the Armistice. To us, de Gaulle was a deserter for fleeing to London.' He rolled his eyes. 'And as for French communists, they were the spawn of Satan! They took their orders from Moscow, which is why they only started resisting the Germans when the Nazis attacked Russia in '41.'

'I didn't realise.'

'Oh, indeed. Many thought the real danger was not German Fascism, but Russian Communism. And that wasn't so crazy, was it? When the War was over, NATO came to the same conclusion.' He smiled, ruefully. 'But that's not the … Authorised Version.'

'But you worked with Garnier, even though he was a communist?'

'He was the undisputed head man when it came to the Resistance in this area. Mathieu was the genuine article, a *maquisard*. I respected him. Even so, after I became mayor his activities caused me some sleepless nights, I can tell you. He made a speciality of blowing up the power lines to factories working on German contracts, which made us all nervous. I had responsibility for the people of St Cyriac, you see, and the last thing any of us wanted was reprisals. But Mathieu was clever, and kept his activities out of the area. He died at Dien Bien Phu, in 1954.' He looked quizzically at me. 'There's an irony for you. Killed fighting the communists. A mad world, isn't it?'

He rose to his feet and fetched a tray with a decanter and a couple of squat glasses on it and set them on a small round table between us. He poured two glasses and invited me to take one. We sat in comfortable silence, sipping our armagnac.

'You have to understand the way things were back then,' he said. 'There weren't many heroes of the Resistance of the kind one sees at the cinema. Oh, there were some brave and passionate people. Many. People like Garnier. Certainly I don't claim to have been one of them. Felix might like you to believe otherwise, but the night of your father's escape was the one time I was actively involved. I had my hands full as mayor, trying to keep trouble away from this place.'

I drank some more armagnac. It was as warm as the firelight. I said nothing, but I could feel him watching me over the rim of his glass.

'Confusing, isn't it?' he said. 'But then, war is, especially to Anglo-Saxons. The experience of invasion and occupation wounds the national psyche in a way I don't think the British or the Americans will ever understand.'

I let him refill my glass. 'Can you tell me what it was like?'

He paused. 'Let me put it this way. Did you know that during the defeat of 1940, sixty or seventy thousand French soldiers were killed, and close to two million taken prisoner? In six weeks. On top of that, perhaps eight million French people left their homes ahead of the German advance and fled south. This is from a population of forty million. So in the space of forty days or so, a quarter of all French people were dead, displaced, or held captive. That's more than a defeat: that's the disintegration of an entire society.

'The focus of people's allegiance switched from the state to the community, from the city to the village, from *la patrie* to *la petite patrie*. And not only literally, but inside their hearts. People turned away from great causes and looked after their own. The household, the family, the village. It was all people had to hang onto in the face of chaos. And in this I was the same as everyone else.'

He looked past me at the fire, stooped to move the screen and threw on a log.

'It was at Saumur that I learned my lesson,' he said. 'We were just teenagers, most of us. Cadets. We volunteered to hold the bridges over the Loire. No one could order us to, because Petain had already called for an armistice by then and hostilities should have been over. In fact, we'd been ordered to retreat. Why did we agree to stay and fight? I don't know. We were young and at the time it seemed terribly glorious. We had rifles and a few machine guns from the first war. Our two seventy-fives were so old no one dared fire them. And there were about two thousand of us to face a Panzer Division of 18,000 Germans. We annoyed them for a couple of days and then they brushed us aside. It was all perfectly pointless. The Armistice was signed two days later, on the 22nd of June.'

He leaned forward in his chair.

'But Iain, the thing that struck me most forcibly was that everyone except us *knew* it was pointless. The Loire bridges were crammed with refugees, people on horses, on foot, on bicycles, people pushing their lives on wheelbarrows, some even driving cattle. And among these people – these French people – were some who jeered at us. Can you imagine? They laughed at us for the schoolboys we were. Laughed at us for imagining our sacrifice would make any difference.'

'What happened to you?'

'I was shot through the thigh towards the end of the first day. Painful, but most convenient. Kept me out of things from then on and probably saved my life. And as I lay there I had plenty of time to think. And I saw that those refugees were right, and we were wrong. If the ship is sinking, there's no point trying to drag it back out of the depths. The best you can hope for is to try to save yourself and, if you have the strength, to help a few of those struggling in the sea around you.'

The fire crackled between us. I looked into the flames and thought of people struggling in the sea.

'I saw Robert Hamelin's memorial yesterday,' I said.

He had been in the act of pouring more armagnac but he stopped with the decanter tilted over my glass.

I said, 'The verse carved on the stone is from Psalm 77. My father's favourite psalm.'

'Ah.' He poured my drink, stoppered the decanter and set it down. 'That solves a little mystery. The obelisk was set up in the 1960s with a donation from someone in England. Felix tells me there's no clue in the church records as to who sent the money.'

'Did you ever suspect it was my father?'

'I couldn't be certain. Hamelin was in London for two years with the Free French. Any of his former comrades might have been behind it.' He sat back and the leather of his chair creaked. 'It's satisfying to know the truth.'

I let a few beats pass.

'I saw something else yesterday,' I said. 'A photo of Robert Hamelin as a boy.'

'Oh, yes?'

'Christine Tremblay tells me he lived with the Rosen family.'

'The Rosens were generous people, and he was an orphan. They had a large house, La Division, a few kilometres up the coast. Robert spent most of his time there, I recall, when he wasn't away at school.'

'And he and Lena Rosen became close?'

'You heard that, did you? You *have* done your homework.'

For a moment I thought he might deny the story, or dismiss it as idle gossip, but then he suddenly looked down.

'Tragic,' he said. 'Made for one another.'

'You knew them?'

'Not well. Robert Hamelin was younger than I was and something of an outsider. But I have a vivid recollection of him and young Lena sitting arm in arm on the harbour wall one evening, just where the fishing boats tie up now. The most perfect picture of young love you will ever see.' He hesitated, then went on. 'And yet more than that. They were so very young, but even then it was impossible to imagine anything ever coming between them.'

'But it did,' I said, half to myself, and instantly regretted it, for Dr Pasqual's face clouded.

'Forgive me,' he said, seeing that I had spotted his reaction. 'The topic distresses me.'

I made an attempt to change the subject. 'Is it still there, the house?'

'La Division? Derelict now. Nothing but a ruin.'

'I'd like to go up there one day. Take a look at it.'

He glanced quickly at me. 'Why?'

I thought about this. 'I'm not sure. It's just that Lucien – Robert Hamelin – was the reason my father came here. Yet I seem to know so little about him.'

The old man nodded thoughtfully. 'I don't think you can get to the house any more. Marc Garnier has his scrap metal business on the site now.' He made a disapproving face. 'Uncouth man. He discourages visitors.'

I swirled my armagnac and let my thoughts drift. I said, 'He must have taken it badly.'

'I'm sorry?'

'Robert Hamelin. When the Rosens were arrested.'

'Oh, poor Robert, yes. My word! He disappeared almost at once. I don't know how he got to England but the next time we heard of him he was with the Free French. That was when your father brought him back to us for that one short month.' He paused. 'Though he was a different man by then.'

I wanted to ask him more, but his face seemed so weary and sad that I could not bring myself to do so. Instead I said, 'I'm sorry to have stirred all this up.'

'We have to face these things,' he said, with unexpected firmness. 'We have to close the circle. That's what you are helping us to do, Iain, merely by coming here. To close the circle at last.'

I left Dr Pasqual's house at around seven-thirty, my blood singing with armagnac. I called in at Henri's again and chatted with him and with one or two others over an omelette and a couple of beers. But I could not get the old man out of my mind all evening. I wanted to be back in that warm and firelit study, hearing his stories, sharing the privilege of his trust.

Yet at the same time I knew that there were other questions I might have asked him. I thought of that neglected monument in the churchyard. Robert Hamelin had been one of St Cyriac's own, but I would have known nothing whatever about him if

Christine Tremblay had not shown me that photo. No one had mentioned him. Even Dr Pasqual had never spoken of him, until I did.

I ordered a final drink and sat staring into it for a long while.

20

The next morning was overcast and chill showers were gusting in from the Channel. I drove west out of St Cyriac and along the Côte de Granit Rose, heading towards Morlaix.

My father's sketch was clipped onto the dashboard in its plastic sleeve and my large scale maps lay on the passenger seat beside me, neat rings of felt-tip marking every jetty or pier I had identified along the coast. The filthy weather didn't help my mood. I didn't want to admit it, but I had almost entirely lost faith. I felt a little ridiculous, and I only kept going because of a stubborn sense that I could not leave the search half-finished.

I parked in a rainswept lay-by and for most of the morning I followed endless winding lanes down to the sea, trudging across fields ankle-deep in mud and over wide, windy beaches. I found several houses with jetties but none looked remotely like the one on my father's sketch map. Three were hotels with private landing stages, all of them comparatively modern. Two more were old enough, but were situated in fishing villages, and the sketch didn't show a village. Another jetty formed part of a small marine repair facility near Port Blanc. The last, near Tregastel, turned out not to have a jetty at all. What had looked like one on the map proved to be a line of boulders encased in wire netting and dumped in the water to protect the beach.

I stood on the bluff there for a while, watching the sea burst against this breakwater. I could see the dark mounds of Les Sept Îles far offshore, through the driving rain. I pictured the torn water which stretched beyond, all the way to England. Then I made my way back to the car, knocked the worst of the mud from my boots, and drove back to St Cyriac.

I pulled up on the quay. Le Toque and his son Guy were working in wet weather gear to unload their boat, the boy swinging plastic trays of fish up onto the dock and the old man stacking them. A third man stood at the wheel, blipping the engine every now and then to keep the boat steady. Le Toque heard the clump of my car door, glanced up and raised a hand to me. I was glad of his friendliness after my dismal day, and I strolled over to where he was working. He dropped the last of the plastic trays onto the stack on the dock and shouted instructions. Guy nodded to him and in a moment the boat nosed out towards its mooring against the wall near the harbour mouth. I watched it go, remembering suddenly what Dr Pasqual had said. Just where the fishing boats tie up now. That was where he had seen Lena Rosen and Robert one long ago evening, sitting arm-in-arm. There was no one there now on the cold wet stones.

'You've been exploring, M'sieur Madoc,' Le Toque said, breaking into my thoughts. He jerked his chin down at my filthy boots and mud-spattered clothing.

'Yes. Yes, I have.'

He sat down on one of the iron bollards and took out a tin of cigarettes. He offered one to me, his eyes twinkling. I declined, and he lit one for himself against the rain and wind with the dexterity of long practice.

When he had the tip glowing like a ruby he said, 'And what did you hope to find on a day like this?'

'This house, maybe.' I felt inside my coat and held the sketch out to him. 'I don't suppose you recognise it?'

He squinted at it but did not take it from me. He shook his head. 'Doesn't mean anything to me.'

I put the sketch away.

He took another drag on his cigarette. 'That's your dad's map? Father Felix told me you had a map.' The wind whipped the smoke in a fine grey line over his shoulder. 'Maybe it's not around here at all, this place.'

'Maybe you're right.'

I must have sounded dispirited, for he lifted up his chin in sympathy. It was raining hard now, the drops rattling against our wet weather clothes, but Le Toque didn't seem in any hurry to get under cover. I could feel cold water trickling down my back, but presumably he was used to bad weather. A big flatfish flapped around in one of the trays and then lay still. Le Toque studied his cigarette.

'You want to know how it was for your father,' he said. 'How things were in St Cyriac when he was here. That's natural. A son would want to know.'

'Yes,' I said, surprised by his sensitivity.

'It wasn't like you think. The War. The Occupation. It wasn't like anyone thinks.'

'No? What was it like?'

'I was only eight years old at the Liberation. But I remember bits of it well enough. And I heard stories later from my mum and dad. And from Cousin Guillaume – you know, he was one of the guys who helped your father and his mate that night. About the most unlikely *resistant* you could hope to meet, I'll tell you that!' He laughed. 'Short-sighted, asthmatic, couldn't punch his way out of a wet paper bag. He died of yellow fever in the Congo or some place, trying to educate the blacks about the splendours of French civilisation.' He shook his head and gave a snort of derision. 'Silly bastard. No offence, but if he'd had any sense he'd have kept his head down and let your dad take his chances.'

'Perhaps he didn't feel he had a choice.'

'Oh, he had a choice all right, M'sieur Madoc.'

'How do you mean?'

'Life went on, even under the Occupation. If you didn't cause trouble you probably weren't going to get into any.' He paused, thinking back. 'There were soldiers on the streets, guns all over the place, rules and regulations and big penalties for breaking them. This was the Occupied Zone, remember. Even when the Germans were good about it, there was no escaping that we were under guard the whole time. And yet people still got married, had babies, went to work. Kids like me still went to school, took their exams, got jobs. People got by.

'It was much worse in the cities. My mother had family in

Nantes, and they were on starvation rations. Nantes and St Nazaire and Lorient, they were bombed to buggery. St Malo and Brest too. Not by the Boches. By your people. My mother lost her sister and her niece at St Malo, and never did know who she should curse for it, the Germans for being there, or the RAF for dropping bombs on them.'

I said nothing.

'Personally,' he went on, 'I didn't mind the Germans. We had two Wehrmacht lieutenants foisted on us, because we had a spare room, what with my older brother being away on the forced labour. My mum was upset about that, but I didn't care. I was just a little kid, and it was exciting. One of those officers had a boy about my age back in Leipzig, and I used to sit with this character sometimes and teach him a few words of French. It reminded him of home, I guess, hearing my prattle. He cried once, I remember, when I was reading to him. They weren't much better off than we were, those guys. Worse, really. They knew they'd be lucky to get through it alive. Sometimes it felt like we were all in it together, just waiting for it to end.'

I looked out over the rocking boats. I said, 'The priest was shot in his own church. That can't have done much for good relations.'

'True enough, M'sieur Madoc. But then it took a certain sort of man to get himself into the position Father Thomas got into.'

'What sort of man did it take?'

His voice darkened a little. 'A man who didn't care about risks. To himself, or to anyone else.' Le Toque flicked his cigarette butt into the harbour. 'I'll tell you something, M'sieur Madoc. There were some real heroes about in those days, and they weren't always the ones you might expect. For my money it was the quiet guys in small town jobs – the councillors and the village mayors and sub-prefects – the guys who had to wheel and deal between the Germans and the ordinary French people. They didn't get much thanks for it afterwards, either, a lot of them. If they got too close to the Boches they were accused of collaborating. But if they didn't, they lost their jobs or wound up in jail and couldn't help anyone. It was characters like that who kept the worst of the War away from our doors. If I can sit here now and tell you how I hardly noticed anything, it's thanks to men like that.'

Le Toque fell silent for a moment, then suddenly grinned and slapped my knee. 'But still, there's one thing to thank Cousin Guillaume for, eh?'

'What's that?'

'If he hadn't played the hero you might not be here now, about to buy me a beer.'

Inside Henri's we stripped off our dripping jackets and I left Le Toque at the table and went to the bar. I wanted to prompt the old man to tell me more, but as I came back with our drinks his son Guy and the deckhand came into the café, and by the time I got to the table the conversation had turned to today's catch and the cost of marine diesel. I joined them and drank my beer and ordered steak frites with them and chatted amiably enough, but no more was said about those faraway days.

At about seven I left the café and walked back across the wet square. Le Toque was certainly right about one thing. The Occupation hadn't been the way I had imagined it. Of course he was a mere child in those days, shielded from the worst of it, and yet I found his account compelling. What would any sane person do, but keep his head down and get on with life as well as he could? Whatever revisionists said now, I wondered how people had really felt back then about people like Father Thomas Montignac. I remembered what Dr Pasqual had said, that he neither knew nor much cared who had betrayed the priest.

I turned into the sidestreet and walked down towards the guesthouse. There was a new silver Peugeot 307 parked outside with an Avis sticker in the rear window. I paid no particular attention. I put my key in the lock of Madame Didier's front door and turned it.

'Hello, big boy,' Chantal called to me from the driver's window of the car. 'On your own?'

*

Chantal walked into the Camellia Suite ahead of me and looked around her.

'This place is seriously gross,' she said. 'The V&A ought to buy it as a job lot. This is just the *Rocky Horror Show* of interior design.'

'Think yourself lucky. Kate's got the Lavender Room.'

Chantal gave her big laugh, and a family of crystal animals tinkled in sympathy in their cabinet by the door, which made her laugh again. I pushed her back onto the bed and stretched out beside her, and we both lay there, not speaking.

'It's OK, isn't it?' she said finally. 'Katrine and me turning up like this?'

I nuzzled her neck. I loved the smell of her hair.

'I didn't want to crash in on your *quest*.' She put it in inverted commas with flicks of her index fingers. 'Not if you don't want us around. But we always said we'd start the rest of our lives this Wednesday, and now it *is* Wednesday, and Katrine and I had a talk about it, and—'

I kissed her.

She put her palm in the middle of my chest. ' ...and we thought, Katrine and I, that we should all start the rest of our lives together, just as we'd planned. Wherever that happened to be. And if that meant a little while in Brittany first – are you listening? – well, that'd be fine; we'd all move on after that, whenever we were ready ... Iain? I'm serious.' She was using her headmistress voice.

'I'm serious too,' I told her. 'Very, very serious.'

'Oh! So you are.'

Sometime during the past hour I had heard Kate open her door and make her way downstairs. Now, as Chantal and I came back to the world we could hear Twenties jazz music from below and Madame Didier's unexpectedly full-throated laughter.

'We had a look around St Cyriac while we were waiting for you,' Chantal said. 'It's a special place.'

'I thought so too.'

'I'd forgotten that villages like this existed. They have a kind of magic about them.' She turned in the bed and saw my face. She cocked her head. 'What?'

I got up and went over to the window.

'Iain?'

She sat up. I went back and sat beside her in the evening light.

'Tell me,' she said.

So I told her about Felix and Dr Pasqual and Father Thomas Montignac. About the Rosens, and Robert Hamelin; about the party at Henri's; about Dominic and the boat.

She listened quietly, and when I'd finished, she stayed silent for a little while. At last she looked up at me. 'Does it feel strange?'

'Does what feel strange?'

'To have cracked this little mystery of yours so soon?'

I looked at her. 'Cracked it? It feels like I haven't even started.'

She frowned. 'You came to St Cyriac to find out why your father doesn't want to talk about what happened here. Right?'

'Right.'

'And you haven't heard enough good reasons for that?'

'I've heard good reasons,' I said. 'I'm just not sure they're the real ones.'

She tilted her head. 'Something about this doesn't sit right with you?'

'No. Not entirely.'

'Try me.'

'The old boy down at the boat, Dominic. He talked about something that happened here. Something my father blamed himself for. Something bad, he said.'

'The loss of his boat. His crew. The priest's death. They're not bad enough for you?'

'I asked him that. He meant something else. He won't tell me what.'

'Maybe you shouldn't put too much store by what one funny old boy says.'

'Then there's the memorial in the churchyard, to Robert Hamelin, the agent they came to pick up. Lucien. My father paid for that monument.'

'I'd have thought that was rather … touching.'

'It was put up in the 1960s. Why would he pay for a memorial to this man, twenty years after the War was over?'

Chantal was quiet for a moment. 'Your dad had a hard time here, Iain,' she said. 'A really hard time. People have been thrown off balance by a whole lot less. Believe me. I've seen it happen.'

'He was a tough guy, my old man.' I said. 'I never realised how tough. He'd seen plenty of war and death. After five years, he was used to it.'

'It happens to tough guys too,' she said. 'Sometimes especially to them. And nobody ever gets used to it. Not ever.'

'If people hadn't got used to it in World War Two, half the population would have been screwed up.'

'Maybe they were.'

I didn't answer. I thought of that photograph of my father on the beach, smiling, his arm around my mother. I could not imagine what it must have taken to break his spirit.

Chantal looked up into my face. 'Iain, when in doubt, take the simple option. He blamed himself for losing the launch and his crew, and for the death of the priest. Never mind what Dominic or anyone else says. That's what it comes down to.'

'He had no reason to blame himself. He was a hero. Everyone says so. He risked everything to get Hamelin out, and when things went wrong he survived to bring another man home, against all the odds.'

'You have a theory?'

'That something else happened to him here,' I said. 'Something I haven't heard about yet.'

She pursed her lips, but said nothing.

'He was afraid, Chantal. That's what Mum said. He was pursued by something. Like a wolf in the forest.'

She looked at me, startled. 'A *wolf?*'

I stared out over the rooftops. I could see it again in my mind: flotsam on grey water, an upturned boat, weed-encrusted timbers looming in the rain. And I could hear my father shouting, and feel his strong arms around me in the cold sea.

Much later I awoke to feel the night air, sweet with the rain on the fields and hedges, flowing into the room. I knew Chantal wasn't asleep either, and after a while she gave up pretending and nestled against me in the darkness. Her long hair drifted against my chest.

I said, 'I heard a bell the other night. From that window. A warning bell, out on the Shoals.'

'Something odd about that?'

'It isn't there. The bell. It was taken away years ago.'

I could sense her picking through the options.

'Church clock?'

'At two in the morning?'

'Some sort of weird echo, then? Ship's bell?'

'Or maybe I imagined it.'

'Maybe you did.' She propped herself up on one elbow, setting the glass menagerie tinkling in the corner cupboard. 'Loosen up, sweetheart, all right? You're under a lot of stress right now.'

'Me? I'm rich and I'm on holiday for the rest of my life.'

'Your mum's been dead two weeks,' she said patiently. 'Now

you've discovered all this stuff your dad never told you about.' She poked me hard in the ribs with her forefinger. 'This is not rocket science.'

I ran the heel of my hand down her spine. 'I think maybe I was dreaming. When I heard the bell. It's like I was still half asleep.'

She pulled herself up a little and kissed me. 'You rationalise it any way you like, *chéri*.' She yawned and nestled down against me and was asleep almost at once.

22

I got up and quietly dressed, though there wasn't much need for stealth as far as Chantal was concerned. She could sleep like a baby under artillery fire, and it would take more than me padding around to disturb her. I left her a brief note propped against the mirror, picked up my things, and let myself out.

'Dad?'

Kate was standing in her bedroom doorway, just across the landing. No one could look imperious quite the way Kate could when she put her mind to it, and I felt as if I'd been caught by matron, sneaking out for a cigarette.

'Going for a walk,' I said. 'Couldn't sleep.'

Her eyes flicked down to the maps in my hand. 'Just a walk?'

'There's a place up the coast I want to take a look at.'

'What place?'

'A place called La Division. Just an old farm.'

'Is it far?'

'Four kilometres or so.'

'I'll come with you.'

'Were you planning on getting dressed first?'

'The square in five minutes,' she said loftily, and closed the door.

I emerged into the chill morning street. My walking boots were in the back of the Discovery, so I crossed the road, got the boots out of the car and sat on the rear bumper while I laced them on. Henri's place wasn't open yet, so I went over to the Bar des Sports and bought thick coffee in a paper cup and leaned against the wall outside. I pulled out my new map. I'd circled the place in pencil. The map showed a single rectangular building on a minor lane which snaked down from the coast road.

Kate appeared beside me, took my coffee cup and drained it. She flicked the edge of the map. 'Let's go.'

The cliff path led steeply up from the village and we climbed it in the rising light, breathing hard. An old Celtic cross stood at the summit, hidden by gnarled hawthorns. The weather had eaten away the reddish stone. Kate and I stopped in the shelter of the trees as the wind rushed in from the Atlantic. Behind us, St Cyriac's pink and white cottages huddled around the church. On the shore immediately below us waves boiled among rocks the size of houses. In the distance the black shoals were already breaking the surface. Soon the whole expanse would be a maelstrom of booming surf.

I let my gaze wander back inshore. A little way up the coast to my left I could look down on what must be La Division. A single shabby, tin-roofed barn stood a couple of hundred metres back from the shore. There was a truck with a crane on it in the yard, what looked like a couple of big steel hoppers, and a huge pile of glinting rubbish.

The wind dropped as I followed Kate down the path. It led us through stands of pine along the cliff edge and, at the bottom of the slope, through clumps of oak and ash. The track emerged on the low earth bluff above the beach. The sand above the high tide mark was littered with dried rashers of weed and the shells of crabs and razor clams. A shingle bank held back the sea. I could feel the tide shoving at it, and could hear the long rattle of stones as each retreating surge gathered energy to push forward again.

Kate walked ahead of me, along the bluff above the sea. We both saw it at the same moment. A small boat with an awning was tied up a few metres out from the beach, where a rough line of boulders formed a miniature anchorage. A bare-chested young man in shorts was standing alongside the boat, up to his waist in the water. It must have been cold enough in the April sea but as we watched he ducked under the surface, stayed down for a few seconds, and came up with a bunch of weed in his hands. He tossed it out over the rocks, flicked water from his hair, took a deep breath and ducked down again. He did not see us.

Kate walked to the water's edge, and stood poised like some long legged seabird while the grey water shouldered the rocks at her feet. The boy still hadn't seen her and he didn't hear me come down the shingle bank to join her. Water beaded on his brown arms and shoulders. He had given up duck diving, and was now standing in the water, bending at the knees and groping around under the boat with both hands.

As he worked he was singing some jazz number I didn't recognise, in a voice which tightened to a rhythmic grunt every few bars as he gripped something underwater and tugged at it. He reached a crescendo and marked it with a burst of air guitar, then he saw us and stopped singing as if a plug had been pulled.

'Who the fuck are you?' he demanded, and crossed his hands over his bare chest in a curiously vulnerable gesture.

I said, 'And good morning to you, too.'

'Sorry. Didn't hear you coming.'

'Is there a problem?' I nodded at the boat.

'Kelp round the prop,' he mumbled. 'Fixed it now.'

He levered himself cleanly out of the water and onto the rocks, reached for his faded denim shirt and dragged it on. He did this very quickly, but not before I saw the white scar that writhed across his chest, livid against his tan. He stood up in front of us, buttoning the shirt; he was of medium height and well built, with dark eyes and very dark hair worn rather long, which gave him a buccaneering look. I guessed he was about eighteen, but he had a few days' stubble and this gave him a year or two. He stepped across the rocks towards us.

'You're the English guy,' he said. 'Dominic told me about you.'

'You know Dominic?'

'Everyone knows Dominic. He's a great old dude.'

'Everyone knows everything, apparently.'

'This is St Cyriac.' Unexpectedly he stuck out his hand. 'Serge Baladier.'

His skin was cold and wet and fragments of crushed shell rolled between his palm and mine.

'I'm Iain Madoc. My daughter, Kate.'

'Katrine,' she corrected, too quickly.

He solemnly shook her hand too. The formality seemed to embarrass her and she snatched her hand away and hid it behind her back.

'Come aboard,' he said.

'You're busy.'

'Nobody's that busy.' But then perhaps he saw my reluctance. 'Hey, wait.' He waded out a few steps, untied the boat, and towed it a little way into shallow water, mooring it again up against a large boulder almost on the beach. He jumped aboard and held out his hand to me. 'Just watch the rock, it's slippery.'

I stepped up onto the boulder and focused my attention inside the boat, forcing myself to notice details – the engine cover which formed a low table amidships, and the leather-backed notebook which lay on it, and next to that a fisherman's knife, a tumbler of red wine and some bits and pieces of fishing gear. I got as far as putting one foot on the top strake. It stirred under my weight, and I stopped with one hand on the stanchion of the boat's awning. I started to sweat.

'I have a fear of boats,' I told him, and my awkwardness made me gruff. 'It's ridiculous, but there it is.'

'There's nothing ridiculous about fear,' he said, and added gravely, 'Me, I've got a morbid terror of caterpillars.'

'Of *caterpillars*?'

'Only green ones.' He took my forearm as I grappled with this concept and before I realised it I found that I had been drawn smoothly and safely onto the boat. Serge smiled – his first smile – as if he had just performed a conjuring trick. I was inclined to think he had.

I sat down on the locker with a bump and tried not to register the small rise and fall of the boat. Serge stretched out his hand to Kate but she wasn't about to be helped. She stepped easily over the gunwale and sat down beside me.

Serge said, 'You'll have a drink, of course.'

'It's early, Serge.'

'You're English, M'sieur.' He grinned again.

He got into the half-crouch that was all the awning would allow him and began clearing a space by moving hooks and floats off the engine cover onto the locker beside him. I glanced around the little boat. Up in the bow lay a crab trap, a couple of nylon nets, a diving mask and snorkel and a pair of blue rubber flippers. Two buckets with lids stood in the stern, and I could see the shadows of things moving sideways through the semi-translucent plastic.

'Are you a fisherman, Serge?'

'Some of the time.' He rummaged in the locker beside him, found a canvas satchel, and took out a bottle of red wine and a couple of tin mugs. He filled the mugs and handed us one each. 'I'm a student.'

'So the crabs are a sideline?'

'Crabs. Lobsters. I dive for them out on the Shoals.'

'On your own? At this time of year? Isn't that dangerous?'

'Yes,' he said.

'You're mental,' Kate told him shortly.

He raised his glass ironically to her. She tossed her head. I watched the exchange with amusement. I was fairly sure Kate had never met anyone quite like this kid, with his attitude and his dynamite smile.

'You know how it is, M'sieur,' Serge said. 'Struggling students need money, and the restaurants in Lannion and Morlaix pay a good price. Henri's place in St Cyriac too, sometimes. And people down the coast.'

The boat moved slightly under us and the awning popped in and out in the breeze. I took a couple of deep breaths to calm myself. The wine helped. Serge bent forward to pour some more and Kate watched him.

'Your dad was skipper of that launch, right?' he said. 'They say he sailed some bath tub down the Vasse and back across the Channel? Took a wounded man with him?'

'That's how I hear it.'

Serge sat back on his haunches. 'He must have been a pretty

cool sailor, your old man. The tides can be awesome in the mouth of the Vasse.'

'He's not *dead*,' Kate put in, testily. 'You don't have to talk about him in the past tense.'

Serge kept his eyes on her but at the same time carved a couple of hunks of cheese with the fisherman's knife and sliced a loaf and set it on the engine cover. Finally he shifted his gaze and looked at me. 'What brings you up to La Division, M'sieur?'

'I wanted to see the old place. I gather it has a history.'

'Yes. A sad one.' He nodded towards the shore. 'The house is in the trees there, what's left of it.'

'I didn't see it.'

'It's set back a few metres, bushes all around it.'

The boat bumped and rasped against the rock and I clutched instinctively at the gunwale.

'It's OK,' Serge said quietly. 'It's just the tide dropping.'

My heart was thudding and I was furious with myself. I glanced over the side to avoid his eyes. But then I saw it, and for a second I forgot to be scared. Beyond the boat a line of rocks was almost fully exposed by the falling tide. They formed a low wall of black granite, weedy and barnacled, crumbling in places, but quite straight, and reaching out to where the deeper water swallowed them.

'What's the matter?' Serge asked.

'This is some kind of a jetty.'

'They say the Romans built it, but I don't know if anyone's ever proved that. You can only see it at low tide.'

Low tide. Low water. *LW*.

Kate half stood and followed my gaze out over the rocks. 'Show him the map,' she said.

I took it out and handed it to him. 'The place on this sketch,' I said. 'I've been up and down the coast looking for it.'

'Well, you just found it. This is La Division. Where we are right now.'

'There are farm buildings on the sketch. Barns, or whatever. Four of them. There's only one here.'

'There used to be three others. They were pulled down years

ago, but the concrete bases are still there. It's a pretty old map, right?'

'Nineteen forty-four. I think my father drew it.'

'He did? Why did he want to draw a map of the Rosens' old place?'

'Good question,' I said.

He must have sensed something in my tone, because he didn't pursue this. Instead he took out his knife and began to slice some salami into a tin dish, busying himself for perhaps a full minute at this task. I put the map away.

He placed the dish of sliced salami in front of us and looked up at me, flashing very white teeth. 'Excuse me asking, but are you really English? You do have a bit of an accent but your French is amazing.'

'*He's* English,' Kate said. 'My mother's French.'

'Ah.' He passed her a hunk of bread. 'Then you're only half English. That explains it.'

'Explains what?' she demanded.

Serge sat back and speared a chunk of cheese for himself on the tip of his knife. He seemed suddenly very sure of himself. 'The English have lots of qualities,' he said, 'but the French do have a certain style.'

Something about his new-found confidence threw a switch in me. I drained my wine, set the mug down and got up. 'Kate, let's get going.'

She stared up at me in surprise, the bread still in her hand. 'I thought we were—?'

'Another time.' I stepped off the boat with reasonable aplomb, feeling the solidity of rock underfoot with a rush of relief. I crouched so that I could see under the awning and into the boy's face. 'Thanks for the drink, Clam Baron.'

Before Kate could protest I stretched out my hand to her and took her wrist. She rose, flustered, and followed me off the boat. The boy sat looking at us, taken aback at the abruptness of our departure, but half amused too.

I said, 'See you again, maybe.'

I took Kate's arm and walked her quickly back along the ancient jetty and over the shingle.

'Dad?' Petulantly, she pulled her arm free. 'Wasn't that a bit rude?'

'I think the Young Man of the Sea can take it, don't you?'

She glanced back towards the boat, but I guided her quickly up the bluff above the beach and soon the water was out of sight.

Just behind the beach we pushed through a screen of bushes and came up against a rusty chain link fence, collapsing in places, which ran parallel to the path. Sure enough, a large, old stone building stood among the trees a few metres inside the fence line. Slates lay scattered on the ground and the walls were nearly smothered in bramble and alder.

Two glossy horses cropped knee-high grass in a paddock that stretched beyond the shell of the house. The shabby corrugated iron barn I had seen from the clifftop was maybe a hundred metres further inland. I could see now that the glittering mountain beside it was made up of wrecked cars, tyres, and stacks of rusting refrigerators. There was no sign of life, but the truck with the crane mounted on it was still parked in the yard, and a chained dog was stretched out asleep on the bare earth beside it. Black crows and white gulls picked among the junk.

Kate was still annoyed with me. 'Dad, where are we going?'

'Quiet a minute.'

I started to walk along the fence line, and came to a place where the fastenings had rusted through and a panel sagged inward against its iron supports, leaving a gap just wide enough for me to squeeze through. Kate clicked her tongue in irritation but followed me. Inside the fence, the thick grass was dotted with spring flowers coming into bloom, blue periwinkles and scarlet poppies. The horses watched us curiously, their ears flicking. But they were merely inquisitive creatures, not friendly, for when we got within a few metres of them they shambled away, their big hooves clopping on the turf.

La Division must have been a handsome property once. At the heart of it was a typical Breton homestead built of granite blocks which had been extended into a residence of a dozen rooms. The roof was entirely gone. An ash tree sprang up from within the house itself, shouldering aside what was left of the rafters, and a bank of bramble had wrapped itself around one end wall.

'That Jewish family lived here?' Kate asked from behind me, falling under the spell of the place despite herself.

'That's right.'

'It's so sad. And they've let it go to ruin.'

I stepped up close to the door. 'The whole thing's sad. More than sad.'

The windows were boarded, but the massive oak front door had only been padlocked shut, and where the planks had shrivelled I was able to get a glimpse inside. Daylight flooding through the open roof showed me the remains of a farm kitchen with a shelf or two holding jugs and jars smothered in cobwebs, and a fireplace in which an iron pot still hung from chains above the grate. The floorboards had rotted and the remains of the furniture had slid down into a wine cellar beneath. I could see bottles scattered among fallen slates and debris on an earthen floor.

'Dad!' Kate cried in sudden fear, and I spun round.

Two figures were standing just a couple of metres away, a young and burly man in front holding a German shepherd on a chain, and an elderly, gaunt man behind him. I didn't pay much attention to either of the men. I was too focused on the dog as it lunged towards us on its chain. I grabbed Kate and pulled her back beside and a little behind me.

The younger man shouted, 'This is private land. You know that?' He was about twenty-five, and had tattooed forearms as thick as my thighs which bulged with the effort of holding the dog. 'Fucking private, all right?'

I was suddenly furious. I said, 'You just keep your bloody dog—'

The old man came up at that moment, his hand cupped around his ear. It was only then that I realised he was Marc Garnier, whom I had last seen at Dr Pasqual's dinner, and I stopped speaking. He recognised me in the same instant and dismay filled his face.

'M'sieur Madoc, is it?' He spoke sharply to the younger man, who grunted and dragged the dog back a few paces. Old Garnier's eyes shifted past me and Kate, and next I could see him checking the farmhouse door and the padlock. 'You haven't been inside, have you?'

'No, I—'

'Because it's not safe, see?'

Garnier came forward and took my arm and with surprising strength began to draw me away. Kate followed closely, frightened into silence.

'The old place is falling down,' Garnier went on. 'There's been accidents.'

I was angry and upset and I disliked the feeling of his hard fingers locked on my bicep, steering me along as if I were an erring schoolboy. I disliked his sour body odour too, and as soon as I could decently do so I stopped and twisted my arm free of his grip.

'You didn't need to bring the dog down here,' I said. 'That wasn't necessary. My daughter and I were just taking a walk.'

He faltered. 'It's my boy here, Yannick. He's touchy about people sniffing around. We get a lot of thieving at the yard, see.'

Yannick took a turn of the chain around his fist to remind me he still held the dog. I saw him look speculatively at Kate and I felt a fresh spurt of rage. But before I could speak, Yannick demanded, 'What d'you want here, anyway? Poking around.'

I told myself to keep calm. 'I want to know why my father drew a map of La Division,' I said, pointedly speaking to old Garnier.

'A map? Of here? That can't be right.' The old man sounded harrassed, fretful. 'No, no, M'sieur Madoc. There's been some mistake.'

'It's this place,' I said. 'The jetty. The farmhouse. The barns.'

I thought about getting the map out and showing it to him, but for some reason which I could not quite define, I decided not to.

'I don't know about any maps, M'sieur Madoc.' Old man

Garnier shook his head. 'But this is private land. No one's allowed in here. It's dangerous. Somebody gets hurt in there, and I'll be liable. Besides, it's not right to just walk onto someone else's property.'

My indignation was leaking away and I was beginning to feel foolish. 'If I'd known you were there, M'sieur Garnier, I'd have come up to the yard and asked. The place looked empty.'

'Well, it isn't,' Yannick said. 'It's private. Now get off our land.'

The dog, sensing renewed tension, burst into a fresh frenzy of barking.

'Have we got a little misunderstanding here?' Serge said easily, strolling up from the fence. He whistled at the dog, which instantly sat down on the grass, looking at him as if for instruction. 'What's up, Yannick? Afraid this gentleman and his daughter are going to steal some of your garbage?'

Yannick backed off half a pace. 'You'd know all about that, gipsy boy.'

'You haven't got one thing I'd bother to steal.' Serge stooped to stroke the dog's head: it wagged its tail. 'Certainly not good looks or a bright idea.'

I said quickly, 'If M'sieur Garnier and his son care so much about privacy, maybe we should let them keep it.'

Serge shrugged. 'Fine. So let's go.'

He beckoned to Kate and me and the three of us started to walk towards the fence. Garnier came after us a little way, hurrying to keep up.

'Listen, M'sieur Madoc,' he said. 'No offence, but it's for your own good. That old house is dangerous. Falling down. I got safety to think of.'

'Right,' I said, without looking at him. I stepped out over the sagging section of chain link.

'There's different rules in France, M'sieur Madoc. Maybe you didn't know that. You can't just go looking around where you choose on other people's land. That's just how it is. It's …' he searched for the word, unaccustomed, I guessed, to deploying it in his own defence ' … it's the *law*.'

'Right,' I said again.

We left him standing by the gap in the fence, watching us unhappily, a mean old man in greasy clothes.

'Jesus, Dad,' Kate said, when we were out of earshot. 'What was all that about?'

'Nothing. Forget it.' My bad temper was pretty obvious and Serge and Kate followed me in silence as I marched back up the track. I turned to Serge. 'Gipsy boy?'

'Romany, to be precise. Half, anyway.'

'And was that some Romany magic you did with the dog?'

'Not really. I've been feeding him chocolate biscuits for the last week.'

I glanced at him. 'Why?'

'So he doesn't bite my balls off while I'm stealing Garnier's garbage.'

We both laughed and some of my tension evaporated.

'Why were they so stirred up?' I asked him.

'The Garniers? They're just peasants. It's the way they're wired. They're territorial, like their dog, but not so smart.'

'There's more to it than that.'

He took a moment to answer. 'It's because of that house. Nobody ever goes near it.'

I tried to gauge how literally he meant this. 'Because of the Rosens? People are superstitious?'

'I don't know about superstitious. Ashamed, maybe. People here have long memories, M'sieur Madoc. Nobody wants to remember La Division after what happened to that family.' We had reached the pine trees. Serge said, 'Well, guys, I've got a tide to catch.'

I hesitated and then said, grudgingly: 'I owe you one.'

He grinned a little bashfully, gave us a mock salute, walked to the edge of the bluff and vanished like a genie. We heard his footsteps ringing through the shingle below. I had walked some distance up the cliff path before I realised that Kate was hanging back, leaning against a pine trunk. I heard the burble of Serge's boat starting up down below and I caught her moving a few paces between the trees to keep it in view as it headed out to sea. Only when the sound of the motor began to fade away did she hurry along the path to catch up with me.

I thought she would say something about the boy, something nonchalant perhaps, something designed to reveal and disguise at the same time. The old Kate would have done that. Instead she strode past me without a word and away up the slope.

23

Chantal came in from the bathroom wearing a white cotton bathrobe and rubbing at her hair with a towel.

'Where did Kate get to?' she asked.

'Keeping vigil, in case Tidal Serge comes sailing in from the sunset.'

I meant that to sound lighthearted, but some edge in my tone made her stop and look at me closely.

'Not good enough for Daddy, huh?'

'I didn't say that.'

'Better get used to it, sweetheart,' Chantal laughed. 'Kate's seventeen and gorgeous. That package comes with attendant risks.'

When I didn't answer, Chantal walked round to look into my face. 'Are you OK?'

'Of course. Why?'

'You don't seem exactly overjoyed with your little pilgrimage today. Is it just this Serge kid? You know you won't be able—'

'It's not that.'

'What then? I thought you'd be over the moon, finding your mystery farmhouse.'

'It wasn't quite what I expected, that's all.'

'That's the trouble with revisiting the past. It's never the way it ought to be.' She started rubbing at her hair again with the towel but didn't take her eyes off me. 'You worried about your little showdown with these Garnier people?'

'I didn't handle it too well,' I said. 'In fact, I made a bit of a prat of myself, wandering around on their land, dragging Kate along, getting us caught like trespassing schoolkids.'

She tilted her head. 'And?'

There was never any point in lying to Chantal. 'And they scared the pants off me.'

'Ah,' she nodded, understanding at last. 'In front of Kate. In front of the boy. I see.'

I looked glumly out of the window.

She tossed the towel away. 'You were only looking, weren't you?'

'That's all.'

'Fuck 'em, then,' she said, savagely. 'Forget about it.'

Chantal had a happy knack of closing down minor problems like this. To her my little drama was trivial. She wouldn't have hesitated to walk onto Garnier's land if she'd felt the need, even if it had been ringed with barbed wire and *Keep Out* signs. Especially then.

She walked a couple of paces towards the bathroom and then came back. 'Iain, how about you tell me what's really churning around in that twisted brain of yours?'

I stared out over the canted roofs. 'I just can't work out why Dad would have drawn a map of that house in the first place.'

'How does anyone know why anyone did anything sixty years ago? I don't know what I did last Tuesday, let alone why I did it.' She crossed to the blue chest of drawers. 'You can ask the Lord of the Manor tonight. Maybe he'll know.'

I looked at her, puzzled. 'Who?'

She held up a white card. 'A real, grown-up invitation. *Dr Yves Pasqual requests* ... Tonight at eight. All three of us.'

'Where did that come from?'

'Father Felix delivered it about an hour ago. I'll tell you something – they didn't make priests like that when I was going to confession.'

Dr Pasqual's table had been set in the bay window of a pleasant room at the back of the house, overlooking the garden. It was a pale blue and white space with a beechwood table which the five of us filled without crowding. Candles gleamed on silver and in the dark windows and Bach was playing softly in the background.

Jeanne had produced a rabbit casserole with garden vegetables and Felix had been serving us discreetly copious quantities of red wine for some time.

The old man had asked to see the map again as soon as we took our seats, and propped it in front of him against a water glass, but hadn't mentioned it since. Instead, father and son deftly tossed conversational balls from one to the other, Dr Pasqual feigning disapproval of Felix's racy style, and Felix making fun of the old man's formality. Now, when Jeanne had collected the dishes and bustled out, Dr Pasqual moved the drawing under the light.

'Those barns ... I'd forgotten they were ever there. The Garniers pulled them down years ago.' He shook his head. 'And the jetty; I never even thought of that old relic as a jetty. It's underwater most of the time. I simply didn't recognise the place when you showed this to me last time.'

'When did the Garniers buy La Division?' I asked.

The memory obviously pained him. 'After the Armistice in 1940 the Vichy French Government passed laws which prohibited Jews from owning businesses. Alphonse Garnier was head of the family then; Marc and Mathieu's father. Gustave Rosen was majority owner of a fruit packing plant at La Division, and old Alphonse was his business partner. When Gustave was dispossessed by the Vichy laws, Alphonse was only too happy to take over the entire operation. Of course, there was bad blood between them after that, especially since the Rosens' home stood on the property.'

'And the Garniers held onto the place after Liberation?'

'The Rosens had no family, so after the war the Garniers' ownership was never challenged.'

'The business failed,' Felix said. 'The boys closed it down and set up their scrapyard there after old Alphonse died. It's limped on like that ever since.'

Jeanne reappeared with a jingling trolley laden with dishes of lemon sorbet and the conversation became inconsequential again while she fussed around the table. Felix leaned over and cracked a joke with Kate, and they both laughed. Dr Pasqual spoke to Jeanne as she bent to set down his plate, thanking her quietly so that she glowed with pleasure. She clinked away down the corridor to the kitchen.

When she had gone, Dr Pasqual took up the sketch map again. 'The drawing of the farmhouse is quite precise, but this peculiar device in the centre, three bars … some sort of a grating, perhaps?'

'I'm afraid I've no idea, Dr Pasqual. I hoped you had.'

He moved the map a fraction closer to the lenses of his glasses, and then away again. 'Another mystery, then. Although the greater mystery remains: how and why your father drew this. He could never have seen La Division. His entire time here was spent in the crypt. Is it possible that it's someone else's work?'

'It's possible, but I can't think of who.'

'It did occur to me that Robert Hamelin might have drawn it. La Division was certainly important to him. It was his home. He might have given the drawing to your father when they crossed the Channel.'

'But why would he do that?'

'Might they have agreed a rendezvous, after the war?' Dr Pasqual looked up at me and pulled down the corners of his mouth. 'Who knows?'

I thought about this. Two young men, fixing a meeting in the future, as if the simple fact of it might pull them safely through what lay ahead. I couldn't decide what I felt about the idea. Billington had described the man he knew as Lucien as sinister and unstable. He said my father had felt the same way about him. Would my father have exchanged confidences with such a man? On the other hand, he had paid for a monument to Lucien, though for some reason that was only years later. And there was the matter of the sovereign. Probably Hamelin had given him that. Why not a map too?

I let the conversation grow lighter as dessert was followed by armagnac and coffee.

A little after eleven we gathered in the hallway and Jeanne fetched our coats. Felix opened the front door and strolled up the drive arm-in-arm with Kate and Chantal, chatting easily, but as I turned to go Dr Pasqual laid a hand on my arm.

'I didn't want to mention this during dinner, Iain, but I understand that you and your lovely daughter had some unpleasantness with the Garniers at La Division today?'

I covered my surprise with difficulty. How had he known this?

'They didn't like us on their property,' I said. 'You did warn me.'

'Neverthless, it's unforgiveable that they should have behaved in that way. And with young Katrine present, too.' He drew himself up a little. 'I should like to apologise for the incident.'

'Apologise?' There was something so wonderfully antique about this that I wanted to smile, and yet I knew the old man was serious. 'Dr Pasqual, why should you apologise for anything?'

He seemed about to say more, then he relaxed, and when I gave him my hand he enclosed it in both of his. 'Goodnight to you, Iain. And God bless you.'

We didn't speak on the walk home, Chantal and I arm in arm, and Kate a few paces ahead. At first sight the village square was as empty as an abandoned stage set, the wind rushing through the rose bower over the Rosens' monument, shaking the heavy blossoms. Glimpsed between the buildings, sodium lights swung on their poles down on the esplanade, and boats in the little harbour rocked on black water.

We turned the corner into Madame Didier's sidestreet and at once I saw a motorcycle parked in the shadows by the kerb. A young man was kneeling on the tarmac beside the machine, working on the engine with a spanner in one hand and a pencil torch in the other. Serge. Kate saw him at the same moment and froze like a deer. He got to his feet with elaborate astonishment.

'Mr Madoc! And Katrine. Well, how extraordinary.' He stepped forward, smiling his dynamite smile. 'And Mrs Madoc?'

Chantal disengaged herself from my arm and glanced in amusement from the boy to Kate and back again. She gave the boy her hand in queenly fashion.

'I was heading home,' Serge explained. 'Bit of a problem with the fuel line. Fixed now.'

'At five minutes to midnight,' I said. 'At the bottom of our street.'

His smile grew a little fixed. 'Actually, there was something I wanted to ask Katrine.'

'Imagine my surprise.'

'There's a dance. In Lannion, tomorrow night. Just a local thing. And – with your permission, of course – I wondered if—'

'Pick me up at seven-thirty.' Kate said. She strode past him without another word, and let herself in through the front door of the guesthouse.

'Great,' Serge said to the door, as it swung to behind her. He turned to us and grinned. 'Great!' He fumbled his crash helmet on and swung himself into the saddle. 'Until tomorrow, then.'

24

The next morning Chantal and Kate took a trip to St Malo.
They asked me if I wanted to go, but they could see I was restless and I guessed that they were trying to stay out of my way.
When they'd left I walked to the library, took my seat at one of
the blond wood tables, and asked Christine Tremblay if I could
see the diaries again.

Dr Pasqual's reference to the anti-Jewish laws had sparked my
interest again, and I flicked through Father Thomas' entries for
autumn 1940 until one caught my attention.

Sunday 6 October
*The Government in Vichy has finally found the will to address the
problem of the refugees from Eastern Europe who have infested our
cities since the debacle of France's defeat. It's harsh on the Jews, of
course, but it cannot be denied that a great many of these newcomers
are of the meaner sort, and a very great strain they place on our poor
country, at a time when it should be harbouring all its strength to
heal itself.*

*Dominic drove me in the trap to market in Lannion, fuel now
being too severely rationed even for the local bus to run. It was while
haggling over some miserable mackerel with Gaspard that I was told
of the Statut des Juifs which was passed by the Vichy Government
two or three days ago. As I understand it, the Statut bans Jews from
senior positions in government and the law and other professions.*

*I am not so foolish as to imagine the Jews are responsible for all
our problems, and of course they are part of God's creation, as are we
all, and thus deserving of compassion. But I hardly feel they can be too
surprised if some of their advantages are stripped from them. If the*

Socialist Government of that libertine Leon Blum – a Jew, advised by Jews – had not so weakened the country five years ago, we should not be in these straits now. This is only to be expected if one elects to a position of great authority a person of alien race and culture. How could a man like Blum have had the interests of the true France at heart?

I closed the black-backed journal.

'I hate it when he writes like that,' Mlle Tremblay said. 'The way he just refuses to see what Vichy was really doing.'

'Under pressure from the Nazis ...'

'Vichy was the legal government of France,' she said, with a bitterness which made me wary, 'it wasn't some puppet regime.'

'There were plenty of racist pigs in Britain too. There still are.'

'Should that reassure me?' She caught herself. 'I'm sorry. It's just that I'm Jewish myself, you see.'

'Ah.' To change the subject I said, 'I went to take a look at La Division yesterday. I got a distinctly unfriendly reception from the present owners.'

She gave a tight little laugh. 'I wouldn't take it personally, M'sieur Madoc. The Garnier family don't need a special reason to be rude to anyone. It comes naturally to them.'

She moved away to attend to a woman at the front desk but soon she was back.

'I nearly forgot, I came across something that might brighten your day. You were looking for details of the other survivor? The man your father saved?' She laid a sheet of paper on the table in front of me. 'It was in my file at home all the time. The RAF must have sent it with the others, but I'd forgotten all about it.'

The page was similar to the ones I had seen, a photocopy of typewritten personal data on speckled wartime paper, the shadow of a paperclip in the corner.

'M'sieur Madoc?' Christine Tremblay asked.

I could not take my eyes off the name on the form. I picked up the paper and peered closely at it, but there was no mistake. The name was Billington. Rodney Billington.

25

I folded some clothes into my pack and zipped it.

'I shouldn't be more than a week,' I said.

Chantal came out of the bathroom with my razor. 'If you're going, just go. You don't have to keep apologising about it.'

I took the razor from her, unzipped my washbag, put the razor inside, put the washbag in my pack. She watched me do this, her arms crossed, but she didn't speak. She was not happy.

'I've got to run this to earth, Chantal. You'd have to if it was you. You know you would.'

'I'm a journalist,' she retorted. 'It's my job, or it was. What's your excuse?'

'I don't need an excuse.' My own fuse was just beginning to smoulder. 'But I want to know why Billington lied to me. He told me he'd never even been to sea.'

'His face was burned off, you said.' She opened the pack on the bed, forcefully rearranged something inside, zipped it up again. 'It could just be he didn't want to talk about it. Had you thought of that?'

'Then why not say so? Why shoot me some line about car crashes in Weston-super-Mare and his brother-in-law's Hillman, or whatever? Why try and cover up the fact that he was ever even here with my dad?'

We stood glaring at one another for a few moments. I hated arguing, especially with Chantal. I suppose she hated it too, but she always seemed better at it, quicker at it. But now she was silent: perhaps it was the mention of my father that did it.

At last she said, 'You've got to be careful about this sort of thing, Iain.'

'Careful?'

'I learned a few things over the years. One is that people never tell the truth about the past. Another is that there are some stories that don't have happy endings.'

'Meaning?'

'Whatever happened involved this little village. This is France, remember? And you're English. They won't like it if you poke around in their past, and especially not if you sit in judgement.'

'Who said anything about sitting in judgement? I just want to find out what happened to my father here, that's all. It's my history as well as Billington's. As well as St Cyriac's.' I hefted the bag off the bed and dumped it on the floor at my feet. 'And you think I should just forget about it?'

'I think you should keep your eye on the main game, that's all.'

'Chantal, I'm sorry if this delays things for us. I know you had more exciting places than St Cyriac in mind—'

She shook her head impatiently. 'Iain, for God's sake. I'm only trying to say that maybe it doesn't matter a whole lot what these scared kids got up to all those years ago. What does matter is that you and your dad make contact before it's too late.'

'But that's exactly what I'm trying to do. Don't you see that?' She did not reply, and I picked up the bag and walked to the door. I stopped there, miserable about leaving things like this. I said, 'You'll be all right here for a few days?'

'I survived Baghdad and Kabul,' she said tartly. 'I might be able to hack St Cyriac.'

'And Kate?'

She snorted. 'Something tells me you don't need to worry about her. I'm sure that she'll find something to amuse herself.'

I didn't like the sound of that, as she knew I would not. I gave up, and felt for my car keys. 'Maybe when I get back we can begin the rest of our lives,' I said.

'Just get back here as soon as you can, Iain, so we can all move on.'

26

I spent the night in St Malo and caught the morning ferry. I drove up the ramp at Portsmouth at a little after two the following afternoon and ground through snarled-up traffic to join the A27. Within an hour I was driving down the lane to Tangmere Military Aviation Museum.

'He's gone,' the elderly woman at reception announced with grim satisfaction, as soon as I pushed in through the door.

I stopped dead. 'What?'

'Billy's gone. So, no, you can't see him.'

I walked up to the desk. The lobby was empty and my footsteps sounded ominous on the lino. 'Gone where?'

'New Zealand,' she said. 'He has family. He won't be back.'

'That was … sudden.'

'Very. And we're going to miss him. A great deal.' Abruptly, tears filled her eyes and she cried out, 'Why couldn't you leave him alone?'

I stood there like a fool, dumbstruck. She reached under the desk and pulled out a white envelope and flipped it across to me, so that it fell on the floor at my feet.

'Now go away. Please. Just go away.' She swivelled her chair away from me so that I could not see her face.

I picked up the envelope and retreated through the glass doors into the dull afternoon, shaken by her news and her distress. I walked around the buildings, tapping the letter against my thumbnail. The sea of long grass swayed and rolled where the Spitfires and Hurricanes had once stood. I imagined the sun flashing on their Perspex canopies, and jaunty pilots leaning against the wings.

I tore open the flap. The single sheet had been typed on an old-fashioned manual typewriter, three neat paragraphs, with a signature scrawled at the bottom. It was dated two days after my first visit to Tangmere.

Young Mr Madoc:
The fearsome Merrill will have told you that I've absconded to the colonies. Not quite true, I'm afraid, but she believes it is, so I'd be obliged if you wouldn't tax her for more precise information. I have, however, gone overseas for a while, perhaps forever. At my age, everything is perhaps forever. Your visit wasn't the only cause of my departure, but it certainly precipitated it. I expect you could track me down if you tried hard enough; I ask that you do not do so.

You must know by now something of the tragedy at St Cyriac. If you are reading this, you have returned with more questions, and you must also know that I was less than honest with you during our last meeting. I regret that. I saw much of your father in you, and I would have preferred to have been straightforward. But I still feel that I had no choice. I ask you to remember that all those years ago, your father had no choice either. I am not God and cannot judge. But I do know that a man can do no more than act on his beliefs, and on the information he has available to him at the time. Very often, and especially in wartime, he has only a split second to make his decision. He's not always right.

I have no more to add on the subject of St Cyriac. Suffice to say that your father was a good and brave man. I don't put so much weight behind the 'brave', for we are all cowardly and brave by turns, often in the wrong proportions and in the wrong order. But he was a good man, and – however it may have seemed – I am sure he never wished you anything but happiness.

And there I, Billington, rest my case.

27

I drove through narrow lanes of cow parsley and hawthorn blossom. Early moths siphoned into the headlights. Past Exeter I emerged on the moorland road, high above the shore. Seaside towns dazzled in folds of the coast below me. Beyond the frivolous lights glimmered the sea, stretching out to the curve of the earth, black and unknowable.

When I got to the cottage it was in darkness. My headlights swept across, illuminating it like a plywood stage flat. I saw at once that the front garden was untended, and that there was litter on the step – uncollected papers, a Yellow Pages directory in a shrinkwrap cover, advertising flyers. Loose sheets had blown in among the ragged flowerbeds.

I got out of the car and stood for a moment, taking a couple of breaths to steady myself, and then walked around the side of the house.

I could see the glow of a candle at the kitchen table, and the shape of the old man, hunched over the flame. I pushed open the back door and walked in. My father looked up unhurriedly. Twin miniature candle flames burned in his half-moon reading glasses, and amber light shone on the folds of his face and his neck and on the Bible which lay open in front of him. I couldn't imagine that there was enough light to read by, but somehow he seemed to have been doing so.

He met my eyes steadily. 'Hello, Iain boy.'

I leaned back against the door to close it. The air was musty and smelled faintly of fish. In the garbage bin under the sink I could see two or three empty sardine cans. A solitary plate stood on the surface beside the cooker, and an untouched fruit cake was shrivelling on a breadboard next to it. I guessed it had been donated by Betty Coleridge from the guesthouse. She was the only person who would bother to come here now. It was cold in the house and I tugged my jacket around me. The silent, candlelit face in the darkness unsettled me, and I reached across and flicked on the light switch. Nothing happened. I snapped the switch up and down uselessly several times.

'I had it cut off,' he said.

'You *what*?'

'I had no need of electric.'

'What about heating? What about hot water?'

I strode noisily around the kitchen without waiting for a reply, opening and slamming cupboard doors. I found a box of candles under the sink, lit three more of them from the stub on the table and set them up on the draining board, on the mantelpiece, on the windowsill. I could see by the way the flames trembled that my hands were shaking. I pulled out a chair and sat down.

'Dad, what are you doing to yourself?'

'I wasn't expecting no company.' He took off his reading glasses and set them on the open page of the Bible. 'It's not like you to come unannounced. It's not like you to come at all. What brings you here now?'

The moment had arrived. I waited a couple of seconds, centring myself, letting the words form in my mind.

'A couple of weeks ago,' I said, 'I met a man who wanted to thank you. I should have given you that message before, probably.'

'And yet I know of no one who owes me thanks.'

'His name's Billy. At least that's what they all call him. Billy Billington.'

I was aware of a tap dripping into the sink.

'Billy wanted to thank you for what you did for him,' I said. 'He wanted to thank you for all the men you saved, too. All the men you never abandoned. What he meant was, that you never abandoned him.' I paused. 'I've been to St Cyriac. You must have known I'd find my way there.'

'And why was it so needful to do that?'

'Was I supposed to pretend she'd never spoken to me?'

'That would have been a kindness.'

'She did more than speak to me, Dad. She gave me some things. Some things of yours.' I put my hands on the table and leaned forward on them. 'Why don't you tell me the real story?'

'It seems you know enough already.'

'I don't know anything. I don't know why Billy didn't say straight out that you'd saved him. Why he was so desperate to convince me he was never in St Cyriac. I don't know why you brought back a map of La Division. And I don't know why being a hero should have screwed up your life.'

He looked up quickly at me, and there was a great sadness in his eyes, but he didn't say anything.

'Let's not pull back now, Dad. Not when we're so close. I've found the boat. I've seen the graves. I've even met Dr Pasqual – Mayor Pasqual as he was then.'

'I don't remember their names. I never wanted to remember.'

'No? Well, they remember you. Just like Billy Billington does. Even Dominic remembers.'

A light leapt in his eyes. 'Dominic? He's still alive?'

'So you remember him well enough. He says you're a great patriot, does Dominic. A great hero. They all think that.'

'Did you ask them why?'

'For trying to save Lucien. For justifying the risks they all took. For making Father Thomas's death worthwhile. For saving Billington. How many more reasons do you need?' I pushed my face towards his. 'Isn't it worth something to be a hero to these people?'

'It's the greatest blasphemy of all …'

He rubbed the bridge of his nose between thumb and forefinger. I moved back a little.

'Dad, something happened there, didn't it? Something really bad, that no one's talking about.'

He didn't answer.

I said, 'You can't be responsible for everything that went wrong. No matter what it is, why can't you tell me about it? Why have you never been able to tell me about it?'

'You think you would have benefitted from such talk?'

'Yes. I would have had a chance to understand why things were the way they were between us. We'd both have had a chance to put it right. We both wanted to.'

He sat quietly watching me. I knew he wouldn't speak until he was ready, and after a while I could no longer bear the weight of his gaze, and I looked away, out through the window and over the black sea.

'That day when you were a little lad,' he said at last. 'Out in Tom Blake's boat. You remember?'

'Oh, I remember.'

'You heard it that day, Iain. Out there on the waters.'

I felt something cold trickle down my spine. I kept my gaze fixed out over the sea. 'What should I have heard?'

'The voice of one who would have told you that your father isn't a hero and never was.'

'I didn't hear any voice,' I said, but I felt the hairs on the back of my neck stir. 'How could I have heard a voice? Out there?'

'That's not what you said back then, as I recall.'

'I was eight years old, for God's sake. I was terrified. I imagined it.'

'What difference would that make?'

I looked back at him, and we sat with our eyes locked, like two checkmated chess players.

'You let it be, now,' my father said. 'It'll be over soon with me. I'll be gone, and it will all be gone with me, and that's as it should be.'

I did not then know his whole meaning, but I could see that things would be just the way he described them. He was shutting down, as he had shut down the house around him. One day quite soon Betty Coleridge would come rapping on that window and, peering through the glass between her cupped hands, would see him here, his head bowed onto the open Bible, her untouched Dundee cakes rotting around him.

I could already hear Betty's tearful, accusing voice wavering down the phone line. And what would I be doing when that call came through? Sipping wine in some French café with my daughter who loved me, and my wife who loved me, watching the setting sun, looking forward to tomorrow.

'Dad, who says we can't have another chance?'

'It's too late for all of that, Iain.' He moved a leather bookmark into place and closed the Bible on it with a soft thump, so that the candle flames trembled. 'I expect you've come here meaning well enough, but now you've had your say you must leave me with such peace as I can find. And don't trouble to come back no more.' He looked up, unblinking. 'Believe me, it's better that way; for both of us.'

I wanted to fight him, to rage against him, but when I saw what lingered in his eyes I knew I had lost. There was pain there, and loss, and something else, something deeper than both of those. I remembered my mother's words – that he loved me, that he had always loved me. Perhaps that was why I was incapable of resisting him. He was my father and, face to face with him, I was not strong enough even now to overcome the hold he had on me. He wanted me to walk out of that door and never see him again in life, and that was what I would do.

I got to my feet. I opened the door a fraction and the cold night wind fluttered the candle flames so that shadows swooped and lurched around the kitchen. I stepped out into the darkness. When I got to the corner of the house he was still sitting there in the window, motionless.

28

I found a red brick pub along the coast road, tricked out with a lot of fake copper and brass. A darts tournament was under way and the bar was a deafening crush of sweating men drinking pints. The landlady was a tough woman in her fifties with mauve hair.

I paid for the room in advance, bought half a bottle of scotch and took it straight upstairs, feeling the woman's eyes on my back, part suspicious, part concerned.

The bedroom had a view across dark fields to the open sea. I poured myself a massive slug of scotch, took off my shoes, rested the glass on my chest and stretched out on the bed, listening to distant roars of triumph and despair as the darts duel was fought out below. I could see the moon from where I lay, paving a path of beaten silver to the edge of the cliffs.

He used to ride that trackless sea, my father, in all weathers, in storm and rain, and sometimes with people trying to kill him while he did it. He and his crew would blast out into that lurching darkness, looking for lost men who were no longer friends or enemies, just men who were cold and despairing and utterly alone. My father hadn't abandoned them. He never abandoned anyone.

Now he was himself alone, and fearful. And I knew that, no matter how hard he struggled against me, I must not abandon him. I thought of the carefree buccaneer in the photograph I carried in my wallet, a young man full of the love of life. I had not seen that smiling, courageous man since I was a small boy, and very soon I would lose my last chance to catch the merest shadow of him.

I shifted my weight on the bed and felt something slip from my pocket. The sovereign lay there on the counterpane, denting the material with its weight. I picked it up and turned it between my fingers, rubbing the gold thoughtfully until it winked at me in the soft light. I could feel my mind casting about to make the last connections, as a spider casts about to anchor its web. I thought of Lucien. Robert Hamelin. I thought of a fare paid and a debt called in.

In the morning I ate a huge and unnecessary English breakfast in the bar. The room looked tawdry in the sunshine and smelled of stale beer. The landlady served me the greasy food with a rough motherliness and I stayed at the table for some time, listening to the peaceful sound of the country birds in the trees outside.

I made a couple of calls on the mobile and it wasn't until about nine-thirty that I drove off. I stopped at a supermarket on the outskirts of Plymouth, and not long after that I pulled up on the gravel outside my father's cottage. I carried the boxes of groceries one by one over to the front porch and stacked them up there. He opened the front door as I was lugging the fourth and last one from the car. He was unshaven and in the hard daylight he looked haggard and pale.

'Hello, Dad.' I put the box down and stood up.

He peered down at the cartons and back up at me.

'The store will send the same again every fortnight. If you need anything meanwhile, ring them up. Here's the number.' I held out the supermarket's card and stock list but he made no move to take these things. I tucked them into the top box. 'It's all paid for, this and whatever else they send. You want me to take this stuff inside?'

He stared down at the boxes.

'You can let it rot on the porch, Dad. But it'll pile up after a while, and then Betty will have the Council round here, and the ratcatchers and the dog patrol and the health people and the SAS and a squadron of Challenger tanks. You know what she's like. Oh, and by the way I've had the power put back on.'

'I don't need no electric,' he said vaguely.

'So don't turn the lights on. Walk round blindfolded if you like. I've sorted the phone and gas too, for the next year.' I took the first thing that came to hand from the top box – a milk carton – and thrust it at him. 'Here. Go to town. Have some milk in your tea while you're locking yourself away in this morgue. What the hell, treat yourself to a ginger nut too. Live a little.'

He looked at the container in his hands as if he had never seen one before. Condensation made the surface pearly and he ran his finger through the drops.

'I'm not going to leave this alone, Dad,' I said quietly. 'You know that.'

I waited until he looked at me, and I could see that he understood.

29

I put the Discovery in the underground car park at Clerkenwell Road and took the lift up. The flat echoed with our absence. It had always been crowded, full of Kate's music and my computer gear, of Chantal's camera equipment and half-packed bags. Now the rooms felt hollow.

I shut the door behind me, gathered up a sheaf of mail, walked through to the kitchen and checked the phone. There was a score of messages on the answering service. I didn't listen to any of them. I made myself a coffee and walked through into my study. I switched on the computer and the green-shaded desk lamp and opened the window a little on the cool spring afternoon.

I took Billington's letter from my wallet and smoothed it out on the desktop. *A man can do no more than act on his beliefs, and on the information he has available to him at the time. He's not always right.*

The space beside the monitor was clear and I set the other relics out there: the sketch map of La Division, the sovereign, the box Brownie photograph of my parents on that empty beach, and even my mother's yellowing newspaper cutting about Sally Chessall which I had put aside when I first left for France. I moved the pieces of the puzzle around on the desk, as if a new configuration might suggest a new approach. I knew I must have overlooked something.

I stopped.

I took the old cutting out of the pattern and pulled the keyboard towards me and keyed in Sally Chessall's name. It failed to get a single hit. I tried the two names separately, and got pages of information, none of which looked relevant. I linked the name with Dover, with World War Two. Still nothing. I tried 'wartime crimes' and got everything from local historical societies to research material for teachers. I scrolled rapidly through, but almost all of it seemed to refer to London. I could find nothing about any Sally Chessall.

I tried the Women's Royal Naval Service. Their website invited queries about World War Two personnel, and for a moment my hopes rose. But the link took me no further than the Ministry of Defence's Veterans Agency site, which told me that only the barest details of rank and postings were available for personnel who had left the WRENs before 1972. I couldn't see how that would be of any use, and even to get that far I would need permission from Sally's next of kin.

I tried 'Kent Police Service'. The homepage displayed a rearing white horse on a seven-pointed shield. It boasted photographs of smiling officers of both genders and various racial backgrounds chatting to residents, directing traffic, kneeling to comfort lost children. Running 'Sally Chessall' in the site's search box drew a blank. I wasn't surprised: I didn't hold out much hope that a modern police force would provide links on its website to a sixty-year-old murder.

I typed in 'archive' and was given a link to Kent Police Museum. The web page contained a brief history of the museum's collection and of its installation in the restored Royal Chatham Dockyard. The place didn't look much use as a source of information. It was run by volunteers, and was only open three or four half-days a week. Visitors were asked to ring first, or risk finding the place locked and unattended. I imagined something like the Tangmere museum, but on a smaller scale.

I played around on the museum's site for a few more minutes. At least there was a photo gallery which I could access online; I did so, turning up agreeable studio pictures of self-conscious constables with large moustaches sitting stiffly next to aspidistras, and shots of Wolseley patrol cars, antique handcuffs and truncheons. There was no search box, but I'd started now and was reluctant to give up. I picked up the phone and tried the number.

I had been expecting an answering service, but to my surprise a man's voice came on the line at once. He introduced himself as John Cruikshank. He had a lugubrious voice and an estuary accent. I told him my name, mentioned the newspaper clipping. He was quiet for a moment.

'Chessall, you say?'

'Sally May Chessall, yes.'

He waited, as if he expected me to go on. I found this oddly intimidating.

'I'm not entirely sure what I'm after,' I started to say. 'I believe there's some kind of a connection …' But then I trailed off, hearing how absurd this already sounded, one stranger calling another about a murder more than sixty years ago.

'A connection with what?' he asked.

'With my mother,' I said. 'Look, I realise—'

'She wasn't one of the victims, was she? Your mother?'

'I beg your pardon?'

'Sorry if it's a delicate subject at all, Mr Madoc, but I wondered if maybe your mum …' His voice trailed off.

'You've lost me, Mr Cruikshank.'

'It's just that they were never entirely sure they identified all the victims. You didn't know that? He was what they now call a serial killer, see. The one who did Sally Chessall.'

'Are you saying this was a famous case?'

'I don't know about famous. The killings were a bit notorious at the time. But I only know that because we've got a file on them. They were known as the Gold Sovereign murders.'

I took the phone away from my ear and looked idiotically at it.

'It's kind of a nickname they got after the event,' Cruikshank was saying. 'Sally May Chessall was the last victim. Or they think she was.'

I was silent for so long that he prompted me.

'Mr Madoc?'

'I'll be there in an hour,' I said.

30

High brick walls encircled the old dockyard at Chatham, now a heritage site packed with museums and galleries and cafés with nautical names. I drove in through the archway only an hour after leaving London.

As their museum space, the Kent Police had been allocated a handsome yellow brick building with a blue 1930s police box standing outside. At a reception desk sat a solidly built man of about sixty with two cardboard folders in front of him. He had pepper-and-salt hair and steel rimmed glasses. He looked up as I came in and held out his hand to me.

'John Cruikshank.'

'Iain Madoc.'

'I gathered.' He gave me a wry look. 'I was going to tell you we were about to close, Mr Madoc, but you didn't give me the chance.'

'I'm sorry.'

'Not a bit. It's nice to hear a bit of enthusiasm for all this ancient history. Gets the old juices flowing a bit.'

He stood a cardboard sign on the desk, picked up his folders and led me between glass fronted cabinets of police memorabilia – helmets, medals, photographs – and into a study space at the back. There was a single table with a light over it and a couple of chairs and some shelves of books and a touchscreen computer with an 'Out of Order' sign stuck on it.

We sat. Cruikshank lowered his head so he could see me over the top of his glasses and tapped one of the folders in front of him.

'You can read this one for yourself, but it's mostly photocopies of old newspaper articles you've probably seen already.' Cruikshank handed it to me and the chair creaked under his weight as he leaned back. 'Funny, isn't it? There's a World War going on, and the greatest seaborne landing in history just about to be launched, yet people still liked to get their teeth into a nice juicy murder.'

There were half-a-dozen articles, four from the *Kent Courier* including the two I had already seen, and two more from the national papers, all of them dated March and April 1944. I scanned them rapidly. Several reproduced the same fuzzy picture of Sally May Chessall, a laughing, round-faced girl in uniform. They all told the same story, with hardly any variations. She was nineteen, she had served at Dover for just under a year, she had been the subject of a frenzied attack, probably with a dagger or bayonet, and she may have been dead for two days or more by the time she was found.

The later articles were more or less the regular fare of crime journalism when there's not much new to report: horrified quotes from neighbours, a statement from the girl's commanding officer, a photograph of her family home in the Cotswolds taken through locked iron gates. All repeated the same account of the discovery of the body. Only the latest, from the London *News Chronicle* of 18th May 1944, carried one extra detail, and then I almost missed it.

The alarm was raised by Miss Chessall's colleague Leading Wren Joan Fordyce, who visited her friend's flat when she grew concerned. Receiving no answer at the door, Leading Wren Fordyce left and returned with her fiancé, Pilot Officer George Madoc of the Royal Air Force, who effected entry and made the grim discovery.

I re-read the words. Again. From a distance, I became aware that Cruikshank was speaking again, that he was sliding the second folder over to me.

'This is what they didn't release at the time. Got a strong stomach, Mr Madoc, I hope?'

Dully, I opened the folder. They were crime scene photographs, stark black-and-white and revolting in their clarity. Sally Chessall had died in a mean room which had peeling wallpaper and stains on the ceiling. A plywood wardrobe stood in the corner with one door hanging loose. A chipped sink was streaked and dribbled with what must have been blood, ink black in the camera flash. A jumble of smeared handprints on the wall looked like Stone Age cave paintings. And on the bed, on blankets black and clotted, lay a very young girl with a face as white as paper. Her eyes were bulging, and her intestines were festooned over the edge of the mattress. A close-up shot showed her gaping mouth. A coin lay on the cushion of her tongue, a shiny coin.

'Nutcases like this often leave some sort of signature,' Cruikshank said, and then glanced at me. 'Madoc. Unusual name.'

I lifted my eyes from the awful pictures. 'It was my father who found the girl.'

'Thought so. I read the article.'

'It did something to him.'

'I'm not surprised.' He took off his glasses and folded them on the table in front of him. 'They retired me two years ago with a leaking heart valve, of all things,' he said, as if this somehow followed from our conversation.

I looked at him.

'I never knew I had it,' he went on. 'I ran marathons and all sorts. Would you believe it? Felt as fit as a fiddle, but I could have dropped down dead any minute. So these days I amuse myself in here, helping out, getting the files in order. It keeps me off the streets, as the wife says. But an old copper's instincts die hard. I could tell this was personal with you, so after you called I read through this stuff, and made a couple of inquiries of my own.'

'And what did you find out?'

'Another kid might have got pregnant and caused a scandal. Young Sally May gets disembowelled by a maniac. Them's the breaks, I suppose. She wasn't the only one, like I told you on the phone.' He looked down at his notes. 'There were two more of these so-called Gold Sovereign murders that they knew about. A housewife in Canterbury in October '43, and a prostitute in Deal, about a month before young Sally. Same MO in each case.

Sexual assault. Mutilation with a knife, probably a commando dagger. And a sov left in the mouth.'

'No one was arrested?'

'Not so far as I can see. But no wonder. Our Sally, by all accounts, liked to have fun, and there was no lack of volunteers. In 1944 the whole of the South of England was packed with young blokes armed to the teeth, all juiced-up about the Landings, half of them fearing they were going to die. You know they used to give gold sovereigns to behind-the-lines types?'

I nodded and stared down at the vile pictures and at the murky photocopies. I thought about a girl who liked to dance and drink, a girl who liked to make love. A girl who ended up torn apart in some shabby basement, with a gold sovereign in her mouth. When I looked up I realised Cruikshank was watching me across the table.

'Mr Madoc, let me take a guess. You know something about this crime you haven't told me yet.' He smiled and sat back in his chair, his hands locked behind his neck. 'Why don't you tell me now?'

I took out my wallet and tipped my own sovereign onto the table.

He unfolded his glasses again and leaned forward.

'My father brought it back from France in March 1944. I believe he was given it by an agent he ferried across to Brittany.'

Cruikshank looked at me over his glasses. 'Very good. Do we have a name?'

'Robert Hamelin. Long dead now.'

'Did he tell you all this, your dad?'

'Not in so many words. But I do know that a month later he didn't want to go back to France to collect this man.'

'That would be logical, if in the meantime he'd found the body.' Cruikshank closed the file. 'Oh, yes. That would be logical, all right.'

A few minutes later, we pushed through the doors and walked down the steps to the car park. Evening had fallen while we had been inside. It was chill and dark and the masts of the ships on the Medway stood like gallows against the fading sky.

'Take a tip from me,' he said, as we reached the car. 'I was thirty-seven years a copper, and if there's one thing I learned, it's that nothing ever really makes sense.'

I unlocked the car and rested my hand on the driver's door handle. I was anxious to get away, to think things through, but Cruikshank didn't show any sign of wanting to go back into the building.

'It's like my dicky heart,' he said.

I took my hand away from the car door.

'See, I was lucky,' he went on. 'Someone thought things weren't quite the way they ought to be, and took the time to ask why. Next month I'll have a little operation, and more than likely I'll be right as rain after that. But it could've been the other way so easily. A little thing like that meant life and death. What I mean to say, Mr Madoc, is that it's not the times when we're in doubt that we do most damage. It's when we know something for certain sure. That's when we make the big mistakes.'

He put out his hand and I took it. He must have thought it strange, because his words struck me so forcibly that I forgot to let go, and stood there pumping his hand absently as the patterns shifted in my head. He finally withdrew it as gently as possible and shoved it into his jacket pocket in case I might be tempted to seize it again. He kept it there and watched me cautiously as I drove past him and out of the car park.

31

I went back to London and ate at a local pub and spent the night in the empty flat.

The next morning I drove down to Plymouth again. I got there in the early afternoon. A wind was picking up, and a few petals from the apple blossom in Betty Coleridge's orchard whirled across the windscreen as I came up the lane and parked in the lay-by opposite my father's cottage. I saw him at once. He was standing in the vegetable garden, leaning on a hoe. There was some broken soil at his feet and a small pile of dislodged weeds at the end of the trellis. He watched me expressionlessly as I got out of the car. I stopped a few feet in front of him.

'She loved the roses so,' he said, as if his presence in the garden needed to be explained. 'Useless bloody plants. But she loved them so.' He looked into my eyes, and his gaze carried such pain that I thought it would break my heart. 'I never thought to see you again, Iain.'

I put my hand on the hairy sleeve of his jacket. 'Dad, let's go inside.'

He rested the hoe carefully against the trellis and I followed him into the house. The kitchen was tidy this time, and no longer smelled of fish and mould. The candles had been removed and I saw that the groceries I had delivered had been put neatly away. The Bible lay closed on the table. He led me through to the main room and stumped over to his old leather chair in the bay window. The space was pleasantly melancholy at this time of day. I remembered from my childhood that this was the only time that I had liked to be in here, with the afternoon sun throwing dusty bars of light into the dim house.

He slumped into his chair and stared out at the sea, his shoulders rising and falling. I sat down opposite him. I pulled out my wallet and emptied it, setting out the map of La Division, the sovereign, the photographs, the old newspaper cutting, on the wide window ledge. He didn't watch.

'I know about Lucien,' I said. 'I know about what he did.'

'Do you? And what else do you know?'

'I know about what you did. Or didn't do.'

'And what was it I didn't do?' His voice was very soft, as if he was tempting me to say it aloud, as he himself could not say it.

'You left him. Or maybe you just didn't try hard enough to save him.'

I lifted the sovereign so that it shone in the light. His gaze settled on it and it seemed to cost him an effort to look away and meet my eyes again. When the silence had gone on for long enough I spun the coin and caught it and closed my fist around it.

'You knew Lucien was more than half mad when you ferried him over to Brittany,' I said. 'He gave you this coin during that trip. So when you got home, and you found Sally Chessall, you knew he'd killed her.'

He held back a moment longer, but then a barrier inside him collapsed and something of the architecture of his body sagged. His eyes shifted away from mine and focused in the past.

'We saw that child, your mother and I,' he said. 'She was gutted like a fish. Like a wild animal had been at her. Dreadful to see. Dreadful.'

'Dad, nobody blames you for not saving Lucien.'

'Don't they, now?' he said, wearily.

'Nobody ever did blame you. Billington doesn't. The lads on the launch would have said you made the right decision. You tried to get them all to safety.'

'I failed *him*,' he said. 'I was sworn to save life, and I failed. I could see him. I could hear him screaming for help, and I turned away.'

'And that's why you had the memorial put up all those years later? Out of guilt? Jesus, Dad, you'd saved other men. Good men. You'd saved many of them. But this man? When you knew what he'd done? What could you owe him?'

'I owed him that I should do my duty,' he said quietly.

'So you turned away a little earlier than you would have done otherwise. So what?' I gave him space to answer, but he didn't take it. 'For God's sake, Dad, you were under fire. You had a choice to make, a split-second decision. To take the one chance of getting away with your crew, or of sacrificing them for this maniac.'

'They were sacrificed anyway.'

'How could anyone know that? You still had to make that choice. You still had to try.'

He kept his steady gaze on me for a very long time. 'You think too well of me,' he breathed at last. 'I suppose I should be grateful.'

'It's the truth, isn't it?'

I couldn't read the expression in his eyes. 'I failed,' he repeated, very quietly. 'That's the only truth that matters.'

'And because of *that* you couldn't look yourself in the eye? Couldn't look me in the eye?'

'That's right,' he said at last. 'How could I? I sat in judgement on that boy.'

'But he was a psychopath!'

He lifted his head and his voice took fire. 'Don't you understand what an awesome thing it is to sit in judgement, no matter what I thought of him? And if it had only stopped there. But good God, look at the vileness that flowed from it. You must know all the things that turned bad after I did what I did. How I let in the evil to corrupt everything that followed.'

But I was hardly hearing him by then, which is perhaps why I did not register the strangeness of that reply.

'Dad, why didn't you talk to me about this earlier?'

'What good would it have done? Talking?'

'It would have given us a chance to put things right.' I pushed my hand through my hair. 'Maybe it could still do that.'

'What?' He was scornful, incredulous, as if I had said something inane. 'Don't be foolish. How could such abominations ever be put right?'

'I worshipped you – don't you know that?' I felt my voice begin to escape from my control but I didn't much care. 'I still do.'

'You think this is just about you and me?'

The incredulity had not left his voice. In the silence that followed I grew aware that he was watching me with a new keenness. Just for an instant I was surprised by something in his eyes that flickered like a compass needle, and then settled.

'No,' he said finally. 'You wouldn't have understood. And no more do you understand now.'

I did detect it even at the time – an odd timbre to his voice as he spoke this phrase – a hint of relief, like a suspect who, under questioning, realises that his interrogators can't prove a thing after all. But at that moment I was wound too tight to trust my own perceptions.

I got up and paced away across the room. I found myself standing at the bookcase in front of the photograph of 2548 and of her crew with their cocky grins, crowded onto the waist of the craft with the English Channel glittering behind them. I picked up the frame and turned it in the light. I thought of the grave mounds in St Cyriac churchyard, the clipped grass and the daisies and the squabbling starlings and the beech trees shifting in the sea wind above them. Not a bad spot to come to rest, I thought, if you had to come to rest at seventeen or twenty-one, or twenty-five or even thirty-eight years old.

'St Cyriac's a pretty place now,' I said. 'It's a peaceful place.'

I glanced over at him, but his gaze was directed somewhere very distant, out beyond the shining estuary.

'Dad, why don't you come back with me?'

He lifted his head slowly. 'To St Cyriac?'

'Why not? We could do it. We could find a place that was big enough for all of us. Even if it was just for a while.'

He looked at me as if I might be mad. 'You want me to go back to that place?'

'But why not, Dad? There's nothing in this house to keep you.'

He gazed at me in disbelief. 'Sixty years we lived here, your mother and I. I didn't always give her a good life, but such life as we had was planted here, and grew here. It was here she brought me when she led me back to the light. It was here you were born. And you say there's nothing to keep me?'

'Nothing but ghosts now.'

'That's where I belong. Among the ghosts.'

I had a lurching sense of loss. I had thought that unlocking the past would unlock the present too. It had never occurred to me that I could learn what there was to learn and that nothing would change. I turned away from him again, not knowing what else to say. The photograph was still in my hands. I gazed at it. What would these young men have said? How would MacDonald and Billy Billington have handled this? Would they have known how to reach him in a way that I had never been able to? I stared at their smiling faces as they pushed their shoulders towards the camera, MacDonald flaunting his three stripes and Billington his two.

The image before me suddenly bloomed into yellow flame. I stared at the reflection, uncomprehending, and then whirled round. I was too late: he held the burning map until the flame licked at his fingers and then dropped the charred corner of cardboard onto the floor, where it curled and smouldered.

I put the picture down and stepped quickly across and picked up the sovereign and the photographs and the cutting from the window ledge and held them out of his reach. I knew that if he had been quick enough he would have grabbed for them all.

'Why did you do that?' I said.

'Best all this is forgotten,' he said.

'How can it ever be forgotten?'

We stood looking at one another while big sooty flakes drifted down over us.

'Best you go now,' he said. 'Best you go.'

'Dad—'

But in a gesture, for him, of extraordinary intimacy, he groped for my hand, gripped it hard then released it. 'Best you go now.'

I walked back to the car. I could still feel his hard old hand on mine.

It was a cool, breezy afternoon and the apple blossom swept across the windscreen in a blizzard, piling in a pink and white drift against the wipers. I started the engine. My father had not come out with me, but now I could see him in the mirror standing in the doorway, his face turned towards me but his eyes focused somewhere far away, while the petals whirled around him like spindrift out at sea. He didn't move as I pulled away slowly down the hill. The windscreen was blurred. I flicked on the wipers to clear it, but they didn't make any difference.

I knew it wasn't right. Even as I drove back across the moorland roads with the flinty light riding up over the bonnet and dazzling my eyes, I sensed I had missed something important. That doubt nagged at the back of my mind, just out of reach.

But for the moment it was drowned out by the renewed pain of his rejection – rejection at the very instant when I had hoped at last to close the gap between us. It was a cruel refinement of that pain I had felt all my life, and it blinded me to everything else.

32

That pain had receded to an ache by the time I drove into St Cyriac the next morning.

Hoardings had gone up outside the Hotel de Ville, advertising a local carnival in a couple of weeks' time. Girls in bright tee-shirts were handing out flyers about it and a team of men with a cherrypicker were fixing up bunting. The innocent energy of the preparations came as a relief to me and I felt my spirits lift.

They lifted still further when I saw Chantal standing at the corner by the Café des Sports, waving me down, waving so vigorously that her black hair flashed about her face. She was in blue jeans and white tee-shirt and her backpack was slung over her shoulder. She looked like a student hitch-hiker about to set off on the adventure of her life.

I had been unsure of my reception after the tension of our parting, and now I was achingly glad to see her. She wrenched the car door open before I had properly stopped, tossed her pack over the back of the seat and threw herself across me, hooking her arm around my neck and pulling me down into a long kiss.

'It is so bloody good to see you!' she said, then kissed me again, and her body moved against mine. The driver behind us blasted his horn and pulled out to swing past. It was Le Toque, in his battered white Landcruiser, a mermaid painted on the door and the back of the vehicle piled with plastic boxes and tackle. I glimpsed his laughing red face as he made a cheerful and obscene gesture in my direction.

'Chantal? I think maybe we ought to move out of the middle of the square for this.'

'Last of the great romantics,' she sniffed. She sat up and

slammed the car door. 'OK. Down to the front and turn right.'

I had no idea why she was directing me this way, but I did as I was told and drove the length of the seafront. The road curled back to follow the river bank for a little way before petering out.

'Stop here.'

I pulled up. To our left a strip of shingle sloped down to the water and I could see out across the narrow mouth of the Vasse to the willows on the far bank. On our right stood a weather-board cottage with a slate roof and a veranda, half hidden behind a neglected garden.

'Evangeline Didier's owned it for years,' Chantal said.

'Oh, yes?'

'She said that if we were staying on for a while it would be more comfortable than the guesthouse.'

'Are we staying on for a while?'

'Of course we are,' she said airily, as if there had never been any question over the matter. 'The place is a bit tatty, but it's really quite sweet. Drive on in.'

I put the car into gear and drove down the rutted track to the front of the house and pulled up next to an elderly motorcycle. I recognised it at once.

'Serge is helping out around the place,' Chantal said, glancing at me to check my expression. 'That's his excuse, anyway.'

The front door was open and in the hallway, between step-ladders and paint pots and dustsheets, I could see Serge and Kate at work. Kate came to the top of the veranda and stood there, in paint-spattered jeans, her hair tied up in a scarf, waving and smiling at me. I turned back to Chantal. She was grinning like an idiot.

'What have you done?' I said.

'Bought it, obviously,' Chantal replied. 'Signed the contract, anyway.'

'You are one crazy bitch,' I said. 'You know that?'

'I try,' she said. 'I do try.'

I dumped my bags on the old brass-framed bed and started

to unpack while Chantal lounged in a wicker chair under the window, her long legs over the arm. She and Kate had given me a breathless tour of the place. Three bedrooms with wooden floors and tall shuttered windows, and a grand old kitchen with a pine table and an iron stove. The plumbing looked as if it had been installed fifty years ago, and the whole place badly needed redecorating. The floors sagged, the plaster was peeling, and not all the angles were entirely square. I carried my clothes over to the chest of drawers and put them away. I opened the wardrobe to stow away the empty bag. The door handle came off in my hand.

'It does that.' She twisted a strand of her hair around her finger and looked the other way. 'Serge'll fix it. He's really good at that sort of thing.'

I tossed the handle onto the bed and started on my second bag, taking out parcels and papers and books and putting them on the bedside table. I unpacked the model ship I had bought in Portobello Road, checked to see that it was still intact, and set it beside the other things. The light winked on its green glass. I could feel her watching me.

'It's for Dominic,' I said. 'I'll take it over to him in the morning.'

'He'll love it. He's a sweet old man.' But we both knew that neither of us was thinking about Dominic. Finally she said, 'Iain, I know the place isn't up to much. But it's going to be, you'll see. I've got Jean Bonnard coming in tomorrow to fix up the roof. Felix says he's an OK builder if you keep an eye on him.'

'I'm sure it's going to be great.'

'Even if we only use it as a holiday cottage every now and then. And this village is just so special. You feel that too, don't you?' She hesitated, losing a little of her confidence. 'It's not like it was expensive.'

'I don't care about expensive,' I said, 'but why did you do it?'

'I was such a bitch before you left,' she said. 'I gave myself a good talking to afterwards. Beat myself up a bit.'

I shook my head in wonder. 'So you bought a house?'

'Iain, I'm on your side,' she said simply. 'Always have been, always will be. Before you left, I just forgot it for a minute, that's all.' She bounced up from her chair and came across the room and took my hand. 'There's something else. Come along.'

We edged down the half-painted corridor, past the stepladders, and out of the front door. She pulled me along the veranda and down the steps. There was a small wooden cabin standing a few metres clear of the side of the house. She opened the door of the cabin and led me in. There was one room, almost square, cluttered with broken furniture, boxes and old garden tools. The window in the far wall was cracked, but through the smeared glass I could see across the road to the sea.

'I did some thinking while you were away.' She dragged aside a beer crate and an old chair, found a scrap of rag among the litter and rubbed at the filthy glass. 'If it hadn't been for your dad, we'd never have come here …'

'And?'

'I thought … this cabin …' She looked at me in mute appeal. 'I thought maybe we could bring him back to the beginning again. Help him make his peace with St Cyriac, and with you.'

I pictured the old man as he had been two days before, standing at the open front door of his cottage, gazing into the past while the petals whirled round him. 'It's a wonderful thought,' I said. 'But I don't think he'd look at it that way.'

'How would he look at it?'

I hesitated. 'I think he'd rather no one ever mentioned St Cyriac to him again.'

Her face fell. 'When I saw this place, it seemed so natural. I suppose that was stupid …'

'It wasn't stupid. I hoped the same thing for a while. I even asked him.'

'You got somewhere with him, then?'

'I found out some things.'

She regarded me carefully. 'Do you want to talk about it?'

I told her. And as I did so I saw my father again, willing himself into the darkness where none of us could follow him, taking his ghosts with him.

'Do you want to know what I think?' she asked quietly, when I had finished. 'I think perhaps it doesn't matter so much what the old man decides to do. It just matters that you don't give up on him. In here, I mean.' She tapped her breast. 'In here.'

33

Moonlight sliced through the shutters and zebra-striped the tangle of sheets on the brass-framed bed. I guessed it was an hour or so before dawn. The window was slightly open and I could smell the tang of seaweed from the foreshore and hear the wavelets slapping against the stones. In the distance a trawler, perhaps Le Toque's, was thudding out to sea. I settled back with Chantal's head in the crook of my arm, and listened to her breathing as she grew calm again.

'Does that mean you're glad to be home?' she whispered.

When I didn't answer she propped herself up on her elbow and looked at me questioningly.

I said, 'He burned the map.'

'What?'

'His old drawing of La Division. He burned it. I was too slow to stop him.'

'But why?'

'Because there's a connection between him and that house.'

She searched my face. 'Where are you going with this, Iain?'

'He hasn't given me the whole story. Even now he hasn't.'

'You can't be sure of that,' she said. 'Maybe you already know all there is to know. He abandoned Hamelin, and he's been haunted by that one act all his life.'

'Haunted …' I said.

She hesitated. 'Is there something else?'

I looked at her in the greying light. 'Do you want me to tell you a story I've never told anyone before?'

She met my eyes uneasily. 'I'm not sure that I do,' she said.

*

I was eight years old and walking along the beach at Torpoint. It was the first really hot day of the summer. I had known from the start that it was going to be a special day. Telephone calls of any kind were unusual in our home, especially on a Sunday. But this one had been very unusual indeed: it was from Chief Inspector Myers, my father's boss – a terrifying man with glittering buttons. My parents had talked between themselves for a long while in an odd, urgent fashion after that phone call.

I must have overheard some of this, because I knew my father would be *Sergeant* Madoc from now on, and wear stripes that were almost as impressive as Chief Inspector Myers' silver buttons. I had worked all this out even before my mother had flung her arms around my father's neck and kissed him, right there at the breakfast table. That was extraordinary enough, but it was even more extraordinary that he had laughed aloud and called her a silly maid.

'Take him down to the seaside, George,' my mother had said then. She looked happy and flustered. 'It's a shame to shut him up inside on a day like this.'

'We should be off to church,' he had said, but without much conviction.

'Go on, buy the boy an ice cream.' She added daringly, 'God won't mind.'

So we trudged along the shingle past the beach huts and the sunbathers behind their windshelters until I could see the moored yachts of the marina, the ferries, and the creamy hotels on the seafront. To my right, beyond the distant grey line of the Plymouth Breakwater with its spike of a lighthouse, the blue Atlantic stretched out to a horizon lost in a summer haze.

I was happy, because my hand was in my father's hand. A man was backing a Land Rover and trailer down a ramp and across the narrow strip of beach until the back wheels were up to the axle in the sea. On the trailer was a tubby blue-and-white motorboat with a half-cabin. Three more fat little boats were riding in the water a few yards out. The Land Rover's driver hauled on the brake and jumped out of his cab.

'George Madoc!' He was a big man with sun-whitened hair

189

and a red face and he carried a sign attached to a sharpened stake. 'Or is it Sergeant Madoc, now?' When my father looked bashfully away the man grinned and stuck out his meaty hand. 'Congratulations, I say. I heard a whisper. For once they promoted the right bloke.' Still grinning, he took his signboard and rammed it into the sand and admired it. It read: *Tom Blake: Motor Boats For Hire*. The sight of his own advertisement seemed to give him an idea. 'Take the lad for a spin around the bay. My treat, George; my way of saying well done. And here's to a new start.'

I felt my father's grip tighten on my hand. 'I don't go out no more, Tom. You know that.'

'A Madoc who don't go to sea? That's like a bird that don't fly. Your people have been sailors since before Francis bloody Drake, so don't try that one on me.'

Tom Blake knocked the ratchet of the trailer winch free and the wooden boat rattled down the ramp and splashed into the sea and sat there rocking prettily, blue hull on blue water.

I sat on the bench in the half-cabin with coiled ropes and a steel anchor at my feet. The little space smelled of diesel and dead crabs. I had never been on a boat before and I could not decide what I thought about it. It was wildly exciting to sense the living water beneath me and to feel the breeze from the open sea. I hadn't realised that it could be so windy out on the water and the spaces frightened me, the shining space opening up between us and the shore, and the dim space I could feel plunging away below.

The sea had a strange and muscular rhythm out here. It took me some minutes to accept that waves running higher than the sides of the little boat would always, by some magic, pass harmlessly underneath. My father sat easily on the transom, holding the tiller against his knees, his head up, his eyes narrowed into the wind and sun, riding the motion of the boat like a horseman. He looked younger than I had ever seen him look, and more relaxed. He looked in command.

The boat moved in a wide arc across the estuary, the inboard diesel thudding comfortably. Mount Edgcumbe rose green and sunlit to our right, Drake's Island slid past on our left. I moved gingerly out of the cabin and leaned on the gunwale. Three times in quick succession the bow butted the water and sent up a little spray. I felt my stomach lurch.

'No need to have fear of that,' my father told me, ''tis just where the river kisses the sea. It will pass.'

And, sure enough, very soon the water was smooth again, smoother than at any time since we had left the beach. We moved past a wooden tripod standing high out of the water. A red beacon shone from the top of it, weak in the sunshine. My father barely glanced at it as we passed, but it made me feel uneasy to see the tresses of dark weed moving just under the surface, coiling around those massive legs. I wondered how far down they went.

Two large ships rode at anchor far out to sea. They had seemed impossibly distant at first, but gradually I could make out more and more detail – steel gantries, portholes, streaks of rust along the hulls. I did not look back to the shore. I did not want to see how distant the land had become. Perhaps my father had not intended to come this far, for I saw him look up and scan the horizon, squinting into the sun. He grunted and swung the tiller, taking the boat around quite sharply, so that it bucked against the broadside sea for a few moments before steadying again. The land seemed to have vanished, leaving us alone. Plymouth and the long green coast were lost in a grey mizzle. I began to be afraid.

'Summer rains. We'll likely get wet, but it won't last.' My father settled himself on the transom and opened the throttle slightly. 'Still, we'd best get back.'

The squall met us when we were still some hundreds of yards short of the tripod channel beacon, a curtain of rain and blustering wind sweeping out from the estuary. I was astonished at its force. In an instant the sunlight vanished and the surface of the sea turned to pewter. The boat was lashed by rain and everything more than a few yards distant was swallowed in a grey murk. It grew startlingly cold. I felt the water move beneath us, more restlessly now. I tried to remember the comforting phrase my father had used: this was where the river kissed the sea.

The engine died.

It did not splutter or cough. It simply stopped, between one thudding beat and the next one that didn't come, and the noise of it was instantly replaced by the silky run of the tide against the hull and the moan of the squall. My father leaned forward and tugged a couple of times at the starter rope with his free hand. The movement was awkward and he released the tiller and crouched over the engine to pull on the rope with both hands. Immediately the wind caught us and we swung broadside on, and the sea began to slap noisily along the side, rocking the little craft. He cursed and went back to the tiller.

'I'll take it,' I said.

He glanced at me, hesitated, but then he stood up and without a word I slid onto his warm patch of bench.

'Just hold it so. Keep her pointing round into the waves, not beam-on. She don't rock so much then, see? I'll have this fixed in a jiffy.'

I took the tiller under my arm, bursting with pride and fear. I could feel the living sea through the wooden bar, making it quiver, and I was awed at its strength. I leaned on the bar and the boat's prow moved from one side to the other.

My father knelt and took off the engine cover and tugged on the starter rope twice more. When that didn't work he found a spanner and deftly undid a nut and freed a tube and blew down it. The rain made his black hair slick and water ran down his neck.

Up ahead, I could see a smudge of red light. Soon I could see the ghostly outline of the timber tripod. The structure swayed as we approached. I knew that it could not be, that it was the boat that was moving – quite fast on the inbound tide – but I couldn't shake the feeling that we were standing still and the marker had broken loose and was lurching towards us.

My father sat up, grimacing at the taste of fuel from the pipe he had sucked. He caught himself doing it and grinned at me. He did not often smile, but when he did it felt like a blessing. He jerked his thumb at the tripod as if I might not have seen it. 'See how the tide's carrying us in? We'll be back on the beach in ten minutes, motor or no motor.'

I nodded. I felt tense and focused. He was rarely so talkative and I knew he was trying to reassure me. He bent over the engine and reconnected the fuel line and began to tighten the nut, first with greasy fingers and then with the spanner.

The channel marker was only a few yards ahead of us now. I leaned on the tiller but this time the bow would not come round. I pushed harder. It did not move. It felt heavy and sluggish, as if invisible hands were clutching the rudder below. The slimy pillars rose above us, a dim cavern between them. I braced my feet against the gunwale and strained against the tiller bar.

My father dropped the spanner and jerked his head up, and said, quite clearly, 'No.'

The tiller bar twisted out of my hands and the boat was inside the black triangle of timber, knocking against the posts, dragging against them as the sea rose and fell. Water gurgled around us and dripped on us and my father was shouting and the red light was flashing on and off above us, turning the sea lurid. The boat tilted and lurched and I let go the tiller and slid in terror into the shocking water and it closed over me.

I was in daylight again and my father's arms were around me, dragging me upwards, and I clutched the material of his coat, coughing and retching, the salt water stinging in my mouth and nose and roaring in my ears. The grey sea lifted me on its back and I caught a glimpse of the upturned boat swaying in a litter of flotsam and the tripod tower tilting away in the murk towards the open ocean. My father's rough jacket was crammed against my face and the world beyond was cold and charged with dread.

And I heard my father shouting, shouting and sobbing, freeing one fist to shake it and hurling his words at the indifferent sea.

'You'll not take him!' he bellowed, over and over again, his voice cracking. *'You'll not take him from me!'*

Chantal nestled closer to me. 'He wasn't just shouting at the sea, was he?'

'No. He wasn't.'

'He was shouting at someone,' she said. 'Calling to someone.'

'Yes.'

She hesitated. 'Who?'

'I don't know. But it wasn't Hamelin. I think it was a woman, a girl. He could hear her sobbing. Wailing.'

'So he did tell you that much, at least. He did talk about that.'

'He didn't need to,' I said. 'I heard her, too.'

34

I could hear scaffold poles ringing and clattering as workmen unloaded a truck, and Kate's voice as she issued orders.

By the time I got downstairs the kitchen was full of the aroma of coffee. Bonnard and his three workmen nodded to me from the veranda and I nodded back. But I wasn't watching them. I was watching Kate hand the mugs around. She was wearing khaki pants, a man's blue denim shirt knotted around her waist, and open sandals. I noticed the way the men looked at her as they took their coffee.

She came back to the door with the tray. 'What are you staring at?'

'Nothing. Thanks for keeping these guys sweet.'

A brown paper bag full of croissants lay on the draining board.

'I thought maybe you needed a lie-in.' Kate gave me a schoolmarmish look. 'You want to be careful, at your age.'

I grinned, took a croissant and ate it wolfishly.

'Dad!' She put her hands on her hips. 'They were for Serge! He's coming over for breakfast.'

'Oh, yes?' I licked my fingers. 'I'll have another one, then.'

She was about to protest when we heard the motorbike in the driveway. I could see her quicken, and knew she was forcing herself not to run outside.

I slapped crumbs off my fingers. 'You like him, don't you?' I said.

She clicked her tongue. 'God, Dad.'

'Am I embarrassing? It goes with the territory. For the record, I quite like him, too.'

'Dad likes him!' She rolled her eyes. 'Well, that's the kiss of death.'

The engine cut out and the bike came trundling past the back door, squeaking on its springs. I caught a glimpse of Serge in a black helmet and old-fashioned goggles. His shirt was open and his forearms were taut and brown. Kate turned away from me and ran outside. I waited a decent interval before I sauntered after her.

'Kate's short-changed you on the croissants, Serge,' I said.

'This is Dad being funny.' She tried to look haughty, but she shone at the boy's side.

Serge smiled uncertainly at me and leaned over to shake my hand. He took off his helmet and goggles, and rocked the bike up onto its stand, sitting astride it with an old canvas satchel resting on the seat in front of him. The bike was a very old BMW, heavy and angular, nothing at all like the sleek rockets on which I saw kids of Serge's age blaring around London.

I poked at the stuffing escaping from the pillion seat. 'Where did you get this thing?'

'They don't make them like this any more.' He pulled a wry face, clipped his helmet to the handlebars and lifted the canvas bag. 'I brought a few extra tools.'

I stepped away from the bike. 'Stay for dinner tonight, Serge.'

'Dad,' Kate said, pink with embarrassment. 'Serge stays for dinner nearly every night.'

'He may do,' I said. 'But I've never asked him before.'

I walked around the corner of the house, my coffee steaming in the cool morning. Jean Bonnard was standing in the front yard, peering up at the roofline, making notes on a clipboard.

'Needs a bit of work, that roof,' he said.

'Something told me you'd say that.'

He chuckled; we understood one another. He was in his fifties and solidly built, his face nutbrown from the weather and creased with smile wrinkles.

'Ah, but you can't go wrong with these old places, M'sieur,' he said. 'Especially not this one. My grandfather built it.'

'He did?'

'My grandfather on my mother's side, that is. He built a lot of the places around here during the War.'

'He could find work here then?'

'It was the War that made him. There were lots of opportunities for a smart builder during the Occupation. New barracks over at Lannion. Prison compound down near St Brieuc. He did all that. He even built that old blockhouse on the point across the estuary. The Germans used forced labour for most of this stuff, but you still needed someone to manage things.'

'I didn't know that.'

He glanced at me. 'There wasn't much future in refusing, M'sieur. Every company in France worked for the Germans, and the Government encouraged it. How else were they to pay their workers, keep everyone fed? Mr Churchill wasn't going to do that.' He took hold of a drainpipe running down the wall and shook it experimentally. 'Lots of people did well in those days. Especially the shipyards and the munitions works. Now my other grandfather, Paul-Louis, he was a different animal altogether. Well, you know he was in the Resistance. He helped your father.'

'What was he like?'

'A bit of a lad, was Paul-Louis. It suited him, the War. He and Mathieu Garnier got in with a group who used to blow up the power lines. Mathieu was the brains, of course. That's what really did for the Germans in the end; they couldn't get power to run their factories and such. Mind you, it was risky stuff. You'd get shot for that kind of thing, and get other people shot too.' Bonnard pointed at the house. 'Now *this* granddad, the builder, he did his bit without ever touching a gun. He nearly bankrupted the Third Reich all on his own.'

We walked on a few steps, around the corner of the building, Bonnard poking the clapboard planking here and there and clicking his tongue in disapproval.

I said, 'I suppose the Germans kept a pretty close eye on this coast?'

'Oh, Christ, yes! They had every bay and inlet guarded in case the Allies landed here. All the locals were praying they wouldn't, or so my dad used to say. Anything to keep the War away. Luckily for us it was Normandy that copped it. Once the British and the Yanks had broken out of the bridgehead in August '44 things eased off a bit here, but up until then the coast was stiff with Boches, all of them getting jumpier by the minute.'

Something began to spark in my mind, some connection not quite made. I gazed past Bonnard's bulky shoulder to the sea. I could just see the corner of the old blockhouse. I said, 'And yet in June that year my father managed to sail out of the Vasse estuary, right under their noses.'

'Fortune favours the brave, M'sieur.' Bonnard wagged his head. 'But I must say I've often wondered how they got away with it. Your dad and his pal must have sailed so close to that blockhouse that the Krauts could have thrown frankfurters into the boat.'

35

About midday I parcelled up Dominic's present and walked into the village. As I approached the bank of the river I spotted him sitting at one of the wooden picnic tables overlooking the water. There was a children's playground here, with plastic swings and slides. A few early tourists sat at the nearby tables, nursing takeaway coffees they'd bought at the kiosk while their children squealed in the sandpit. Dominic was alone, contentedly eating a lurid ice cream from a cone. He was enjoying himself, laughing at a group of kayakers who were trying unsuccefully to paddle against the in-streaming tide.

He saw me and jumped up. 'Hello, Iain!'

'Dominic. I was just coming to see you.'

'Yes,' he agreed, as if he had known this all along. He finished his ice cream and dropped the wrapper neatly in the bin.

I put my backpack on the table.

'What have you got there?' he asked artlessly. 'Is it a present for someone?'

'It's for you. From England.'

He looked at me wide-eyed. 'For me?'

I held out the parcel.

He rubbed the palms of his hands a couple of times down the seams of his overalls, took the box gingerly, and began to unpeel the wrapping.

'Go on, rip it,' I urged him. 'It's more fun if you rip it.'

He glanced at me with shy pleasure, but folded the wrapping paper into a careful square and set it aside before he eased off the lid. He lifted out the bottle and held it with both hands and gazed at it with rapture, turning it with infinite care to look at it first from one direction and then another. It was a ship in a bottle with calico sails and a blue wooden hull. His enchantment was so intense that it attracted the attention of the families sitting nearby. I could see them nudging one another and smiling the way strangers will smile at the delight of a child.

'You told me you liked models,' I said.

He put the bottle back in the box with infinite care and cradled it in his arms.

'I'm glad you're pleased,' I told him. 'It was made by an English sailor a long time ago.'

'Perhaps your papa made it,' he suggested, 'when he was here in St Cyriac?'

'I don't know about that. But it was probably made by somebody a bit like him.'

He rocked his gift for a few seconds longer, smiling his gentle smile. At length he picked up the folded square of wrapping paper and tucked it inside his overalls.

'Come along,' he said brightly.

'Where are we going?'

He was already striding away down the riverside track, and hurriedly I got up to follow. This time he didn't turn left across the pontoons at Bourgogne's yard, but kept along the path for a few hundred metres. I felt like a kid on a surprise outing. The track followed the river between poplars and ash trees. The cottages at the edge of the village gave way to patches of open ground, smallholdings and vegetable gardens, and I could see the mill beyond them.

Dominic turned down a narrow path to a gate in a chain link fence, and let me in through it. We crossed a carpark and walked through a brick archway into a courtyard surrounded by balconies on three levels. Groups of elderly people and their younger relatives chatted around tables and a giant chess board was set out on the paving in one corner. A plump woman in a blue housecoat appeared carrying a thermos of coffee.

The woman put the thermos down with a thump and bustled over to us. She gave me a look of frank appraisal.

'You're back early today, Dominic. Fish not biting?'

'This is my friend Iain, Madame Duquesne,' Dominic told her, in the voice a nervous schoolboy might use to a headmistress. 'I'm going to show him my models.'

'Well, isn't he the lucky one?' Whatever she saw in my face seemed to satisfy her and she held out her hand. 'I'm the caretaker here. I like to keep an eye on my old folks.'

We shook hands.

'You have to watch them,' she went on. 'Watch 'em like a hawk, I do. Not that this one's any trouble – are you, young Dominic? Your visitors are always *most* pleasant and respectable.'

He beamed at her.

'You run along and play with your boats, then,' she told him, and as he started to lead me away she gave me a wink.

The doors and the balcony rails were painted in primary colours. Dominic's bright blue door was on the second floor. There was a lift but we climbed the concrete steps. Dominic trotted spryly ahead of me, chatting as he went.

'There,' he said proudly, pushing the door open for me.

I walked into a short passage with coats hung on a rack and a bag of carpenters' tools stowed behind the door. It opened into a pleasant room with double windows looking out at the branches of a lime tree. Under the window was a large wooden desk with butcher's paper spread over it. Dominic's blue china elephant sat in an alcove above it. On the desk itself, brushes, chisels, and pencils were neatly arranged around a half completed model of a sailing ship. There were thirty or so completed models arranged on fruit boxes, on trestles and stands and on the floor, models of everything from ships of the line to tea clippers in full sail to humble fishing boats.

The detail was astonishing. Dominic had reproduced every cleat and block and every thread of rigging. Through the ports of the warships, miniature guncrews polished their cannon; on a quarterdeck a blue-coated officer gestured up at the maintop. On the deck of a merchant ship I could see livestock in cages and hessian bales stacked in the waist, each of them intricately lettered, though it would have taken a magnifying glass to read the words.

Dominic reached past me to place the gift I had given him on the desk.

'You like my boats, Iain?' he asked, his voice full of innocent pride.

'I've never seen anything like them. They're wonderful.'

He gave a little grunt of pleasure and moved away, and when I turned, he was standing in his little kitchen area, smiling at me. Just behind him was a small two-ring cooker with a pan placed ready for use, and on the surface beside the cooker was a plate with four plump sausages on it under a transparent cover. One of the kitchen drawers was open, and I glimpsed bank notes in it, large denomination euro notes in bundles. A lot of them.

I said, 'Dominic, you shouldn't leave that stuff lying about.'

'It's OK. I only just took them out of the fridge.'

'Not the sausages. The money.'

'Oh, that! Madame Duquesne tells me the same thing. But the cheques keep coming from the Government, and she tells me I have to cash them.' He slid the drawer closed, as if that closed the subject, too.

He came back to stand beside me at the desk and made a play of admiring the ship in its bottle. Beside his own work it now looked clumsy to me, yet he seemed to love it just the same, and as far as I could see his delight was genuine.

'I'm glad you like it,' I said, 'but I think I'd better be going.'

'Oh, you can't go!' He looked shocked at the idea. 'I've got something for you. That's why I brought you up here.'

He ducked down behind one of the tables and lifted out a varnished wooden box. It was about a metre long with a rope handle and a lid with brass catches and hinges. He manoeuvred it out and set it on the table in front of me, next to his ship in its bottle. He snicked the catches and folded back the lid. The model was, as far as I could see, perfect in every detail: radio masts, Oerlikon cannon above the stern hatchway. And the number 2548 in yellow on her hull.

'This is for you,' he said.

A crewman in oilskins manned the gun – a figure no more than a couple of centimetres tall – and another crouched in the forepeak hatch with binoculars raised. Through the wheelhouse windows I glimpsed the bearded skipper in his white sweater, his feet apart and hands on the wheel.

'I can't possibly accept this.'

'Oh, yes you can! Besides, it's not for you, really. It's for your papa.'

I stroked the smooth curve of the hull with a fingertip. 'I don't know when I'll see my father again, Dominic. Perhaps never.'

'You'll see him again,' he told me with complete confidence. 'You just keep this for him until he comes.' He leaned across me, closed the box and clicked the brass catches into place. And then, as if the question were connected to what he had just said, he asked, 'Have you finished reading Father Thomas's diaries?'

'Not quite, no.'

'So Father Thomas hasn't spoken to you about your papa yet?'

'I'm not sure he's going to be able to do that, Dominic. The diaries finish before my father got here.'

'Oh yes,' he said. 'That's true.'

I looked at him narrowly. 'Dominic—'

He smiled up at me. 'Fancy a sausage?'

I left him an hour or so later, and lugged the mahogany box back down the track. It was heavy and awkward, so I stopped for a couple of minutes at a bench near the mouth of the river. The remains of the old German pillbox on the opposite point were just visible in the undergrowth. I could see black gunslits and rusting strands of reinforcing steel where the side wall had begun to crumble.

The kayakers I had seen earlier had been replaced by a group of kids in wetsuits learning how to sail catamarans. The bright craft had green-and-white hulls and bottle green sails and re-minded me of dragonflies. Every now and then one would tack a couple of hundred metres to seaward and edge quite close to where I sat, and an instructor in an aluminium dinghy would call it back. But his caution was unnecessary. The in-rushing tide was beginning to slacken but, even so, none of these fleet little craft looked as if it could come close to crossing the bar and breaking out to sea.

36

The next morning, Serge arrived while we were finishing breakfast. Bonnard and his crew came bouncing up the drive in their truck a minute or two later. I felt bad about leaving now, just as the working day was starting, but I knew I had to. I walked through to the bedroom to fetch a jacket. Chantal leaned against the doorframe and gave me a quizzical look.

I said, 'I'll start pulling my weight this afternoon. Promise.'

'That's fine.' She plucked at a loose thread on her shirt, but kept her eyes on mine as she did so.

'There are just a couple of things I want to get out of the way first.' I checked my wallet and slipped it into my pocket.

'Iain, I do understand how important it is.'

'I know you do.' I leaned forward and kissed her.

Christine Tremblay looked up from her monitor.

'Welcome back.' She got up, smiling, and shook my hand. 'I'd never have imagined the good Father's diaries were quite so interesting.'

'Oh, real page-turners. You've no idea.'

She laughed, and led the way, her heels tapping on the parquet. 'And you've become a genuine St Cyriac resident, I understand? Now that shows devotion!'

'You know how it is. We liked the village so much, we bought a bit of it.'

'Well, now you're one of us, perhaps I can stop calling you Monsieur Madoc.'

'Please do. My name's Iain.'

'I know it is. And mine's Christine. You must come over for

dinner one night. I have a little place in Lannion.' She made innocent eyes. 'And your wife, of course, if she's free.'

I sat at the desk and watched her speculatively as she tapped away to the archive room. In a moment she came back with the journals. I avoided her eyes and opened the one for 1941.

Sunday 5 June
I was in the vestry after Mass, believing myself alone in the church, when I was disturbed by the sound of weeping. I emerged to find Madame Rosen in a state of considerable distress. In my presence the lady had always previously been high spirited to the point of disrespect, but despite the coolness between us I conceived it my duty to approach her and offer solace. To my astonishment she fell to the floor and threw her arms about my knees in a most undignified manner.

She insists that her family are in terrible danger. Apparently a second Statut des Juifs was passed a few days ago by the Government in Vichy, barring Jews from practising at all in a wide range of professions and excluding them from most public office. Her husband must give up his work as notaire, which his family has practised for generations.

Madame Rosen says she has heard dreadful stories from the east, stories of purges and extermination. I urged her to stand, afraid that someone might come. I told her she must be mistaken, for France was the first nation in the world to emancipate Jews. The Vichy Government might wish to clarify the place of Jews in society, but it would never visit actual persecution on them. I reassured her that France had much to be proud of in her treatment of alien peoples.

At this she stood shouting at me in the aisle, quite hysterical. "Aliens?" she cried. "Are we not as good a French family as any in this village?"

I told her this was the House of God, and no place for such unrestrained emotion. She controlled herself with an effort and left with some dignity.

I have now seen the second Statut des Juifs, passed on the 2nd June, and its restrictions are certainly harsh. However, my own belief is that this is mostly political posturing, and the Statut's full stipulations could never be put into effect. I wish I had been able to reassure Madame Rosen on this point, but she would not listen to reason.

I packed the diaries away in their box, and walked back to the reception desk.

Christine Tremblay looked up brightly at me, the same coquettish sparkle in her eyes. 'And did you find what you were looking for this time?'

'What *did* happen to the Rosens, Christine?'

Some of the light went out of her. I think we both knew that the moment for banter had passed.

'Everyone knows what happened to the Rosens,' she said. 'They were arrested in 1942.'

'But who arrested them? Where were they taken afterwards?'

'Auschwitz. Most French Jews went there.'

'Are there any records?'

She sat up very straight and her voice grew guarded. 'I won't be able to help you with that. We don't keep that kind of thing here.'

I retreated a little. 'Look, I don't mean to—'

'Can I tell you something, Iain? Between friends?'

'Please.'

'Some of the older inhabitants are really touchy about the Rosen story. I think they're ashamed that it could have happened here in St Cyriac.'

'I see.'

'And after all, it was a very long time ago.'

'Right.'

But I didn't move. She looked unhappily at me, and in a moment she sighed, picked up her bag and opened it. She took out a white business card and handed it to me across the desk.

'Rabbi Silbermann in St Malo,' she said. 'He's built up an archive of all the Jewish families around here. Nothing formal, but it's a passion of his. Tell him I asked you to call.'

'Thank you,' I said. 'Thank you very much.'

When I got to the door I glanced back and found she was still looking at me.

I wanted a moment to think and, flicking the business card idly against my nail, I made my way up to the churchyard. I had almost reached the iron bench by the graves of my father's crew before I saw Dr Pasqual. He smiled at me and patted the bench beside him. I sat down.

'So very young,' he said, and nodded at the gravestones. 'Nineteen years of age. Twenty-two. Seventeen. But that's how it works, Iain. The rich send the poor to war. The clever send the stupid. But most shamefully of all, the old send the young.' He rearranged his slender hands in his lap. 'You've been away?'

'For a few days. To see my father.'

He turned to look into my eyes. 'Your journey did not bring you the answers you sought, I fear.'

'No. Not all of them.'

'There comes a time when it's better to let the past rest in peace, Iain,' the old man said softly. 'We lived it once, your father and I, and these lads lying here, and Mathieu Garnier, and Paul-Louis Bonnard, and Guillaume Le Toque. And millions of others like us. We hoped those who came after us wouldn't have to live it again. Indeed, I seem to remember that was the whole point.'

I thought he was going to say more, but instead he got to his feet. He rested his thin old hand on mine for a second, then moved off down the gravel path, like some ancient and courtly ghost drifting between the gravestones.

When I got back to the square, kids were skateboarding on the paved area at its centre, performing impossible leaps over the low railings. A group of men were playing *boules* opposite the Hotel de Ville. More pretty girls in tee-shirts were moving among the early holidaymakers, handing out leaflets about the carnival.

I spent a moment by the rose arbour, looking in at the Rosens' sculpture.

At Henri's place I sat at an outside table, took out Rabbi Silbermann's card and called him on the mobile. He picked up almost at once.

'I don't think I shall be able to help you very much, Monsieur Madoc.' He had a measured voice – not unfriendly, but giving nothing away, like the voice of a doctor or a lawyer. 'But of course if Christine suggests it, you must come over and see me. I shall attempt to find something on the Rosen family before you arrive. Tomorrow morning? Say ten o'clock?' He gave me precise directions and rang off.

It was windy out on the terrace. *The Gay Dog* was rolling in the restless water just beyond the wall of the quay, sleek and polished amongst the sober workboats alongside. The hatch was open, and I could hear the whine of machinery from inside. Gunther appeared from the cabin, bare chested and beautiful, a sander gripped in one hand.

Henri came bouncing out of the café, apron flapping, seized my hand and welcomed me back. He set a silver tankard down before me with a flourish.

'A little something for our new resident!' he cried. 'On the house.'

I thanked him, and tried to make small talk, but he must have sensed that I wanted some time to myself, because he pretended to hear a summons from inside and quickly vanished again. The concoction was delicious – champagne and something peppery which I couldn't identify. I drank again, then reached for Henri's menu in its imitation leather cover and pulled out the sheet announcing today's specials – *moules frites, bouillabaisse, tartes aux pommes*. I turned it over, found a pen, and began to draw.

My map of La Division didn't look much like the smudged and wavering sketch my father had destroyed. Mine was clear and bold. Some hidden mechanism in my memory must have been at work, because it showed more detail than I consciously recalled seeing in the original. I drew the plan of the farmhouse with particular precision, and within it a box inside a box, the inner rectangle dissected by three firm lines, even the scribbled numbers. I still didn't know what it all meant, but at least I had a map again. My father had not been able to obliterate his own trail entirely.

37

The house was full of builders and noise, the smell of paint and the din of power tools. Two trucks were parked at odd angles just below the veranda steps, and the drive was stacked with timber and slate. A skip had been dropped on the overgrown flower-beds. I could taste plaster dust and crushed vegetation. I climbed the three steps to the front door and looked in. An internal wall came down in a cloud of plaster. In the back bedroom Serge and Kate were ripping out the plywood partitioning. I could hear Kate shrieking with laughter as they did it.

I retreated to the cabin. Dominic's model sat in its case in the corner where I had left it, but the rest of the place was still cluttered with junk, old crates, rusted bicycle frames and bits of broken furniture. I carried the model outside, put it out of harm's way on the grass, took off my jacket and got to work. I moved crates and cartons and rolls of felt and ancient gardening tools and tubs of potting mix and a box full of hardened paint cans and worked my way gradually through to the end wall. Then I scrubbed the whole place, walls, windows and floor, sluicing it all through three or four times. When the floor was dry I brought the model back in, set it up on a crate by the door, and constructed a makeshift table under the window by resting an old cupboard door across a couple of trestles.

I could see straight out across the coast road to the beach from the newly cleaned window. I opened it and spread my hands on the sill. The breeze flickered in off the sea, shivering the foliage in the garden, cooling the sweat on my forearms.

The latch clicked behind me. Chantal had untied her hair and it flowed over her shoulders. She carried two tumblers of white wine, and wordlessly gave me one of them. She sipped hers and began to prowl around, running a fingertip along the timber walls, and, when she reached it, over the smooth varnished wood of the model's case, leaving a dark track in the film of dust there. There was something langorous about the way she moved.

'Just imagine, if you turned out to be good at all this,' she said. 'Carpentry. Fixing things.'

'Doesn't sound much like me.'

'That'd be great, wouldn't it? To be married to someone for eighteen years and start discovering new things about them.' Her prowling had taken her back to the door, and now she leaned against it until it clicked emphatically shut. She said, 'I had a little piece of news to tell you. But something's put it clean out of my mind.'

I moved forward and put my hands up under her hair. The skin behind her ears was warm and moist. I could feel her pulse beating. I bit the lobe of her ear. I heard her draw a deep breath and she put her glass down clumsily and her arms snaked round my neck. She kissed me and then broke free, moved into the centre of the room and stood in a patch of afternoon sunlight. She pulled her shirt up over her head and unbuckled her jeans and stepped out of them and stretched herself out on the boards like a cat in the sun, and reached up her arms to me.

I undressed quickly, and knelt over her. The sun fell through the open window onto my back. I was conscious from time to time of the sounds from outside – early evening birdsong, murmured banter between Serge and Kate in the house. Then these sounds receded. Chantal's skin smelled of sunlight and sweat. I stretched myself deep inside her and her arms locked hard around me and she gripped the flesh over my shoulder blades and I felt her mouth open under me.

The noises of the world crept back gradually, a distant tractor, waves on the beach. And then a new sound: the hum of Kate's viola. It was the first time I had heard her play since we'd come here, even though she had started lessons again with Sylvie Bertrand.

'He sits and watches her play,' Chantal said. I could feel her smile against my shoulder. 'It's sweet.'

'He's supposed to be working,' I said darkly.

She kissed my neck. 'Yes. Just like us …'

She stood up and gathered her clothes, dressed and walked over to the open window, shivering a little in the cool breeze. She glanced down at the map, which I'd left on the tabletop, and stiffened.

'I made a copy,' I said unnecessarily. 'I pinched one of Henri's menus.'

She stood looking at the drawing without speaking.

'Is this a problem?' I asked.

'No,' she said. 'Not yet, anyway.'

'I just need to close the door on it,' I said, getting to my feet.

'I understand that.' She looked at me. 'The past's important. But we have a future as well.'

'I'm sorry. Am I getting too caught up in all this?'

'I know how much it means to you. I won't stand in your way.' She walked across and took my face in her hands, shaking my head with a little jolt to emphasise her point. 'Just don't forget to spend some time in the here and now with me, OK? I'm not used to you as a man with a mission.'

'Right now my only mission is to crack a bottle of Burgundy.'

Her brow furrowed. 'That reminds me of what I came to tell you. We're going to Paris.'

'We are?'

'You aren't. I'm taking Katrine for a couple of days. Do some mother-daughter bonding. You'd hate it, and anyway you need to stay here and play foreman.' She gathered up our empty glasses and walked to the door. 'All you have to do is suck your teeth and shout a lot. And keep young Serge from pining away.'

'Maybe he'll do the same for me.'

'Ahhh,' she said, and blew me a kiss. She stopped at the door. 'This is OK with you, isn't it, sweetheart?'

'Except that the last time I left you and Kate alone you bought a house.' I bent down to lace my trainer. 'When are you leaving?'

'In a couple of hours.'

'Well, I'm glad you could fit me in.'

She raised one eyebrow, but I hadn't meant it like that.

38

I dropped Chantal and Kate at the rail station in St Brieuc. They were cutting it fine for the seven o'clock train and I watched them race across the concourse with their bags bouncing and their hair flying like schoolgirls. I waited until I saw the sleek locomotive draw out.

When I pulled up in the drive again it was dark, but I noticed that the light was still on in the cabin. I walked over, pushed open the door and reached for the switch.

Serge stood up hastily. 'Monsieur Madoc.'

He was as surprised as I was. I saw that he had been kneeling on the floor in front of Dominic's model. The varnished case stood open. His canvas satchel and his tool belt lay on the floor.

He said, 'I saw you'd left the window open. I came in to close it. Then I couldn't resist taking a look at this. It just knocks me out.'

'It does that to me too.'

'Old Dominic made this? It's just amazing. I'd heard he made models, but I never knew he had this kind of skill.' Serge shook his head. 'He's a character, isn't he? I sometimes think he's the only sane one and all the rest of us are nuts.'

'You know him pretty well, then?'

'I see him down at the launch from time to time, when I bring my boat into the estuary. I've never been to his place, though. Never seen his models.'

'You should ask him to show them to you. He'd be pleased.'

'*He'd* be pleased? I'd be bloody delighted.'

He bent down again in front of the model. 'Did he make this for you, Monsieur Madoc?'

'For my father. Dominic seems convinced he's going to come to St Cyriac and collect it one day.'

'And you're not?'

'I think my dad was glad to get out the first time. I would be too. I'm still not sure how he did it, getting away in an open dinghy, and taking an injured man with him, right under the noses of the Germans.'

'Forget the Germans.' Serge closed the model's case reverently. 'In the Vasse the tides are the big danger.'

I remembered him saying something like this to me before, and a picture came into my mind of kayakers and kids in catamarans fighting against the current.

'Tell me about that, Serge. Tell me about the tides.'

'Your dad must've been lucky, that's all. Nobody could sail out of the Vasse against a flood tide – when it's coming in, that is. The current would be too strong. And the Vasse is special. It's even got a bore sometimes.'

'A what?'

'A bore. The river's quite deep, but it's narrow, and the riverbed takes a couple of sharp turns up beyond Bourgogne's boatyard, where the cress beds are. When the tide comes in the river holds back the sea for a while, then the tide gets the upper hand and it rushes in like a big wave. That's called a bore. When the tide turns the other way, all that water rushes out to sea again really fast.'

I'd heard about a similar phenomenon on the River Severn, and the image of it had always given me the creeps. I pictured a wall of water, swift and soundless and sinister, rolling mud and dead branches.

'The bore on the Vasse isn't much,' Serge said. 'It's only about half a metre high even at the fullest tide. But the point is, once that tide turns, it ebbs fast.'

'So my father must have caught the ebb?'

'Sure. That would have whisked him out to sea like a cork in a millrace. That'd be why the Germans didn't see him. Blink and he'd be past. But the timing had to be absolutely right.'

'I suppose there's no way of knowing what the tides were actually doing that night?'

'Oh, yes. I'll look it up for you.'

'You can do that? Look up one particular night? After all these years?'

'The rhythm of the moon and the tides doesn't change. You get one reading, and you can work back as far as you want. Computers make it easy. I'll get onto it.'

He scooped up his bag and his toolbelt.

I said, 'There's no rush, Serge.'

He stopped, uncertain now whether he should go or stay. His satchel was a shabby army surplus affair, and it lay unbuckled and open. A well thumbed textbook and two leather-backed sketchbooks were visible inside the flap. I noticed that the bigger of the two was open and I caught a vibrant flash of colour from the page. I reached over and touched the cover.

'May I look?'

He hesitated, but did not quite refuse, and I lifted the book out of the bag and turned it to the light. The watercolours were exquisite. I could see at once their inspiration – the spiral structure of shells, tresses of weed, the angular armour of crabs – handled in a startlingly abstract fashion which was both sensuous and precise.

'Serge, these are beautiful. Surely they're not coursework?'

He shook his head. 'These are just for myself.'

'But you are studying? Isn't that what you said?'

'Oh, yes,' he said quickly. 'I'm doing marine biology at IFREMER. Do you know it? The marine science institute.'

'Isn't that in Paris?'

'They've got five centres. The closest one's in Brest. I do it by correspondence, mostly.'

He took the book from me a little roughly and stuffed it into his pack. 'The Shoals are my special project. I go out there whenever the tide is low enough, early in the morning or at night. That way I can get here during the day.'

'You go out in the dark? In that little boat of yours?'

His chin came up. 'I know what I'm doing.'

'I'm sure you do.' I remembered what I had read about the Shoals; that they became quicksands with the incoming tide, capable of swallowing people, wreckage, even ships. 'You must have a passion for wild places.'

Serge shrugged, but I could see that I had struck a chord. He fiddled with the buckles of his bag for a while and then stopped, staring not at me but at the wall.

'There's such beauty out there, Monsieur Madoc. On the Shoals. On the sea. There's such beauty all around us, and we never see it. We never see the pattern in it. It's as if we're too close. As if the rhythm's too slow for us to hear the music.'

I had not expected anything like this from Serge, and I could see all at once what it was about him that Kate found so attractive. He was an outsider. He might act tough, but that was because his sensitivity to the world made the rougher contacts painful and he had to fend them off.

'Where do you live, Serge?'

'Oh, down the coast a bit. My family owns some property outside Lannion.'

'A farm?'

His defences came up at once. 'You were expecting a gipsy caravan? All campfires and duelling violins?' He hefted his backpack and gestured at Dominic's model. 'Sorry. I should have asked you before opening it.' He walked to the door.

'Serge?'

He turned back. 'Yes?'

'You'll be here tomorrow?'

'Sure.'

'I've got an appointment in St Malo in the morning. Can you keep an eye on things here?'

'Of course.'

'And maybe we can grab a bite to eat tomorrow night, if you're free.'

The invitation clearly surprised him, but I could see it pleased him too. He ducked his head shyly and stepped out into the night.

39

I had expected Rabbi Silbermann to be a scholar in his sixties, but he couldn't have been much over thirty-five. He reminded me of a middle ranking bank official, careful, meticulous, and dark suited. He took the sheets from the printer and flicked rapidly through them, peering through polished glasses. He marked a passage here, a line there, in yellow highlighter.

'There's not much, Monsieur Madoc, I'm afraid. I was hoping I could show you more. But this is mostly background on the Rosen family from before the War. Certificates, qualifications and so on. Let me just make sure I haven't missed anything.'

I waited patiently, gazing out of the window of his office at the ramparts of the old city. Holidaymakers were walking in the morning sunshine, posing and photographing one another in their bright clothes. Above the battlements the masts of ocean-going yachts trembled against an azure sky.

'You've seen this photograph?' Rabbi Silbermann showed me a print-out of the Rosen family group.

'Yes. I have a copy.'

'It was taken in February 1939. Gustave, Rachel and their daughter Madeleine. Christine tells me the boy was a local lad who lived with them. But perhaps you knew that?'

'His name was Robert Hamelin. My father ferried him across the Channel a few years after this picture was taken, when Hamelin was with the Free French.'

'And that's why you're interested in the Rosens? Because your father knew this boy?'

'It's one of the reasons.' I opened my wallet. 'This is a copy of a map my father brought with him when he escaped from St Cyriac in 1944. It's La Divison, the Rosens' family home.'

He took the sketch and studied it. 'Why did he have this?'

'That's something I'd really like to know.'

He handed it back to me. 'I wish I could help. I'm afraid I haven't found much about the Rosens at all. Although I can tell you they were extremely unlucky.'

'Why do you say that?'

'Jews were being systematically marginalised almost from the start of the Occupation. There were *Statuts des Juifs* in October 1940 and June 1941 and all kinds of other regulations restricting their business activities. But they weren't rounded up en masse until July 1942. Even then it was supposed to be only foreign Jews that were taken, although in practice any Jew who fell into the net was fair game. Still, I'd have expected the Rosens to be relatively safe until at least then. They were French citizens, with a strong tradition of service to the state. Gustave had been mayor, after all, and was a decorated veteran of the first war. So why were they arrested in May 1942? It sounds as if someone had a grudge against them.'

'That sort of thing happened?'

'Oh, certainly. A lot of betrayals were motivated by simple jealousy. Many of the Jewish doctors who were turned over to the Nazis were shopped by their own colleagues. Restaurateurs were betrayed by rival restaurateurs, housemaids by rival housemaids.' He looked up. 'You find that surprising?'

'I guess we'd all like to think we'd behave differently.'

'Sadly, we wouldn't. None of us can imagine what it was like to live through those years. It was utter moral chaos.'

'What do you mean by that, exactly?'

'Have you ever seen photographs of St Malo in 1944, Monsieur Madoc? It was flattened. This ancient town you see from the window is entirely rebuilt, stone by stone. It took them nearly thirty years. The original city was bombed out of existence in a few weeks in 1944. Medieval churches, ancient houses, the twelfth-century Cathédrale St Vincent – not to mention the homes of tens of thousands of people – bombed flat. Not by our enemies. By the Allied airforces, who wished to deny the place to the Germans.

'St Malo wasn't alone, of course. Scores of other Norman and Breton cities were destroyed, too. No doubt the cause was just. As a Jew, I would say it was. But it's easy enough to understand how, if you lived here, you might believe yourself to be in the grip of insane forces against which no code of honourable conduct could prevail. You might look upon other people's heroism as folly. You might be prepared to pay almost anything just to keep your wife and children safe. Forgive the lecture, but I repeat it every now and then to remind myself that these were just ordinary people. That it could just as easily have been us who sold out the Rosens and thousands like them.'

'They were sent direct to the camps?'

'Most of the Jews rounded up in France were taken to Drancy in northern Paris. It was a French-run transit centre. Over a period of months the inmates were sent by train to Auschwitz. Very few came back.'

He held up a single sheet of paper. It was the scanned-in print of an original document, and I glimpsed blockish type, an official crest, and the claw of a stamped swastika.

'It's a transit order,' Silbermann said, 'made out by one Oberleutnant Diermann, at the local Waffen-SS HQ. Two Jewish adults and a juvenile. Family name: Rosen.'

'That's all there is?'

'After they left St Cyriac, that's it.' He put the paper with half a dozen others and handed them to me. 'It's unusual for a family to disappear quite so completely. The check-in system at the camps was pretty meticulous. And a lot of effort went into tracking down missing Jews after the War – by the Jewish community, the police, various charities, family members. But there were thirty million displaced persons floating around Europe in 1945. A lot of people just vanished.'

'Did no one know the Rosens outside the village?'

'No one who chose to remember, it seems. They weren't active in the Jewish community, they had no surviving family. There was no one to bear witness. They were just shoved onto a railway truck, and dropped off the edge of the world. It's not the most dramatic story from our archive, but it's no less tragic for that.'

'Did anyone witness the arrest?'

Silbermann lifted his index finger. 'Ah, now, that at least *is* documented. May I?' He took the papers back from me. 'A local man saw the SS arrive at the Rosens' home, bundle them into a car and drive them away. All over in a few seconds. The house was left open, a meal still cooking on the stove. The witness went in and turned the gas off, he says. The least he could do. That kind of thing.'

'Who was he, this witness?'

'It's here somewhere.' As he thumbed awkwardly through the papers they slid from his hands. 'Damn.' He got down on his knees and gathered them.

'And who took his statement?'

He looked up at me. 'A Red Cross mission after the War. The witness says he wanted to intervene, but didn't dare. Not that you can blame him. Half-a-dozen armed thugs in uniform turn up and arrest your neighbour, you'd be a brave man to get in the way. And it wouldn't have made any difference if he had.'

Silbermann stood up, took out his glasses and put them on.

'Here we are.' He traced his finger down to the bottom of the page. 'Your witness was a chap called Garnier. Mathieu Garnier.'

I drove back towards St Cyriac with Silbermann's photocopies on the seat beside me and the image of the Rosens' arrest in my head – Rachel and Madeleine clinging together, portly Gustave struggling to retain some dignity. And young Mathieu Garnier watching helplessly as they were driven away, then entering Rachel's neat kitchen to turn off the gas under the dinner the family would never return to eat.

I pulled up on the verge just above the bridge over the Vasse. Here and there weekend anglers sat with picnic baskets and iPods. I stood at the parapet and gazed down towards the mouth of the river. To my right the water rushed through the antique sluices which fed the pools where cress grew in vivid green carpets. The air was filled with flashing dragonflies and birdsong.

40

Henri's place was half-empty when we arrived at a little after eight that night, but was beginning to fill up by the time Serge had finished his second plate of *frites* and was working on his third. I had stopped eating some time before.

We were sitting at a window table, just beside the door. Boats jostled in the little harbour. *The Gay Dog* was moored against the staging directly opposite the restaurant. Gunther had been working on a splendid wooden figurehead now mounted on the bow – a bare-breasted woman, almost lifesize, with golden tresses and blue saucer eyes. This vision rose from time to time above the edge of the quay, glanced coquettishly at me and dropped out of sight again.

Conversation between Serge and me had been stilted at first, but a couple of glasses of wine had loosened him up and we'd been chatting about the house and the building work. Quite suddenly he put down his knife and fork.

'I do love her, you know,' he said.

He sat very straight and stared defiantly into my eyes.

'Love,' I repeated. The word hung in the air between us.

'I don't suppose I'm exactly what you hoped for. Not for Katrine.'

'Is that what you are, Serge? For Katrine?'

'For as long as she wants, I am.' His chin lifted. 'I don't imagine you think I'm good enough.'

'Lighten up, Serge,' I said. 'I'm her father. Nobody's good enough.'

'After what you'll have heard about me, I mean.'

I said nothing.

'It's not all true,' he blundered on, 'though some of it's true enough. And I just want you to know that all that's behind me. I haven't been in any trouble for three years, Monsieur Madoc, and there isn't going to be any more of it. I've worked really hard. I'm going to graduate, and when I do ...' He faltered as he saw the look in my eyes. 'You haven't heard?'

I couldn't help smiling. 'Not a thing.'

'You will,' he said, hoarsely.

'I don't pay much attention to gossip.'

I poured us both another glass of wine. He drank some but didn't say anything. The silence lengthened and became awkward. Finally, when I was on the point of making some flippant remark just to break the tension, Serge pulled a couple of sheets of paper out of his jacket pocket and handed them to me across the table.

'I nearly forgot, Monsieur Madoc. These are for you.'

'What's this?'

'Tide tables. For the night your father escaped – the 14th of June 1944, right? The night the priest was killed.'

I glanced at the sheets with their dense columns of figures. 'Jesus, Serge, this looks like nuclear physics ...'

He moved his chair around so that he could see the print-outs. 'Here. On the 14th of June, 1944, low tide at St Cyriac was 22.31 hours.'

'And high tide?'

'About six hours later, obviously. Here: 04.15 on the morning of the 15th of June.'

'But it would have been light by then.'

'Pretty much broad daylight, at that time of year.'

'So all that time, between ten-thirty on the night of the fourteenth and four-fifteen the next morning, the tide was running *into* the estuary?'

'That's what it says here.'

'And they couldn't have got out against the tide?'

'No chance in a sailing dinghy.'

'But Dr Pasqual heard the church clock strike twelve on their way through the village. And Mathieu Garnier told him that as soon as my father saw the boat they couldn't hold him back. So we're talking one or two o'clock, latest, when they set sail.'

Serge frowned. 'But –'

A battered Chrysler truck drew up outside and parked carelessly between the iron bollards on the quay. The Garniers got out. There were three of them this time, the old man, his son Yannick, and a second younger man, whom I took to be Yannick's brother and was cast in the same mould: big, powerful and shabby. Serge stiffened. I felt the same way.

The three men came into the restaurant, laughing loudly at some shared joke. As he closed the door Yannick's gaze brushed across me, and then on to Serge. But he kept his eyes stony and followed the others wordlessly to the bar.

'Are you still hungry?' I asked when they were out of earshot.

'Lost my appetite.'

I took out my wallet, and looked around to catch Henri's eye. I couldn't see him at first, but then he appeared from the crowd around the bar carrying a fresh bottle of Muscadet. He cracked his napkin like a whip and set the bottle down between us.

'From the gentleman at the bar.' Henri splashed a little wine into each glass. 'Using the term somewhat loosely.' He stalked away.

Serge and I looked at the bottle and at one another.

'You could always send it back,' he suggested.

'Discretion is the better part of valour,' I said majestically. I filled his glass.

'What does that mean?'

'It means I haven't got the balls to make a scene. You stay here. I'd better find out what this is all about.'

The Garniers were at the far end of the bar, the boys either side of the father. There were beers set up in front of them. The room was crowded now and there was a steady burble of conversation and laughter, but it petered out as I made my way between the tables. Yannick was in the middle of a story, but he stopped as I approached, his mouth still open. He nudged his father, who glanced up, put down his glass and slid from his bar stool to face me. The old man bared yellow teeth.

'Monsieur Madoc,' he said, and stuck out his hand. 'Hope you enjoy the wine.'

I took his hand, not knowing what else I could do. 'I'm not sure I know what I've done to deserve it.'

'Oh, just being neighbourly,' he said. 'I want to put that little misunderstanding behind us. I had a word with Dr Pasqual, see, and, well, he's a wise old bird. Pointed out that me and Yannick were out of order that day. That you probably didn't know the way things were done around here.'

'Did he?' I said.

I tried to imagine frail Dr Pasqual dressing down this old villain, like some kindly headmaster reprimanding the school bully.

'Now don't get me wrong, Monsieur. Private property's private property, when all's said and done. But we weren't very welcoming. What with the dog and all. Yannick feels the same way.' He turned to the bar. 'Yannick?'

His son lifted his beer glass the merest fraction in my direction. The other boy stared fixedly at the counter top in front of him.

'Matter of fact,' Garnier said, 'you've done us a favour. We could never decide about La Division, but it's high time we did something with it. And now we will.'

'Will you? What will you do?'

'It's a danger to life and limb, that old place. Like I said, that's why we don't want people poking around it. We'll have it pulled down. My younger boy, Stephan here, he's going to build a bungalow, when the weather improves. He's getting married, see.' Garnier leaned forward and gripped my elbow. 'You go back and drink your wine now, Monsieur Madoc, and we'll forget that little spot of unpleasantness, eh?'

I made to pull back but he tightened his grip and brought himself close enough for me to smell his sour breath. 'But a word to the wise. If I was you I wouldn't trust that gipsy kid. I wouldn't trust none of them, but especially not him.'

He released me and turned away before I could reply. I went back to the table. After a few minutes the Garniers trooped out again, nodding to us as they passed, and drove away into the night.

'Monsieur Madoc?' Serge ventured after a while.

'I'm not supposed to trust you,' I said. 'That's according to the Pillar of the Community.'

'Well, there's a surprise.' He took a sip of wine. 'Anything else?'

'They're going to knock La Division down. Knock the old farmhouse down and build a bungalow.'

'Why now? After all this time?'

'It's young Stephan. He's in love too. There's a lot of it about.'

Serge opened his eyes very wide.

'I know,' I said. 'I don't believe it either.'

41

Wind rattled branches against scaffolding. I glanced at the glowing numerals of my watch: 4.32. I was keenly aware of the emptiness of the house around me, of the noises and unfamiliar shadows.

I knew that I would not be able to sleep again, so I got up and made some coffee and drank it at the kitchen table. When it grew light enough, I took the map from my wallet, grabbed my fleece, and let myself out of the house.

The last streetlamps of the village fell away behind me, and the dawn sky opened like a vault, a quarter moon riding between ribs of cirrus. After fifteen minutes I stood panting by the Celtic cross on the clifftop while a startlingly cold wind hissed through the hawthorns. At the bottom of the slope I moved into the trees and followed the path until I could see the paddock at the back of La Division.

The entire seaward fence had been replaced. The new barrier was higher than before and topped by razor wire. I rested my hands against the cold metal and this small and almost silent contact triggered a frantic barking. The dog came bounding through the grass, teeth bared.

I stood back.

I could see the old farmhouse away to my left, half smothered by the undergrowth, now utterly unreachable. Soon it would be gone altogether, and some breezeblock cube would squat over the site of the Rosens' home. I turned and walked away towards the beach.

I took out the gold sovereign and rolled it between my fingers. A fulmar sailed across the sky high above, touched by the rising sun. I watched it for a moment then sat against the grass bank that edged the sand, drinking in the sounds of the sea, trying to order my thoughts.

I sat up sharply, sure I had seen something just beyond the stone jetty, but light flared on the broken surface now and there was only churning water. I moved my head, shielding my eyes against the glare, and saw it again, this time quite clearly. A man floating face down, almost submerged, his black-clad body made lissom by the sea.

I opened my mouth to shout – I don't know what or to whom – but at that moment the figure lifted its head clear of the water and looked directly at me. The eyes were startlingly white against a face streaked by light and shadow. My cry locked in my throat.

I put my hands down beside me in the cold grass and felt the coin slip out of my fingers. I scrabbled for it, found it, and when I looked again the lithe shape was sliding through the surf beyond the jetty. A seal; that seemed quite obvious now. It vanished, then reappeared a metre or two further on among a jumble of rocks. It lifted its slick black muzzle and looked directly at me once more before diving again. This time it did not reappear.

I got to my feet and walked onto the landward end of the jetty. I did not dare go further, but it didn't matter. There was no sign of the seal in the fractured water, nor of anything else. I stood staring at the waves thudding against the stones.

I went back through the pines to the fence line and paused to take a last look at the ruins of the farmhouse. Two men were standing in the long grass beside the building; Bonnard and old Garnier. They must have seen me come through the trees but both stood staring at me without any sign of greeting. I held their cold gaze for a moment and then walked away up the cliff path towards St Cyriac.

42

Dominic was squatting on the foredeck of 2548 when I arrived. Around him lay piles of coloured tissue paper, a box of sequins, and a green costume of some kind with spangles sewn onto it. He was wrapping a long handled toasting fork in silver baking foil. He didn't speak as I arrived, just smiled his peaceful smile and gestured for me to come aboard. I settled myself against the hatch cover. I noticed that in the shallows a few metres beyond the bow stood the heron, its dagger bill poised to strike.

'You're worried, Iain,' he said, before I could speak. He put down his roll of foil and his toasting fork and looked at me. 'You've heard the warning bell again?'

'Dominic ... I know you can't talk about the old days unless Father Thomas says it's OK. But can I ask you just one question? You once knew a man called Robert Hamelin, didn't you?'

'You've seen Robert?' His voice was level, giving nothing away.

'I can't have, can I?' I spoke as gently as I could. 'He's been dead for years.'

'Still, you've seen him,' he said. 'He was a great patriot, you know.'

'I'm sure he was.' I was suddenly uncomfortable with his tone, which was no longer light and breezy. I had an urge to leave at that moment, and I half rose. 'I'm sure they were all great patriots.'

'Was it at La Division?' he asked.

I sat down again. 'Yes.'

'Robert goes back there. He's looking for someone who used to live there.'

'Lena Rosen?'

'That's right.'

'Did you know her, too?'

'Of course. I liked Lena. She was very pretty. Robert came back for her, all the way from England. But he couldn't help her.'

'No. She'd been taken away long before.'

'It's a sad story,' he said, and his voice quivered. 'A very, very sad story.'

'I'm sorry, Dominic. I shouldn't have asked about this. Don't worry about it any more.'

He looked up at me, his eyes bright. 'But I'm not worried, Iain. You are.'

'Yes,' I said. 'I am.'

'Father Thomas used to tell me that it was no good looking backwards at bad things when you could look forward to good ones.'

'He was a wise man.'

He smiled, his light spirit returning. 'I'm going to speak to Father Thomas tomorrow. I've got something special for him. Look.' He opened a paper bag on the deck beside him and held up a fat purple candle, studded with glittering spangles. 'I just bought it in the village. Do you think he'll like it?'

'He'll love it, Dominic.'

'I think Father Thomas doesn't want you to worry any more.'

I said nothing.

He said, 'I think that's why Father Thomas needs to speak to me, so I can give you a message from him. Of course, I couldn't be sure. I'd have to ask him.'

He let the silence stretch between us, and then took up his toasting fork again and continued to wrap the shiny foil around it. When he had finished he shook the costume out and smoothed it lovingly on the deck. It had patches of bright green cloth sewn onto it like fish scales.

'Guess who I'm going to be,' he said.

'King Neptune?'

'That's right!' he laughed, delighted at my cleverness. 'At the carnival on Sunday. I'm King Neptune every year. Daniel and Marie-Louise let me ride on their float. I have a big net and everything. You have to come! Everyone will be there. It's in the afternoon, in the square, and there's a party afterwards.' He added, suddenly serious, 'Please come, Iain. I'd really like you to.'

'Of course I will.' I tried to sound eager. 'How could I miss seeing you in your Neptune outfit?'

He smiled, happy again. 'And then I can tell you what Father Thomas says.'

I got as far as the boatyard on my way home, and didn't see Marie-Louise Bourgogne until I had almost walked into her.

'Iain?'

She had moved a director's chair down beside the track, as if to enjoy the view, but I had no doubt that she had been waiting for me.

'Hello, Marie-Louise.'

She smiled, but only with her mouth. 'Did you enjoy your visit? With Dominic?'

I didn't reply.

'What *do* you find to talk about?'

'One thing and another.' It didn't seem appropriate to tell her to mind her own business, but I hoped she was getting the message.

'I worry about him being bothered, you see,' she said, holding her smile.

'By me?'

'I realise you're curious about the old days, but I don't think it's good for Dominic to talk about such things. He's such a gentle soul, don't you agree? He should be much too busy enjoying himself, getting ready for the carnival, helping us with the float.'

'For the record,' I said, 'Dominic hardly says anything about those days.'

She picked up my irritation. 'I'm so sorry, Iain. I don't want you to think I'm prying. But if you knew the way he is after these visits of yours. I know you don't mean any harm, but ...'

'Marie-Louise, the last thing I'd want to do is upset him,' I said, more gently. 'I'm very fond of him.'

'Yes, of course, we all are.' She looked helplessly at me. 'Iain, I don't know what else to say. But I'd so much rather you didn't see him any more.'

Before I could find a reply she gathered up her folding chair and hurried away across the lawn.

43

I knew something was wrong as soon as I walked into the drive. Bonnard's trucks were no longer parked outside the house. The front door was open and the lights were on, but I could hear no hammering from inside, no drilling, no blare from the workmen's radio. The scaffolding had been dismantled from the gable wall. A metre-square hole gaped in the kitchen roof. Serge was up on the ridge, unfurling a tarpaulin.

'Serge? What the hell's going on?'

He looked down at the sound of my voice, but before he could answer me Chantal came striding out onto the veranda.

'I was going to ask *you* that.' She put her hands on her hips. 'Oh, and by the way, thanks for picking us up. I've been calling you since eight this morning. What's the point of having a mobile if you don't turn the bloody thing on?'

'You weren't due back until tomorrow.'

'Well, I beg your pardon—'

But as I approached her and she could see my face, her expression flickered from anger to concern.

'I had a bad night,' I said. 'I'll tell you about it later.'

I took her arm and drew her into the house. The partition wall in the second bedroom was a pile of bricks and plaster. The floorboards were up in one corner with a few new joists in place and others left scattered. Everything belonging to the builders was gone – tools, trestles, dustsheets; even the clamps that had held the joists in place. I moved through into the kitchen. Kate was at the foot of the ladder. There was a small pool of rainwater near her feet.

She pulled a face. 'Dad, they've left a real mess.'

'I'll call Bonnard.'

'I already have,' Chantal said. 'I've been calling since we got in, but his phone's ringing out.'

I thought of Bonnard and Garnier at La Division, and a vision of Marie-Louise on the towpath jumped into my mind.

'I'm really sorry, Monsieur Madoc,' Serge said, coming down the ladder. 'The guys were here until a couple of hours ago, and then Bonnard showed up and told them all to pack their gear and move out.'

I scuffed my boot through the water on the floor. 'Do you have any idea what this is about, Serge?'

'I asked Bonnard, but he wouldn't tell me a thing.'

An empty paint tin lay close to my foot and I kicked it savagely down the hall. I knew that I was behaving like a child but I couldn't help it. I stalked out of the house and up the steps into the cabin and slammed the door behind me. I went over to the window and leaned against the sill. Almost at once the door handle turned and Chantal came in and closed the door behind her. I swung to face her.

'Jesus, Iain,' she said. Quite suddenly she started to cry.

I put my arms round her. 'I'm sorry. It was wrong of me to go away and leave Serge in charge.'

'Serge isn't the problem,' she said, her voice muffled against my shirt.

'I'll sort it out, Chantal,' I said. 'First thing tomorrow I'll get us another contractor. Someone reliable.'

She sniffed. 'The things I've seen, without turning a hair. And look at me now, just because the builder's fucked off.'

I held her tight. 'I told Pablo I wanted to build something with my own hands. Now might be a good time to start.'

She didn't laugh.

After a few moments she looked up at me. 'Iain, what's happening?'

I avoided her eyes. 'I'm not sure.'

'Where *were* you this morning?'

'I went to La Division.'

She frowned. 'What for?'

'They're going to pull it down. The Garniers. They've owned it since the War, since they as good as stole it from the Rosens, and now, all of a sudden, they're going to pull it down and build right over the top of it.'

'So?'

'So I went up there to take another look. Maybe a last look. And guess what? Garnier's got security around that old ruin like it was Fort Knox. And Bonnard just happens to be up there visiting.'

She looked hard at me. 'You have to tread carefully, *chéri*. You know the history that house has. You can't make waves about this sort of thing in a place like St Cyriac.'

'We walk around on eggshells, just in case we hurt someone's feelings?'

'Do you think this only happens here?' she flared. 'Try it in Northern Ireland. Try asking about people there who disappeared and never came back. Or in Bosnia. Or Sicily. Or Argentina. This isn't *history*, Iain. Not in this country. It isn't Trafalgar. It isn't at a safe distance.' She turned away and stared out of the window. 'You're going to have to stop this. You'll ruin everything. I don't know what questions you've been asking, but you're really pissing somebody off. Promise me you'll stop.'

'No.'

'What do you mean, *no*?'

'I just can't promise you that.'

She stood facing me, her chest rising and falling.

I said, 'Look, you're right. I've upset somebody, that's for sure. And why do you think that is? Because I've started picking holes in their comfortable fucking fiction about the past.'

She shook her head in bewilderment. 'What are you talking about?'

'For a start, the tides don't fit. My father and Billington couldn't have got out of the Vasse on the night of the 14th of June, 1944. It would have been a physical impossibility. The tide was flowing in. And that's not guesswork. That's a fact. Maybe they got out some other night, but not *that* night.'

She stared at me. 'Do you seriously think the whole village

235

would have got the date wrong? It was the most important bloody date in their history. Iain, just leave this alone.'

'I must be pushing some of the right buttons – look what's happened here. And now you want me to walk away from it? You could never have done that, and you know it.'

'I'll tell you what I know. I know when it's time to pull the plug before you get hurt – or you get somebody else hurt.'

The door of the main house crashed open. Chantal and I both looked round. Serge stamped down the steps into the garden and marched past the window of the cabin.

Kate shouted after him: 'Go and drown your bloody stupid self, if that's what you want!' She threw something out after him, his backpack probably, which thudded into the turf.

Serge took a couple of steps to retrieve it. He said, 'Katrine, come on. This is ridiculous. You know I have to go.'

'Look at the weather! Even I can see it's breaking up. You're going out in this?'

'It'll blow itself out. For God's sake, I've been out in worse.'

'Fuck off, then!' she screamed. 'And don't bother to come back!'

I pushed the door open and stepped outside. Serge had already reached his bike. He revved the engine fiercely and took off up the drive, lifting the front wheel, spraying mud and gravel. Kate came down the steps and ran past me, shouting, suddenly pleading with him not to go. Serge swerved out of the gate and careered off down the road, leaving her standing there, her hands opening and closing at her sides. I could see from the heaving of her shoulders that she was sobbing.

Chantal moved past me and took a couple of steps towards her. 'Katrine?'

Kate turned and fled past us into the house, white-faced and wild.

Chantal and I looked at one another.

I said, 'Maybe we could both use a drink.'

'You go ahead. I'll just see how she is.'

In the kitchen, with the wind tugging at the tarpaulin above me, I opened a bottle of Medoc and set it on the pine table. Chantal came in as I was pouring.

'She's pretty cut up,' she said.

'He'll be back in the morning.'

She sat down and toyed with her glass. She didn't look convinced.

I said, 'I want to know what really happened in this place during the War, and what Dad had to do with it. That's all.'

She put her chin in her hands and gazed gravely up at me. 'No, Iain, you want more than that. You want what everyone wants – you want it to make sense. You want to see some order in it, some truth. That's what people like me fool ourselves we bring into people's living rooms, from Iraq or Afghanistan or Darfur. But we don't. Maybe we never have.' She reached out and touched my hand. 'You know what none of us can bear? The thought that it's all so random. That our sons or sisters or fathers were destroyed by people who didn't know them, didn't hate them, sometimes never saw them, and often didn't even know they'd done it. Because that would be mad, wouldn't it? That would just be pointless bloody lunacy.'

I stared down into my wine. I could feel her eyes on me.

'You asked me once if you should stop, and I said no then. I'm saying yes now.'

Over the patter of the rain and the bustling of the wind we could both hear Kate weeping.

44

I sat on the iron bench by the graves of my father's crew while the congregation filed out of morning Mass. The worshippers were mostly elderly, their faces shining with virtue. Many of them nodded to me as they passed. I nodded back, and when I thought they had all gone I walked over to the church door. One parishioner, an old lady in a mauve tweed suit, must have lingered behind, because I nearly collided with her in the porch. She smiled and held the church door for me. I thanked her and stepped into the cool stillness.

I could smell candlesmoke and the scent of the flowers arranged in vases either side of the altar, fountains of white and purple and blue in the half light. Between them I saw Felix, kneeling before the altar. He got to his feet, crossed himself, and came down the steps towards me.

'I gather Bonnard's left you with half a roof,' he said. 'I've a good mind to excommunicate the bastard.'

'Chantal thinks it's my own fault for asking too many questions.'

'It's not illegal to ask questions, though it's not always a great idea to drag up the past when no one can benefit from it.' He paused. 'Some of these guys are just bigoted old farts, Iain. They'll piss on an outsider soon as look at him. You don't want to read too much into one incident.'

'Not just one. I had that run-in with Garnier before I went to England. Then yesterday I got a lecture from Marie-Louise, warning me off Dominic.'

'Marie-Louise?' He looked puzzled. 'What was her problem?'

'She seemed afraid that I'd upset the old man. But maybe there was something more.'

'Something more like what?'

'I don't know. But whenever I poke around under the surface of my father's story, something comes up and bites me.'

He looked at me, his brow still furrowed. 'One problem, of course, is that it's not just your father's story.' He squared his shoulders. 'But leave this to me. I'll have a quiet word here and there.'

'Felix, this isn't just a case of giving the foreigner the cold shoulder.'

'What, then?'

'I looked up the tides for the night Father Thomas was killed. The tide was coming in. I don't see how my father could have got away in a sailing dinghy that night. Not from the Vasse.'

'Come on, Iain.' He leaned across and clapped me on the shoulder. 'Can any of us really know how a bunch of desperate young guys pulled off something like this sixty and more years ago? Maybe they carried the boat past the point. Or maybe it *is* possible to sail against the tide if you're a good enough sailor. And ...'

'And?'

'And maybe you have been treading a bit heavily. My friend, people here have the past in order. They've cast your father and mine as heroes of St Cyriac. They don't want you to rewrite any part of that script. Relax. You leave it with me. I'll make sure everyone knows you don't mean any harm.' He looked into my face. 'You don't, do you?'

I'm not sure if he expected an answer, but I didn't give him one.

He slapped his thighs and got to his feet. 'Look, forget about all this nonsense. Come along to the carnival this afternoon. We'll have a few drinks, build some bridges with the locals. Let your hair down. They'll like you all the better for it.' He grinned at me. 'You might even enjoy yourself.'

45

I spent the rest of the morning clearing up the mess the builders had left, and running makeshift repairs – plugging leaks, nailing boards over joists, shifting rubble. I took an hour in the middle of all this to call a list of contractors in Lannion and St Brieuc. Being Sunday, most were closed, but I felt better for making the effort.

Chantal busied herself cleaning the bathroom and kitchen. I heard her make a couple of attempts to look in on Kate, who had not emerged since the night before, but she got no encouragement. I doubted that she would until that beaten-up old BMW came grumbling up the drive again. But it did not come.

We stopped for a baguette at lunchtime and were gentle with one another. Neither of us mentioned Serge, or Dominic, or Bonnard. I went back to work afterwards, but at about four I took a shower and walked into the village.

Last night's spring rain had passed over and the afternoon had turned out fine for the carnival. A dozen stalls and sideshows had been set up on the gravel of the square, and a sizeable crowd of tourists and locals lined the esplanade and gathered on Henri's terrace. I saw Felix there, moving among the tables, laughing and joking, holding court to one group of visitors after another. He saw me, took a bottle of rosé and two glasses as Henri cruised past with a tray, and pushed through the throng.

'Good to see you made it.' He sat on a bollard on the quay and poured for us both, put the bottle on the ground, and rang his glass against mine. 'And you're in luck. The parade's about to start.'

I said, 'Have you seen Dominic?'

'He makes his big entrance on the Bourgogne float.' He drank. 'He'll be prancing about in his Neptune outfit, jabbing people with that damned trident of his. Does it every year.'

A loudspeaker crackled and an announcement rang out, and an ancient red tractor came chugging down the esplanade, coughing fumes. The crowd gave a cheer. More elderly farm vehicles followed, some lovingly restored, the drivers in smocks and straw hats and neckerchiefs, waving at the crowd.

Felix topped up our glasses. He shouted some ribaldry at one of the drivers, who threw back his head and laughed.

'They have their own way of doing things,' he said, still looking at the tractors. 'It's not London or Paris, but it's a real community. You know what that means, Iain? Maybe you don't. Maybe that's what you've come here to find out.'

'I'm sorry if I've been clumsy, Felix. I just can't get this stuff out of my mind.'

'St Cyriac's survived all kinds of difficult newcomers.' He smiled at me. 'And, in time, taken quite a few of them to its heart.'

The first of the floats was coming through now. An enormous plywood fish, painted silver and blue and pivoted in the centre, was mounted on a flatbed truck. Le Toque, his son Guy, and two deck hands, all dressed in yellow oilskins, capered around tossing sweets into the crowd.

Two or three other floats followed. I craned my neck to get an early look at them. The Citroën dealership had entered a trailer with two shiny new hatchbacks on it and girls in bikinis sprawled over the bonnets. On the farm cooperative's float, piled with hay bales and fruit and vegetables, kids in peasant gear shrieked as they squirted the crowd with water pistols.

And there were more, crawling into view: a cider maker's float boasting a huge barrel and free samples, a band in twenties costume playing Dixieland, a clown on stilts, a truckful of teenage beauty queens in sashes and tiaras.

'There they are,' Felix said, and from the relief in his voice I realised he'd been watching too. 'There's Daniel.'

The boatyard float had been rigged like a galleon in full sail, with wooden cannon along the sides and a dozen flags flying. On the makeshift quarterdeck Daniel and Marie-Louise Bourgogne were both dressed like pantomime admirals, in cocked hats and blue frock coats heavy with medals.

'He's not there,' I said.

Felix stood up. 'He must be. He's always there.'

The float moved abreast of us. We both pushed through the crowd to the kerbside. Daniel was making an effort to wave and smile at people, but Marie-Louise was tightfaced at the wheel, staring straight ahead. I had the impression she had been crying. Daniel caught sight of us and beckoned us up to the float and crouched to talk to us as we walked beside it, speaking loudly over the laughter and music.

'Have you seen Dominic?' he said.

Felix rested one hand on the trailer. 'We were going to ask you that. He's never missed this before, has he?'

'He usually comes over about an hour before the start,' Daniel said. 'We waited as long as we could. Maybe somebody should check on him.'

'I'll go,' I said. 'You're both busy here.'

Felix looked uncertain. 'I can come if you need me.'

'I'll sort it out, Felix.'

He touched my arm. 'It's probably nothing. He forgets things, loses track of time. Come back for a drink afterwards, and bring the old bugger with you. We'll all still be here.'

I took my now familiar route across the pontoons by the boatyard, past the Bourgognes' cottage and down the river path. It was just before six o'clock by now, a warm spring evening – the warmest of the year so far – with the westering sun angling across the water and through the trees. The tide was out, and I could smell dank river mud and rotting vegetation. I didn't think I had ever noticed this rank smell before. It was very quiet where the bend of the bank smoothed the current, and I slowed my pace. Two swans were feeding in the shallows. I could hear them dibbling among the weeds, could hear the trickle of water from their bills in the stillness. The slanting light was gauzy with insects.

I stepped up to the launch and rested one foot on the gunwale.

Dominic was not here. There was no need for me even to call out; I could feel he wasn't here. And yet I had pictured him so very clearly riding the prow with his fishing line in his hand, smiling his childlike smile. I waited there in the warm evening, disappointed, wondering what to do next.

It took me a couple of moments to see the heron, standing in the shallows just in front of the boat, much closer than before. It was watching me, unmistakably watching me, its shortsword of a head slightly on one side and one white-ringed eye fixed on me. The river was so still that the bird was perfectly mirrored. Only the faintest ripple of water around its legs betrayed the sliding of the current.

And then without warning the heron rose. The rush of it startled me, and I felt its broad wings thumping, banging up into the air above the launch. The bird circled once under the trees, and then beat away low over the water towards the open sea, *whump whump whump*, the sun flashing on white and slate grey.

I started back down the track, paying no attention now to the sound of my footfalls or to the speed of my going. I was ill at ease, and unnerved by the heron, and I felt like an alien creature, something that didn't belong here. I crossed back over the river, and after a moment's hesitation I set off upstream on the opposite bank, past the cress beds and towards the mill.

I walked in under the brick archway, crossed the courtyard with its tables and giant chess set, and started up the stairs. Madame Duquesne was in her back garden, taking in her washing. She called something up to me but I didn't catch it, and I didn't stop.

Some visitors' cars were in the parking area below and old people were pushing children on swings in the playground. On the second floor a scruffy man of about sixty was hanging over the balcony rail sucking on a very thin cigarette. He grunted to me as I passed. The door to a flat was open some distance down the walkway and I could hear a shouted conversation over the noise of a television.

I walked on down the passageway and found Dominic's bright blue door and tapped on it. I could hear nothing from inside, and

I knocked again, more loudly. Madame Duquesne came puffing up the stairs behind me, her flat shoes slapping on the concrete walkway.

'He'll be off at the carnival by now,' she said.

'Did you see him leave, Madame Duquesne?'

'Why, isn't he there yet? He'll be late for his own funeral, that man. Man? Child, I should say.' She shouldered past me and dragged out her keys. 'Goes off in a dream, making his little ships or stitching his costume. Oh, I have to watch him!' She tapped the side of her nose. 'Watch him like a hawk. He's in another world, that man.'

She pushed open the door and shouted Dominic's name a couple of times through the gap, then shrugged and stood aside for me.

I knew at once that he was dead. He was curled on the bed fully dressed, facing me, his lips slightly parted, eyes open and unfocused. There was dried vomit crusted over the sheets and on the floor and splashed over the half-dozen wine bottles which lay scattered there. Dominic's skin was the colour of paper with bluish shading around his mouth. The still air in the room stank of puke and stale wine. I heard Madame Duquesne gasp. I leaned across and touched the skin of his neck. It was mutton cold. I stood back. The chill seemed to linger on the tips of my fingers.

'Oh, he's not, is he?' Madame Duquesne asked. 'Oh, the poor soul! He's not, is he? And wine? He's not allowed drink! He *can't* drink. He knows that!'

She stepped up beside me, panting a little. I glanced into the kitchen area. A small frying pan stood beside the gas hob, and in it were two pink sausages with half a dozen fat flies droning around them.

'Aren't I always telling him?' Madame Duquesne cried, as if Dominic might still be susceptible to scolding. She made to push past me, but I stopped her.

'Better leave him,' I said. 'The police won't want anything touched.'

'The police?' She looked at me, disbelieving, and then back at

244

the dead old man, and her chin began to wobble. 'But I watch them like a hawk, Monsieur Madoc. Just like a hawk.'

'Why don't you call Sergeant Freycinet?' I said gently.

'Yes.' She took a deep breath. 'Yes, of course. I'll go and do that right away.'

She bustled out of the room. Somebody – perhaps the cigarette-smoker leaning on the rail – asked her a question and got a terse reply. I nudged the door closed. I realised that I had my mobile in my jacket pocket and could just as easily have called the police myself, but I was glad I had sent her away.

It was very quiet. A couple of pigeons were murmuring in the lime tree outside the window. I could faintly hear the TV from the neighbouring flat, studio laughter and a game show klaxon. Dominic's green Neptune costume was draped over a chair, and his silver foil-wrapped trident was leaning against the chairback. I could hear a faint hiss and I checked the gas stove. But the sound was coming from Dominic's portable radio, up on its shelf above his head. If I concentrated fiercely I could just hear dance music through the static.

Only then did I see that the china elephant lay shattered on the tiled floor. *They'd broken Jumbo's trunk. But I've made him better.* Not any more. Dominic wouldn't be making Jumbo or anything else better, ever again.

I felt glass crunch under my feet and, looking down, I saw chunks of a thick greenish bottle, some bits of coloured wood and small pieces of calico. I looked into the living room, already guessing what I would see. Every one of his models had been smashed. The floor was littered with splintered wood, tangles of rigging, and the tiny figures of crewmen. The models had been systematically broken apart.

I stood there until I heard the sirens and the sounds of men hurrying up the steps and along the walkway. The door opened and the flat was full of clumping boots and Madame Duquesne's pleading voice and Sergeant Freycinet's gruff replies. He stood beside me, staring at Dominic, breathing heavily from his climb up the steps.

'Poor old sod,' he said finally. 'We used to throw stones at him, you know, when we were kids. Village idiot, sort of thing. Awful cruel, kids.'

'Yes,' I said.

'Not this cruel, though.' Freycinet looked at me curiously. 'Did you find him, M'sieur Madoc?'

'Yes.'

'We should sign you up. You're better than a sniffer dog.' He laughed, vastly amused at his joke, then touched the cold skin of Dominic's neck, as I had done. He stood up. 'Wine, eh? Dominic didn't know much, but I thought he knew better than that. Sent him crazy, drink did.'

He walked back out into the living area and I followed him. He saw the destruction and whistled softly. 'How would you call it, Monsieur? He goes on a bender, blows a gasket, breaks everything up, then has a fit and chokes.'

'That would wrap everything up very nicely.'

He gave me a narrow look. 'You have a better idea?'

'Sergeant, you see that drawer? That middle one. Could you open it?'

'Why?'

'Last time I was here it was full of money.'

He lifted his eyebrows, but produced a handkerchief with something of a flourish, wrapped it around his hand, and slid open the drawer.

'Not any more,' he said.

It was late by the time I got home. Chantal was standing at the stove. I had called her from Freycinet's office and she must have decided to keep herself busy while she waited for me, because the kitchen was clinically tidy. She was wearing a cheerful cartoon pinafore which was at odds with the expression on her face. It was at odds with everything.

'Are you all right?' she said. 'That poor old man.'

I went to the fridge and took out a beer, offered one to her. She shook her head. I sat down at the table and poured it, taking a lot of care.

'The place has been turned over,' I said. 'Everything's smashed. All his money's gone.'

She took a couple of breaths. 'It must have been horrible. Finding him ...'

'I expect you've seen a lot worse. In all those war zones.'

She blinked. 'You're upset.'

'Yes.' I looked away. 'I'm sorry. I don't know what made me say that.'

'I do,' she said.

I drank some beer and stared into the glass. Chantal came over to the table and sat down opposite me and caught my right hand in both of hers. I could feel her eyes on me, and the pity in them, but I couldn't meet them, which made me sad, because I badly wanted to say more to her. I wanted to tell her that Dominic was a nice old man who liked sausages, that he repaired broken elephants and made beautiful model boats, and he never hurt a fly in his entire life and the birds loved him and he would even throw back the fish he caught and for all I knew perhaps they loved him too. I wanted her to put her arms around me. I wanted to pull myself against her waist and sob for Dominic and tell her about the terrible feeling that was growing within me, the feeling that he was dead because of me.

'I'm going to bed,' she said, and got up clumsily. 'Are you coming?'

'Not just yet.'

46

I sat in the dawn garden. Across the seafront road the sun struck fire from the Channel. I could hear the village coming to life – a car starting, the clatter of a steel shop shutter, the tolling of the church bell. Felix would have heard by now. And Dr Pasqual. And Le Toque, and Garnier, and Madame Didier. The whole damned village would have heard by now. Nothing would ever be the same here again.

'Dad?'

Kate stood a few feet away, beside the trunk of the poplar, a steaming mug in each hand. Her face was blotchy and her eyes red.

She said, 'You look like you haven't slept.'

'You look like that makes two of us.'

Her face crumpled and I walked quickly over to her and took the mugs out of her hands and set them on a paving slab on the ground and took her in my arms.

'I feel such a bitch,' she said against my shirt. 'That poor old man's dead, but I'm not crying for him.' She took a step back and found a wad of tissues and scrubbed at her face with them.

A dark blue Peugeot came sliding down the road from the direction of the village. It passed the ragged hedge bordering the garden, stopped a little further on, and backed up, coming to a halt half up on the verge just a few metres from where we stood. A man emerged from the passenger door and looked over the hedge.

'Monsieur Madoc?'

'Yes.'

He gave me an electric smile. He was in his late thirties, dark and good looking in a way that reminded me of 1950s movies, with a charcoal cashmere coat and beautifully creased trousers. He hopped across the drainage ditch, keeping his shiny shoes out of the mud, and stepped through the gap in the hedge.

'Inspector Sharif,' he said, peeling off a black leather glove to offer me his hand. 'It's about Dominic Charpontier, naturally.'

I took his hand. 'Charpontier? Was that his surname? I never knew.'

Kate turned away. 'I'll leave you to it.'

'No, please, Mademoiselle,' Sharif said quickly. 'Please do stay for a moment.'

Kate looked at me for guidance.

I said, 'I don't think my daughter can be of much help, Inspector.'

'Please. I'd be very grateful.'

He worked his hand back inside his glove and gave a wry little grin to Kate. That grin said *yes, this is all nonsense, but you know how it is.* She did not respond, but she didn't move either.

I said, 'Shall we go up to the house and talk there?'

'No need,' Sharif said. 'It's very pleasant here. I like to get out in the open air myself.'

I had rarely seen anyone who seemed less like an enthusiast for the outdoors than Inspector Sharif. I noticed that under his coat he was wearing a lavender shirt and a dark blue tie with a silver clip. I couldn't remember when I had last seen a man wearing a tie clip. It was some time since I'd seen anyone wearing a tie.

'I gave a statement to Sergeant Freycinet last night,' I said.

'So you did, Monsieur. And I came along partly to thank you for your help with this. If you hadn't been there, I'm not at all sure the estimable sergeant would have noticed the money was missing.' He broke off a twig and examined it minutely. 'And if it hadn't been for the money, we might have thought poor Dominic had got drunk and had some sort of a brainstorm. But thirty-nine thousand euros is a powerful motive for robbery. That's how much seems to be missing.'

We were all quiet for a few moments.

I said, 'Inspector, what do you think happened to Dominic?'

'We're still waiting for forensics, and the rest of the witness statements, and a full pathology report. But I can tell you there's some bruising to the back of his head.'

'Somebody hit him? Dominic?'

'We won't know for sure until the pathologist's finished.'

'But he was in bed when I found him.'

'Conceivably someone put him there after he was struck. Or he dragged himself there.' He shrugged. 'Anything's possible at this stage.'

'How long had he been dead?'

'Twenty-four hours or so by the time you found him.'

'That long?'

'Madame Duquesne thought he was at the Bourgogne place, getting the float ready. So did everyone at the carnival. The Bourgognes thought he was already there.' He spread his hands. 'Everyone thought he was somewhere else.'

'Saturday, then.'

'Probably Saturday night. We'll know more precisely when we get the last of the test results through. We can already say that he seems to have put down a heroic amount of alcohol in quite a short time.'

'I never saw him drink anything.'

'According to Freycinet he'd drink when he was upset about something. That was rare, but when he did, he couldn't stop. It was dangerous for him, because of his condition.'

'What condition?'

'He was a severe epileptic. Didn't you know?'

'No.'

'Alcohol interferes with the drugs, apparently.'

'Why don't you say what you're doing here?' Kate demanded in a tight voice.

'Mademoiselle?'

'You didn't come for this. Not to make small talk and pretend you like the birds and the bees. Why don't you say it?' Her voice started to rise. 'You're talking about Serge, aren't you? Everyone knows he's been in trouble before, so let's all point the finger at him.'

I said, 'Kate, no one's talking about Serge.'

'I'm sorry to say your daughter is right, at least up to a point.' Sharif's voice carried delicate regret. 'Serge Baladier has indeed been in trouble before. Quite serious trouble. And it could be complete coincidence, of course, but as it happens he is also the only one of Dominic's visitors on Saturday whom we have so far failed to trace.'

'You see?' Kate cried. 'The usual suspects.'

'Serge went to Dominic's flat?' I said.

'According to Madame Duquesne he was there briefly, close to midnight on Saturday evening. Drunk, she thought. She was in bed in her apartment, reading, but she heard something and saw Serge Baladier going up the stairs. Apparently Dominic's light was still on, but that wasn't unusual. She watched for a bit, but the boy left not long afterwards and she thought no more of it. Do you know why he'd have gone there?'

'I had dinner with Serge last week, Inspector, and I did say he should call in on Dominic, to see his models.'

'You think he'd do that at midnight? Drunk?'

'I've really no idea what he was doing there.'

'Neither have I. It would be nice to ask young Monsieur Baladier himself, but somehow our Serge isn't anywhere to be found.' Sharif looked from Kate's face to mine and back again. 'I hate to ask anything quite so predictable, but when did you last see him? Either of you?'

Kate turned and walked sobbing towards the house. Sharif and I gazed at one another in silence until the door banged behind her.

'Saturday afternoon,' I said. 'They had a row.'

'What did they argue about?'

'He wanted to go out in his boat. She wanted him to stay with her. I didn't think it was serious.'

'They were ...' he searched for the word, 'attached to one another?'

'She loves him,' I said. 'And he loves her.'

I was aware that in saying so I had allowed the truth of it to take root in my mind. Perhaps Sharif sensed this, for he lost some of his polish for a moment and looked hard and weary.

'I'm sorry,' he said. 'I don't take any pleasure in this.'

'Inspector Sharif, anyone could have come into Dominic's room and found him that way. Anyone could have taken that money. One of the old derelicts in the other flats. Thirty-nine thousand euros is more cash than many of us see in our entire lives.'

'You're quite anxious to defend the boy, aren't you?'

'Serge and Kate had a fight, and he took off in a temper. That's all. What can I say? I like him. And I just can't see him doing anything like this.'

'You knew he had a police record?'

'He hinted at ... some trouble in the past.'

'You didn't ask what?'

'No. Kids can make mistakes, can't they? Even gipsy kids.'

All at once he didn't seem smooth and urbane at all. 'I'm Algerian, Monsieur. I don't care if he's a Hottentot with a bone through his nose. But if he was screwing *my* daughter it would worry me that he'd been arrested three times.' When he saw he had my attention he held up his gloved hand and counted on his fingers. 'Car theft at fourteen. Drug dealing at fifteen. Malicious wounding at seventeen.'

'Malicious wounding?'

'Yannick Garnier's missing a kidney, thanks to him.'

'But he's a bright kid. A student.'

'Is that what he told you?'

'He's at that marine science place. I've seen his work.'

'He told other people that, too. The place we're talking about is IFREMER, Monsieur Madoc, and it doesn't have students. It's a research institute, not a university. Not a college. And for the record, they've never heard of any Serge Baladier.'

'Maybe I misunderstood—'

'You didn't misunderstand. The boy lied to you. Almost certainly he lied to your daughter too.' He relented a little. 'Look, I appreciate your liberal sentiments, Monsieur. It's true, the boy might have nothing to do with this, but we won't know until we talk to him. And he doesn't seem to welcome that prospect.

We have a witness, a police patrolman who spotted him and that BMW motorbike of his in a service station outside Rennes at five o'clock on Sunday morning. That's before we even had an alert out for him, but the patrolman was an enthusiast and noticed the old bike. Rennes is a long way to go to make a point after a lover's tiff, you'd have to admit.'

I stood looking at him, not knowing what to say. I couldn't fault his logic, but equally I couldn't believe the conclusion he'd reached. I hardly noticed that Inspector Sharif had wished me good morning and was already walking away.

I called to him, 'Why were Dominic's models smashed?'

He turned back. 'What?'

'Why would anyone break up his beautiful models?'

'The thief did it,' he said impatiently. 'In case the old boy had more money hidden away.'

'His money wasn't hidden away. It was lying in the drawer. When I went there the drawer was open and anyone could see it. Dominic didn't care about money. He'd have given it to anyone who'd asked.'

Sharif stepped back through the hedge. 'So have you got another suggestion?'

I hesitated. 'Not right now,' I said.

I found Kate in the cabin. She was sitting with her back to me on the single bed we had put in there. The bright counterpane had been Kate's own contribution. I think secretly, like me, she had never entirely given up on the idea that the cabin was my father's room, and that one day he would occupy it. She was staring out of the window over the shining sea.

'It's all right,' she said, without turning. 'I've finished with the crying business.'

'How much did you know, Kate? You need to tell me.'

'About Serge? Everything. More or less from the start.'

'You knew he'd been in trouble with the police?'

'Yes, I knew.' She looked defiantly at me. 'You must have guessed something. Don't say you didn't.'

I sat down. 'Yes, something. He hinted at *something*. I thought

253

maybe some petty crime. But drug dealing? Malicious wounding?'

'Yannick Garnier and his brother attacked him. Didn't you ever see that scar he has? The families had some kind of a feud. It went back years.'

'Kate, you've got to admit this is all a bit heavier than teenage high spirits.'

'He didn't hurt poor Dominic. I know he didn't and so do you.'

'How do I know that?'

'Because he couldn't have!' Her voice rose. 'Serge, do a thing like that? It's crazy! He's the gentlest, sweetest—'

'All over the world, Kate, there are the mothers and sisters and lovers of people who've done awful things, and half of them say, "Oh, he was the gentlest, the sweetest".'

'Don't you talk like that!' she shouted suddenly. 'Don't you point the finger like all the others! Not you!'

Her anguish silenced both of us.

She went on, more quietly: 'I'm not a fool, Dad. I'm not talking this way just because he was mine for a while. He didn't do this thing, that's all. It's not right they should say he did.'

I said, 'If only he hadn't run away. And why did he lie? About being a student – at IFREMER of all places?'

'He didn't lie, Dad,' she said. 'Not the way you mean.'

'What other way is there to lie?'

'His project on the Shoals was real. I saw it. You saw it too. Notes, photos, maps, drawings. He virtually had to teach himself to read and write to do that, but he was going to present it to IFREMER in the summer. He'd even fixed the meeting.'

'But they don't have students at IFREMER, Kate. That's what Sharif says.'

'I know that. But Serge had this dream that they'd give him a job on one of their research boats. Anything. He'd have done anything. He'd work his way up. Maybe later they'd help fund him through college. It was all he wanted. A step on the ladder. All he wanted …'

She turned back to the window. I got up and walked to the

door, letting my hand rest briefly on her shoulder as I passed. I knew as well as she did that she hadn't finished with the crying business yet.

The kitchen smelled of coffee and bacon. Chantal turned from the stove and gave me a tight little look as I came in.

'Hi,' she said.

'Hi.' I sat down at the pine table.

She pointed at the stove. 'I thought we ought to eat something. I seem to have gone a bit over the top. I don't quite know how it happened.' She looked sadly at the food. 'Do you want some of this, now it's done?'

'Why not?'

She brought me a plate of bacon and eggs and spent some time loading the table up around me: toast rack, marmalade, coffee pot. We never ate breakfast like this, and she would never normally wait on me in this way, but I could see that this morning she wanted to be busy. At length she sat down opposite me, nursing her coffee cup.

'I heard you talking, with that cop,' she said. 'It was good of you to stick up for Serge. That would have meant a lot to Katrine.'

I looked at her. 'Do you believe Serge did this, Chantal?'

'I don't know. I don't know anything any more.' She stared down into her cup. 'Except that right now I wish we'd never come here.'

I couldn't find an answer to that.

In a moment, Chantal went on, 'Sylvie Bertrand rang about an hour ago.'

I glanced at her, wondering what the connection was.

'She's cancelled Katrine's music lessons.' Chantal lifted her head. 'Oh, she was awfully correct about it. Unexpected pressures of work. Only so many hours in the day. Katrine deserves someone's complete attention. All that.'

'And?'

'We made him one of us, Iain. If there's a shadow over Serge it's bound to fall on us too. When things go wrong in a community like this, someone has to get the blame, and it's usually the outsider.'

She came round the table and pulled up a chair next to me and put her arm around me. There was no mistaking the protectiveness of that encircling arm, and no denying the message it conveyed: that she would stand by me, no matter what.

I said, 'This is my fault, isn't it?'

'Don't be ridiculous. Do you think I'd listen to that kind of talk? Even for a moment?'

Her vehemence told me that she had already had to listen to that kind of talk, and that whatever Sylvie Bertrand had wanted it was more than a chat about music lessons. I kissed her hand where it rested on my shoulder, got up and quietly left the room.

47

I took a shower after that, scrubbing savagely at my skin.

I kept telling myself that the world was still the same as the one I had occupied yesterday. The sun still streamed through the frosted glass window, and the clunking of the pipes in the half-painted bathroom was just as it had always been. Surely the village too would be just as it had been, and the people in it.

But I knew that everything had changed, had flipped from positive to negative. Under the too-hot water I spooled through an endless litany of self-justifications. But there was no escape. If I had never come here, if I had never started asking questions, poor Dominic would still be sitting on the prow of the old boat right now, dangling his line into the bright river, smiling that guileless smile.

I dressed quickly and walked through the house. I could hear Kate and Chantal in the kitchen, talking softly, Kate's voice shuddering a little, Chantal's soothing, sympathetic. I was glad they were together but I didn't want to interrupt them and I didn't want to know what course their conversation was taking. I was afraid it involved me. I shut the front door quietly behind me.

Three shiny tourist buses stood outside the Hotel de Ville and cars with foreign plates were parked under the plane trees. A Dutch driver had got his caravan stuck in the alley next to the photo shop and people were shouting instructions to him in three different languages. The square was noisy with strangers eating ice creams and taking photos of one another while their kids splashed in the fountains. There was not a face I knew among them, hardly an expression I recognised. These people knew nothing of Dominic, or St Cyriac, or the past.

At first sight the church appeared to be empty. I closed the door behind me as quietly as I could, but the iron latch clicked like a pistol shot. Felix was sitting on a chorister's chair near the altar, looking at me. From the angle of his body I knew he had been holding his head in his hands. Light glinted on the silver thread of the cross woven into the chasuble he wore and on the amber beads of a rosary hanging from his fingers. This formality, and the fact that he looked ten years older than when I had last seen him, made me stop at the foot of the altar steps, suddenly unsure of my reception.

He came down and put his hands on my shoulders. 'St Cyriac without Dominic. Can you imagine such a thing?'

I shook my head.

He stood back half a pace, letting his hands slip away. 'Everyone's in a state of shock. Papa's here now. He's been in Father Thomas's chapel for hours.'

'How's he taking it?'

'Papa's still a bit of an old-world aristo when all's said and done, and Dominic was just a funny old guy who wasn't all there. But they shared so much history.' Felix gave a strained little smile. 'And they were the only two who used that chapel. They'd both be in there, communing with Father Thomas. Dominic used to annoy the hell out of Papa by praying out loud. You know how he was.'

'Yes, I know.'

He was quiet for a moment. 'If I hadn't been so busy here, Iain, I'd have called round to see you before now.'

'Did you think I needed special attention?'

He gave me a quizzical look. 'We all need special attention. But the police said you found the body, and that must have been terrible for you.'

I realised how defensive I had sounded, but Felix waved away the moment of awkwardness and sat down on the end of the front pew, gesturing for me to sit too. We faced one another across the aisle.

'I was also concerned for Katrine,' he said. 'People have been peddling stories about young Serge Baladier – I suppose you've heard? And the police haven't done much to dampen that down. It must be very distressing for her.'

'She won't believe Serge had anything to do with it.'

'Neither do I,' he said. 'Surely you don't?'

'No,' I said. 'I wasn't sure at first, but I've given it a lot of thought since then. No, I don't believe he could hurt Dominic.'

'Good. Wherever he is, he'll need us to believe in him.'

I felt a rush of affection for Felix; sitting there half lost in his splendid robes, a sad, weary and loyal little man with a bald head. I thought now that I should have had more trust in his generosity from the start.

I said, 'Thanks, Felix.'

He widened his eyes. 'For what?'

'For keeping the faith.'

I knew he wanted to say something in reply, and that he couldn't decide how to proceed. I didn't know how to help him. Doves fluted in the beech trees outside and the wind shivered among the spring leaves.

At length he said, 'Shall we pray together? For Dominic?'

I stared at him.

'It's a priest thing,' he said. 'A lot of us do it.'

I had been so at ease with him over the past weeks, so seduced by his refusal to take himself seriously, that the idea of him formally practising the rituals of the church had never really crossed my mind.

He smiled. 'Did you think I didn't really believe all this stuff?'

'I don't know what I thought.'

'We all need faith, Iain. Stories we can believe in. Myths, if you like. That's what keeps the darkness at bay.'

'Will any myth do?'

'Meaning in life is created, my friend, not discovered. The answers may or may not be at the back of the book, but the best we can do in the meantime is find a myth that fits, and commit to it. I'm not a romantic. I don't believe in things that go bump in the night. But to take a myth and make it real, that makes sense to me.'

'Like the myth St Cyriac's built up around itself since that night in 1944?'

'Yes.' He kept his eyes steadily on me. 'Precisely like that.'

I got up and stood in the aisle, gazing up at the altar, the glorious light dazzling on the white cloth and on the silver and gilt of chalice and crucifix.

'I've been exploring a little myth of my own,' I said. 'It's not a very pretty one.'

'I can handle ugly myths too.'

'Felix, when I got to Dominic's room last night it was ransacked. He wasn't just burgled for a miserable wad of euros.'

He raised his eyebrows.

I said, 'I think someone was looking for Father Thomas's diaries. The missing ones.'

He kept his eyes on my face. 'You're serious?'

'It's a possibility, isn't it? At least a possibility.'

Felix put his head back and breathed deeply. Then he looked at me, but didn't say anything. As the seconds dragged by I began to regret that I had spoken at all.

I said, 'Sorry. Maybe I should have kept my mouth shut.'

I started to walk away down the aisle.

'Iain?'

I swung round.

'Have you told Inspector Sharif about this?'

'No.'

'You should. You must.' He stood up. He tossed his rosary from one hand to the other. He looked harassed and tired. 'Iain, I have to go. Would you look in on Papa in the chapel? I'm worried about him, and he'd appreciate seeing you, I know.'

'Of course.'

He made to leave and then hesitated and opened his hands in appeal.

'I'm just the parish priest, for Chrissake. What would I know? But out of our love for Dominic we shouldn't leave any stone unturned. Speak to Sharif.'

He swept out past me, gripping my arm briefly as he went.

I heard his car start up and stutter away, but I stood for a while longer, savouring the sense of tranquil space around me. I had never had much time for the church, but it seemed to me now that this place, with its air of continuity and calm order, was indeed sanctuary from an incomprehensible world. I walked back down the aisle and past the Lady Chapel, its altar banked with late spring flowers, their fragrance floating on the still air between the pillars. The heavy door to Father Thomas's chapel stood half open, and I could see the glimmer of candlelight from within.

Dr Pasqual sat on one of the hardback chairs towards the back of the little stone cell. His hands were clasped in his lap and his head bowed, the candlelight glinting on his white hair. He must have heard me, but he made no move of any kind as I stepped quietly into the room. I sat on a chair close to the door, unwilling to interrupt him.

An uneven row of candle stubs stood in the sand tray at the foot of Father Thomas's plinth. I recognised the stubs of Dominic's candles – pink and green and yellow, and a pool of hectic violet studded with silver spangles where one had melted quite away. Also in the tray stood a few conventional and austere tapers of ivory wax. I glanced up at Father Thomas's bronze bust in its alcove. It was as unsettling as I remembered. The face was gaunt, the eye sockets black pits.

'You must not give up,' Dr Pasqual said from his chair. His voice had a disembodied quality. 'You must not abandon your quest for the truth. Especially not now.'

I turned towards his shadowy figure. He got stiffly to his feet and walked the length of the room, his eyes on Father Thomas's bronze face. He stopped and faced me.

'I heard you talking to Felix,' he said. 'You know, Iain, the older I get, the less I know about anything. I seem, after all, to be just an old fool like all the other old fools. I allowed myself to believe I understood this village and the people in it. But the St Cyriac I knew, the St Cyriac I fought to preserve and protect, could never have done this thing to poor harmless Dominic.' He was standing very erect, as if on parade, a small neat terrier of a man with only his eyes betraying the pain he felt. 'Don't give up now, Iain. Your father would not want you to.'

'My father never wanted me to start this in the first place. I'm coming to think he was right.'

'It is a son's duty to make his father proud,' he said, 'even if it's despite both of them.'

48

I sat opposite Inspector Sharif at the window table in Henri's café. He was immaculate in a midnight blue shirt, charcoal jacket hung carefully over the free chair between us, and I felt scruffy and unshaven. He set his cup down gently, taking care that it made no sound as it settled in the saucer.

'Naturally, I understand that you'd very much like to prove that Serge Baladier isn't guilty of anything. The idea that the love of your daughter's young life …' He brushed his perfect moustache with the tip of one finger, checking unnecessarily for flecks of cappuccino foam.

I said, 'You haven't been listening to me.'

'Oh, but I've listened to every word.'

Sharif made a serious face and tapped his notebook with his slim gold pen as if to emphasise how much attention he had paid me. The notebook was a handsome leather affair which seemed unlikely to be regulation police issue. As far as I could recall, he had not opened it once while I had been talking.

'Monsieur Madoc, do you honestly believe in these missing diaries?'

'I'm not the only one who does.'

'Dominic confirmed their existence, did he?'

'He certainly never denied it.'

'Ah well, of course that settles it.'

'Inspector, during the War he used to sit and watch Father Thomas writing his journal. If there were more diaries, nobody was more likely to have them than Dominic, or at least to know where they were.'

'That's a big if,' he said.

I made to rise. 'I'm sorry I've wasted your time.'

'Sit down, please, Monsieur. I mean no offence, but you must know how these folk tales grow in a community like this. For Dominic, those diaries were a harmless bit of make believe. He had the intellect of a child. Children make up stories.'

'You didn't know him, Inspector. He wasn't like that.'

I looked around the café, so that I wouldn't have to see the pity in his eyes. There were a score of people in for breakfast and morning coffee, a couple of tourist families and several locals whose faces I recognised – one of the check-out girls from the mini-market, the pharmacist, the chain-smoking bus driver. None of them looked at me. At first I had told myself that I was being too sensitive, but a few moments earlier Sylvie Bertrand had put her head round the door, caught sight of me, and immediately left again without a word. Henri was standing by the bar. He met my eye but kept his expression blank.

'Look at it from my point of view,' Sharif was saying. 'I've got an old man dead and forty-odd thousand euros missing from his flat. Oh, and that head injury was a skull fracture, by the way, so now I've got not just a robbery but a homicide. And I have a boy on the run – a boy with a record of violence who was seen visiting the victim the night he died. I've got the kid's fingerprints from inside the flat, and I'll give you fifty-to-one that his DNA turns up there too. I've got everything except a home movie of Serge Baladier committing the crime. I ask you, Monsieur Madoc, what conclusion would you draw from this?'

'I hope I wouldn't jump to any conclusion at all.'

'Well, *touché*. But it's not as if I'd have to jump very far to reach this one. And you're not offering me any kind of alternative.'

He shifted his notebook to one side, placed his pen neatly on top of it, and tugged down his crisp cuffs, signalling that he was ready to leave.

'Inspector, do you think it's likely that Father Thomas would suddenly give up writing his diary at the end of 1941, and not record the biggest thing that had ever happened in St Cyriac?'

'Which was, in your opinion?'

'The arrest of the Rosen family.'

Sharif narrowed his eyes but he remained seated.

I said, 'Father Thomas sent Rachel Rosen away when she came to him for help. When she told him the *Statuts des Juifs* would bring death to the Jews, he wouldn't believe her. So when the SS arrived to arrest her and her family, how do you think Thomas felt? That was 1942, and I'd say it's no coincidence he joined the Resistance that year. He confided everything to those little black books, Inspector. Everything. Do you think he'd have left all this out?'

'Even if the diaries did exist, no one would care about them now.'

'Someone might, if they revealed who'd betrayed the Rosens.'

'The Nazis arrested all Jews. Nobody needed to betray them.'

'The Rosens were French citizens. Gustave was a war veteran. They should have been safe at least until July '42, and probably beyond that. They might have got out of the country in that time. But somebody had them taken away in May. Why?'

'I've a feeling you're going to tell me.'

'Did you know La Division was confiscated from Gustave Rosen, and handed to the Garniers? Gustave would have reclaimed it after the War, if he'd lived.'

'You're suggesting that over sixty years ago old man Garnier sold the Rosens out?' Sharif made incredulous eyes. 'And the connection with Dominic is …?'

'The Rosen affair is in the diaries. But nobody except Dominic knew where they were. Then, all these years later, I come along, asking questions, reopening old wounds. I get friendly with Dominic. So somebody makes a last ditch attempt to find the diaries before he gives them to me.'

He looked at me steadily. 'M'sieur, it's a beautifully constructed theory. The trouble is, you've absolutely no proof of anything. No proof anyone betrayed the Rosens. No proof the diaries ever existed. All you've got is a small-town legend and some hints dropped by a simple minded old man. This is a house of cards. Remove a single doubtful premise, and the whole structure collapses.'

'Father Thomas wasn't the only one who knew the Rosens' story,' I said stubbornly. 'I think my father did too.'

'Your father? Back in England?'

'He was hidden here by Father Thomas in 1944.'

'Yes, I know the story. But that was two years after the Rosen affair.'

'There has to be a reason why my father drew a map of La Division. Perhaps, while he was in hiding, the priest told him what had happened to the Rosens, and who had sold them out.'

Sharif raised his eyebrows. 'So he drew a map of their house?'

'I don't know yet why he did that. I'm just sure there's a connection between him and the Rosens. Something's haunted him ever since, and I think it was to do with that family.'

'Perhaps. And perhaps you should ask your father.' Sharif raised a hand to silence me. 'No, let me guess. He won't talk about it.' He removed a shred of cotton from his perfectly tailored sleeve. 'I'm sorry, Monsieur. I know you mean well, but why don't we do a deal? You play Sherlock Holmes on this imaginary crime of sixty years ago, and leave the real investigation to me.'

I didn't watch him leave.

I grew dimly aware of an argument taking place on the pavement immediately outside the window, a woman's belligerent and tearful voice, and a man's weary responses. Then the woman shoved open the door and Henri moved swiftly across from the bar to try to intercept her. He was too late.

'I don't know how you can face yourself in the mirror!' Marie-Louise spat at me, placing both hands on my table and pushing her square face aggressively into mine. 'Didn't I ask you to leave the poor old man alone? Didn't I beg you? And now look what's happened!'

'Marie,' Daniel pleaded. He hurried up behind her and took her arm.

'Don't *Marie* me!' she shouted and shook herself free. 'I *will* have my say!'

'Marie-Louise,' Henri said, jovially. 'How wonderful to see you! Why don't you both come on over to the bar and have a drink?'

She swept Sharif's empty coffee cup into my lap. I clutched at it clumsily and the saucer shattered as it hit the floor. The café fell silent.

'Dominic was just a child! Why couldn't you leave him alone instead of stirring up poison from the past? If only you hadn't come here!' She was screaming at me now. 'If you'd just left us alone!'

She barged past her husband and back out onto the esplanade. Daniel hovered by my table for an anguished moment, on the point of going after her.

'Let her go,' Henri told him gently. 'You can't help. Gunther will make sure she's all right.'

Daniel's shoulders slumped.

'Why don't you sit down?' I said.

'No. No.' He passed his hand distractedly over his short cropped hair. 'I'm sorry about that exhibition, Iain. Dominic was like a little boy to her. The son she never had.'

'I understand.'

He looked at me. 'You don't understand at all. How could you understand?'

'Daniel, I grieve for him too.'

He didn't answer, but gave an incredulous shake of his head, a gesture which seemed to say that it wasn't my place to claim a share of the communal grief, but that if I didn't realise that, there was no point arguing about it.

The door behind us jangled again as another customer left the restaurant, and someone else called for the bill.

'You're going to have to do something about the boat,' Daniel said abruptly.

'Something like what?'

'Get her moved away from my yard. Marie can't bear seeing her there. Every time she catches sight of that old wreck it reminds her of Dominic. It's too painful.'

'Daniel, what's this all about? Move the boat after sixty years? How am I supposed to do that?'

'I'm doing you a favour,' he said. 'For your father's sake I'm giving you the chance of saving her. Otherwise I'll take a torch to her. It's as simple as that.'

'I don't know a damned thing about boats. I wouldn't have a clue how to get her moved.'

'That's not my concern, is it?' But then some of the fight went out of him. 'All right, Iain, all right. I don't want to be unreasonable. I'll move her myself if you really can't get it done. On this afternoon's tide. There's an inlet we use for temporary moorings, out near the point by that old blockhouse. You can get to her by the footpath that leads from the bridge around the back of our place. But I don't want any more to do with the damned boat after that, you understand? She's your responsibility now, as far as I'm concerned. Have her towed away. Sink her.'

'Christ, Daniel.'

'I'm sorry it's come to this.' He straightened his back, relieved to have said his piece. 'I'll see that she's properly moored up. But you'll have to do something about her before long. If any kind of weather comes through I'm not sure how much punishment she'll take, and if she slips her moorings she'll end up on the Shoals inside an hour and that'll be the end of her. If I were the superstitious kind I'd say that might be best.'

A taxi driver and a mechanic from the Citroën garage got to their feet, tossed money onto the counter top and walked out. Daniel nodded curtly to me, and strode out after them, catching the door before it closed. After that it was so quiet in the café that I could hear the halyards tinkling from the harbour. In the hush Henri cruised up with two gleaming silver tankards on a tray. He banged one down defiantly in front of me, and raised his own.

'Iain,' he said, with a toss of his head, 'we must drink a toast.'

A group of half-a-dozen men at a table on the far side of the room began to get to their feet. I recognised most of them – two crewmen from the charter boats, a deckhand from Le Toque's trawler, the manager of the marine chandlery. They left their drinks half-finished, feeling in their pockets for change.

'It's on the house!' Henri boomed at them with magnificent disdain. 'And if that's your attitude, you can take your miserable custom somewhere else!'

The men slunk out, muttering, but no one had the nerve to confront him.

I said, 'Henri, I'd better go. You won't have any customers left.'

'Don't you dare leave! This is a free country, despite all appearances, and nobody tells me who my friends are.' He raised his voice to carry around the room. 'Especially not a bunch of small-minded village prigs. And if there are any more of *them* here, they can leave right now.'

Nobody moved.

Henri looked me firmly in the eye, and lifted his tankard. 'To Dominic!' his voice rang out. 'Who never harboured a mean thought about anyone.'

My throat clenched, and I looked quickly down at my tankard, concentrating on the dribbles of condensation on its mirror surface.

'Drink!' Henri ordered me.

I raised the tankard. 'To Dominic,' I said quietly.

At the other tables people repeated the toast – even a family of bemused German tourists repeated it – and the tension seeped out of the room. A hum of conversation began. The concoction was as delicious as the last time I had tasted it, on my return from England, and the chill of it brought back my composure.

'You remember the day you first came in here?' Henri asked.

'I remember.'

'And I told you to forget that old wreck?'

'Yes, you did.'

'Get Bourgogne to build you your own boat, I told you. Something with a bit of class. Something like *The Gay Dog*, I said.' He gripped my shoulder with one hand and gestured expansively out of the window with the other. 'Just look at what you might have had!'

I followed his outstretched arm. *The Gay Dog* lay at the quay, her timber decks gleaming the colour of port wine, her big breasted figurehead rising and dipping on the swell.

'All finished, and ready for her maiden voyage,' Henri said. 'Once Gunther and I find someone to take us out.'

'Can't you take her out yourself?'

'Good Lord, no. Too busy running a restaurant to learn all that salty seafarer stuff. We'll get round to it, though. We thought we might drive her over to Rio for the Mardi Gras one day.'

'Isn't there a fairly large ocean in the way?'

'Iain, don't be so negative!' He put his arm around me and gave me a hug. 'Just look at her! Forget about that worm-eaten old tub of yours. Sneak down to the inlet one night and cut her loose, I would. *The Gay Dog* is yours for the asking. Any time you want to go out for a spin.'

From the pocket of his apron he pulled a pigskin key wallet embossed in gold with the boat's name. He jingled the wallet at me invitingly.

'Thanks for the offer, Henri, but I'm no good with boats either.'

'Nonsense! With a father like yours? The sea's in your blood.'

He grabbed our tankards and cruised off towards the bar, smiling benignly on the customers he had just intimidated, and detonated a second bottle of Moët.

49

I came out of Henri's place half an hour later. After the champagne, the day sparkled. I had parked the car on the far side of the square and I strolled towards it under the plane trees, taking my time. I needed some fresh air before I drove home. A group of men were at a game of *boules* and I stopped to watch. Visitors, I thought, not locals; people who didn't know anything about Dominic, or about wartime mysteries, or about me.

I enjoyed the musical clink of the balls and the players' gasps and groans and laughter. A shining *boule* rolled across the gravel towards me, pursued by a man in a blue check shirt. I moved back and he thanked me and I smiled at him with a warmth which must have puzzled him. I felt better after that, and headed to the car.

The gouge ran from the rear light cluster, across both doors and on to the front wing, scoring the blue paintwork down to bare metal and pushing in both door panels. When I ran my fingertip along it, flakes of white paint came away on my skin. I looked around. A few tourists were wandering in the sunshine outside the Hotel de Ville, and a yellow Renault mail van was parked opposite. Some kids on bikes were performing dramatic wheelies in the grit. The postman returned to his van, opened the back door and tossed in his satchel. I caught his eye questioningly. He glanced at the damage, made a sympathetic face, and drove off.

I parked in the drive. The afternoon had clouded over, and the half-renovated house looked sad under the overhanging trees. There were no lights on in the hallway. Chantal was sitting on the veranda steps. She had been reading, or pretending to read, but now her book lay face down on the boards beside her.

'Hi.'

She shifted around so that she could look directly at me. 'Hi.'

I said, 'How's Kate?'

She flicked her hair over the nape of her neck. 'She hasn't been sleeping. So I gave her a couple of my special downers.'

Chantal could always lay her hands on emergency medical fixes. I wasn't sure that all of them were strictly legal, but they always worked. If Kate had taken one of Chantal's knock-out drops she would be anaesthetised from both love and loss for the foreseeable future. Part of me envied her.

'The world will still be there when she wakes up,' Chantal said. 'Maybe they'll even have found Serge by then.'

'I've been talking to Sharif,' I said.

'Was he any help?'

'No.'

She looked out over the garden. 'I know you're having a hard time, *chéri*. And I know I'm not being much use to you at the moment.'

I sat down on the step beside her. 'I haven't been a barrelful of laughs myself.'

We were quiet for a moment.

She said, 'This came for you.'

The envelope had British stamps on it and a handwritten address. I didn't recognise the writing. I slit the flap and pulled out three or four smudged copies of newspaper articles in old-fashioned type with almost impenetrably dark photographs. A sheet of notepaper was attached, from the Kent Police Museum in Chatham. It was signed by John Cruikshank. *I found this in the files*, he had scrawled. *Nothing's ever quite the way it seems, is it?!*

The front page of the *Kent Courier* for the 12th of July, 1966 read:

A manhunt spanning twenty years and two continents came to an end

272

in New Zealand today when an Auckland post office worker, Clive Adrian Parslow, was charged with Kent's notorious 1940s 'Gold Sovereign Murders'.

Parslow pleaded guilty in Auckland Crown Court to killing three Kent women: Edith Violet Morgan, 41, a Canterbury housewife, in October 1943; Astrid Hellaby, 27, a prostitute from Deal, in January 1944; and Sally May Chessall, 19, a Wren, in Dover, in March 1944.

Parslow, 57, gave himself up at a central Auckland police station ...

'What is it?' Chantal asked.

I handed it to her. She took her time reading it.

She said, 'Hamelin didn't kill her.' She looked at me.

'That's right.' I didn't meet her eyes. 'And, yes, as a police officer himself, my father would have heard about this.'

'He thought he'd left an innocent man to drown. Isn't that what it means?'

I got up and walked down the veranda steps and stared out through the trees at the choppy water.

She said, 'This is why he'd never talk about St Cyriac. Why he paid for a memorial to Hamelin, twenty years late.' She got up and stood beside me and held my arm. 'This answers all your questions, Iain. Doesn't it? Please tell me it does.'

'Why did he behave the way he did when he got back from France in 1944?'

'We've been through this,' she said, her voice hardening. 'He felt guilty because he failed to save this man when it was his duty to save him. That's why.'

'Guilt doesn't quite cover it. He was in an agony of remorse. It blighted his life. At the time he hid himself away even from the woman he loved. You think he'd do that because he'd failed to save Lucien?'

'He might. You can't tell how he'd feel or what he'd do.'

'Well, I don't believe it. I never really did.' I pointed to the sheaf of photocopies in her hand. 'This explains why the monument went up twenty years late. But back in 1944 my father still thought Lucien had butchered this poor girl in Dover. Do you

273

think he would really react the way he did, just because he didn't save a man like that?'

She gave a little groan. 'Oh, Iain. I don't know.'

'And the map ... why did he burn it? Why did he have it in the first place?'

'I don't know that either.'

'And now this so-called escape down the Vasse? The escape that couldn't have happened? What does all that mean?'

She sighed. 'I don't know, and I don't know.'

She walked a few steps away, stopped by the car and touched the gouge in the bodywork. She came back and looked me in the face.

'Iain, I'm on your side. I always have been and I always will be. But in this life we don't get all our questions answered, and there comes a time to stop asking them.'

She touched my cheek, and went into the house.

50

Just beyond the bridge the footpath branched left, down the spine of the headland. The way was overgrown with nettles and brambles, but I followed it without much difficulty for a couple of hundred metres. It took me behind and above Daniel Bourgogne's house. I could see the roof through the trees. A little further and the track began to drop downhill towards the estuary again. I passed the overgrown concrete walls of the old German blockhouse, and emerged through a screen of gorse.

In my mind I still saw 2548 as she lay sleeping, tilted to one side in the mud. Now, with the rounded swell of her hull beneath the water, she looked lighter, sharper, sleeker. Daniel, as good as his word, had moored her hard up against the bank, where the curve of the shore protected her. I could see her quivering in the current.

I walked up to the edge of the bank, a step away from the deck, swallowed hard and clambered aboard. I sat down heavily on the hatch, gripping the edge of the coaming and shutting my mind to the muscular stirring of the launch beneath me. Sweat prickled on my face and neck. I bent down and unfastened the ties that held the tarpaulin over the hatch, and peeled it aside. Dominic's makeshift wooden ladder was still in place. I swung myself over and climbed clumsily down into the hull.

I stood there, trying not to think of the weight of green water pressing on the frail skin of the vessel around me. I could hear the mooring ropes groan. There wasn't much sign now of Dominic's presence. The tin box containing his little camping cooker was upended on the floor and a scatter of *Tintin* comics and sodden biscuits lay in a pool of bilgewater which rocked at my feet.

Light spoked in around the edges of the forepeak hatch. I walked unsteadily towards it, running my hand along the hull for support and reassurance. Every few paces I stopped to tap at the hull, or to turn over some litter with my toe, or to run my hand behind one of the ribs or under the plywood fittings. I knew it was hopeless, but I had to try.

I was turning back towards the ladder, empty handed, when I heard a soft thump somewhere ahead of me. I froze, feeling my stomach clench. Quiet footsteps moved along the deck above my head, and paused at the main hatch. I stood utterly motionless, unwilling to acknowledge even to myself what I was so afraid of. A pair of expensive trainers appeared on the top rung of the ladder.

'Felix,' I said. 'For Chrissake ...'

His own surprise was so complete that he stumbled and slid down the last two rungs.

'Iain! You frightened the life out of me.'

'Ditto.' I walked towards him, my heart banging in my chest. 'What are you doing here?'

'Daniel wanted to put a new lock on the hatch. The police busted the old one.' He took a shining padlock and key from his pocket, detached the key and dropped it into my palm. 'I told him I'd do it, so he asked me to pass the key on to you.'

'Couldn't he manage that himself?'

'I think he'd rather steer clear of you at the moment.' He walked a few steps down the hull, kicking at the timbers, scuffing his trainers through the water which lay along the centreline. 'Well, I'm no expert, but the hull seems sound enough to me. She's taken a little water, but being afloat will close her up.'

'Is that good?'

'Yes, Iain,' he said. 'It's good.'

'Felix, what the hell am I going to do with her?'

'Oh, she'll keep for a week or two.' He came back and clapped my shoulder in that familiar gesture of his. 'Don't worry about it. We'll work it out.'

I couldn't imagine how, but I was grateful for his encouragement.

'Come on,' he said. 'Let's get out of here. I've seen livelier corpses than you.'

I didn't need to be asked twice. I went up the ladder into the daylight and jumped the small gap onto the bank, leaving Felix to close the hatch and fix the new padlock. When he had finished he stepped ashore beside me, and we stood gazing at the old launch and out over the glittering water. We were only three hundred metres or so further along the estuary from her original resting place, but the prospect from here was quite different. The bend of the bank made it impossible to see back up the river towards the boatyard, and to our right the view opened directly out to sea.

Felix said, 'Are you going to tell me what you were really doing on board? Or shall I guess?'

'It was a shot in the dark.' I gave him a neutral look. 'The boat's got a double hull. There are a thousand places you could lose little black diaries.'

Felix sighed, and shook his head. 'Those damned diaries.' All at once his voice trembled and he turned his face away from me.

'Felix?'

'They're going to release his body tomorrow. So the village can bury him.'

I struggled to find the right response, but then I heard again in my mind the words he had used, and I realised that Felix's distress was not just on Dominic's account, but on mine as well.

'You don't want me at the funeral,' I said.

He swung back to look at me, his eyes shining. 'I hate to do this, Iain. But I have no choice. He deserves to be seen out of this world in peace, especially after the violence of his passing.'

I stared out towards the Shoals. 'Do they all blame me?'

'Iain, I know you're hurting too. If it's any comfort to you, I don't believe you have a single thing to reproach yourself for.'

'When will it be?'

'Tuesday.'

'Well,' I said. 'I'll be thinking of you both.'

He couldn't find a reply to that, and presently he touched my arm and left. I let him go.

I had thought solitude might be welcome, but the sight of the launch creaking against her new moorings unnerved me. Quite soon I followed in Felix's tracks, only stopping when I reached the bridge over the Vasse.

51

The house had a sad and abandoned air to it, as if had just been vacated rather than recently occupied. Evidence of Bonnard's unfinished building work was everywhere – raw new timber on the veranda, a stack of slates, a blind window roughly covered with black plastic.

The impression of emptiness was so strong that when I reached the kitchen I was surprised to find Chantal seated at the pine table, her chin in her hands. Small intricate objects were spread on the tablecloth in front of her. Despite the daylight flooding through the window, she had set up a desklamp which threw a brilliant glare over her work.

'You've been a while,' she said.

'I went to check on the boat. And to see Felix, as it turned out.'

I saw for the first time what she was doing. She had arranged the components of her Hasselblad camera with geometric pre-cision on the folded white tablecloth, lenses and shutter and half a hundred tiny cogs and screws and springs. Metal and glass gleamed. Chantal had never lost her love for the Hasselblad, now virtually an antique. It had been her first serious camera, and had been with her in deserts and shell holes and burning buildings, through flood and famine and earthquake.

'I'm thinking of going back to work,' she said. 'Part-time, maybe.'

'I thought that was all behind us.'

'Iain, we can't go on like this indefinitely.' She sighed. 'What did Felix want?'

'Among other things, to tell me not to come to Dominic's funeral.'

She lifted her head sharply. 'Felix said that?'

'He said he had no choice. I can see his point.'

She got to her feet, took both my hands in hers and looked up into my face. 'This is my fault, Iain. I made us buy this place. We'd have been dining out in Paris or cruising the vineyards in Provence, if it hadn't been for me.'

'Is that what you want?'

'There's no joy for us here.'

I said nothing.

She let go of my hands. She said, 'We'll get someone to patch the house up, put it on the market. And we'll get out.'

'I'm not sure I'm ready for that.'

'You're not the only one involved, *chéri*.'

'Chantal, Dominic gave the diaries to my father.'

She stared at me.

'I just worked it out, walking back from the boat,' I said. 'After the priest was killed, Dominic gave the diaries to my father for safekeeping. He probably hoped he'd take them to England. But Dad wasn't sure he'd get across the Channel, so he hid the journals at La Division.'

'Iain—'

'I thought maybe they were in the launch, but all the time the answer was staring me in the face. They're marked on the map. A box within a box. Those three lines aren't bars or a grating, or whatever. They're three objects. Three books. Under the main room at La Division. That's where he must have hidden them.'

She closed her eyes. 'Please, Iain.'

'Of course I can't be a hundred percent certain. But I think that's what happened. One thing is for sure: he and Billington didn't sail from the Vasse estuary. The tides are wrong, I told you that. They sailed from La Division, and before they did, he hid the books.'

'Everyone knows how they escaped,' she said tightly. 'Dr Pasqual stood on the bridge and watched them sail down the river. He said so. Tides or no tides, he saw them go.'

'I stood on that bridge just now. You can't see the boatyard from there. You can't see the estuary, even in broad daylight. You can't see more than fifty metres down the river.'

'So the old man lied about this, did he?' Her voice was high with disbelief. 'The whole village conspired to lie about it?'

'Not the whole village. Four men. That's all it took. Four men who had a secret to keep, so they made up their own story about that night, and passed it on. And that's the story everyone believes.'

'Why would they do such a thing, Iain?'

'I don't know yet.'

'You don't *know*? You dream this thing up and haven't even got a motive? Listen to yourself!'

'My father and Billington must have been taken to La Division, and for some reason the four guys who took them there had to lie about it. The answer must be in the diaries. What's more, they're still at La Division, which is why Garnier wants to bury the place in concrete.'

'Iain, that's insane. If the diaries are there, and if they say anything so damaging, why wouldn't Garnier just find them and destroy them?'

'Maybe he doesn't know exactly where to look. Maybe that's why it's panicked him, me turning up with the map. Serge didn't do this, Chantal. Whoever killed Dominic was looking for the diaries, and thought the old boy had them. But all the time they were up at La Division.'

'Nobody will believe that, Iain,' she said wearily. 'Serge has a bad history, and he's gone on the run from the police. They don't need another suspect.'

'They might have to look for one if the diaries turned up, and we could all see what Father Thomas wrote in them. There might be another motive then.'

She put her fingertips on my lips.

'I'm sorry, Iain. This has gone on too long.'

'No, listen—'

'I've listened enough. Too much. I want us out of here. And

I don't want to wait. I mean, right now. Tonight.' She moved back to the table. 'I'm serious,' she said.

'This is you being on my side, is it?'

'You have the nerve to say that to me?' Her voice dropped dangerously. 'I never wanted to stay here, you know that. But I bought this place for *you*. So that you could get this out of your system. I must have been mad. I thought the past would set you free. But instead, you're trapped in it.'

We glared at one another.

I said, 'Take the car.'

'What?'

'You're right. Everything you say is right. I'm sorry.' I took the keys out of my pocket and held them out to her. 'You have to go, you and Kate. Take the car. Go now.'

'Iain, you can't stay here alone. What on earth have you got to stay for?'

'I just want another day or two, that's all. Go on. Take the keys.'

'What do you think this is? Fucking *High Noon*? What do you hope to achieve by staying?'

'Just a couple of days. Tie up some loose ends.'

'Keep your bloody keys. I'm going to pack.' She took two steps towards the door and swung back. 'I'm not coming back, Iain. You do understand that? If you don't come with me, I'm out.'

'Just a couple of days,' I repeated.

She held my eyes for a moment longer and then stalked away through the house.

I sat at the desk in the cabin I had once hoped would be my father's. I had lost track of how long I had been here, watching the day fade into night. Two hours, perhaps. Every now and then Chantal would cross in front of one of the windows in the main house, carrying a case or folded clothes. Soon she would be finished with packing. I had several times been on the point of going back inside, making some fresh overture. But I knew Chantal meant what she said. And so did I.

I heard a light footfall on the step and swung round, but it was

Kate who pushed the door open. She was pale, her hair scraped back from her face.

I said, 'Come and have a seat, sweetheart.'

'Just chill, Dad,' she snapped. 'OK?'

She stood over by the model of 2548. I had opened the mahogany case as I always did when I came in here. It was a ritual, opening the case, opening my father's story. Opening the past.

'Mum's in a state,' she said finally. 'I'm not helping much.'

'Me neither, I'm afraid.'

'She's told me to call a cab.'

'You'd better do it, then. And Kate? I want you to go with her.'

'And you?'

I didn't answer.

She touched the model's wheelhouse roof, leaned a little closer to look in through the windows at the bearded figure which stood at the helm. 'This is meant to be Grandad, isn't it?' she said.

'That's how Dominic saw him, so I guess that's how he was.'

She blew a little dust from the wheelhouse windows and squinted in again at the carved figure which represented her grandfather. She walked up to the desk and stood beside my chair.

She said, 'What are you doing out here, anyway?'

'Trying to convince myself I'm not completely nuts.'

'Is it working?'

'No.'

'We should all go, Dad. Everything's gone wrong since we got here.'

'I can't argue with that. But I need a little time.'

'So you can stay here and solve your precious mystery?'

I covered her hand with mine. 'It's not my mystery, Kate. It's your grandfather's. And he's not telling how it all started, far less how it's going to end.'

She was quiet for a minute, thinking that through.

'If you're right about those diaries,' she said, 'that would put Serge in the clear, wouldn't it?'

'I don't know. But at least there'd be a possible motive for someone else to have killed Dominic. So, yes, it could help Serge if I was right.'

She reached past me to touch the map where it lay on the desk. She said, 'A box within a box. That just about sums up this whole village.'

Chantal called Kate's name and we both went outside. Chantal was standing on the veranda with four bags at her feet.

Kate said, 'I'll call that cab.'

'I've already done it,' Chantal told her, avoiding my eyes. 'Get your things.'

Kate looked from her mother to me and back again. 'I'll just …' she began, but didn't finish the sentence. She made a vague gesture and went into the house.

Chantal swallowed and raised her eyes to me with an effort. She said, 'We'll go to London. To the flat. Yes. That's what we'll do.'

'That would be best.'

'I'll make …' she hesitated, her voice quivering, 'I'll make other plans then.'

The lights of the cab were already coming down the road and had almost reached the drive.

'Chantal …'

'I can't talk about it any more now.' She let out a long breath as if it hurt her. 'Please don't stand there and watch us. I couldn't bear it.'

I went back into the cabin and listened to the cab's wheels crunch on the gravel, and heard them lug their bags down the steps. I stayed there even when the car doors clumped shut and the diesel clattered away into the night. I couldn't watch it go. I had never been able to watch Chantal leave.

When it was quiet again I went through to the kitchen. I took a bottle of scotch and a glass from the cupboard and sat at the kitchen table, listening to the nightwind as it flapped and rattled around the house.

52

I surfaced into something like wakefulness and got shakily to my feet, feeling stiff and nauseous. The kitchen was rinsed in cold grey light. I lurched to the phone and grabbed the receiver before it could shriek at me again.

Chantal's voice was hollow. 'It's me.'

I opened my mouth to answer, but no sound came out. I tried again. 'Where are you?'

'We're at the ferry terminal at St Malo. We're OK.'

I could see the clock on the kitchen wall. It was seven-thirty in the morning. I shook my head, trying to get my brain to work.

'We stayed in some awful little dive,' she said. 'I didn't want to call you until this morning.' She waited. 'Did you get any sleep?'

My head ached and my mouth was dry. 'It doesn't feel like it.'

'Same here.'

'Chantal—'

'Be quiet a minute.'

I could hear her breathing, readying herself for some announcement. I clenched my fingers around the phone.

'I wasn't sure you'd be there,' she said. 'I hoped maybe you'd … come to your senses. I lay awake all night wondering if you'd come after us. Hoping you would.'

'Chantal—'

'I don't know what you think you're doing there, but I want you to remember this, Iain. You never needed to play the tough guy. Not for me. You never needed to throw it all away for that.'

She hung up without waiting for a reply.

I put the phone back on the hook and felt a loneliness I had not experienced since childhood. For a second I was tempted to follow her, right now, and to hell with it. My head was beating like a triphammer. I put the scotch away, and went into the bathroom for a couple of paracetamols. In the mirror I looked exhausted, battered. But I knew I wouldn't follow Chantal to London. I knew I couldn't.

I washed and changed, went back into the kitchen and forced myself to eat. At about nine I locked up, went out to the car and drove through the bright morning to St Brieuc. I found a shop selling outdoor gear and bought myself a backpack and a torch and a folding spade and a dark, zip-up windbreaker. I loaded them in the back of the car and went into a hardware store on the square and bought a pair of heavy duty wirecutters.

I got back about three in the afternoon, took my purchases through into the bedroom, locked the house and slept for a couple of hours. When I came round I found a bottle of Chablis in the fridge, poured myself one, and carried it out onto the veranda at the front of the house. The light was beginning to soften. I stood leaning on the wooden rail with my glass in my hand, letting the sea breeze cool my skin, listening as it stirred the bushes in the garden. The shadows lengthened around the house. I sipped the wine, put the glass down, and went down the steps into the garden.

I found what I was looking for in the lean-to toolshed beside the house: a pick-axe handle in smooth white wood. The balanced weight of the hardwood in my hands gave me reassurance. I took it into the house and leaned it against the wall inside the bedroom door. After that I came back out to the kitchen, heated something in the microwave, and took my time eating it.

I didn't want any interruptions, nor any further demands on my resolution. I unplugged the phone from the wall and turned my mobile off. I went to bed early and set the alarm for two in the morning.

*

In the event it wasn't the alarm that woke me. It was the cigarette smoke.

It hung in the darkness, raw and pungent. I lay with my eyes open and slowly raised my head. Moonlight fell through the window and across the foot of the bed and over the floor. The red numerals of the digital clock beside the bed told me that it was a little after one o'clock. I eased myself into a sitting position, placed my bare feet on the floor and stood up. I grabbed the pick handle and soundlessly opened the door.

The hallway was flooded with moonlight. A trail of wet footprints led from the locked front door. They had paused at my bedroom door, just where I now stood; their owner had looked in on me while I slept before heading down the dark corridor towards the kitchen. I felt the short hairs rise on the back of my neck. I breathed steadily for a minute, and then followed the tracks.

The kitchen door stood half open. I nudged it with my shoulder and it swung noiselessly inwards. A rasher of cigarette smoke slipped sideways through the kitchen window. A man sat with his back to me at the kitchen table, a pool of water gathering beneath his chair. I stopped breathing. I glimpsed dark hair, dark sodden clothes. I shifted my grip on the stave and the figure rose with astonishing speed and turned to face me. I saw white eyes and a smeared face.

'Christ, M'sieur Madoc!' Serge blurted. 'Who were you expecting?'

53

My hands shook as I poured him a scotch. I took a few more deep breaths and steadied myself, though Serge probably didn't notice. He was spent, soaked and filthy. There was mud in his hair and on his face and he stank of the estuary. His canvas backpack lay in a wet mound on the floor beside him.

'I came down the track beside the river,' he said. 'I waded the last bit, where it comes round the point, so I couldn't be seen from the village.'

I poured myself a drink and sat down. 'How did you get in?'

'I still have a key. I was going to wait till morning, but it's cold out there. Sorry. I didn't mean to wake you. I thought I'd been as quiet as a mouse.'

'It was the smoke that woke me. I didn't know you smoked.'

He looked puzzled. 'I don't.'

I said nothing, my drink halfway to my mouth.

'And who was this for?' He touched the pickaxe handle with his fingertip.

'It doesn't matter. It wouldn't have been any use.'

He didn't pursue that. He cupped his glass in his hands and drank gratefully.

'She's gone, hasn't she?' he said.

'They left last night.' I got up and pulled down the kitchen blinds. 'Things got … difficult here.'

'I just wanted to see her again, Monsieur Madoc. One last time.'

'One last time before what?'

'Before going to the police.' He saw the way I glanced across at him. 'This mess won't sort itself out, will it?'

288

I primed the percolator then went to the fridge, found cheese, olives, a cold lamb joint, and dumped it all on the table with some bread. He fell on it as if he hadn't eaten for months.

'You're going to give yourself up?'

'I should, shouldn't I, Monsieur Madoc?' His mouth was full and his voice muffled, but the appeal was clear. 'Should probably have done it before. I mean, they're not going to stop looking for me.'

'Serge ... What happened on Saturday night?'

He swallowed and put down the wad of bread and cheese that was folded in his fist. 'I got drunk,' he said. 'Kate and I had a row, so I went out and got drunk.'

'There are witnesses?'

'I was feeling pretty bad. I took a couple of bottles down to the beach and got blasted all on my own.'

'Christ, Serge.'

'I didn't know I'd need an alibi,' he said, his resentment sparking up, 'or I'd have got drunk in better company. Anyway, when I came to my senses it was about midnight. I wanted to come back here, but didn't think I'd get much of a welcome.'

'Why didn't you go home?'

'There was no way I could use the bike. I left it in the village and started walking. I got as far as the old mill, saw the light on in Dominic's apartment. It was the only light on in the whole place. You said he'd be glad if I went to see him, and I had some crazy idea that maybe he was sitting up there, all alone, working on his models. The door was open, and off the latch. I knocked and the door just came open. I went in. And there he was.'

The percolator began to gobble.

'What did you see?'

'He was in his bed with all these bottles and stuff around him. But he was dead.'

'You're sure of that?'

'Of course I'm sure,' he said sharply. 'If he'd still been alive do you think I'd have left him there drowning in his own puke?'

He was getting his strength back, and his attitude with it. I poured two mugs of coffee. 'How could you be sure?'

'He had no pulse in his neck or his wrist. He was almost cold. His eyes were rolled back. His bladder had released. I thought those were pretty bad signs. What would you think?'

I handed over his coffee.

He looked away. 'I'm sorry. I shouldn't have spoken that way.'

I suddenly saw that beneath the dirt and the commando outfit he was just a frightened kid. I saw too that he had not come here just to find Kate. He had come to find me; to ask me to take charge.

I said, 'Go on.'

'His place was destroyed. All his beautiful models. Everything; just smashed up. I didn't know about the money, not until I read about it in the papers. But anyone could see he'd been robbed. That sobered me up pretty quickly.'

'Then what?'

'I panicked, I suppose. I went back the way I'd come, picked up the bike and headed east. I didn't know where I was going. I just rode until I had to stop for fuel. I sat and thought about it then, but it was too late to go back. That's what I figured at the time, anyway.'

'You thought they'd blame you?'

'Was I wrong?'

I drank some coffee.

'I did do right, didn't I, Monsieur Madoc?' he said. 'Coming back, I mean? I know I shouldn't have bolted. But now I've come back they'll sort it all out. They'll find out who really did this. Won't they?'

'I honestly don't know,' I said quietly. 'They've developed a habit around here of avoiding the truth wherever possible ...'

He stared at me. 'So what should I do?'

I reached across and poured him another scotch, then put the cap on the bottle and moved it away from both of us. 'The first thing you should do is drink that coffee. Then this stuff. Then go and stand under the shower for ten minutes and I'll find you some dry clothes.'

He picked up his bag and looked at me uncertainly. 'And after that?'

'After that we're going out.'

54

I drove through the sleeping village with Serge crouched low in the passenger seat. The square was empty, the buildings dark and silent. A halo of moths swung around the streetlamp outside the school gates. I headed past the shuttered minimarket and the garage and up to the junction with the coast road. I turned right and drove on for a kilometre or two. Black woods crowded in on us from the seaward side, punctuated occasionally by the glitter of water.

'Here,' Serge said, and sat up.

I would have missed it if he hadn't spoken: a narrow lane that forked down towards the sea. I killed the engine and let the car coast on parking lights through the tunnel of conifers.

After a couple of hundred yards he touched my arm.

A fire trail crossed the lane just ahead, and the trees had been cleared for a few metres on either side. I pulled onto the wide, soft verge, stopped the car and turned off the lights. The numerals on the dashboard clock were the last to fade: it was 2.56.

We climbed out and stood in the mild and aromatic night. There was no sound except the ticking of the engine and the faint rush of the wind through the trees. Bars of moonlight fell across the clearing and along the trail but the woods around us were solid ramparts of darkness. I heard Serge move and a second later the tailgate clicked and he appeared beside me with the two backpacks. I swung mine onto my shoulder. The clink of metal sounded loud in the night.

'Let's fix this now,' he said softly. 'We don't want a big conference when we're close.'

'Go ahead.'

'You follow me,' he said. 'It'll take us about ten minutes. Stick as close as you can. We'll come out by the fence near the old house, not far from the beach. It'll take me a few moments to make friends with the dog again, then I'll come back and whistle. That's when you come through.' He looked at me anxiously in the darkness. 'I hope you're right about this, Monsieur Madoc. It's a big old ruin to go poking around in.'

'It'll be light in about two hours and the workmen will be here,' I said. 'Then it won't matter one way or the other.'

He hesitated for a second longer and then slid away between the trees. He moved fast and I felt clumsy behind him, snapping dry branches and dragging through underbrush. After a minute or two my eyes adjusted to the darkness and I found some kind of rhythm and gradually closed the gap between us. When he reached the edge of the trees and raised a hand to stop me, I almost collided with him. He crouched down and I did the same.

The fence glinted in the moonlight. Beyond it, the rear wall of the Rosens' old farmhouse was a dark blur against the undergrowth. A hundred metres away, on the far side of the field, cold light lay along the ridgeline of the corrugated iron barn, but the other buildings and the junkyard itself were in darkness.

Serge unslung his pack and unclipped the straps. He waited for a few seconds and then crept across the strip of bare earth, carrying the pack under one arm. I heard the snap of wirecutters and a twang from the first strand. He was very quick after that. Half-a-dozen sharp snaps later he folded back a square of fence and slid through it. He didn't look back.

I lost sight of him almost immediately in the long grass, and hunkered down on the soft pine needles to wait. I took out a bottle of water and drank. I imagined my father and Billington waiting in that old house sixty and more years ago, listening as I was now to the the waves bursting against the shingle just beyond the bluff.

I heard Serge's whistle, and scrambled through the hole in the fence. I waded through the long grass towards the old farmhouse and plunged into its shadow. I stumbled on a root and the dog barked quite close by. I heard Serge calming it. He was crouching in the litter of broken tiles at the front of the house, behind the bushes that shielded us from the open paddock. The dog stood beside him. The animal gave a low growl as I rounded the corner, but lost interest in me as Serge conjured up the lamb joint from his backpack. The dog froze for a second, ears pricked, not quite able to believe its luck, then disappeared into the undergrowth with the bone.

'If we're going to go in,' Serge said, 'it might as well be now.'

I stepped through the litter to the door, felt in my pack for a tyre lever, slipped it through the hasp of the padlock, and snapped it off. The door wouldn't budge. I put the tyre lever in against the jamb and splintered the wood. The first plank tore away in my hands, and then Serge was beside me and between us we heaved the door outwards. The dog whimpered once, but when the noise stopped it went back to its meal.

The roofless kitchen was still and warm, sheltered from the wind. The ash tree whispered in the moonlight above us, but here at floor level it was quiet and dark. I snapped on the torch and swept its beam across the debris. Serge's torch sprang on beside me.

The kitchen was larger than I had realised. A dresser, once full of china, had collapsed in the far corner and its contents had slid across the floor. A rack which had held pots and pans on butcher's hooks above the range had fallen against the far wall. The range itself, an ancient cast iron affair, had collapsed through the floor under its own weight, and lay at an angle in the cellar below, its rusted doors hanging open.

I stepped onto the rubble slope and started to edge down towards it, then half-slid, half-clambered the rest of the way. My torch beam wavered in front of me and dust rose in the light like smoke. I had the map in my shirt pocket but I didn't need to take it out. I could see it with perfect clarity in my mind.

I set my backpack on a mound of fallen bricks and got down on my knees in the damp earth and thrust aside some of the rubbish – old dark wine bottles, tiles, a rusted saucepan, bits of worm-eaten timber, pebbles, roots. An orange centipede stumbled over the dirt. A very large spider scuttled into a crack in the brick foundations of the chimney. The light of my torch blazed briefly on its battery of ruby eyes as it sidled into the darkness.

'Monsieur Madoc—'

'Get down here, Serge.'

He did so at once, bringing a small landslide with him. He was breathing hard. 'It'll be light in just over an hour ...'

'If it's here at all, it's somewhere in this corner, up near the chimney breast.' I pulled out the map. 'See these measurements? If I copied them down right, it should be a couple of feet in from this wall and maybe four or five feet from that one, which means between here –' I scuffed the soil with my heel ' – and there ...'

'That's under the old cooker,' he said.

'Sod's Law.' I crawled over to my pack and threw him one of the trowels. 'Shift some of that junk and dig around the edges of the thing. I'd guess we're looking for a box. A biscuit tin, or maybe an ammunition box. Possibly a leather or oilskin packet. Anything you could keep a couple of journals in. If we don't have it in a few minutes we're out of luck, and we're out of here OK?'

I took the other trowel, and shaved off a layer of soil and then another and another. I could hear Serge dragging aside the debris behind me.

In the next twenty minutes I carved a hole nearly half-a-metre deep in the sandy soil. I spent a few more minutes widening it, throwing the spoil behind me. The earth was clean and un-disturbed. I worked until my muscles ached and I had to stop. Sweat was running down the sides of my neck and I threw my head back and let the night air cool my face.

Above me, the leaves of the ash tree glittered in the moonlight. I don't know what it was about that sight, the tree shivering against the stars. Something changeless and huge. Whatever it was, the full absurdity of what I was doing suddenly overwhelmed me. We would not find anything here. No cashbox, no leather packet, no diaries. Perhaps they never had existed after all. I tossed aside the trowel, and wiped my forehead with my sleeve.

I turned to see that Serge had stopped working too. He was on all fours, and his torch, lodged in the oven door of the rusted cooker, shone on his face as he peered down at the floor between his hands

'Monsieur Madoc?'

I crawled over to him, shoving aside a mound of wood and bricks and old bottles. One of them rolled and broke and the air was filled with the tarry bouquet of sixty-year-old claret. I aimed my torch into the pit he had scraped. A cracked grey paving stone lay half-exposed at the bottom of it. A corner of the slab had broken away and I saw a patch of rusted metal underneath.

I took Serge's trowel and tapped the metal with the base of the handle. It gave a hollow thud. My mouth went dry. I levered up the rest of the slab and heaved it aside. Underneath it was a recessed circular handle, which the paving stone – flush with the original floor of the cellar – would have concealed. I prised up the handle and got two fingers through the ring and lifted. It groaned a little but did not give.

Serge craned over my shoulder. 'What is it?'

'It's not a tin box, that's for sure.' I dug away at the dirt and found an edge, then a corner. 'A hatch, maybe?'

Serge and I dragged aside a jumble of old boards and joists and between us we revealed a small trap, less then a metre square. I could lift it only an inch or two before it clanged against the side of the range. I did this a couple of times, experimentally, and let the door fall back, then got up and put my shoulder against the stove and pushed. It moved only a fraction.

Serge shuffled up beside me and as the dead weight of the stove lifted a few centimetres he kicked a loose brick under it. We heaved again and this time I managed to shove the broken corner of the paving slab into the gap and won us another small space. We were making a lot of noise by now, but the excitement of the discovery deafened us to it, and it was only when the dog barked that we both froze. We waited perhaps thirty seconds, leaning against the old range, filthy and sweating and out of breath, listening for any sound over the hissing of the trees, but there was nothing more.

'He's finished his dinner.' Serge smiled wanly in the torch-light. 'I hope he won't want us for breakfast.'

A faint wash of dove grey light was stealing into the eastern sky above the walls. I knelt down again and cleared the last of the dirt from the trapdoor. I got my fingers through the ring again and this time it lifted, groaning against rusted hinges, and released a gust of stale air which enveloped us both.

I flicked the torch into the darkness: three stone steps down, a narrow space with a concrete floor, litter, an old shoe. There was very little headroom, certainly not enough for a man to stand up comfortably. Some sort of an emergency bunker, an air-raid shelter, maybe, dug beneath the floor of the wine cellar. A box within a box. I swung my legs in and rested my feet on the top step. And I thought: a *shoe*?

I dropped down onto the floor below, pulling my arms in after me, and reached up for the torch. It was a second or two before I could bring the beam to bear. After that I didn't move for quite a long time.

The man lay face down, shreds of what must once have been a black suit still clinging to the bones of his legs. The shoes, perfectly preserved, looked comically big, clown-big, on the thin branches of his ankle bones. I could see the jagged hole in the back of his skull, and the glint of a gold watch chain between his ribs.

His outflung arm rested across the lap of the woman who sat slumped against the far wall, a bundle of sticks half-wrapped in dark rags. Her eyesockets had been knocked together into one long hole and her bottom jaw lay detached on the floor beside her. The girl lay in her arms, partially mummified and her hair still horribly abundant, faded to blond, cascading over her shrivelled face. The claw of her right hand was hooked through the chain of a pendant or locket of some kind.

I heard Serge drop down beside me and catch his breath.

'Jesus Christ!' He crossed himself, and did it again, backing off until he sat down on the steps. 'Jesus Christ!'

I stepped around Gustave's sprawled body and noticed for the first time that the floor was littered with tarnished silverware – candlesticks, a wine cooler, a scatter of cutlery. Mouldered documents, leather satchels and deposit boxes were piled on steel shelves along the wall. I took another step. My foot rolled across a brass shell-case. There were more of them, a lot more. I saw now the pock marks in the cement wall behind Rachel Rosen's back, and the dark stains in the render.

Serge said fearfully, 'Shouldn't we leave them alone?'

I knelt beside Madeleine, forced myself to look into her ruined face. 'She was the same age as Kate.'

The boy stood behind me, breathing hard.

'Go back, Serge,' I said. 'I'll be up in a second.'

I heard him scramble gratefully back up the steps. I stretched out my hand and touched Madeleine's locket. I couldn't make out details in the torchlight but I could see that it was damaged, the edge of the metal smeared over by one of the bullets which had ended her young life. I wondered what talisman had been so precious she had clutched it to her in this last moment. I reached out and let the weight of it rest in my hand.

Up above, the dog suddenly set up a frantic barking and Serge anxiously called my name. I half-turned, and the movement tugged on the chain of the locket and Madeleine's dry face and hair fell against my wrist. She felt as light as a moth's wing. I laid her gently back in her mother's arms, stood up and backed away to the steps. I had reached the top before I realised that Madeleine's locket was still in my hand. Serge called again, more urgently this time, and I stuffed the locket into my jeans.

When I pulled myself up through the trap Serge was already out of the cellar, crouching just inside the front door. He waved me to silence as I came up behind him, but he didn't need to. Headlights raked across the paddock and I could clearly hear the vehicle's engine.

'The Garniers,' I said. 'They mustn't find you here, Serge.'

He looked wildly at me. 'Shall I go back to the house?'

'That's too risky. Hide out in the woods for a few hours, and this evening, when no one's about, go to the launch.' I gripped his shoulder. 'She's at the inlet near the point, near that old blockhouse. When it's safe, get inside, close her up, and wait for me to come. This is the key to the lock on the main hatch. I'll be there after eight o'clock tonight.'

He took the key, tossed aside his torch and slipped through the gap in the door. The dog, seeing his new benefactor running for the fence and freedom, bounded gleefully after him for a short way and sat down, confused. I sat down too, in the doorway. Below me I could see the black square of the trapdoor in the gathering light. I dragged my backpack towards me and took out the water bottle and drank, sluicing some over my face.

The four-by-four came bouncing across the paddock and pulled up outside the farmhouse. Yannick wrenched the door open and a moment later he stood over me, a torch in one hand and a hunting rifle in the other. His brother pushed past into the old farmhouse.

'You're a very persistent type, Monsieur Madoc, aren't you?' Yannick said. 'But trespass? In France? We can do pretty well anything we like to you.'

'He's not alone.' Stephan called up from the cellar. 'Two torches.'

'No. I'm not alone.' I tilted my head towards the trapdoor.

The brothers exchanged glances. Stephan slid down over the rubble to the trap, and flashed his torch into the darkness as I had done. He waited for a moment and then swung himself down.

'What's there?' Yannick called.

But Stephan was already scrabbling up out of the darkness, whimpering, his arms and legs pumping to carry him away as fast as possible from what he had seen.

'What the fuck have you been up to?' Yannick knelt down and knocked me hard on the side of the head with the barrel of the rifle. 'I said—'

But he stopped then, because I was sliding the pickhandle out of my pack and the smooth haft was in my grip, and he knew what was coming and that he would not be quick enough to stop it. I swung the stave hard against his kneecap. I didn't hear him scream, although he certainly did. I didn't even notice when his gun exploded quite close beside my head, because I was too busy lifting the pickhandle high and bringing it down again, this time very hard indeed.

55

Inspector Sharif and I sat in folding chairs, sipping coffee from paper cups while police specialists in white coveralls moved around the ruins of La Division. There seemed to be a lot of them, carrying bags in through the front door, rigging tarpaulins, taking photographs.

I was giddy with exhaustion. The caffeine had not yet kicked in, and I badly needed it to. I drank some more. It was a little past eight in the morning and I was glad of the light and the fresh air.

'Storm coming in, do you think?' Sharif squinted at mountainous clouds building up over the Channel. 'Just my luck. I left my umbrella at Madame Didier's. I'm staying there, you know. You're acquainted with her, I think?'

'Oh, yes. I'm acquainted with her.'

'Extraordinary woman. When I got the call this morning she was already up. Or perhaps she hadn't been to bed. She offered me Amontillado for breakfast.'

'Albert Camus used to insist upon it.'

'She speaks very highly of you, Iain.' It was the first time he had used my first name. 'Which is encouraging, because it's getting a little difficult to find people around here who speak highly of you. I don't think the Garniers would fall over themselves to sing your praises, for instance. Particularly not Yannick. I doubt he'll be dancing the tango any time soon.'

'Such a loss.'

'He's legally entitled to use force if he finds you on his land, so I expect there'll be some boring questions asked about what you did to him. But then I understand that his firearm isn't licensed, so it will probably all come out amicably in the end.'

Sharif put down his coffee, inspected his nails and buffed his expensive sunglasses.

'I must say I take my hat off to you, Iain. Your conspiracy theory had some truth in it. Something certainly did happen in St Cyriac. And it did involve the Rosens, poor people. You were right about that. That's an apology, in case you didn't recognise it.' He leaned forward in his canvas chair. 'I am puzzled, though. How did you know where to look?'

I took out my sketch, grimy now, and gave it to him. 'This is a copy of my father's map. They must have brought him and his crewman here the night the priest was killed.'

'Brought them here? But I thought—'

'They can only have sailed from here. And he marked where the Rosens lay. Three lines in a box ...'

Sharif frowned at the paper. 'But your father escaped in 1944.'

'Yes. And the Rosens were supposed to have been taken to Auschwitz in 1942 ...'

'Well, well. A little conundrum. How do you explain it?'

'You're the detective.'

'So I am.' He gave me back the map. 'Well, perhaps the SS decided to save themselves some paperwork. Didn't trouble with an arrest. Shot the Rosens on the spot, and left them in the strongroom where Gustave kept his valuables, hoping they'd never be found.'

'And forged the transit order to Drancy.'

Sharif nodded.

'And then my father stumbled across the bodies two years later – have I got this right? – even though everyone says he'd never been to La Division. Oh, and then he didn't mention it to anyone. Is that your theory?'

He shrugged.

'Then there's Mathieu Garnier's witness statement,' I said. 'Why did he lie? Why did these four guys want everyone to think the escape had been from the Vasse, instead of from here? And how come the Garnier family suddenly decided to erase this place the moment I showed up with the map?'

'Excellent questions.' Sharif slung the remains of his coffee into the grass and got to his feet, closing his chair with a snap. 'Perhaps your father knows the answers. Or the saintly Dr Pasqual. Why don't you ask them? And while you're about it, ask yourself what good could possibly come of stirring all this up.'

'Three people are dead,' I said. 'You can't just forget about it. That's been the problem all along: that people have tried to forget about it.'

He stowed the chair neatly in the boot of his glossy Peugeot, and stood there dusting his hands as if he had just completed an hour of physical labour.

'Leave well alone, Iain,' he said. 'You weren't even looking for these people when you came here last night. You were after your legendary diaries. The diaries that will Tell All.' He sighed. 'So you can show me that we're wrong about Serge Baladier.'

'You are wrong about him.'

'Maybe so, but this won't prove it. This has nothing to do with him.' He closed the boot. 'Oh, and by the way – you did come here alone, didn't you? The Garnier brothers seem convinced you had company …'

'What on earth makes them think that?'

He lifted his eyebrows. 'Two torches?'

'I like to be prepared.'

'Your Boy Scout training, no doubt. Just out of interest, how did you get past the dog? The Garniers say he's quite fierce.'

'I give money to a dog charity. I showed him the receipt.'

'Oh, you English. How you make us laugh.'

Two overalled *gendarmes* came out of the ruined farmhouse carrying a stretcher. We both watched as the men crossed to the corner of the paddock where the police vehicles waited.

I got up.

'Be very careful, won't you, Iain?' Sharif said pleasantly. 'You're a smart guy. But a bit too smart, maybe. Good morning to you.'

I didn't attempt to go back into the ruins to pick up my gear. I walked out past the police cars and vans and across the paddock

301

and on through the yard towards the gate, past the small mountain of rusting car wrecks and a white ziggurat of old refrigerators. It was spitting with rain now, the fat drops kicking up the
dust around me.

'Monsieur Madoc?'

Old man Garnier came out of the barn and shambled over to
me. He had always made me nervous, despite his age, but now
he looked shrunken, too small for his greasy coat. He stopped in
front of me, breathing hard, as though the mere effort of crossing the yard had tired him.

'He should've had the *Croix de Guerre*,' he said.

'What?'

'Mathieu. My brother. He earned it. Though I don't expect
you to believe that.'

'It doesn't matter much what I believe, Monsieur Garnier.'

'I didn't know him real well. Funny that, isn't it? Not to know
your own brother. I was much younger than him, and most of
the time he was overseas with the army. But he was a hero to me.
And not just to me.'

I should have let it go, probably, but I was tired and on a short
fuse and I turned on him.

'Your brother signed a witness statement. He said how guilty
he felt that he couldn't help the Rosens. He said how he went
in and turned the stove off for that poor woman, after she was
arrested. And it was a lie, from beginning to end. What kind of
a man would lie about a thing like that?'

Garnier coughed. 'I was just a little kid back then, Monsieur
Madoc. I don't know what happened here. I'm not saying it was
good. But it's not right Mathieu should carry the can for it.' He
shuffled a step closer to me. He was unshaven, and his bristles
were grey against his sallow skin. 'What you've done to Yannick
– he deserved that. I know it. But it's not right what you're
doing to Mathieu. Kick a man who can't fight back. It's not fair.
Someone has to say that.'

He turned and stumped back to his shabby little office.

I walked along the fire trail to the car. I didn't start the engine
at once, but sat listening to the rain drumming on the roof and

watching it run in dusty streaks down the windscreen, carrying the pine needles which had gathered on the roof overnight. The exchange with old Garnier had rattled me. The wind was strong enough now to whip the top branches of the fir trees, and I watched them through the wavering screen until I calmed down a little.

I thought of Serge, hidden away on the launch, and the wind and the tide rocking the hull and making the moorings groan. That wouldn't worry him. He wouldn't be concerned about the sea. He'd be thinking about me, about how I would come to him as he hid there, hungry and alone, and tell him what to do for the best. He had put his trust in me, and when I arrived he would be crouching there inside that swaying hull, trying to second guess what news – what hope – I would bring him.

56

I let myself into the house and snapped on all the lights. I turned on the shower and took off my filthy clothes. As I dropped my jeans onto the tiled floor I heard the clink of metal. I reached into the pocket, drew out Lena Rosen's locket, and put it on the bathroom shelf. I couldn't bring myself to look at it.

I stood under the water at full blast for five minutes.

It didn't help much, not even when I'd towelled myself dry and changed into fresh clothes. I took the locket through to the kitchen and laid it on the table under the light. I turned it slowly in my hand. It appeared to be silver. I took it to the sink and ran the hot tap and rinsed it gently, rubbing at it with my thumb. The accumulated dirt and corrosion of six decades crumbled and swirled against the porcelain. I dried it carefully and took it back to the table.

I could see now that it had a substantial silver case, perhaps originally for a gentleman's pocket watch. I touched the dented metal where the bullet had clipped it. I tried prising the clasp open with my thumbnail but the damage had jammed it shut. I tapped it smartly on the table top, several times, but it remained as solid as an oyster.

I put it on the table and stared at it. The room was dim and the rain had started to trickle in under the tarpaulin which covered the hole in the roof. I found a kitchen knife in the drawer and took it and the locket across the sodden garden to the cabin, hoping the light would be better in there.

I sat at the makeshift desk under the glare of the tablelamp and worked the point of the knife into the clasp of the locket. Losing patience, I twisted hard. The case sprang open and a yellow disc fell with a clatter onto the desktop. I picked it up and held it in the light.

It was a gold sovereign, one edge bent and smeared where the bullet had compressed the soft metal. Otherwise it was in mint condition, and it shone as if it had just been buffed. King George VI's profile, the delicate milling of the edge, and the tiny letters and numerals of date and inscription were all as sharp as the day they had been stamped. As sharp as those on the sovereign Hamelin had given my father. I closed my eyes and opened them again and examined the coin afresh, but its message remained the same.

Madeleine Rosen was supposed to have died in 1942. But around her neck she wore a coin minted in 1944.

I felt dizzy and a little nauseous. The light hurt my eyes and I turned it off and stumbled over to the bed and sat heavily on it, my head in my hands. My mind was full of images which lurched and flickered and would not come to rest. She had vanished in 1942, this girl, and her parents with her. I saw them in my mind's eye, lost and alone, as if in another dimension. And then, two years later, they materialised just long enough to be cut down, in a miserable cell beneath their own home. I didn't know how they had got there. I didn't know where they had been in those two years. But I knew what had happened to them at La Division. And I knew my father had witnessed it.

The rain boomed on the roof of the cabin.

I closed my hand over the sovereign and felt the cold kiss of gold, the only kiss Lena Rosen had enjoyed for over sixty years.

57

I sat up sharply on the bed, convinced that I had overslept. It was gloomy enough in the cabin for the numerals on my watch to stand out like neon, but they showed me it was only six in the evening. I stretched and massaged my neck and shoulder. I had slumped awkwardly against the wall and my muscles were locked stiff.

Outside, the rain was roaring against the shutters and chattering in the downpipes. It was cool in the cabin, even cold. I was hungry and chilled. I rubbed my face hard and tried to wake up.

Then, on the far side of the room, I saw the bulky shape of a man hunched near the model of the launch. I jerked to my feet.

'Hello, Iain,' my father said. He reached across and flicked the light switch, blinding me.

Before I could recover, the door opened and Kate put her head into the cabin. Her hair was in rats' tails and she looked white and strained, but her face filled with relief when she saw me.

'I brought Grandad,' she said.

'Yes, I spotted that.' I squeezed my eyes closed, but the world didn't make much more sense when I opened them. 'How did you get here? And where's your mother?'

'She ... she didn't exactly know I was coming. Not at first, anyway. She found out pretty soon, though. I took her car.'

'You *took* it?'

'I kind of ... stole it.'

'Kate, you haven't got a licence.'

'I only went as far as Portsmouth. Well, I picked up Grandad first, obviously. Then we took the ferry. I called Mum from St Malo. I told her we were fine, but she's … a bit upset.'

'No. Really?'

'She said she'd been trying to call you, but she can't get through.'

'The phone's off the hook.' I shook my head. 'Kate, what did you think you were doing?'

'What did I think *I* was doing?' She tossed her head defiantly. 'I've brought the two of you together. That was supposed to be impossible, wasn't it? Now what are *you* going to do?'

She banged the door behind her so hard that the cabin shook.

I looked across at my father. Neither of us spoke. He took his eyes off mine at last, got to his feet and turned his ponderous attention to the model beside him. He found his glasses inside his hairy jacket, put them on and began tracing the line of the boat's hull, bending to squint through the wheelhouse windows.

'Near perfect,' he said, straightening. 'All bar the Oerlikon, that is.'

'The what?'

'The cannon. The Oerlikon cannon. He's got a left hand magazine on it.'

'For God's sake. Does anybody care about the bloody Oerlikon?'

He faced me. 'The maid said Dominic built this for you. Is that right? He was always good with his hands was Dominic, even as a lad.'

'He didn't build it for me, Dad. He made it for you. He told me I should keep it for you.' I pictured Dominic smiling his soft smile in the sunshine. 'He said you'd come, one day.'

'He knew more than I did, then. But there again, perhaps he always did.' He paused. 'So they came for him at last, did they?'

'They?'

Though he had invited the question, he did not respond to it.

'Not fourteen years old, that boy,' he said. 'They said he wasn't the full quid, but I'll tell you this: he wasn't scared of nothing. Not the shooting, not the priest's screaming and his blood running down the steps into the crypt.'

'Dominic was with you the night Father Thomas was killed?'

'He shamed us all. More loyal and steadfast than any of us.'

Silence gathered in the room. We each waited for the other to make the first move. The rain drummed on the shingles overhead and the cabin creaked like a ship at sea. I could hear the surf bursting against the beach.

'I found the Rosens, Dad. But you knew where they were all along, didn't you?'

'I knew.'

'Because you were there when they were murdered.'

'Yes.'

'You couldn't stop it …'

'I didn't stop it. That's the truth.'

'How could you?' I said. 'But you've blamed yourself for it ever since.'

The locket was still in my hand. I held it up for him to see, the sovereign in my palm beside it.

He was quiet for a while, gazing at it.

'He'd given her that,' he said at last. 'Lucien. She told me so. He gave her the sovereign, after I first brought him over in March. He promised to get them out. All of them. This was his token.'

'But he couldn't do that. Get them out.'

'No. How could he?' His eyes were stony. 'I left him to drown the night he would have brought them to freedom.'

'You tried.'

'Did I?' He took a breath. 'It was later that same night, when Billy and I were taken to the crypt ourselves, that we found the Rosens. They'd been there for nigh on two years.'

Two years. I felt again the clammy and claustrophobic darkness.

'Father Thomas hid them,' I said, and all at once I understood.

'That's right. Before the Jewish round-ups began in '42. Couldn't find a way to smuggle them out after.'

'And Lucien knew they were there all along.'

'Of course he did. He'd helped hide them.'

'So in 1944 he was coming back for them.'

'He fixed it somehow. Got himself sent here. But no matter what he told me or those who sent him, when I brought him back in March of '44, he came to find Lena and her parents. Do you see it now? Lucien was their last hope, and I snuffed that out when I came back to get him.'

My father paused. 'Me and Billy, we were down there with the Rosens for eight weeks after I lost the launch. Eight weeks they nursed us, that girl and her mother. The father helped, too. Billy was in a bad way with the burns. If it hadn't been for the Rosens, I doubt either of us would have survived. And mark this: young Madeleine knew I'd failed Lucien. She knew one way or the other his death was my fault. But she never uttered a word of reproach. Never a word. Instead she'd tell me of the times they'd spent together when they were growing up. The beach. Family picnics. And then, as they got older, learning what was happening between them, making plans for the future. Then she'd tell me how she'd lost him when they went into hiding, and how precious it had been to see him again for that month after I brought him over. She'd thank me for it. *Thank* me! Can you believe that? It went through me like a sword.'

'You did give them that month, Dad.'

'Aye. And took away the rest of their lives.' His eyes closed for a moment. 'She nursed me and Billy like we was her brothers. They all treated us the same. We shared their food. We shared their fear and their hardship. Then the Germans came for the priest, and while we was wondering what was to become of us, those four French lads broke in and took us up to the farmhouse. All five of us, and Dominic tagging along. And in the night ...' His voice locked. 'The boat was too small ... It couldn't take all of us. It could barely take two, and we all knew it. And in the night ...'

'In the night,' I said, 'the Rosen family were pushed down into the cellar and shot.'

He swayed a fraction and I reached out to steady him, but he opened his hands as if to ward me off, as if he could accept no help for this, as if this were something he had to do alone. 'Just one of them done it. The leader.'

'Garnier.'

'I didn't know their names. I didn't wish to. But it was just him. The others never knew it was going to happen. No more did Billy and me.' He gathered himself. 'What became of that one? The leader?'

'He's long dead.'

'He was spared, then. Spared all this.' My father drew himself up and looked me in the eye. 'No, it won't do. I'll not pretend I didn't know something evil was going to happen that night. The girl cried out to me as she was pushed down the steps. She begged me not to forget. And I never have. I never have. I've never forgotten that I didn't raise a finger.'

'What could you have done?'

'I make no excuses for myself. Don't you make none for me.'

'Dad, it wasn't your fault.'

'It was my fault,' he said sharply. 'All my fault. Because I'd abandoned him. I'd abandoned Lucien. It all sprang from that.'

'No. You made a mistake.'

'You're wrong. It wasn't that I didn't try hard enough to save him. I didn't try at all. Can't you get that through your head? I judged him, and condemned him for something he hadn't done.'

'I know that, but at the time—'

'And having condemned him I left him there, out on the Shoals, clinging onto that damned bell. Screaming at me. I didn't even have ears to hear what he was shouting. Not till later.'

'You were under fire.'

'Is that what Billy said? He was staunch, was Billy. Staunch and grateful. But it's not true. I saw Lucien hanging onto that bell-buoy – we all did – and I cruised past him without so much as cutting speed.' He looked at me. 'I could have taken him off, but I left him there to drown. It was only afterwards that the Germans saw us and the shooting started.'

'Dad—'

'And now you know what Lucien wanted, what he was

screaming about. He didn't want to save himself. He'd come out in that rowboat to tell me about the Rosens. He'd come out to beg me to pick them up, off the old jetty at La Division. Father Thomas was going to take them there later that night.'

'No one could have done that.'

'Oh, I could have done it. I was perhaps the only skipper on the South Coast who could have brought her in there, in barely four foot of water. They might all have got free, and that would have been a glorious thing. But in my heart I'd damned him for what I thought he'd done to Sally Chessall, and I left him there screaming, on that bell. And after, when the firing started, I panicked. I took the wheel from MacDonald and ordered full ahead, and got it wrong for once in my arrogant bloody life, the only time it mattered. And we struck. And instead of that glorious thing that might have been, I end up with seven of my lads dead, and Lucien dead, and me and Billy in the crypt with the people I might have saved.' He looked at me. 'I lost most of my crew that night, Iain. And very soon I lost the Rosens. And with them, I lost myself.' He glanced at me. 'And I lost you.'

I reached across and took both his hands in both of mine, and this time he didn't recoil.

'I meant to come back after the War,' he said. 'Find Lena and her parents. Take their bodies from that miserable cellar. Give them back to their people. I thought I could at least do that much, and that's why I drew the map. But I kept thinking of this village, and the people who'd risked themselves for us, and I kept thinking of the harm it would do them, the innocent as well as the guilty. And more than that, I was weak. I couldn't bear that your mother should know. Still, for years I told myself I'd do it one day. Then you were born, and such resolve as I had went out of my world as you came into it. I didn't want you to grow up beneath the burden of such things. I didn't want that to be your legacy.'

He straightened, easing his hands gently from my grip.

'Besides, I'd made promises that night, and they were not to be broken lightly. Not just to ease the weight on my own soul.'

'What promises?'

'Promises to the men who saved us. They had a few words of English between them, and they begged us not to speak of it, for it could help no one. And how could I point the finger of blame at anyone? Me? After what I'd done to Lucien? Without that, none of this would have happened.' He looked past me, out at the storm. 'I'll tell you one thing I learned in my long life. All the vileness that smites this world, it don't spring from Satan and his demons. It springs from ordinary men who fail to do what they know they ought to do.'

'Why have you come here now?'

'Because Dominic's dead. Because the innocent are suffering for the guilty once again, and on into the next generation. Because it's time for this to stop.' He lifted his shoulders and let them fall again. 'And because the maid said you needed me.'

'I've always needed you, Dad.'

The door opened and Kate backed in carrying a tray of coffee mugs. The wind caught the lid of the model's mahogany case and blew it shut with a bang.

'Is it safe?' she said, looking from one of us to the other.

I nodded and took the tray from her.

She closed the door behind her and sat on the bed, still watching us. She was wet through, her hair plastered to her skull and her clothes clinging to her body. She didn't seem to notice.

I took my jacket from the back of the chair and draped it around her shoulders. She didn't seem to notice that either.

'Serge has been here,' she said. It wasn't a question. 'You've seen him.'

'Yes, I have.' I picked up my coffee and drank a little, grateful for its warmth. 'He's on the boat. It's moored up near the point. I'm meeting him there sometime after eight tonight. Then he wants to go to the police.'

'In that case we'll all go to fetch him,' Kate said with calm certainty. 'And we'll all go to the police. And he'll be free.'

I put my coffee cup down. 'It's not as simple as that—'

'Yes, it is,' she snapped, cutting across me. 'Grandad's here now. I didn't bring him all this way for *Auld Lang Syne*. I brought him so the two of you could go and tell that Algerian

312

cop about what happened all those years ago. Then everyone will know why Dominic was killed. And they'll know it wasn't Serge. Won't they?'

She started to cry then, the tears running soundlessly down her face, and I saw how very near the edge she had been. I made a move towards her, but she waved me impatiently away. There was a tense little silence. Over to my right, my father folded open the model's case again and bent low over it, examining it minutely.

I said, 'Sweetheart, I know what you hoped would come of this. But we have a problem here.'

'A *problem*?' she said, losing her fragile control. 'It's simple, isn't it? It'll all be in the open, won't it? They'll know it wasn't Serge who hurt Dominic. It was someone trying to find the diaries, like you always said!'

'But Kate, I don't have the diaries. I can't even prove they ever existed. And without them there's no motive for anyone to have hurt Dominic.'

She stared at me in desperation. 'So what's Serge supposed to do? Cower on that bloody boat until they find him?'

I reached for her wrist and tried to take her in my arms, but she writhed away from me.

'Kate—'

We all heard it. A sharp click and the snap of a spring releasing. Kate stepped back from me, letting her arms drop to her sides. We both turned towards my father. He was crouched over the model. The wheelhouse section had folded back to open the centre of the hull.

He lifted them out reverently, and laid them on the table beside the boat. Small, black leather books. Three of them. I stepped up to the table and picked one up. Gold numbers were embossed on the spine: 1942. I riffled the leaves. A little dust escaped. The pages were feint lined, and Father Thomas's tight and crabby handwriting filled them densely.

I looked at my father.

'I knew that Oerlikon was wrong,' he said.

I turned to Kate. She stood with my jacket rucked over one shoulder, her eyes huge.

'Go and find him,' I said. 'Go and get him off the boat and bring him back here.'

'Yes.' She took a couple of deep breaths, steadying herself. 'Yes, of course.' She walked to the door and opened it against the wind. 'What are you going to do, Dad?'

'Your grandfather and I are going to church.'

58

The rain drove horizontally across the village from the sea, and the beech trees in the churchyard surged against the sky. I checked my watch. It was just gone seven and what light there was had begun to fail. We stopped at the iron gate. The west window of the church glowed like the stern gallery of a man-of-war. I glanced at my father, but his face revealed nothing, and neither of us spoke. We walked the last few metres up the path.

I caught the west door before the wind did, and closed it gently behind us. We stepped into the body of the church. No one noticed us at first, though there were twenty or so men and women there, and the space was full of quiet activity and soft light. They were preparing the church for Dominic's funeral. Candles were already lit, bright little flags of flame fluttering in the eddies which chased us in. More were massed near the altar steps. The taste of hot wax hung in the air, and behind it the smell of damp clothing.

My father set off down the aisle without waiting for me, his stick clacking against the flagstones. I moved up beside him, aware of a buzz of surprise. They registered my presence, but I was not the focus of their attention. Perhaps they wondered who this gnarled old man was, with his coarse coat and his stick. Or perhaps they already knew.

My father reached the end of the aisle, and sat down in the front pew, staring straight ahead, his hands crossed over the head of his stick. For all the attention he paid to anyone else, he might have been alone in an empty church.

Felix was up at the altar on his knees, his back to us. He rose slowly and turned, his robes swinging around him. His eyes flicked from my face, down to my father's, and back to mine. I stepped close to him.

'So he came at last,' Felix said, so quietly that only I could hear.

'Yes.'

Felix passed his hand over his pate and sighed. 'What am I to say to you, Iain? I'm happy for you that he's come. I know what that means to you.'

'But?'

'Do you suppose it's going to make any difference now? What either of you say? It's a bad idea for you to be here tonight. Please, go home.'

He turned his back on me. The dismissal was so unmistakable that when I didn't move there was a brief murmur of concern from the body of the church. They hadn't been able to hear what we were saying, but they could read the body language well enough and they didn't like it.

I glanced round at them. I glimpsed familiar faces, hostile faces, tilted up towards me – Daniel, Freycinet, Bonnard, old Garnier. Leaning against a pillar, watchful and sardonic, I caught sight of Inspector Sharif. More people were coming in now. I could hear their feet on the flagstones and their whispered questions and the answers that came hissing back to them. I blocked my mind to that. I took the diaries out of my jacket and laid them gently on the white cloth of the altar table between the communion chalice and the crucifix. Felix looked down at them. His expression did not change, but I saw hope die somewhere behind his eyes.

'So you finally found what you were looking for,' he said.

'I think we've all been looking for these, Felix. I think you've been looking harder than anyone else.'

He held my gaze.

'Tell me you didn't mean to hurt him, Felix. Tell me it was an accident.'

He held out for a moment longer, but then, quite suddenly, his resistance crumbled. He groped for the rail and sat down untidily on the altar steps.

'Iain ...'

'Something wrong, Father?' Sergeant Freycinet called, his voice hard. 'Want us to get rid of him?'

'Get on with your work,' Felix snapped back with more force than I thought he could muster just then. 'Please. All of you. This is a private matter.'

The moment passed. Sounds of grudging activity began to build up again behind me.

Felix licked dry lips and looked up at me. 'Have you known for long?'

'Not long.'

'How?'

I hunkered down in front of him. 'Who could have known for sure that Dominic was going to talk to me about the diaries the day of the carnival? You knew, Felix, because he asked Father Thomas for guidance. When I came to see you here, the day after I'd found him, his special candle was in Father Thomas's chapel. He'd prayed out loud, the way he always did, and you overheard him. You thought he was going to give me those journals. You thought they'd be in his flat.' I looked at him. 'Felix, Felix. Was it worth it?'

'Of course it wasn't worth it. How can you ask that?'

'So how did it happen?'

He screwed his eyes closed and breathed deeply. 'I gave him some wine. I told him it was all right to drink it, and he believed me. I thought ... I'd get him drunk, get him to tell me where the diaries were. He'd pass out, and I'd take them. It wouldn't matter what he said after that, nobody'd believe him.'

'You knew he couldn't drink.'

'I thought a couple of glasses wouldn't hurt, and I figured that was all it would take. And it worked – he started to tell me. In the boat, he said. He kept saying that. But then he had some kind of a fit. He fell and struck his head on the edge of the desk. I got him onto the bed. I waited with him, tried to help, but the fits wouldn't stop. I went to get Madame Duquesne. But just as I got to the door, he shrieked out. It was the most horrible sound ...' He swallowed. 'And when I got back to him, he was dead. Just like that. It all happened in a couple of minutes.'

'In the boat. You thought he meant they were in one of the models?'

He nodded. 'I just didn't know which one ...'

'You were right. They were in the boat he gave me.'

'My God.' He closed his eyes. 'He didn't know how to tell a lie, poor Dominic. Afterwards I decided he must have meant they were in the launch. When I went to look, you'd got there before me. Remember how we met there? I had to give you that story about changing the lock. Not that it mattered. If the diaries were hidden in that launch, neither of us was going to find them.'

'And the money?'

'I went a little crazy when Dominic died. I had some idea it would look like a burglary.' He reached up and grabbed my wrist. 'Iain, believe me. I never meant any of this to happen. I wouldn't have hurt Dominic for the world. And it never crossed my mind they'd blame Serge.'

'You didn't come forward to clear him, though, did you?'

He gazed at me in anguish. 'I won't try to excuse that. How could I? I'd have come forward if they *had* arrested him. I like to think I would.'

I stared at him for a long time, at the smile wrinkles around his eyes sagging in despair.

'Felix, you bastard. I trusted you.'

'I know,' he said, and his voice firmed as he said it. 'Help me up.'

I took his arm and he got to his feet. He brushed down his vestments.

He said, 'There's just one thing I need of you. I'll tell Sharif what happened to Dominic, that it was my fault, that I wasn't man enough to own up to it. But destroy the diaries. Let the past rest in peace ...'

I picked up the three black notebooks from the altar and weighed them in my hand.

'Please, Iain. Please. For my father's sake. You love him too, don't you? And this has all been for him. Everything I've done has been to protect him. Hasn't he earned that?' He kept his eyes on me, but shouted over my shoulder. 'Inspector Sharif? Could I have a word with you?'

The words echoed through the stone vaulting. The hall fell silent again, and I heard the detective making his way down the aisle towards us.

'Please.' Felix gripped my arm. 'I beg you.'

I heard Sharif climbing the altar steps. I slipped the diaries into my pocket.

Sharif came up beside me.

'Father Felix has something to say to you,' I said.

I stood back a little as they spoke. Down in the body of the church the people were gathered in small suspicious knots. Their eyes were hard when they met mine.

My father still stared straight ahead, his hands knotted like hickory. As I looked down at him, I heard the handle turn on the door of Father Thomas's chapel. Dr Pasqual walked out of the darkness and into the space in front of the pews, as if stepping onto a stage. He saw my father at once and stopped a couple of metres away, standing very erect, staring at him. There must have been some reaction from the congregation in the body of the church, but I wasn't aware of it. I was aware only of this small, neat old man standing to attention in the light thrown by the banks of candles which flanked the altar steps.

Beside me Felix and Sharif stopped speaking. In a wrenching voice, Felix cried, 'Papa!'

But the old man didn't seem to hear him. He moved towards my father, who had risen to his feet and stood there motionless. Dr Pasqual looked up into my father's creased face, and when he spoke it was in a precise and elegant English I had not heard him use before.

'Pilot Officer George Madoc. Welcome back.'

'I never thought to meet you again,' my father said. 'Not in this life.'

'I know. But I've been waiting for you. And for the message you bring me.' Dr Pasqual smiled sadly. 'And what is that message, Pilot Officer Madoc?'

My father looked into his eyes. 'That it won't ever go away,' he said. 'That we were fools to try to hide it. That we're all to blame.'

Dr Pasqual took a small, sharp breath, and his composure faltered. 'I was so very frightened,' he said, quietly. 'So very frightened.'

'You were not alone in that,' my father told him. 'No more you are now.'

Dr Pasqual touched my father's hands where they lay locked over the head of his stick, then went down like a marionette when its strings are cut.

My father reacted with an agility I didn't expect from him. His stick clattered onto the floor as he caught Dr Pasqual awkwardly in his arms. I heard gasps from the front pews and before I could move people had clumped around the two figures. A woman – it might have been Marie-Louise – was screaming for someone to call an ambulance, and I saw Bonnard talking urgently into a mobile.

I tried to get closer. My father knelt with Dr Pasqual's head in his lap, while Daniel Bourgogne tugged at the fallen man's collar. Dr Pasqual's lips were blue and his face the colour of parchment. There was a lot of shouting, echoes of shock and distress amplified in the stone cavern of the church. Sharif turned away from Felix and strode past me.

Felix still stood by the altar steps, one hand on the rail. His gaze was directed away up the aisle and over the ranks of pews, now empty of people and littered with fallen prayer books, hymn sheets, discarded coats.

I walked over to him.

'Is he dead?' he asked. He did not meet my eye.

'I don't know, Felix. They're getting help.'

'If he died now,' Felix said, 'he'd die without ever knowing what happened at Dominic's.' He clutched at my arm. 'That would be best, wouldn't it?'

I turned unhappily away from him, letting his hand slip from my arm. On the edge of the clustered group I could see Sharif, his charcoal cashmere coat slung over his shoulders, talking on his phone. He snapped it closed, and began moving people aside, speaking calmly to them, reasserting order.

Sergeant Freycinet was in the porch, marshalling help to wedge open the main doors. The wind came swooping in and riffled through the pages of the prayer books and made the candle flames shiver, so that shadows loomed and shrank between the pillars.

It must have taken at least a few minutes, but it seemed that almost at once a siren was wailing and spikes of blue light, dulled by the stained glass, were lancing into the church. Four *pompiers* in blue uniforms came clattering up the aisle and took over, moving the helpers back, easing the old man from my father's lap and setting down boxes of equipment beside him. Almost at once, two SAMU specialists hurried in after them. One of them put his ear to Dr Pasqual's chest. Another drew Sharif aside and they held a low, urgent conversation.

A minute or two later they lifted the stretcher, and bore the old man out. One of the *pompiers* held high a bag of liquid and light glinted on a plastic oxygen mask. Everyone followed the little cortège out into the night. There was a brief press around the door as they funnelled through and then they were gone and someone closed the door behind them. I heard an engine rev, and the siren slowly receded. The candle flames steadied and it grew quiet again.

My father was seated once more on the front pew, his hands again locked around his stick. I took a step towards him as Sharif reappeared. The big west door crashed open again and the wind seemed to carry Kate in with it. She flew up the aisle towards us with raindrops spinning off her clothes and hair. She was filthy and scratched and frantic.

'It's not there!' she shouted. 'The boat! It's gone!' She stood with her fists clenched. 'The boat is gone!'

I turned back towards Felix and saw bewilderment, suspicion, horror pass across his face. I grabbed him by the folds of his splendid vestments.

'What have you done?'

His mouth came open and he began to breathe rapidly. I shook him hard. Sharif tried to step between us but I brushed him aside.

'Serge is on the launch, Felix,' I said. 'He's there right now, waiting for me. What have you done?'

'I've cut it free!' he hissed into my ear, as though the words had been forced out of him under pressure. He looked wildly at me, sweat running down his face. 'I cut the moorings. I set it adrift.'

'Why, for God's sake?' I shook him again and heard his teeth clack together.

'I thought the diaries were on board. I told you that ... So I waited for the storm and I cut the moorings and I thought the damned boat would be on the Shoals in an hour and that would be the end of it, at last.'

'What's he saying?' my father called. He got to his feet.

Sharif said, 'I'll get the coastguard.' He pulled out his phone and snapped it open.

'What did he say?' my father demanded again, and grabbed my arm. 'The little priest. What did he say?'

'The launch is adrift,' I told him in English. 'He cut the moorings. The boy's aboard.'

'When? When did he do this?'

'Since an hour.' Felix spoke in English too, directly to the old man. He seemed to come back to his senses as he did so, as if the effort needed to communicate in a foreign language had focused him. 'An hour ago. No, not so much. Three quarters, only.'

Kate looked wildly around the group of us. 'He's going to drown!'

Nobody answered her. She ran to my father and seized his arm with both hands. He did not look at her.

'Don't you understand?' she shouted. 'Serge is going to drown while we stand here!'

Felix stared dazedly from Kate to my father and back to me, perhaps realising for the first time what he had done. He said: 'The currents. It will be ... on the Shoals ...'

'Not yet,' my father said. 'Not with an onshore blow like this.'

Kate shook at his arm like a child trying to shake an oak tree. 'Grandad!'

I released Felix from my grip and turned to her. 'Kate, Inspector Sharif is calling out the coastguard right now.'

My father said, 'From where?'

Sharif looked up from the phone and answered for me. 'Roscof. They have fast ships. And …' he circled his forefinger rapidly until he found the word ' … helicopters.'

'Not fast enough,' my father said. 'Roscof's too far.'

He put his arm around Kate's shoulders as if to shield her from this truth.

'Please, Grandad,' she whispered, and, burying her face in his coat, she began to sob. 'Please. Please.'

She wanted more than mere comfort from him, I knew that, she wanted something that only he could give. I didn't know what that something was – perhaps I didn't let myself know it just then.

My father kept his eyes fixed on mine and there was silence in the church except for the moaning of the wind outside and the girl's soft keening. Then with his free hand my father smacked his stick down hard against the paving.

'Listen. Once the tide starts to ebb, the Vasse runs out at eight knots, maybe ten after this rain. It sweeps round until it comes up against the southern end of the Shoals. It's like a living thing, that current. It tries to get over the Shoals. It tries to reach the open sea. With a storm like this, it'll be a cauldron out there. Nothing can survive in it.'

Sharif looked at him. 'You know this coast?'

'If it hasn't changed in the last sixty years,' my father said. 'That current will carry anything with it, and deliver it up to destruction on the Shoals sure as fate, and there'll be an end to it. But with luck it will take some time, with this wind against it.'

Kate stopped sobbing abruptly and turned her stained face up to him.

'How much time?' Sharif asked my father.

'Maybe long enough to get a boat out to her from St Cyriac before she strikes, if it put to sea now.'

'That is not possible,' Sharif said. 'A man could never find it in this darkness.'

'A man might,' the old man told him. 'If a man knew where to look.'

Sharif narrowed his eyes. I could hear his mobile squawking in his ear, demanding his reply. In the end he shook his head. 'We have no vessel here. We have no ...' he groped for the word again, 'we have no sailors. None who will go out in such a sea.' He walked away up the aisle, talking rapidly into his phone as he went.

Beside me, Felix slid to the floor, his head in his hands.

'Grandad,' Kate said softly.

Her voice sounded odd to me and I looked sharply at her. I could not see her face.

'There's nothing to be done, my maid,' my father said, not meeting her eyes. 'Except perhaps to pray.'

'But I love him, Grandad,' Kate persisted in that same quiet voice, 'I love him, and I can't lose him again.'

A cold fingertip ran down my spine. For an instant it was as if someone else was speaking, not Kate, in a voice only half recognised from long ago. I saw that the same strangeness had touched my father too, for he looked down into her face for the first time, and as he did so his eyes grew distant and hollow.

I stepped up to them. I took Kate roughly by the shoulders and moved her to one side.

'I can get us a boat,' I said.

59

Henri felt inside his apron and tossed the leather key wallet onto the bar.

'Like I told you,' he said, 'I don't know how to make it ... *go*.'

My father picked up the key.

I said, 'He knows how to make it go.'

I turned to follow the old man and reached the door.

'So I was right,' Henri called to me. 'It's in the blood.'

My father was already moving along the quayside, the wind whipping at his coat. I hurried past him, hoping to outrun my fear, and jumped down onto the slatted walkway between the boats. They tossed and moaned each side of me, and the black water slapped eerily beneath my feet.

I stepped onto the deck of *The Gay Dog* before I could think twice and started to rip the tarpaulin cover from the cockpit. Even here, within the shelter of the harbour walls, the little antique cruiser heaved, jostling the boats to either side. I closed my mind to it. My father tossed down the keys and I fumbled through them until I found one that would unlock the cover over the control panel. I opened it and flicked switches at random. Lights sprang on, revealing the inside of the cabin with its polished timber and brass.

My father stepped into the cockpit beside me and checked the controls. He planted himself at the wheel, turned the key and the engine grumbled into life. I leaned forward and placed my hands on the cabin roof. I could feel sweat mixing with the rain and running down the sides of my neck and inside my clothes. I became aware of my father watching me, waiting, his hand on the throttle lever, his white hair plastered to his skull.

'Get back up there and cast off,' he said, 'or we'll take the dock with us.'

I went unsteadily to the edge of the cockpit. If I climbed off I didn't think I could summon the courage to get aboard again. I could feel my father's eyes on me. I heard the rasping of my own breath. I reached for the lip of the dock as it lurched up past me, got my hands on the wet timber.

'Stay there,' Felix shouted from above me.

He was crouched over the bollards, tugging at the mooring, his sodden robes hanging around him. I could see other figures hurrying down the quay behind him. I let go and fell back into the cockpit while he cast off the stern line and freed the bow rope. Felix walked forward a couple of steps, taking the tension in the line, guiding the bow out between the other vessels. He hesitated, and I knew it was in his mind to take that last small step down into the cockpit beside me. But then I saw him shake his head, defeated. He tossed the wet line down at my feet and stepped back. I met his eyes, and saw nothing but pain in them.

My father eased open the throttle. We slid quickly out between the rocking boats and in a moment were thudding through broken water at the harbour mouth, the beacons painting us alternately ruby and emerald. When we were clear the old man pulled back the throttle and the cruiser surged forward, chopping through the swells. The engine note climbed and the bow lifted and spume flew up in sheets.

I crouched in the cockpit, clutching the edge of the locker. I could smell diesel, and feel the juddering of the engine beneath me. The sky was wild with torn clouds and the moon plunged like a silver horseman through cannon smoke. The boat pitched and the world spun and my head beat like a drum and I retched a couple of times.

When I looked up again I saw that my father was standing braced against the wheel, gazing along the elegant curve of the cabin roof, his face creased against the spray which lashed over the low windshield mounted there. He took his eyes from the sea ahead and looked down at me, and I was conscious under that steady gaze of how I must appear to him, huddled here, sick and terrified. Some shackle in my mind abruptly snapped. I stood up, and gripped the rail on the cabin roof, and turned to face the bow, where the buxom figurehead was plunging in and out of the swell. I glanced back. The harbour wall was receding over black water, silhouetted against the lights of the village.

The wind burst open the cabin door. I heard glass smash and a rattan tray came clattering out between us and was whipped overboard. I dragged the door shut and latched it as the boat plunged again and green water sluiced over the cabin roof and mounded against the Perspex screen. The bow rose again, and I saw for the first time the line of white surf far ahead, luminous against a graphite sky.

I shouted, 'How will we find her in this?'

'If she stays afloat there's a chance we'll see her against the white water.' My father gripped the wheel, glanced sideways at me. 'It'll be calmer here for a space,' he called over the wind, and indeed the confusion of the inshore waters had settled a little and the boat was moving now to some sort of rhythm. 'When we get close, it'll grow rougher again. But we shall manage.'

I nodded. The wind buffeted me, and on the bow the figure-head plunged and rose, grinning idiotically.

'It was Madeleine Rosen I heard,' I told him.

'What?'

'It was Lena. I know that now.' I raised my voice. 'Out on the sea that day. I heard her as you held me, just the way you heard her. I was eight years old. I thought it was all in my mind.'

My father shook the water off his face. He stared forward over the cabin into the darkness and spray. A wave came rearing out of the blackness and broke like a bomb over the foredeck, sluicing over both of us as we clung on. I choked and spat out salt water. A second and larger wave smacked into us and for a second I was sure we were going over. As I clambered upright I saw that my father had slid down onto one knee under the force of the water and was gasping, struggling to haul himself up again, the wheel skidding under his grip.

I shouldered past him and took the wheel. He groped his way to his feet and clutched at it again but I shoved him roughly aside. 'Get out of the way, you crazy old bastard.'

He stood back and gripped the rail, steadying himself, breathing heavily. 'Take her up into the wind, then,' he growled at me.

'Do what?'

'Starboard a couple of points. Take her starboard.'

I looked at him. 'Left or right?'

Then the stars ahead were blotted out and I found myself fighting with the wheel, instinctively bringing the bow round so that we rose crazily up the wave and came over and corkscrewed and twisted through it into a few seconds of comparative calm.

'Here,' my father said, quite gently, and he placed his big rough hands over mine. 'Here. Let me show you.'

I stared straight ahead into the wind. 'You picked a fine time to start teaching me, Dad.'

'I know it.' His hands guided mine. 'Maybe you wouldn't have listened before.'

'You never gave me the chance,' I shouted, suddenly furious with him. 'You pushed me away at every turn.'

The boat writhed under us, thudding forward into heaving water. His hands tightened over mine, edging the wheel round a fraction.

'It's true enough,' he said at last. 'I was wrong. I own it.'

'Then why?' Our lashed faces were just inches apart in the light through the cabin doors. 'Why?'

'It was Callum,' he said, simply.

My anger evaporated in an instant and was replaced by bewilderment. 'My brother?'

'Your brother who was taken.'

'What are you talking about?'

'That's how it settled in my mind, at least. And perhaps it was so. Callum was taken from your mother and from me at his birth, that little child. That was my punishment. To suffer and to see your poor mother suffer, whom I loved better than myself.'

'So you turned away from *me*?'

'I couldn't let you be taken from me as Callum had been. Don't you see? Out on the water that day when you were little I so nearly lost you. I knew then you'd never be safe with me. No matter what it cost me, no matter what it cost you, I had to turn away from you.'

We both stared at one another in silence. The wind screamed around us, but it passed somehow unnoticed for those few moments, as if we were sealed inside a glass dome and its force could not touch us.

'Left or right,' he repeated at last, as if in wonder. 'Jesus Christ Almighty!' And all at once he began to laugh, a huge, booming laugh I hadn't heard since I was a little child. 'My son!' he bellowed, and he turned his shining face up to the swinging stars and shouted again, 'This is my son, who doesn't know port from starboard!'

He wrenched back the throttle with one hand and swung the wheel with the other so that the boat sat down in the water and – his laughter still ringing out into the night – he took her in a long curve towards the bar of white.

The breaking water showed clearly now, not so far ahead, and my father throttled back. I heard and felt it too: the dull boom of the swells driving into the submerged banks. The moon rode free for a moment and in its light I glimpsed the floor of the sea, dark sand just a couple of metres below, a shadowy and alien landscape canting wildly beneath the boat.

The Gay Dog's hull thumped from one roller to the next. I stared ahead into the moaning darkness. The boat yawed and threw us together, and my father's arm came round me, and for a few seconds we clung there.

'The light,' he said gruffly. 'We'll only have one chance.'

He shoved me away from the wheel and I found the switch and the spotlight on the cabin roof shot a trembling finger of white light out into the spray. I gripped the handle and panned it. The sea ahead was a seething cauldron of white, with nothing but blackness beyond.

A sheet of surf broke clear over a bank perhaps a hundred

metres ahead. My father throttled back and the cruiser rocked wildly in the creaming water. Twice the keel touched the sand but each time the old man twisted the wheel and blipped the throttle and she was clear again. There were more of them ahead, black humps of exposed shoal and acres of broken water.

I twisted the spotlight on its mounting. The beam bored into a wall of water which was suddenly there, hanging over us, and then it crashed down, throwing the cruiser so far over that I felt myself weightless and falling. The cabin roof came up fast and clubbed me above the right eye and I tasted blood.

I shook my head, trying to clear it, failing. Beside me the old man was fighting with the wheel and losing the struggle while water sluiced over us. I was on the floor of the cockpit with my face against the cabin window. I could see seawater slopping from side to side in the ruined elegance behind it, a rocking tide of books, ornaments, sodden watercolours floating from their frames.

My father's hand locked onto my shoulder. He was shouting, cursing, though I couldn't make out the words. I got to my knees and tried to concentrate. I could see my blood dropping onto the cabin roof in front of me. Blood was running down my face and into my eyes too. There was a lot of it. I felt no pain, but I knew something was badly wrong.

I hauled myself up the side of the cabin and groped for the spotlight. The beam was poking uselessly at the sky. I fumbled it down again, until it lanced out over the black water, and I tried to remember what I was looking for in the darkness.

I heard it then. It was hard to be sure at first, my head was so full of noise and confusion. But there it came again. The steady and sonorous tolling of a bell.

'You hear that?' I grabbed my father's arm. 'There. Again. It's over there!' I flung out my hand. I could hear it clearly now, from slightly inshore of our course.

He looked at me strangely.

'Can't you hear it?' I cried. 'Can't you hear that?'

I clutched for the wheel. I no longer quite knew what I was doing. He swatted me aside, but he swung the bow in the direction I pointed and pulled back the throttle and the cruiser ploughed forward between the banks, dangerously fast. The keel cracked against something beneath us and the boat canted and slid free and churned onward again.

2548 lay silhouetted against the white water. She had been driven hard up onto the shoal, and her back was broken, but most of her hull was out of the sea and tilted to one side, so that she looked almost as she had the first time I had ever seen her. Her stern was still in the water and the breakers were smashing against her and pouring in through the splintered hull, but she was resisting bravely, stubborn to the last. Beside her, just clear of the bow, the boy stood chest high in the sea, one hand hooked through the launch's riven planking, the other stretched desperately towards us.

My father ran the cruiser against the sand and Serge was hidden by the swinging bow and its absurd figurehead. A big sea swept right in behind us and lifted the stern and I had to clutch the gunwale to stay upright. I heard the boy scream and I ran up the pitching deck and leaned over the side, stretching out over the heaving water.

The boat tilted as her keel rolled against the shoal. For a moment, only his hands were visible above the water, clutching like claws at the night sky. I grabbed at him and missed, my strength ebbing away and din and confusion crowding back into my brain. The sea drained back and he stood there half engulfed in the shoal, staring up at me in terror, his hair whipping around his face.

'Take the wheel,' the old man bellowed at me down the length of the boat.

I looked desperately back at him. The boat pitched again, her bow jammed up against the bank as the seas drove in under her, lifting her, hauling her back and swinging her. There was nothing but white surf below me now.

'Take the wheel, dammit!' my father roared again.

This time I obeyed. I dragged myself back up to the cockpit and I took the wheel, astounded at the life and strength of it under my hands. The old man knocked the throttle lever into reverse and I heard the engine scream and race and I guessed the screw was half out of the water. The blades touched, and we juddered back. I saw a pair of hands come groping out of the sea and grip the figurehead and cling there. I swore and fought for control.

Then my father's arm was around my shoulder and his rough face was against mine. 'Take her home, my boy,' he said. 'You take her home now.'

'Dad!'

I clutched for him, but he was already walking easily up the slope of the deck. When he reached the bow he turned and smiled at me in the glare of the spotlight, lifted both arms, and stepped backwards into the sea. I saw Serge lifted in lightly over the gunwale, to fall coughing and retching on the deck. Then a monstrous swell burst over our bows and we were shoved back off the shoal. As the screw caught I could see nothing up ahead but a mountain of crashing water.

The silhouette of the figurehead seemed to tremble and dissolve and reform in front of my eyes. I spun the wheel and jammed it against me and looked back. The old launch was collapsing as I watched, the timbers cracking under the weight of the seas which piled against her.

60

Chantal was asleep on the green plastic couch beside the bed, her hair shining in the moonlight. I watched her for a long time, and then rolled my head a little to look out of the high and unfamiliar hospital window. The wind was still restless, and the glass was streaked with rain, but I could see that the storm had all but blown itself out.

I moved my head again, could feel a heaviness, a tightness, on one side of my skull. I put my hand up and felt a wad of dressing. It didn't seem to hurt much. I tested my memory: the glaring lights of Casualty, the rumble of the gurney, a nurse barking questions at me and confusing me by doing so in English. Blue lights. And before that, the knot of people by the shore, some of them in the water, catching hold of the boat, catching hold of me, a glimpse of Sharif in his swirling cashmere coat with the sea up to his thighs.

And before that …

Yes, my memory worked all right.

'Welcome back,' Chantal said. She got up from the couch, moved a chair next to the bed and buried her face into the bed-clothes over my chest. I rested my hand on her hair.

She looked up, her eyes shining. 'They haven't found him, *chéri*.'

'I'm not sure he wanted to be found,' I said.

I took her hand and stroked it. It seemed she was the one who needed comfort. 'Serge?'

'Exposure. Shock. But he'll be fine. Kate's reinvented herself as Florence Nightingale.'

'And Felix?'

'They've taken him in. I think maybe they thought he might … do something stupid.' She hesitated. 'His father isn't likely to last the night.'

'Where is he?'

'Here. Upstairs.'

Neither of us said anything for a while, then I peeled back the bedclothes and swung my feet onto the floor.

'What do you think you're doing?'

But she didn't expect an answer to that, and she sat and watched me as I stood up. I felt frail and disembodied and I gripped the steel bed end, feeling the chill of the metal, grateful for it.

'Go easy,' she said.

I padded into the corridor. Blue light glowed from the nurses' station, but I could see no sign of life there. I started up the stairs. I could feel the effort of the climb at once, and I took it very slowly, leaning hard on the rail. I pushed open the swing doors that gave onto the top floor landing. At the far end of a long corridor, barred with moonlight, was another nurses' station. A couple of figures with their backs to me were leaning against the desk and I could hear hushed conversation and soft laughter.

Dr Pasqual was in the second room on the right. The door was ajar. I opened it silently. He looked birdlike, far smaller even than I remembered. They had dispensed with the oxygen mask, but he was hooked up to a drip, and there was a monitor of some sort flickering on a stand beside him. I sat on the edge of the bed. I had thought he was unconscious, but he moved his head.

'My son …' The words were barely audible.

I said nothing.

'It's so dark,' he whispered, though the room was brilliant with moonlight.

He breathed deeply, and settled again. I sensed him gathering what remained of his strength.

Suddenly he clutched at my hand. 'God forgive me, for I've never forgiven myself. But I used up all the courage I had on the bridges at Saumur. I never had much, and I spent it all there.' He swallowed. 'We all knew the Rosens couldn't escape. They knew it too. The boat was so small. If they'd been captured, the whole

334

of St Cyriac would have paid the price. What was I to do?'

'You killed them,' I said. 'Not Mathieu Garnier. You.'

'I tried to protect the village – from the Germans, from the Milice, from Vichy itself. Even from the demands of the Resistance. I tried so hard to hold St Cyriac together. And it would all have come to nothing. They all knew that. Yet when it came to it, none of them – not that ruffian Bonnard, not Le Toque, not even Mathieu – none of them could do it.' He paused. 'And it could make no difference to me by then.'

'No *difference*?'

'I was already going to burn in hell.'

My knuckles whitened on the rail of his bed. I said, 'The Germans didn't come to the church that night, did they?'

'You have to understand. The Germans were everywhere along our coast as the Allies were coming ashore in Normandy. They were desperate, their backs to the wall. They were ruthless to any hint of resistance. Oh, that was when our war was at its most brutal. Our only chance was for Thomas to surrender the Rosens. He'd had them there for two years, but it could not go on. Can you imagine what would have happened to the village if he'd been caught hiding them? I pleaded with him. We'd found a small boat. I told Thomas that. We could help the two British airmen. But the Jews? That was out of the question. We had to settle for what was possible, I said. We had to compromise. Everyone had to compromise. It was war.' He moistened his lips. 'He would not give them up. I begged him. But he refused. I had no choice. Do you understand, my boy?' He rolled his head towards me in the darkness. 'None of us had any choice.'

The door swung open and the nurse gave a little gasp. 'You mustn't be here!' she said. 'I'll get into the most terrible trouble. You shouldn't be here!'

I held onto his hand for a few moments more, until I was sure he no longer knew whether I was there or not. The nurse fussed around me, shooing me away. Finally, I backed out of the room and walked away. Before I reached the swing doors I heard the monitor beep. The nurse put her head out of the room and called softly and urgently to her colleague.

61

An enormous van was parked in the drive, and two heavily muscled removals men were making a meal of carting out our few boxes and cases. Chantal had spent her morning alternately shouting at them and making them coffee.

I retreated to the cabin. It was pleasant here, with the birds squabbling under the eaves. This room – my father's room – with its scent of pine, its makeshift desk, and Dominic's model of 2548, was the only corner of this property I knew I would miss. I sat down next to the model, marvelling again at its intricacy. Every plank of its deck was perfect, every cleat and radio antenna. I peered in through the wheelhouse window once again at that small bearded figure behind the wheel.

The door opened and the foreman stuck his head in. 'We're just about done here …'

I swung round on him. 'Ten minutes, OK?'

'Sure. Sure.' He backed off, lifting his hands. 'No problem. No problem at all.'

I turned back to the model, touched the Oerlikon magazine with my fingertip, pressed more firmly. The wheelhouse section sprang open. I lifted out the diary for 1944, and flicked through the pages until I came to the priest's last entry.

Monday 13 June
The Allies are pouring ashore in Normandy, and the Germans cannot stop them. The end must be soon. At least, we must pray for that, my charges and I, for the sake of France, for the sake of the future, for the sake of peace.

But not for ourselves. It will be too late for us, and we no longer

deceive ourselves on that point. Pasqual hounds me night and day,
begging, threatening. He would see this innocent family sent to the
deathcamps so that the rest of us can sit safe here until the Allies
come. But how would we be able to face them, our liberators, if we
betrayed our trust? What kind of people would they have fought to
make free?

Poor Pasqual. It has broken him, this war. Very soon he will
collapse entirely, and in his disintegration we will all be brought down.

There's not a bright day nor a dark night that I do not curse
myself for my foolishness. If I had listened to Rachel Rosen earlier
perhaps we might already have saved them. Now my only consolation
is that I have preserved the life of young Madeleine long enough for
her to be touched by love and hope once again, however fleetingly.

I came upon Madeleine last night, beneath the tiny window in the
east wall of the crypt. This is where she would lie with young Robert
during that one short month, before he lost his life trying to find a
way out for all of us. From where they lay, perhaps they were able to
glimpse the stars, and dream of freedom. Robert once gave her a love
token of sorts, an English gold coin, which she had placed in an old
watch case of her father's. This lay open on her lap as she slept there
last night, her hands joined over it. I could not help myself. I stood for
a long time and watched her. All hope must be gone from her, poor
child, and yet still she looked so innocent, so open to the future.

Ah, well. We must wait for what is to come with such fortitude as
the Lord grants us. I pray that, at the end, we will not any of us be
utterly abandoned.

The door opened again and I closed the book with a snap.
Chantal looked at me. 'You OK?'

'Sure. Of course.'

'The guy said you seemed a bit … edgy.'

'Sorry. I need some air. Maybe I'll take a walk.'

'You feel strong enough for that?'

'I'm strong enough.'

She hovered, unconvinced. 'These boys will be finished pretty
soon. Can they take this stuff? Or do you want to sit and look at
it a while longer?'

'I think maybe I've seen as much as I'm going to see.'

'Right. Well, you know – take it easy.'

She closed the door. I found my jacket and slipped the books into my pocket and left the cabin.

It was a glorious day. The quayside was crowded with holiday-makers. They took no notice of me, except for one or two who glanced curiously at the bandage around my head. I cut through the narrow streets beyond the square, avoiding the church. Soon I emerged onto the cliff path, with the breeze from the Channel flattening the grass. I climbed slowly, stopping every few yards and gathering my strength, but at length I reached the old cross on the summit in its thicket of windswept hawthorns. I started down the far slope towards La Division.

I stood above the beach for a while, recovering my breath. Sweat cooled on my skin. I did not turn to gaze at the ruined farmhouse but made my way down the bluff and across the shingle to the stone jetty. This time the water thudding against the blocks did not trouble me as I walked out along them. The seawind bathed my face and filled my lungs.

The diaries floated for a while, their covers spreading like the wings of shot birds and the ink wavering from their pages. And then they were gone.

Epilogue

The summer was almost at an end.

I pushed open the iron gate and walked slowly up the path towards the church. The day was warm, and the leaves of the beech trees hung limp in the heavy afternoon air.

There was no sign of Kate and Serge. Maybe they would come up here later. For the moment they were giving me some space. The thought made me smile. They had already moved on, out of my adventure and into their own. I pictured them at one of Henri's terrace tables, braving the torrent of his astonished and delighted welcome, fielding his questions, allowing him to ply them with celebratory silver tankards of peppery champagne.

I glanced back towards the square. Chantal was sitting where I had left her, on the bench by the rose arbour with its memorial to the Rosens.

I headed for the far wall of the churchyard, taking my time. The yew threw a cool shadow over Dominic's grave. They had buried Dr Pasqual very close by. Both plots were neatly tended, and fresh flowers lay on them.

'Good afternoon!' a voice called from behind me. 'Looking for someone in particular?'

I turned. He was a young man, very black and built like a prizefighter. He wore a paint-spattered bright red polo shirt and faded denim shorts, and he leaned against the side of the church at the top of the crypt steps, smoking. A paint roller on a long handle rested against the wall beside him.

He took the cigarette from his mouth and flicked it away into the laurel bushes. 'Filthy habit,' he said, cheerfully. 'I'm Father Joseph.'

I took his hand. 'The new priest?'

'Not so new any more,' he grinned.

I looked down the steps to the crypt. The iron bound door stood open in the sunshine. I could hear a radio blaring – Fela Kuti in full swing. I glimpsed brilliantly whitewashed walls and pillars.

'It needed brightening up,' he said. 'We're going to turn it into somewhere people can be together. Eat, drink, talk, sing. Get some joy into it.'

There was a moment of silence.

He glanced towards the graves. 'Friends and family?'

I didn't bother to confirm it for him. I knew he understood.

'I hear there's a stone,' I said. 'A kind of obelisk.'

'Ah!' He widened his eyes. 'Our mystery monument! There used to be an old one here, but they took it down and put this new one up the week before I arrived.'

It was dark grey granite, the colour of the sea at dawn. They had placed it up against the wall, close to the graves of the crew of HSL 2548, and not far from Dr Pasqual and Dominic. The polished stone was still mirror bright and the lettering sharply chiselled, but time would weather it soon enough.

'It's a fine verse,' Father Joseph said.

'It's from Psalm 77.' I stooped to flick away a beech twig from the turf in front of the stone. 'But I guess you'd know that.'

I stepped back to read the inscription again.

PILOT OFFICER GEORGE MADOC
and LT ROBERT HAMELIN

'Thy way is in the sea, and thy path in the great waters:
and thy footsteps are not known'

Father Joseph cocked his head. 'Be nice to know what it all means.'

'It's a long story,' I said.